STRANGE INK

Coming soon from Gary Kemble and Titan Books

Dark Ink (October 2019)

STRANGE INK

GARY KEMBLE

TITAN BOOKS

Strange Ink
Print edition ISBN: 9781785656439
E-book edition ISBN: 9781785656446

Published by Titan Books
A division of Titan Publishing Group Ltd
144 Southwark Street, London SE1 0UP

First Titan edition: October 2018
10 9 8 7 6 5 4 3 2 1

This edition published by arrangement with Echo Publishing, an imprint of Bonnier Publishing Australia, in 2018.

Did you enjoy this book?
We love to hear from our readers. Please email us at
readerfeedback@titanemail.com or write to us at Reader Feedback
at the above address.

To receive advance information, news, competitions, and exclusive offers online,
please sign up for the Titan newsletter on our website:
www.titanbooks.com

for Amelia, Eamon and Aurora

Cold dirt pressed against his cheek. Plastic rustled, like a sail shifting, and shades of grey replaced pitch black. A shadow fell over him.

'Yep. He's dead.'

He tried to turn his head. Couldn't. Tried to push himself up off the ground. Couldn't. The shadow moved across the bleak brown landscape. In the distance an ant wandered in lazy circles. Beyond that, only darkness.

'Do you want to cut, or dig?'

He recognised the voice but couldn't place it. A man with an impressive handlebar moustache and an even more impressive beer gut.

The snick of a lighter, followed by the rank odour of cheap tobacco. Feet scuffed. The smoker exhaled.

'Dunno. You sure he's dead?' Another familiar voice. Blond hair. Goatee. Celtic bands tattooed across his shoulders and neck.

'You used a shottie. Half his fucking chest is gone, ya tool.'

Beergut snorted out a rough laugh. Blondie joined in, sucking in breath between high-pitched squeals. The laughter died away. A foot prodded his back. They rolled

1

him over. Silhouettes, backlit by the harsh fluorescent light. Above the men, floorboards.

'Come on, shithead. Cut or dig?'

'Ah, this is bullshit. Cut.'

'Typical. Lazy cunt.'

Beergut reached for his belt. Light gleamed off the hunting knife he slid from its sheath. He handed it to Blondie. The man on the ground felt no fear. He was beyond fear.

Half his fucking chest is gone.

Blondie dropped to his haunches. From behind him came the heavy thunk of a shovel breaking earth. Blondie looked up and light fell across his face, revealing heavy bruising. *I did that*, the man thought, but couldn't remember how.

Blondie sighed, then ripped open the man's shredded, bloody shirt. The man tried to reach out and grab his face. Nothing. Blondie looked down, eyes wide. Close enough that the man could see the sweat on his forehead and the tear tattooed under his swollen right eye. Close enough that he could smell the heady tang of petrol on his clothes.

'Jesus. Lotta ink.'

'Do you want me to dig this hole big enough for two?'

'Keep your head on.'

Blondie pushed the knife into the flesh. There was no pain, just a dull tugging sensation. Blondie sawed away, greasy hair falling around his face. He pulled away a bloody flap of skin.

'What are we going to do with these?' Blondie said.

'What do you think we're gonna do – stick them in your fuckin' family album? Burn them. Idiot. Now get on with it.'

'I wonder how the Chief is getting on with Kyla,' Blondie said. That laugh again: *hyuck, hyuck, hyuck.*

'You know him. Loves to mix his business and pleasure. I'm sure she'll go out with a bang.'

Anger flared. He tried to sit up. Blondie stared down, frowning. With his spare hand he reached down and pressed two blood-tacky fingers against the man's throat.

'What's wrong now?' Beergut said.

'Nothin'.'

'Fucking pussy. Hurry up. I wanna have a few of the old man's VBs when we're done.'

'Yeah, and do you want to explain to the Chief why you're drinking his dad's beer?'

'Well, we *are* concreting his fucking driveway tomorrow.'

They laughed. Blondie brought the knife to bear once more, cutting away a slab of flesh from the man's arm. The rage faded. As the bikie peeled the tattoos from the man's body, the memories went with them. Terrified faces swallowed by a raging sea. Lungs full of water off the coast of Fiji. Blondie rolled the man over and started on his back. The vision of a blood-smeared death room in Helmand province flared, then faded to black.

'I guess I should do the teeth too, right?' Blondie said.

'Yep. Dealin' with a real pro here.'

Blondie disappeared. The man could hear him rummaging around on the tool bench. Then he returned, rolled him over, and hefted the hammer.

Smack. Smack. Smack. Impact, but no pain.

When he was done he reached in, scooped the teeth out. Under the tang of fresh blood, Blondie's hands tasted of unleaded and weed.

Cicadas droned in the trees. In the distance, music

3

played. The White Stripes' 'There's No Home for You Here'. The steady thunk, thunk, thunk of Beergut's spadework lulled the man into a trance.

Beergut grunted, then shuffled over. 'He doesn't look so tough now, does he?' he said.

The plastic flexed around him as the two of them lifted him off the ground, then lowered him into the hole.

Beergut knelt over him, grabbed him by the hair and lifted his head, turning it this way and that.

'You missed one.'

'What?'

'A tattoo. On the back of his neck.'

'Fuck it. No-one's ever going to find this guy.'

'The Chief wanted the tattoos cut off and burned. All of them.'

From the darkness came the sound of a car engine.

'Fuck! Someone's coming!'

The light went out. Pitch black. The White Stripes' song finished. The babble of drunken conversation filled the void. The car edged closer.

'Ah, shit. Quick. Cover him up.'

They pushed the plastic into the hole, then Beergut grabbed the shovel.

'Hurry!'

The dirt fell on his head, and into the wounds on his back. Into his eyes, nose, mouth and ears. He felt its firm weight on his body, like a winter blanket.

The distant stereo cranked up. Powderfinger's 'I Don't Remember'. If he could have closed his eyes he would have. It was time to sleep.

CHAPTER 1

Harry sat in the corner of the lounge room, staring at the packing crates as the hangover squeezed his head and stomach. In one of the boxes he'd find Panadol and Nurofen and Berocca, the staples that would allow him to progress from abject misery to garden-variety misery. He just didn't know which box.

He closed his eyes, but that was worse. The world spun. He cursed the lack of curtains, he cursed the humidity resting on his head and shoulders like a warm, wet blanket, he cursed Dave for the buck's night, he cursed Bec for kicking him out. But most of all he cursed himself for his ability to hoard and his inability to pack in a rational, meaningful way.

Books, he'd found. Stephen King's *Dark Tower* and a healthy collection of Peter Straub were absolutely no help in his current condition. He found bedding, which would have been handy at four that morning, when he stumbled in shivering. He'd been caught in a summer storm while staggering home from… he couldn't quite remember. He vaguely recalled strippers.

VHS tapes, he'd found. *War Games. Beverly Hills Cop 2. Evil Dead.* Videos he'd doggedly held on to all these years, despite Bec's infuriatingly logical argument that they didn't own a VHS player anymore, so there was no point keeping the tapes.

Harry rubbed the back of his neck, which stung for some reason. It felt bruised, sunburned. Rubbing made it worse, which in turn made the headache and nausea worse. He dropped his head between his knees and concentrated on the shapes in the god-awful red carpet. *Who the hell has red carpet these days?*

He tried to remember what happened the night before. Remembering seemed important. He froze, hand resting on the back of his neck, snatching at the memory. A nightmare. Must've been a nightmare. Cold, hard light from a fluorescent bulb. When he thought about it, he recalled his Dad's disastrous Friday-night barbecues after his Mum left. Harry didn't get the sense the nightmare was about the barbecues, per se, but thinking of those nights made him recall damp grass, powdery soil, the stench of tobacco and beer.

Had he been bitten by something? An ant? He remembered an ant walking in confused arcs across a patch of dark earth. The memory faded even as his mind clawed for purchase. No, not an ant. It wouldn't still hurt so much. A spider? No, that didn't feel right either.

Harry leant forward and pulled his shirt off, sniffed it, and threw it across the room, where it landed on a box marked 'PHOTOS'. Of course, it didn't have photos in it. It was one of Bec's boxes, from when they moved in together. She'd turned the middle 'O' into a heart. She'd kept the box because she figured it would come in handy one day. And it had. Harry closed his eyes, squeezed the bridge of his nose with thumb and forefinger, willing the memory away. The one bright spark of sick joy he took from this was that it wasn't part of Bec's life plan, either. She'd be suffering as much as he was.

'Fuck,' he said. He dragged himself to his feet and into the bedroom. He picked his iPhone off the floor, thumbed the button. Dead. Typical. He rummaged through the boxes in his room until he found the charger. He plugged in the phone, waited until it had enough juice, then knelt down so he could hold it behind his head. He snapped a photo. He stared at the screen, not believing what he was seeing. That must've been from the night before. A drunken photo of someone else. But that was his bedroom. His neck. And on it, a tattoo.

'Holy shit,' he said.

You missed one. On the back of his neck.

A bloody knife. An ant crawling in his mouth. He lurched for the front door, bile rising. In the blisteringly hot sunroom his legs gave way. He stumbled onto his hands and knees, crawling, squinting against the sunlight lancing through the craquelure louvres.

He made it. Just. Body flat on the linoleum floor, chin just over the threshold, Harry threw up; water and bile erupted onto the front steps. He dry-heaved a couple of times, then wiped the threads of spit from his mouth. As he looked up, an old man with a ruddy face pushed a green flyer into his letterbox, saw Harry lying there, then hurried up the street.

'Yep,' Harry croaked, pushing himself up onto his hands and knees. 'You've sealed the deal. Welcome to your new home.'

When he had the strength, he crawled back inside and called Dave.

The kitchen's green cabinets and red Laminex benchtops were almost too much to handle in his current state. At least the colours were faded. The original kitchen. Well, original from the '60s. He thought this place, given its VJ walls and the way it creaked at the slightest breeze, dated back to the '30s at least. Back then it was most likely a lonely shack on a dirt track, leading up to more houses on Given Terrace. But unlike most of the houses on the street, in this area for that matter, this place seemed to have escaped the gentrification that was spreading across the city.

The rickety formica table where he and Dave sat was about the same vintage: pockmarked with chips and cigarette burns, the once anodised edging rusting and loose at the back. Harry had fond memories of sitting at a very similar table at his granddad's place at Caloundra, reading old war comics, sea breeze carrying the sounds of gulls and surf. In better condition, it would have sold for a mint at one of the antiques places up the road.

He stared at the photo. The tattoo was a grid – five by five. Each square contained a different symbol. Squiggles. Dots. Circles. Lines. The skin around it was an angry red. He'd never seen a tattoo like it. Although, to be fair, he hadn't seen a great many tattoos.

'It's not that bad, really,' Dave said, taking a sip of coffee to hide the smirk. 'Wearing a collared shirt, no-one will even notice it. With the collar up.'

Harry reached up again and touched the skin. 'Shit! Just... *shit!*'

'Hey, hey! Not so loud,' Dave said.

To Dave's credit, when Harry called he got himself to Harry's place in about ten minutes. He even brought some mysterious pills in a silver packet, but refused to tell

Harry what they were. The benefits of being friends with a nurse.

And to his further credit, he'd managed to keep the grin off his face, mostly, other than the initial burst of hysterical laughter.

'Could have been worse,' Dave said. He pulled up his sleeve. Bart Simpson as Poe's Raven perched on his meaty bicep, clutching a parchment that read 'Nevermore'.

'Yeah, but you asked for that. You weren't drunk.' Harry pushed the phone away, pulled his cup closer. He'd downed another couple of painkillers, topped it off with some coffee, and so far was keeping it all down. In an hour or so he might try some Vegemite on toast. If he could find the Vegemite, and the bread, and the toaster.

'Fuck. This is fucked!' He laid his head down on the table. The surface was cool against his forehead.

'It's okay mate, we'll figure it out,' Dave said. 'What do you remember from last night?'

Harry thought again of flat fluorescent light. An ant crawling in lazy circles. He closed his eyes. Thought harder. Red tablecloths.

'The Indian place. I remember the Indian place,' Harry said.

'Yep. Me too. Shit. How much did we drink there?'

It was BYO. Harry remembered several cartons of beer sitting around the table. He couldn't remember how many they left with, but he knew they wouldn't have been allowed to take drinks on the…

'CityCat! We caught the CityCat!' Harry said.

Dave winced. 'Tone it down, mate.'

'Sorry.'

'But yeah, you're right. We caught the ferry down to

the city. Do you remember Simmo trying to chat up that woman on the Party Barge?'

Now that Dave mentioned it, he remembered the Party Barge drifting past, speakers blaring Rick Astley. Simmo, the best man, was trying to take the woman's photo. He called out to her, asking for her phone number.

'Okay,' Dave said, staring down at the table. He sipped his coffee. 'I know we were heading for the casino, but I don't for the life of me remember what happened there. Hang on.'

He picked up his phone, flicked through the photos. Harry leant over so he could see them. The facade of the Treasury Building, brightly lit by multicoloured spotlights. Inside, people milling around gaming tables. Simmo, at the head of a craps table, beautiful brunette in a low-cut dress beside him. Simmo looked wasted. The woman looked unimpressed.

'What's he doing?' Harry said.

'That's right. He was trying to get her to blow on his dice… so to speak.'

'He's married, right?'

Simmo had gone to school with them both, but Harry hadn't really kept in contact with anyone from those days. He didn't understand why Dave had, although Dave's time at school had been easier. He was one of those people who could cruise through exams and assignments but, crucially, was good at sport, too. He'd led the school's football team to a win at the state finals.

Dave shrugged. 'He doesn't mean any harm. You know how it is.'

But Harry didn't. Not at the moment. He wouldn't have risked his relationship with Bec for a one-night stand.

Dave laughed, flicking through the photos. 'She got really aggro. Security headed over…'

Harry had a vague flash of two beefy Islanders who looked pissed off at having to wear suits on a sweltering Brisbane night.

'… but then he lost anyway. Is any of this ringing any bells?'

'The bouncers. But only because you mentioned them.'

'That's okay, we'll get there. You were still with us when we left the casino, so there was no chance of you sneaking off for a quick tatt then. You had a little hissy fit on the way to Showgirls.'

'Yeah?'

'Yeah, you didn't want to go. You said you were sick of the boys asking you about the break-up.'

'What did you say?'

'I told you to pull your fucking head in. It was my buck's night, after all.'

Harry nodded, sipped his coffee. 'Fair enough.'

'So you were definitely there at Showgirls, although you spent the whole time propping up the bar. Tequila shots, I think.'

'Shit. No wonder I'm so fucked today.'

'Uh-huh. Do you remember anything from Showgirls?'

'No. Wait. Yeah.'

'Girls on Film' on the sound system, a woman in a pink g-string and matching bra cavorting on the circular stage with its shiny brass poles.

'Simmo wanted me to "get it out of my system" with a lap dance,' Harry said.

'Sounds like Simmo.'

Dave consulted his iPhone again. 'Aha. You might have

been shitty but I guilted you into sticking around. Look.'

The photo was blurry. The inside of a MaxiCab. Harry in the back seat, resting his head on his hand, staring out the window.

'Not a happy camper,' Dave said.

'Where were we going?'

'Jamie's place. Do you remember him?'

'From school, yeah. From last night, not so much. He's an accountant, something like that?'

'Stockbroker, mate.'

Harry remembered a towering white apartment building. Remembered thinking that whatever Jamie did, it pulled in a lot more than reporting for a local paper. He closed his eyes.

'Jamie had porn going on his laptop. Kept joking that it was Simmo's mum.'

'Yep, that's right. And check this out.'

Another photo of Harry. In this one he looked much happier, standing on the balcony of Jamie's penthouse apartment, clutching a bottle of Oban. The lid was off, but there was no glass in sight.

'Shit. What a waste of single malt.'

'Yep.'

'And then?'

Dave consulted his phone. 'Dunno. Last photo. I woke up at Jamie's. We'd just had brekky when you called.'

Harry rubbed his face. 'So, somewhere between West End and here, I stumbled into a tattoo parlour and got inked.'

'Probably West End Tattoo. That's where I got mine done.'

'Would they even have been open that late?'

Dave shrugged. 'Got mine during the day. One way to find out.'

'What, now?'

'Yeah, we can get a decent cup of coffee while we're over there.'

Harry dragged himself up from the table.

'Oh, I've got a wedding thing on later, so I'll probably head over straight from West End,' Dave said. 'Are you right to drive yourself?'

Harry gave him a sour look. Dave replied with a wink.

'Legend,' Dave said.

CHAPTER 2

West End was buzzing, people coming alive as the temperature dropped ahead of the incoming storm. Harry climbed out of his car and negotiated a path down the pavement, past an eclectic collection of cafes, bars and grocery stores, to where Dave had parked. Suits sipped wine and imported beer, jostling for space with Gen Y hipsters slurping coffee and jabbing at their iPhones, and world-weary locals who'd seen it all.

West End Tattoo had a low-key shopfront. No gaudy artwork on the window, venetian blinds to discourage gawkers. Harry had walked past the place dozens of times without realising it was a tattoo parlour.

'Now, when we get in there, let me do the talking,' Dave said. 'You don't want to piss them off, okay?'

Harry was angry, but the anger was offset by a sickening feeling in his stomach. He was sweating, his heart racing. It wasn't all the hangover, and he wasn't scared of a looming confrontation. He had to ask plenty of hard questions in his job. Questions people would rather not answer. In his personal life he found confrontation harder to deal with, but he could still flip the 'journalist' switch if he had to.

The place looked just as foreign as every other time he'd

passed it. So much so that as Dave pushed the door open, he knew what the result was going to be. *No. No, we did not do that tattoo. Sorry, pal.* A shrug. A see ya later. Which would leave Harry facing the prospect that he had been so bombed he actually went out of his way to get the tattoo. What else had he done, and couldn't remember?

'You okay?'

Harry jumped. Dave was staring at him.

'Not really. None of this is familiar,' he said, shaking his head.

The walls were covered in framed tattoo designs. On the far side of the small room a woman sat behind a counter. People were crammed in shoulder to shoulder on bench seating around the other three sides of the room. A young guy with bleached blond hair clutched an art folder. A woman with a pram flicked through a magazine. From the doorway behind the counter, tattoo machines buzzed. Stairs led up to the second storey, and Harry could hear more tattooing going on up there.

The woman behind the counter looked up. 'Hey, Dave!'

The ring through the middle of her lip glistened when she smiled. She wore a vintage dress: red flowers on a cream background. Her hair was pinned up, revealing the art that cascaded from her neck down over her shoulders and under the fabric of her dress, before continuing out from under the sleeves and down her arms. Flowers, faces and intricate scrollwork.

'Hey, Sian.'

She nodded at Harry. 'Brought in a convert?'

'Kinda. Um…'

'I've already got a tattoo,' Harry said. 'I just don't know how I got it.'

15

Dave seemed happy to let Harry do the talking, once he realised he wasn't going to explode. When he finished the story, she shook her head.

'Not ours.'

'You haven't even looked at it!' Harry said, a little louder than he intended.

Sian's lips set in a firm line. Dave touched her arm. 'He's a little… Things have been a bit fucked up lately.'

Her eyes flicked to Dave and her face softened a little.

'Well, for a start, we're not some 1950s dockside operation. We don't open at night unless someone's got an appointment. Even if we were open, we wouldn't be doing walk-ins. There's a two-month waiting list for most of the artists here. And even when we do walk-ins, we don't tattoo people if they're wasted. Too much grief for all involved.'

Harry blinked. The rising anger dissipated. Now he could feel a lump in his throat. Sian rolled her eyes.

'Let's have a look at it then,' she said.

She came out from behind the counter, pushed Harry's head forward a little more roughly than was necessary.

'Hmm. I was gonna say you might've got it done at Stones Corner. But this doesn't even look like it's been done with a tattoo machine. The edges aren't defined enough. Looks more like *krob kru*.'

'What's that?'

'Buddhist monks in Thailand have a ceremony where they tattoo people using shafts of bamboo. Mix the ink with snake venom. It's pretty full on.'

'I think I'd remember that.'

'Yeah. You'd think so, right?'

She let go of his shirt, and he turned to face her.

'It's weird though,' she said, frowning.

16

Harry rubbed his neck. 'Oh yeah? It gets weirder?'

'Yeah. They're not *krob kru* tattoos. I mean, it's not a *krob kru* design. In fact, it looks kinda Persian.'

'Persian?'

'Yep.'

'Don't suppose you happen to know what it means?'

'Um. Offhand, no. Sorry.'

Harry stared into his coffee. 'Worst. Day. Ever.'

Dave shuffled his feet under the table, watched the waitress as she delivered another couple of drinks. Tight black t-shirt, tight black shorts. Cars and buses droned past. Up and down Hardgrave Road steel shutters clattered down. The storm was edging nearer, flashes of lightning illuminating clouds in the west.

'Well, she could be wrong,' Dave said.

Harry stared at him. 'Er, she looks like she might know a thing or two about tatts, Dave.' He slurped his coffee.

'Just sayin'.'

Harry searched for a subject that wasn't going to lead back to tattoos or Bec. 'So, you ready to get hitched?'

'Yeah, pretty much. There are some last-minute dramas about the seating arrangements for the reception, but that's about it. Ellie isn't too impressed that I'm on night shifts every night leading up to the wedding but, ah, she'll get over it.'

'No, I mean, are you ready? Emotionally?'

Dave laughed. 'Ha! You know me. I wasn't fussed. It was mainly Ellie's family. I mean, I love her. A ring on the finger is neither here nor there. You live with someone long enough, you just know, right?'

Harry looked into the street; an old guy in a tattered

blue jumper was pawing through an overflowing bin.
Harry thought about the last conversation he and Bec had.
If you could call it a conversation. He provoked her, but
then she really let him have it. About how he was still at
the *Chronicle*. About how all he ever did when he was at
home was watch TV. She even had a go about the middle-
age paunch he was growing.

'Sorry,' Dave said. 'I just mean…'

Harry waved it away. 'I better get going. I've got a big
day at work tomorrow.'

'Oh yeah. Toastmasters' convention? Over-60s Blue
Light Disco?'

'Har-dee-fucking-har-har. You should be a fucking
comedian.'

'That's what the director of nursing keeps telling me.
Maybe I should.'

'Our local MP wants to talk election coverage.'

Dave tipped his head back, offered a fake snore, jolted
awake. 'Sorry. Did you say something?'

'He's not that bad.'

'Ron Vessel. Man of Action,' Dave said, delivered
deadpan.

'Laugh all you want, but Andrew Cardinal is Opposition
Leader, and Ron is his right-hand man. If Cardinal gets up,
Vessel's going with him.'

'Uh-huh. Like that's going to happen. Cardinal would
have to stop running marathons to have a successful run at
the Lodge. And that's not going to happen.' Dave leant in
close, offering a conspiratorial whisper. 'He's addicted… to
the endorphins.'

'Well, I think he'll get plenty of excitement on the
campaign trail.'

Harry stood, started loading his possessions into his pockets.

'Hey, do you want to catch up for a coffee during the week? Last coffee of freedom?' Dave said, picking his wallet, car keys and phone off the table.

'Yeah, maybe.'

'Cool. If not, I'll see you Saturday.'

'I wouldn't miss it for the world.'

Harry turned to leave.

'Hey, Harry.'

'Yeah?'

'Thanks for coming last night. I mean, I know you haven't really had much to do with the guys since high school. It really means a lot to me. And I do feel bad about the tattoo.'

'Not your fault. I'll talk to you during the week, okay?'

Harry was still a hundred metres from his car when thunder boomed through the sky and the heavens opened. He sprinted through the rain, gasping as he fumbled for his keys. He slid into the front seat and sat there for a moment, catching his breath, listening to the rain smashing against the roof.

He opened the glovebox and pulled out a well-worn cassette tape: Counting Crows' *A&EA*. Dave thought it was hilarious that Harry still had the Corolla – his second-ever car – and even funnier that he had never bothered to buy a car stereo with an iPod dock or CD player. Harry wasn't averse to technology. He just figured there was no point putting a new stereo into a car that could die any day now.

He'd been saying the same thing since he bought it, shortly after joining the *Chronicle*. Back then, he didn't have a choice. He needed a cheap and relatively reliable vehicle. These days, he could afford the repayments on something better, but he'd grown fond of the old girl. The Corolla rolled off the assembly line the same year he did.

He keyed the engine, watching the steam rising from the road. As he pulled out into the street the first guitar strains of 'Round Here' came crackling through the speakers. The music, like the car, pre-dated Bec. Dave had introduced him to Counting Crows, back when they were delivering pizzas and Harry was in the process of running his first car into the ground. The music anchored him in a time before Bec, when he was alone, when he was still full of twentysomething angst and thought he'd never find anyone.

Yeah, it was depressing. But right now he needed that. He drove out of West End, eyes tearing up in sympathy with the sky. Across the Grey Street Bridge, the chocolate-coloured waters of the Brisbane River churned below him. City lights refracted off the raindrops on the car's windows.

He made it through Rosalie Village before the tears got so bad he had to pull over. He switched off the engine. The music fell silent but the song played on in his mind. He leant his head on the steering wheel and gave in to it. Tears cascaded down his face and to the floor below, as the storm raged around him.

CHAPTER 3

Harry sat sweating in Ron Vessel's electorate office, staring at the clock on the wall, trying to make it run backwards. He was an hour late. His shirt was crushed. His iPhone was about to die again. He felt very much like the unprofessional hack he was often cast as. Vessel's PA sat behind a faux wood counter, click-clacking away on a keyboard. Ron was behind the closed door at the end of the corridor. It sounded as though he was on a conference call.

Harry had slept poorly the night before, tossing and turning. Every time he slipped into sleep the nightmare returned. The men smoking, the knife slicing slabs of flesh off his body, the feeling of dirt on his tongue, up his nose, in his ears. He'd jerk awake, sweating, thinking he could hear someone or something scratching around under the house. Then he'd drift back to sleep, and back into the nightmare.

He woke as the first rays of daylight crept through the window, his bed soaked in sweat. He couldn't remember where he was. He had a bizarre urge to throw on some shorts and a singlet and go for a run. He hadn't run since he was in the cross-country team in high school. He lay there, listening to the kookaburras, thinking there was no way he was going to get back to sleep. But he did.

He missed his alarm. Ran around the house frantically searching for work clothes and, when he found them, they were crumpled. There was no time for ironing, or breakfast. He couldn't afford to miss the shower though, but then afterwards spent a frustrating five minutes upending boxes, naked and dripping, looking for a towel.

Then the car wouldn't start. *This can't be happening.* The tired old Corolla disagreed, vehemently. Whirr-whirr-whirr... whirr-whirr-whirrrr... click. He pulled out his phone, only to realise it was dead.

Harry resisted the urge to smash it against the dashboard, and instead took it back inside and upstairs, found the charger, and plugged it in. Called the RACQ. During the short wait he sat on the front steps with his bag, watching people dressed in business attire trudge up the hill to the bus stop.

Eventually, the RACQ van reversed down the steep driveway. A man climbed out, shook Harry's hand, and got him to pop the hood. He opened the back of his van and pulled out a multimeter, then pressed the end of each probe to the battery terminals.

'Yep, this battery's dead,' he said.

Harry ran a hand over his face. 'I only got it six months ago.'

'Well, it's gone. Did you leave the lights on?'

Harry shrugged. He didn't think so. Although he was pretty rattled when he'd returned from his visit to the tattoo parlour the day before. Anything was possible.

'I could have.'

At Ron Vessel's office the secretary saw the state Harry was in and took pity on him, telling him to take a seat and she'd see what she could do.

Harry had interviewed Ron a few times over the years; the first time when he was still in state politics. A devout Catholic, Vessel found succour in the Australian Labor Party's ascendant right wing. He survived the infights and bloodletting as the party struggled to reinvent itself in the face of successive losses to a dominant Coalition government, and was now part of what the national media had dubbed 'the Cardinal experiment'.

Cardinal had come out of nowhere, but what he lacked in political pedigree he more than made up for with electoral appeal. A military man, he'd seen action in Iraq and Afghanistan, as well as a bunch of lesser-known hotspots. A real-life action hero. After his honourable discharge he returned to Brisbane, where the ALP offered him preselection. A year later he won his seat, despite accusations from the Liberal Party that he'd been parachuted in (which the political cartoonists had a field day with, given the military connection). The victory was one of the few bright spots for Labor, which was relegated to another term in opposition.

Cardinal made his mark as defence spokesman, and was promoted to foreign affairs by the party leader to assuage his ambitions. The move did just the opposite. The ALP powerbrokers, seeing his abilities at the Dispatches Box, were more than willing to back Cardinal's tilt at the leadership. Cardinal took Vessel with him, offering voters the ultimate one-two of youth and experience.

Ron's door opened, and his mostly bald head poked out. For a fraction of a second Harry saw the true man, the unguarded Vessel, the battle-hardened career politician, and then their eyes met and he lit up. Game on.

'Harry! Good to see you, mate!'

Harry rose so quickly he dropped his notebook on the floor, then kicked it while trying to retrieve it.

'It's okay, Harry,' Ron said, 'I'm not Treasurer yet, no need to bow.'

The secretary sniggered. Harry flushed.

'Just kidding, just kidding!'

Vessel offered his hand. It was a firm two-fisted shake, a farmer's handshake. They stood close enough that Harry could smell the breath freshener, see the broken capillaries on his bulbous nose, the bags under his bloodshot eyes. Scars of a life in politics.

'I'm sorry I'm so late, I…'

Vessel waved away the apology and ushered Harry into his office. He planted his sizeable bulk behind the desk. It was covered in letters, documents, other bits and pieces. In one corner stood a framed photo of his wife and two daughters.

'Come. Sit, sit.'

He laid a meaty hand on the table, his wedding band gleaming.

'You don't mind if I work while we talk?' Vessel asked.

Without waiting for a response, he started tapping away at the keyboard. After every couple of keystrokes he would pause, peer at the screen, then continue. Harry could hardly complain. He was lucky to be here at all. He opened his notebook.

'So, exciting times,' he said. 'Any word on the election date?'

Harry felt almost like a *real* journalist, rather than a hack who worked for the local rag. Everyone was obsessed with the election date, and now he'd had his own opportunity to ask the question.

Ron tapped the side of his nose. 'We have it on good word that they're going to call a December election. Just before Christmas.'

Harry nodded. That's what all the pundits were tipping. It was risky, calling it so close to Christmas, but not unprecedented. Malcolm Fraser defeated Gough Whitlam on an election held on December 13, back in the '70s. They could go as late as March, but there was a raft of hostile reports due in the new year.

'You must be confident,' Harry said.

Vessel shook his head but when he stopped, Harry saw the glint in his eye. He was already measuring up his new office.

'Can't be confident. This is the longest serving Coalition government in Australia's history, with a wily leader. If anyone can pull it off, they can.'

'Unemployment's up. Interest rates are up. The only thing that isn't up is the Coalition's approval rating.'

'Campaigns can do strange things to people. Anything can happen.'

The interview turned out to be as superficial as Harry feared. No big surprises. No big scoops. Andrew Cardinal was renowned for his control of information. His background was in army intelligence, after all. All the real stories would be dealt out to the national journalists on the campaign trail. Vessel talked about his own family but made no attempt to probe Harry about his personal life. There was no doubt that this was all about showing Harry what a great guy he was, how ready he was to help lead the country. But at least Harry had got an interview. It would make a nice page three lead. Front page, if they were desperate.

Harry closed his notebook and smiled.

'Thanks again for seeing me,' he said. 'That just about covers everything for me. Is there anything else you'd like to add?'

He always asked the same closing question. It was one of the few techniques he'd been taught at uni that actually worked in the real world. Harry expected Ron to shake his head, get up, and show Harry out of the office. Instead he paused, shook his head, then took a deep breath.

'No. But there's something I'd like to ask you.'

Harry paused, waiting for the punchline. When it didn't arrive, he shrugged and dropped back into the chair.

'Oh yeah? What's that?'

'Why are you still at the *Chronicle*?'

Harry opened his mouth. Closed it again.

'I mean, shit mate. When we first met I was busting my gut on George Street. And now, let's face it – off the record – I'm about to become Treasurer.

'And you. You're still there. You're polite. You seem bright. Far brighter than some of those dickheads over at the *Brisbane Mail*. That Terry Redwood wanker, for example. What's he got that you haven't got?'

Harry laughed. His face was burning. He remembered being drawn into the story-by-story dogfight with Redwood at uni. He hated himself for it, but Terry really pushed his buttons. At extremely low moments, Harry wondered whether he would have gone ahead with the Cherry Grove story if not for the desperate urge to land a knockout blow on Redwood.

'I don't know. You know what happened, right?' Harry said. When Ron didn't say anything, he continued. 'The uni almost got sued. I almost got sued. I had to put my name to an extremely embarrassing apology. And pretty much every door, except this one,' he threw a hand in the vague direction of his office, 'closed in my face. Before I even graduated.'

Vessel wiped his mouth. 'But the story. The story was *good*. And God knows how an undergrad journalism student got it.'

'Well, I wish you were there back then to tell the Vice Chancellor that.'

Harry rubbed the back of his neck.

Ron shrugged. 'Shit happens, Harry. You've stewed in purgatory long enough.'

Harry stared down at his closed notebook. This certainly wasn't what he expected.

'Harry, why don't you come on the campaign trail with us?'

'What?'

'Why not?'

'Because the *Chronicle* is a local paper. We can't justify devoting basically half our staff to a federal election.'

'This isn't coming from me, Harry. This was Andrew's idea. He wants you on the bus. Local angle, and all that.'

'Thanks for the offer, Ron. But I can't.'

Ron shrugged. He finished the sentence he was typing, then stood up and shook Harry's hand, over the desk.

'All the best for the campaign, Ron,' Harry said.

'Likewise.'

Harry tried to pull away, but Ron held his hand a moment longer. 'I mean it, Harry. This shit is beneath you.'

Harry pulled into the *Chronicle's* undercover car park, head still spinning. On the drive back he replayed the conversation over and over again, vacillating between anger at Vessel for basically reiterating Bec's prime criticism of him, and anger at himself for saying no. He wondered if he could phone Ron back, tell him he'd changed his mind. Then he wondered if he *wanted* to phone Ron back.

The story was good.

Harry rubbed his face. His lecturer had certainly thought so. To begin with. Harry had been looking into allegations that elements of the former Bjelke-Petersen government were engaged in rorting the Brisbane City Council's planning process. The word was, they had the ear of a Labor Party councillor, who was taking kickbacks in exchange for smoothing the approval process for certain property developers. Brian Swenson, then just starting out, was the one developer named in the article.

Joh Bjelke-Petersen's party was kicked out in 1989 after investigative journalist Phil Dickie uncovered widespread corruption throughout the Sunshine State. There was a Royal Commission; people were sacked, disgraced, in some instances jailed. The broom went through. A decade on from the Fitzgerald Inquiry, the idea that someone from the Labor Party – pitched as saviours who promised a clean slate – was in cahoots with the bad boys from the old days was too good to be true. It was the sort of rumour that did the rounds but never went anywhere.

Harry had dug through mountains of newspaper clippings and public documents. Found someone who'd give him details, off the record, and provide documents backing up the claims. His lecturer had insisted that he confirm the information from at least one other source. For weeks it looked as though this wouldn't happen, and the story would never be told.

He remembered Swenson's secretary, breathless over the

phone, telling him she knew the real story. Harry's world exploded. No-one wanted to believe that a journalism student had landed such a scoop. Harry had, in effect, shamed his potential employers.

Then the secretary recanted, saying she'd been taken out of context. No problem, Harry thought, I have a tape recording of the interview. He had the documents. The tape – handed in with the assignment – went missing. The documents were dismissed as fakes. 'Correct' documents appeared. The newspapers and TV stations took great delight in saying, 'I told you so'. Harry's lecturer, who had guided him each step of the way, took a few steps back, scared for his future.

With nowhere else to go, Harry apologised to Swenson. Retracted the story. And lost his taste for investigative journalism. Why put yourself out there when you could earn the same money writing colour pieces and advertorials? He graduated, somehow landed a job at the *Chronicle*, and put it all behind him. End of story.

He walked into the office, relishing the cool air. He sat at his desk, logged on and reached for his glass of water, hand shaking slightly. He took a drink. Christine, the other half of the *Chronicle*'s reporting staff, watched him, peering over the top of her hipster glasses.

'How was the Ronmeister?'

'Yeah. It was… interesting.'

'Interesting? Doesn't sound like our Ron.'

Harry waved it away, and Christine went back to her work. He didn't want to get into it while he was still processing the information himself.

He hadn't told her about Bec yet. Telling her would require admitting that it was not just a temporary thing.

Maybe it *was* a temporary thing. He tried the idea out like trying on a pair of pants. It didn't fit. There were many things he could bounce back from, but not from the bombshell that Bec couldn't imagine spending the rest of her life with him. After six years. Harry had thought that if you could spend six years with someone, you could spend eternity with them, but clearly not. His parents lasted thirteen. He and Bec lasted six.

'You okay?' Christine asked.

Harry nodded. 'I'll be fine.'

'You don't seem fine.'

She peered at him. Harry tried to imagine that there was more in her eyes than concern for a colleague. But again, it didn't quite fit. She was sweet and, yeah, Dave's observation that she was also 'hot' wasn't too far wrong. But she wouldn't be around for long. She was marking time, waiting for her big opportunity. He could picture her on commercial TV, but thought she could do better. He'd miss her, but he didn't want the youngsters to get stuck at the *Chronicle*, doing the same stories over and over again like some journalistic hell.

Youngsters? Fuck me. I'm only thirty-six.

He felt much older today.

'I didn't say I *was* fine, I said I'd *be* fine,' Harry said. He forced a smile, for her benefit. 'Hey, when did you get that?'

He gestured to the gear on her desk. There was a small video camera, and a cordless lapel microphone and pick-up.

'Oh, that,' she said. 'We're trying to get into online video, apparently. Some trial or something. Miles wanted me to give it a go. It's pretty cool. High definition. Streams straight to YouTube.'

She looked embarrassed, as though Harry would be hurt

that he hadn't been asked. And normally he would have. But today he was just glad of the distraction.

'I think you'd look good on TV,' he said.

'Thank you.'

He stared at the blinking cursor on his screen, then opened his notebook. He skipped back past the Ron Vessel notes, to the article he'd been working on Friday afternoon. *Accident waiting to happen.* There were maybe half-a-dozen types of stories he and Christine got to write. 'Accident waiting to happen' was the one about how the council refused to fix a traffic problem that was, in the eyes of the punter, extremely dangerous. Usually it had to do with rat running or traffic calming, or both. An intersection that needed traffic lights. Or an intersection that already had lights, but the lights were the problem. Harry had written thousands of these stories. Sometimes the council did something about the problem – if it was a problem – sometimes they didn't. He doubted it ever had anything to do with his articles.

He started typing, glancing back at his notebook. Normally it was like automatic writing, after all these years. Taking the basic structure of the news story, whacking the slabs of text in, rearranging them and then cutting them down to the required length. Thirty-five column centimetres for a front-page lead, twenty centimetres for a feature, fifteen for pretty much anything else. Knowing full well that by the time the ads were in, at least five centimetres and probably ten would be cut by the subs over at head office, and that there would be no consultation with him, unless it was the front page. And even then only if he happened to be sitting at his desk when they called.

Usually, the familiarity was soothing. But he couldn't

concentrate. The tattoo. If he didn't get it at West End Tattoo, where did he get it? Did he go back into the city? Stones Corner? Sian said it didn't look like it had been done by a tattoo machine. Could that be right? Had he been drugged, abducted? Was that what the nightmare was about?

And now, on top of all that, Ron's helpful advice. His uni contemporaries – some of whom he'd run rings around – popped up all over the place. The *Brisbane Mail*, obviously, but also *The Australian*, the *Sydney Morning Herald*. One had even landed a job with the *Guardian* in the UK. Then he remembered sitting in the Vice Chancellor's office, waiting for Brian Swenson to arrive, wondering how in hell he was going to afford legal representation if Swenson went after him. That sick feeling, frantically looking for a way out and seeing none.

Maybe this wasn't so bad. Telling the same half-dozen stories over and over again. The war veteran, recounting his stories for Anzac Day. The accident waiting to happen. The 60th wedding anniversary. David versus Goliath. Like an incomplete tarot deck, dealing the same fortunes over and over again, fourteen years later.

'… phoned.'

'Huh?' Harry said. Christine was staring at him. 'Sorry?'

'I forgot to tell you – Fred phoned,' she said.

Fred Mackay. World War II veteran. Christine, like all the junior reporters who came before her, groaned when she had to take a call from him, but Harry didn't mind. If you stripped away the conspiracy theories, there was sometimes a nugget of interesting – maybe even useful – information.

Fred wouldn't talk on the phone, because he thought he was under surveillance. But that was okay. Harry liked getting out and about. While Christine was happy to do most of the job at her desk, harvesting news from social media and putting in calls to verify the information, Harry would much rather rack up a few more kays on his Corolla. It was how he'd always done it. He was old-fashioned. To Harry's mind, you couldn't really relate to someone unless you were looking them in the eye, seeing the truth or lack thereof in their manner and surroundings.

Christine gasped. 'Holy crap!'

Harry turned. Christine stood behind him, her coffee mug swinging loose in one hand.

Shit!

'Is that real?' she said.

Harry wanted to deny it, but what good would that do? What was the option? Tell her that Dave had drawn it on with Nikko pen? He nodded.

She walked over to him. 'Give us a look.'

Harry bent his head forward so she could see it better.

'Cool. Kinda retro. Where'd you get it done?'

Now this was something Harry could have lied about. He could have said West End Tattoo, seeing as that was the most likely option. But he was flustered and he blanked.

'I… I don't know.'

Christine backed away, dropped into her chair. 'You don't know. You. Don't. Know?'

'I don't know.'

He told her the story, waiting for the laughter. And to his surprise he got all the way to the end before it erupted between the fingers of the hand pressed to her mouth. She laughed so hard, despite trying to keep a lid on it, that Harry couldn't help smiling.

'Yeah, yeah. Get it out of your system.'

33

'I'm sorry. It's just, you know…'

'Yeah. I do.'

She turned back to her computer.

'If you could keep it under your hat – you know, off Twitter – that'd be good.'

She pouted. 'You're no fun.'

'I'm going to get it removed, so…' he said, not even sure if that was true or not. He didn't feel like it was his tattoo. It made sense to get rid of it. And yet…

'You should keep it,' Christine said. 'It suits you.'

He glanced over at her. She stared at her monitor, slight smile touching her lips. He couldn't tell if she was joking or not, and he didn't want to ask, because he knew he wanted her to be serious.

'Thanks.'

CHAPTER 4

Harry backed into the driveway and climbed out of his car. Despite the heat of the day, it was cool under the house. Unlike many similar homes in the area, it hadn't been built in underneath. Instead of fibro walls, there were just wooden slats, spaced far enough apart to let the breeze through. He thought he might sleep down here on really hot nights, then remembered the mysterious scratching noise. He needed to get some rat traps.

He walked out to the front gate, grass whispering against the cuffs of his pants. He pulled the wad of mail out of the letterbox. Grocery pamphlets. An Indian take-away menu. Three letters, all 'To the Householder'. Christmas toy-store catalogues. And the green flyer. He remembered the man shoving it into the letterbox, after witnessing Harry 'christening' his new place. The pamphlet was crinkled, after being caught in the rain and then dried. He opened it carefully.

SAVE THE TOWER, the headline screamed. It was boxed in by clip art – a cement mixer down one end, a dump truck down the other.

Harry shook his head. Fred. His name wasn't on the flyer but it didn't need to be. And now that he'd made the connection, Harry recognised the guy who'd thrust it into the letterbox. Harry had seen him with Fred once, down the library. Bill, or Bob – something like that. He and Fred had served together. Harry scanned the text.

Swenson Constructions has put in an application to the Brisbane City Council, proposing to replace Paddington water tower with THE TOWERS – an eight-storey apartment complex and retail.

Swenson. That name again. Harry leant over the fence and peered through the drooping purple flowers of the jacaranda trees lining the street. There it was, in all its glory: a stark bulb of graffiti-scarred concrete in the distance, topped with a crown of mobile-phone antennae.

Harry had no interest in going head-to-head with Swenson again. But Fred would want him to. Like every other cause Fred had adopted over the years, this would be the most pressing issue Brisbane had ever faced, and Harry wouldn't hear the end of it until he donated some coverage.

He headed back to the house. In the kitchen, he dumped the mail on the bench and grabbed a beer. He unlocked the back door, and took the beer and the green flyer out with him.

The afternoon sun winked through the mango tree's thick branches and lush green leaves, painting his legs with dappled light. At the bottom of the steps a small concrete path doubled back under the house, to the laundry. The back yard sloped steeply upwards to a mossy picket fence that was falling down in places under the weight of the shrubbery on the other side. Through the gaps, Harry could just make out the back of another Queenslander, although this one had been raised and built in underneath.

He sipped his beer, grimaced, looked at the label. It was a

Corona, the beer he'd favoured since earning a decent wage. It tasted watered down. He took another sip, shrugged, continued drinking. It was still beer.

Up the street there were similar-sized patches of lawn – the same, but different. A greenhouse and a shed at the back of one, kids' toys and a trampoline in another. Further up, a yard was given over to the rusting remains of an old car, partially covered by a fraying blue tarp. Each garden had a Hills Hoist, as though at one point this was a city council planning regulation.

Looking at the state of his own yard, Harry thought it might finally be time to buy a mower. He and Bec had lived in an apartment, and before that a place where the landlord had paid for lawn care. The thought of now having to mow lawn made his stomach churn. Another sign that he was moving on, the things 'he and Bec' had always done would now be decisions he made for himself. Maybe he could get someone to tidy the garden a bit, and then he could reassess.

The general condition of the house led him to believe it hadn't been lived in for a while, which was odd, given the rent was reasonable for what it was and for the location – a short walk to Paddington's fashionable cafes and boutiques. After moving out of Bec's he'd expected to be dossing at Dave's for a week at least. Maybe the woman at the real estate agency had seen the desperate look in his eyes and taken pity on him. She showed him a photocopied flyer for a place that wasn't even on the rental list. He filled in an application right then and there, and they texted him that afternoon to tell him he'd got it. He'd thought about asking, 'What's the catch?' but didn't want to push it. He deserved a bit of good luck.

He sipped his beer. It still tasted odd, but he'd never met

a beer he didn't like. Besides, abandoning the beer would mean it was time to unpack boxes.

Harry focused on the pamphlet. The tower was built in 1927. The only one of its type in Queensland. An iconic part of the Paddington landscape. Fred had roped in his 'IT mate' to do a website, and Harry didn't need to check it out to know there would be plenty of animated GIFs. Fred wanted people to share their stories about the water tower and send in photos.

Good luck with that. Brisbane didn't exactly have a great record when it came to protecting cultural icons, and Fred didn't exactly have a great record when it came to rallying people to the cause. It started with Cloudland dance hall, its picturesque arched entrance torn down by the Deen brothers in the dead of night back in the 1980s. Fred and his wife, June – like many of their peers – had met there. He launched a campaign to bring the Bjelke-Petersen government to account for its actions, or at least the Deen brothers. This was long before Harry's time at the *Chronicle*, of course. Fred failed. Years before he'd told Harry that Joh's secret police had tapped his phone. Since then he'd been iffy about phones, even though Joh was long gone.

Fred had little better luck against subsequent Labor governments. Festival Hall – the birthplace of Brisbane's rock'n'roll scene. Gone. The art deco-style Regent Cinema. Gone. The apartment buildings put in their place always had a 'tribute' to what came before, but a load of photos and memorabilia behind perspex didn't really cut it in terms of preserving cultural identity. The perverse thing was that each subsequent defeat fired up Fred even more. It was as if he'd forgotten why he was fighting. The fight was enough.

Harry laid the flyer to one side. His fingers played gently over the skin at the back of his neck. He thought he could feel the design under his fingertips. He was angry, but didn't know who to direct it at. He pulled out his phone and looked at the photo again. He'd often toyed with the idea of getting a tattoo. He'd once actually stood in a tattoo parlour, looking through books of designs. But he baulked at the thought of having something, *anything*, etched on his body for the rest of his life.

As a journalist, he was a literary omnivore. He consumed a wide range of books, magazines, opinions, commentary. He had engaged in a range of pursuits for short periods of time, usually while researching a story or shortly after writing a story. He'd done some volunteering for Meals on Wheels, delivering food to old people. He'd played beach volleyball for a while, and indoor soccer. But there was no real passion. No one thing that he adored above all else. So anything he got tattooed on his body would be flippant and have no real meaning.

He'd considered something symbolic. When he and Bec moved overseas he thought about two swallows – birds that mate for life – but was put off when she rebuffed without fail any talk of marriage. He'd dodged a bullet there.

He zoomed in on the design. He certainly wouldn't have had some arcane symbol tattooed on his body just for the hell of it. What the fuck *was* that? It was ugly, and kind of creepy. He closed the image and put his phone away.

CHAPTER 5

Harry pulled up outside Fred's house, peering up at the old worker's cottage: flaking paint, weeds growing around the stumps and along the cracked concrete driveway. He couldn't see Fred but he knew he'd be peering down at him through the small gap in the front curtains.

Harry composed himself. It had been another rough morning, after another rough night. The nightmare. The flash of the knife. The dull sawing sensation as Blondie carved the tattoos off. Harry had jerked awake as Beergut and Blondie shovelled dirt onto his face. He came to, shivering, and for a few moments he thought he could see his breath pluming from his mouth. At this time of year that was impossible. He must've still been dreaming. Just as he was drifting back to sleep, he heard the scratching under the house. It was steady, almost to a beat: Scratch, scratch, scratch. Scratch, scratch, scraaatch.

In the end he got up to investigate. He crept under the house, squinting in the morning gloom. Nothing. The sound stopped and there were no obvious signs of rats. After that he was plagued by a restlessness that wouldn't leave him until he pulled on some clothes and headed out the door, into the street. He didn't know he was going to start running until he was doing it. He couldn't face the hill so he took Ozanne Street, making it a couple of hundred metres before he was panting, the taste of blood thick at the back of his throat. Another couple of hundred metres and he was dry-heaving. Harry waited for the nausea to pass, gasping for breath. Then he limped home, wondering what had got into him.

Harry checked his iPhone and pulled out the charger. It had failed him again, the phone's battery dead despite charging all the previous day. But the one upside of the nightmare and the scratching was that he didn't sleep in.

He turned off the car engine. Picked up his phone and called work.

'Hey Chris,' he said. 'I'm at Fred's place. Yeah, yeah, I know. The car wouldn't start again this morning. No, they had to put a new battery in. Anyway, I'll be in later. If I'm not back by lunchtime, send the search party.'

He climbed out of the car, crunched across the lawn. It was ten in the morning and stinking hot and humid. The weather bureau predicted more storms, and the first of the summer cyclones was forming out in the Pacific.

Harry trudged up the steps, and Fred was there to meet him. The door was secured with two deadbolts. The security screen was one of the ones advertised on daytime TV – strong enough to withstand a knife attack. Harry knew for a fact that Fred slept with his old service bayonet underneath his pillow.

'G'day, mate,' Fred said, ushering him in after an iron-clad handshake.

'Hi Fred.'

It took a while for Harry's eyes to adjust to the gloom – Fred didn't open his curtains much – but there were no surprises. Original kitchen. Like Harry's but much better cared for. Green benches, orange cupboards. One clean tea towel hanging from the handle on the stove. Fred's wife had died before Harry could meet her. But unlike a lot of older men in a similar situation, Fred seemed to have kept his shit together. Maybe he'd reverted to his military training. He cooked simple meals, kept his kitchen spotless. But while he'd managed in some areas, he'd struggled in others. The garden was always June's thing, so he'd let it run to seed. It must've been hard. Being with someone for sixty years, and then having to cope alone. Too much time to think.

Every Sunday Fred visited her grave at Lutwytche Cemetery. Best suit. Hair combed. Face shaved. It made Harry feel extremely depressed. When he was with Bec, it made him feel down because he wondered what it would be like to live your whole life, pretty much, with someone, and then for them not to be there anymore. And now, well, now it made him depressed because he could never imagine having something that special with someone. He had thought Bec was 'the one'.

'Take a seat,' Fred said.

Harry sat, placing his notebook and phone next to the porcelain pineapple salt and pepper shakers. June used to collect them – Fred called it 'her vice'. Fred closed and locked both the screen door and the front door, then went to the kitchen to finish the pot of tea. It was part of the ritual, no matter what time of day Harry visited.

The L-shaped open-plan lounge and dining area contained a formica table – again, much like Harry's but in better nick – an old brown lounge suite and a matching sideboard with display cabinet. The cabinet was filled with porcelain figures, books and photos. And even though

Harry had seen the photos dozens of times, he had a look, as he always did. Fred and June on their wedding day. Fred in his army uniform. Fred and June with son Michael – this was one of the few colour photos.

Fred brought over a XXXX tray with the teapot, cups, a milk jug, and a plate of Scotch Finger biscuits. He put the tray on the table, then sat down.

'I saw your flyer,' Harry said.

'This Swenson bloke has gone too far this time. He wrecks Lang Park, turns most of Brisbane's good farming land into housing estates, and now this!'

It was too hot for tea, but Harry took a sip anyway. 'It's a water tower, Fred. It's hardly the Hanging Gardens of Babylon.'

Fred hissed. 'Typical. When you get older, you'll understand.'

'What's that supposed to mean?'

Fred looked away, across to the photos. 'You take these things for granted. But that tower's been there most of me life. June and I used to walk the streets around it when we were courting.'

Harry stared at his tea. 'I'm sorry, I didn't realise it meant that much to you.'

'The bastards got Cloudland. They got Festival Hall and the Regent. They're not getting this one,' Fred said. 'Besides, there's something fishy about it. Prime land. Tower's been sitting there for years. Should have been heritage listed, but no…'

Harry opened his notebook. Fred was known to go off half-cocked, but he also knew a lot about Brisbane. Harry found that writing notes prompted him to talk.

'What makes you think it's dodgy?'

'You hear things. Friends of friends. Bill's daughter's friend works for council. She reckons there were moves to try and get the tower listed.'

Harry looked up. 'Oh yeah? What happened?'

'I heard some money changed hands. And I heard this isn't the first time Swenson has paid his way, if you know what I mean.'

Harry nodded, jotted it down. Fred twisted things to suit his motives, and he saw things through the prism of old age. Fred thought Mrs Dixon up the road was running a puppy farm (puppy farming had been the story of the week on *Today Tonight*) when in actual fact it was just that her bitsa had given birth to a litter of totally legitimate (other than pedigree) puppies. Another time he'd been convinced the guy down the other end of the street was planning to blow up the Story Bridge. This was in the wake of counter-terrorism arrests in Melbourne. Fred called the hotline, reporting a 'Muslim man loading explosives into a white van'. The 'Muslim man' was in fact an Australian-born Sikh, and the 'explosives' were in fact his tools of trade – he was a cable guy. Harry never passed judgement on Fred's claims, not in the first instance. He just accepted them with healthy scepticism.

Harry sipped his tea. Fred wasn't always wrong. He'd been right about the local Meals on Wheels being on the verge of collapse. They hadn't thought to contact the local paper. Harry did a story, it ran on the front page, and the charity was inundated with offers of support. And when Harry heard about a cat called Smokey who had saved his elderly owner from a house fire, and the police wouldn't come through with contact details, Fred was able to put Harry in contact with the woman. It wasn't award-winning journalism, but it turned out to be a nice, offbeat yarn, and he wouldn't have got it without Fred's help.

Besides, Harry enjoyed being with Fred. He reminded him of his granddad, who passed away a few years earlier. After his parents split up, Granddad had been a rock for Harry. Things were different after the break-up. Harry thought that was why he wasn't close with his sisters or his parents. When his granddad passed away, Fred filled the void.

'Anything else you can think of?' Harry asked.

Fred rubbed his chin, rolled his eyes to the ceiling. 'Oh yeah, had some pimple-faced political lackey round the other day,' Fred said.

'Oh yeah? Which flavour?'

Fred laughed. 'Labor. Would've sent the other lot packing. He got hold of one of the flyers that Bill did. Said the ALP were mounting some campaign to save Brisbane's landmarks. Those that are left.'

'Weird.'

'I'll say. Probably nothing will come of it. Probably some New Labor focus group bullshit, if you'll pardon me French.'

'Still, interesting.'

Harry gestured at the somewhat incongruous forty-three-inch TV set in the corner. It was only ever turned on for the cricket, the footy and ABC news.

'How do you think we're gonna go this summer?'

Fred lifted a hand and tilted it side-to-side. 'Depends on whether or not the selectors get some balls.'

As Harry turned to leave, his eye caught the photo of Fred in his wartime gear. 'Hey Fred, I'm sure you've told me this before, but where did you serve?'

'Oh. All over the place. A bit of time in Guinea. Italy. Middle East.'

Harry opened his notebook and pulled out his pen. He quickly sketched the design that was imprinted on his neck. He thought he'd have to consult with the picture on his phone, but he didn't. It was burned into his consciousness. He didn't want to show Fred the tattoo yet, even though he thought the old guy would see the funny side of it. He had a couple of tattoos himself, from his army days.

'When you were in the Middle East, you ever see anything like this?' Harry asked.

Fred took the notebook, slipped on his reading glasses then peered down his nose through them. He shook his head.

'Nah. Not that I can remember. But I spent most of my time in trenches or tanks. Didn't do much sightseeing. Looks kinda like an Arabic bingo card, to be honest.'

Harry smiled. He moved to take the notepad back, but Fred held his hand.

'Can I have the piece of paper?'

'Sure.' Harry tore it out. Fred took it from him, folded it carefully and put it in his top pocket. 'Bill might know. He did a bit of travelling round those parts after the war. His hippy years. Before there were hippies. I can ask him.'

'Thanks. That'd be great.'

Harry didn't even have time to log in before Miles poked his head out of his office.

'Are you two right for the conference?'

'Yep.'

Christine followed Harry into the editor's office, and they both took a seat.

'Right. What have you got for me this week?'

Miles said pretty much the same thing every week, then herded stationery back and forth across his blotter while he listened. Pens to the left, pens to the right. Stapler to the top, stapler to the bottom. When Harry first joined the *Chronicle* he found it extremely distracting. He thought Miles was bored. But no, it was his way of focusing and dissipating some of the nervous energy zipping through his rake-thin body. Harry couldn't see under the desk, but he knew Miles had his legs crossed, the leg on top jiggling up and down so much so that his slip-on barely stayed on his foot.

They detailed the stories they were working on. Possible leads for pages one, three and five, a couple of human-interest colour pieces, advertorials. Sport was centralised so that was the one thing they didn't have to worry about. Harry couldn't remember one edition in all his years with the paper that had come out as forecast at the news conference, but it didn't really matter. Miles really just wanted to know they had a fighting chance of 'filling the holes'.

Harry tried to remember how many juniors had sat beside him. At least eight. Maybe ten. Some shone like a beacon, and were gone in as little as six months. A few decided journalism wasn't for them, and moved to the dark side – government work or public relations. Others struggled but stuck with it. One guy did three years, before moving to another *Chronicle* – the *Menzies Chronicle*, a daily newspaper based a couple of hours' drive west of Brisbane.

He doubted Christine would last another six months. She'd done almost twelve already, and was beginning to realise that, as with most local papers, the news cycle repeated each year. The new year, Australia Day, Easter, Anzac Day, and so on. Regular events that were the staple of the parish pump – that and the dirty half-dozen set stories. It wasn't that Brisbane was boring: two rival outlaw motorcycle gangs – the Dreadnorts and Dead Ringers – had been fighting for turf on the southside a couple of months back; and just weeks ago a guy had been found guilty of bumping off his wife and dumping her body in a creek near Mount Coot-tha. It was just that their patch was more settled than most. Despite the property boom, they had a large proportion of baby boomers who weren't going to sell up. As Fred once said: 'What's the point? Still gotta live somewhere, right?' A couple of times, Harry had caught Christine checking out job ads online. Her heart wasn't in it anymore. Not many Walkley Awards handed out for stories about Meals on Wheels, or accidents waiting to happen, or plans to gentrify some godforsaken shopping centre.

'Oh, one other thing,' Harry said. 'Paddington water tower redevelopment. Fred's arcing up. There're pamphlets and everything.'

'Oh yeah?'

'Yeah. Awful. Comic Sans. Clip art. You know the deal.'

Christine snorted. Miles frowned, then slid some Post-it notes under his monitor, then back out again.

'That's not really our patch though,' he said.

'The developer is Swenson Constructions. Chermside-based.'

Miles dropped the pencil he'd been moving across the desk, then glanced up at Harry. 'Swenson, hey? Could be a story there. Be careful, Harry.'

Harry nodded. 'You know me. Careful's my middle name.'

'Thanks, folks.'

Back at their desks, Christine turned to Harry.

'Why would you need to be 'careful'?' she asked. 'Is Miles worried Swenson's going to drop you into the foundations and dump a load of cement on your head?'

'Something like that,' Harry said. He felt dirt hitting his face and involuntarily shuddered.

He continued with the story he was working on, but he could see Christine in his peripheral vision. He typed another sentence. She folded her arms. Sighed.

'What?' Harry said.

'You never tell me anything.'

Harry stopped what he was doing and turned towards her. 'That's not true.'

'Okay, you tell me stuff, but not the good stuff. Not the interesting stuff. I've been here almost a year, Harry. You need to let me in more.'

'Fair point,' he said. He checked his watch. 'Let's go grab a coffee. A proper one. And I'll fill you in on my history with Swenson.'

On the way over to the shops he told the story. It was something he thought he'd buried, but here it was, clawing its way to the surface. He wasn't sure how Christine would take it. She nodded in all the right places, even threw in a few expletives.

The conversation died while they ordered and paid for their drinks. They switched to safer topics, such as the weather, and what Christine did on the weekend. Clubbing, dinner with friends, a surrealist art exhibition. It made Harry tired just hearing about it. By the time they'd been served their takeaway beverages, Harry assumed the conversation was over. But as they walked back across the car park, Christine wanted to get back into it.

'So that's why you're still here?' she asked.

'Yep. That's it.'

'Harry… I don't want to overstep the mark, but don't underestimate yourself. You've got a lot going for you.'

Harry turned, raised his eyebrows. 'Great. Now I'm getting a pep talk from a Gen Y puke!'

He meant it as a joke, but it came out with an unintended edge. Christine shook her head.

'That's soooo Gen X. No self-belief, but always a sarcastic remark on hand,' she said.

'I'm sorry. Things have been pretty crappy lately.'

'And – *there's* the self-pity.' She grabbed his arm and laughed. 'I'm joking. Before you start sulking.'

The sun gleamed off cars and baked off the bitumen. Harry wished he'd ordered an iced coffee. Ahead, two guys on a stepladder were attaching Christmas decorations to the floodlight poles. It wasn't even Halloween yet.

'At the risk of sounding like I'm digging for compliments – another classic Gen X trait – what exactly have I got going for me?'

Christine considered the question.

Shit, she's trying to think something up.

'You've always helped me out. You know, you haven't held back – in that professional way,' she said. 'I know I came out of uni thinking I knew everything, but I learnt more real-world stuff in that first three months… and most of that you showed me.'

'Uh-huh. So I'm not competitive.'

'Stop it.'

She smiled. He hoped she'd grab his arm again, then pushed the thought away. Flirting with someone so much younger than him. It was pathetic.

'And I think you really showed me the value of community journalism,' she said. 'I didn't really want this job, to be honest. I only took it because my parents hassled me into it. But I can really see now how important the *Chronicle* is to people around here.'

'You're so full of shit!' Harry said.

'It's true! Some people, anyway. You know how true it is once you get a couple of calls from people telling you you've fucked up their Community Diary entry.'

'Yeah. There's that.'

'And that Meals on Wheels story… Don't roll your eyes. It worked, Harry. If you hadn't written that story, it would be gone.'

They walked in silence for a while.

'And, you've got a tattoo now,' Christine said.

'And what difference does that make?'

'You're edgier now! Far more Gen Y.'

The afternoon disappeared in a blur. Christine worked on her stories and Harry on his. He took phone calls and lined up interviews, arranged for photographs to be taken. The TV in the corner was tuned to Sky News, where Andrew Cardinal talked and talked, Vessel nodding studiously in the background. Harry watched for a moment, until the picture cut back to the studio, where Terry Redwood was on what looked like a panel discussion. He was clearly loving every minute. His moment in the sun.

Harry shook his head. All his skeletons were tumbling out of the closet. He tried to distract himself with the to-do list on his screen, and instead ended up thinking about Bec. Part of him hoped she felt as crappy as he did. He hoped she missed him. Part of him nurtured the fantasy that she might call him up and apologise. But while he nurtured it, he recognised it as a fantasy. Like buying a lottery ticket and imagining how you might spend the money.

He flicked to Bec's Facebook page, partly out of habit, partly out of a slightly malicious desire to see her in pain. She didn't mention him. Her relationship status had moved from 'It's complicated' to 'Single'. It hurt that they'd been apart less than a week and she'd found the headspace to advertise it online. He clicked on her photos, knowing how sad it would make him. There were still photos of the two of them in there. From the housewarming party at their apartment. Even some from Europe, all those years ago. She had posted some photos from a work function a couple of nights before. He hovered over the names, prickled slightly when he saw a photo where she was hugging one of her male workmates.

Beside him, Christine stood up. Harry minimised the window, checking to see if he'd been busted Face-stalking.

'Another coffee?' she asked, brandishing her KeepCup.

He shook his head. 'Nah. I'm going to head off soon.'

He watched as she walked away, then returned his attention to his screen. He opened a story at random and started typing, fingers playing over the keyboard, eyes blurring slightly. He could write this shit blindfolded.

When his phone rang, his first thought was Bec. He pushed it away, ridiculed himself even as he reached for the handset, but was still slightly disappointed when he heard Fred's wheezy breathing on the other end of the line.

'Harry? Fred here.'

'Hey, Fred.'

'I got down to the library. Saw Bill.'

'That was quick.'

'Yeah, well, you know me. That symbol you showed me? It's from the Middle East. Some sort of magic apparently,' he said the word slowly – *ma-jick* – as though trying it out. 'From Afghanistan. Harry?'

'Yeah, Fred, I'm here. Sorry, I was trying to multitask.'

'Nope. Blokes don't do that. Is that any help to you?'

'Yeah. Thanks very much for asking him.'

'No problem.'

CHAPTER 6

The Rigid Hull Inflatable Boat skimmed across the waves as the last rays of light drifted from the sky. Rob checked his gear, then glanced back to where Dan and Tim sat. In the sea behind them was another RHIB and, beyond that, the low profile of Christmas Island. Ahead of them, just a dot on the horizon now, the MV Fajar Baru, a tramp steamer with possibly hundreds of Unauthorised Boat Arrivals on board. In the low clouds above it, lightning bloomed.

Tim leant over to him, yelling above the roar of the engine and the solid thump-thump-thump of the RHIB hitting the waves. 'We're gonna have to be quick.'

Rob shrugged. *It'll take as long as it takes.*

There was an election looming; the government had taken a stand on people-smuggling. The PM didn't want any more UBAs washing up on the Australian territory of Christmas Island, demanding asylum. Their mission was to turn the ship back into international waters, and the new Border Protection Bill gave the government (and, by extension, them) the power to use whatever means necessary to do that. They'd all studied the maps during the briefing. It's okay for the Fajar Baru to be here but not there. On one level it was bullshit, but it wasn't Rob's job to question the politics of it. They had a job to do.

Rob was hoping they'd be able to do it the easy way. The Fajar Baru had picked up the UBAs after their small wooden fishing boat foundered off the coast of Indonesia. They'd done the right thing. If not for the crew of the tramp steamer, the UBAs would be dead. Initial radio contact advised the Fajar Baru to turn back into Indonesian waters. They acknowledged the message, but maintained their course for Christmas Island. Further calls had gone unanswered. It could have been that the radio failed. It could have been that the UBAs had disabled the radio. Or it could have been that they had taken over the whole vessel. Rob and his team were prepared for all eventualities.

Yeah, they were armed to the teeth. But Rob hoped it wouldn't come to that. In the RHIB behind them, there was an army medic with as much gear as he could carry. The fishing boat had been at sea for at least three days, and the UBAs aboard the steamer for two days after that. God knew what sort of conditions they'd been living in before they set sail. They'd most likely be filthy, hungry and thirsty.

Ahead of them, the Fajar Baru grew bigger. A rust-streaked bridge rose up at the stern, overlooking the cargo decks below. From here, there was no sign of trouble. The ship was still making good headway, probably hoping to get to Christmas Island before the storm hit. Which wasn't going to happen.

'Get on the radio, Tim, let them know we're coming,' Rob said.

Tim set up his radio. He yelled into the microphone in English, then Bahasa. He screwed his face up. Shrugged. 'Nothing.'

A low crack tore through the air.

'What the hell was that?' Rob said.

But he knew. The dickheads were trying to sabotage the ship. There were people running about on the deck. White splashes as bodies hit the water. Screams.

Fuck. This isn't going to be pretty.

A secondary explosion tore through the ship. Light bloomed amidships. More white splashes as people jumped for their lives when flames erupted from below deck. On the bridge, a flash of frantic movement.

Tim got on his radio again, calling for backup. The HMAS Manoora was in the area. But by the time it got here, it would be too late to do much.

The steamer listed to one side, showing its deck. There was a rupture down the centre, billowing thick black smoke. Occasionally, flames would flare. Charred bodies slid towards the water.

'She's going down fast,' Tim said.

Rob looked behind to check the other RHIB was still with them. The sea was getting choppier. Between the white-capped waves, faces appeared. Crying, screaming. A woman, trying to hold her baby above water. The charred back of a man, floating face-down. The closer they got, the more they comprehended the scope of the tragedy. Hundreds of people in the water.

The ship groaned. An ear-splitting shriek as the deck tore apart. Two splashes of orange, life rafts already overwhelmed by the tens of people struggling to get on board.

The RHIB slowed. Rob turned around. Dan stared back at him.

'If we go in there, we're gone,' he said.

The other RHIB pulled level. Rob had to yell to be heard over the engines and the wind from the approaching storm. John looked over from the other boat, seeking guidance.

'Get in there. We'll do what we can,' Rob said.

Dan cursed, shook his head, but sped up again. They skirted the edges. When the people saw the boats, a dreadful cacophony arose.

'Keep to the edges,' Rob said.

They pulled a woman on board. She coughed and spluttered. Started babbling in Farsi.

'Tim?'

'She wants to know where her son is.'

Tim talked to her, trying to calm her. Dan was right: this had the potential to go pear-shaped quickly.

They yanked a boy from the sea. Thick shock of black hair. Burns on one of his arms.

'A couple more.'

'And then what, Rob?' Dan said.

'Then we get the fuck out of here. Come back.'

Rob watched, horrified, as faces dropped under the waves and didn't come up again. A woman with burns to her face, her hair gone. A man with a thick grey beard. A mob of people, mostly men, were swimming towards the boat. Closer to them, another man dropped below the surface. Rob grabbed his arm.

'Hurry up, Rob,' Dan said.

The hand slipped. Rob reached over the edge, almost sending himself over the side.

'Rob?'

'Throw them some life jackets. Something, for Christ's sake.'

The other RHIB had arrived at the same conclusion,

throwing their spare life jackets overboard. Flashes of orange against the grey sea.

Rob grabbed the man's hand again, pulled back. This time the man came up. At first Rob thought his skin was burned black. Then he realised he was looking at tattoos. Squiggles, lines, dots. On the other side of the boat, Tim helped someone else aboard.

Rob grabbed the man's pants and heaved him over. His shirt was gone. His back was covered in tattoos. Nothing Rob could make sense of.

'Go!' Rob said.

'Got it.'

The RHIB's engine throbbed. Dan brought it around in a tight circle, heading back towards Christmas Island. The front edge of the storm hit, peppering them with raindrops. The voices of those left behind rose, terror and anger and fear. A wounded animal, crying out in anguish.

Rob shook his head. The man rolled over, stared up at him.

'Tashakkur! Tashakkur! Tashakkur!'

Tim translated: 'Thank you, thank you, thank you.'

The tattooed man spoke some more.

Tim shrugged. 'He's Ahmed. He says he owes you his life.'

Harry jerked awake, panting. In those first moments all he could see were the old man's tattoos, imprinted on his retinas. All he could smell was the sea. All he could hear were screams. He blinked his eyes, looked around his room. Then the pain hit him.

'Ow!'

His upper arm felt as though someone had jabbed a thousand needles into it, then set them on fire. He squinted down, trying to find the source of the pain.

Spider? The place wasn't screened. A spider must've… No. Even something like a redback wouldn't be inclined to climb inside someone's room just to bite them.

Snake? He had heard of people finding snakes in their bed, but it was usually in the middle of winter, or in the aftermath of a flood. The only flood Harry was experiencing was his sweat, soaking his t-shirt and sheets.

Harry turned on the light. The skin poking out from the sleeve of his t-shirt was black, blue and green. Not good.

'What the…'

He tried pulling the sleeve up but it hurt too much. He rubbed his face, and his arm exploded in pain again.

'Fuck.'

Harry steeled himself, then pulled his sweat-soaked t-shirt off. He looked down, expecting rotting flesh, an acid burn, shredded skin. *No, impossible.* He walked to the bathroom to get a better look.

A new tattoo: angry waves, white caps. It reminded him of that famous Japanese woodcut. Among the waves, a man: arm outstretched, mouth just above the waterline. Below the waterline, the vague outline of bodies.

Get them into the boat!

For a moment the man seemed to move on his arm, reach outwards, off his skin. Then Harry realised the tattoo wasn't moving, his whole field of vision was ballooning. He gripped the sides of the sink. A wave of nausea washed over him, sweat prickled on his skin. Fear in his gut. The fear he'd dragged from the nightmare coupled with the fear of not knowing what was going on.

He closed his eyes, but found no relief. Instead of darkness, he saw terrified eyes peering out of the darkness. A baby, floating face-down on the churning sea. His stomach turned.

'No!'

He turned the cold tap on, thrust his head down under the water. Kept his eyes open as it washed over the back of his head. He stayed there for a minute, controlling his breathing, focusing on the dark eye of the plughole, clearing his mind. When he felt centred, he stood up again, shivering as water ran down his body.

He took a step back from the mirror, assessed the tattoo again. It was real. Blues, greens, black ink. The detail was amazing. He ran his other hand over it, wincing at the pain. Panic threatened to return, but he blocked it before it could grab hold. There was no point panicking. Panicking wasn't going to get rid of the tattoo. He grabbed a towel, dried his hair. Kept his mind busy with a mental checklist.

Call work. There was no way he was going in to work today. Christine had a handle on things. He could miss a day, given the circumstances.

Make an appointment to visit a doctor. Because something clearly wasn't right with his head. He could wish away that first tattoo, even though the woman at West End Tattoo – what was her name? Sian – even though Sian said she didn't even think it was done by a proper tattooist. Harry had been drunk. Drunker than he'd been in a long time. He had blacked out. While blacked out, anything was possible. But this? Sober. Going to bed at a reasonable hour. This could not be explained away so easily.

He walked back to his bedroom, felt the panic encroaching again, and decided to try and keep it on the back foot until he could go see a doctor. He grabbed a pair of shorts and a t-shirt, pulled on his shoes and headed out the door. He started at a fast walk, then broke into a slow run when he felt his legs had warmed up enough. As the sweat beaded on his brow, he tried to make sense of what had happened.

After work he had stopped off at the bottle shop and picked up a carton of VB. He wasn't sure why he chose his uni beer over Coronas. It just felt right. At the time he'd been thinking about what Fred had told him about his tattoo. *The first tattoo.*

When he got home he cracked a beer. Just the one. He told himself it was mainly because Dave reckoned it was bad luck to put a whole carton in the fridge. Depending on how drunk he was, he would recount several gruesome tales of what had befallen saps who'd dared to refrigerate their whole carton.

He drank it while he unpacked boxes. And, as expected, there were emotional landmines rigged and waiting for him. Stupid stuff. Stuff he didn't think to ditch, well, when his prime concern was making sure he wasn't there when Bec got back.

The tacky t-shirt Bec had bought him that Christmas in London. Rudolf with a light-up nose. They'd been broke, living in the shittiest part of London. And one evening Bec had arrived home with flushed cheeks and a cheeky grin. Harry had been in a foul mood. But then she'd pulled out this stupid t-shirt, and a bottle of cheap whisky, and he'd put it on and they'd gotten shitfaced. It was the only time he'd worn it, but there it stayed, at the bottom of his drawer.

Books. His copy of Stephen King's *On Writing*, with her inscription in the front, telling him she couldn't wait to read his first bestseller. The writing had gone the way of the exercise once they got back from England. He couldn't bear the thought of sitting in front of a computer screen all night after doing that most of the day. But, like the t-shirt, he couldn't face the thought of throwing the book away. Same with all the other books she'd given him.

And the letters and postcards. He had a big golden-hued box full of them. The box itself had memories attached. It had contained a black shirt, her first Valentine's Day gift to him. He'd worn it out to dinner. It was still on when they made love later that night. And the box was full of every letter she'd written him, every postcard she'd sent him when she was away on business. He supposed this box was the first thing that would go. But he couldn't. Not yet. He placed it in the bottom drawer of the crappy dresser that had been in the bedroom when he'd moved in.

Each surprise was greeted with thudding heart, nervous

sweating, shaking hands. Each one carried with it the threat of tears. And yet he stuck to that one beer. In truth, he was still a little bit scared of what might happen if he got hammered again.

And yet… it'd happened anyway. After unpacking, he'd carried himself off to bed, and woken up with this.

Harry stopped at the top of the hill. He leant on a street sign for support, wincing as the muscles in his arm flexed under the tattoo. Catching his breath didn't take as long as it should have. When he felt rested enough, he turned and headed home.

Harry pulled off his sweaty clothes, picked up his phone. Dead. Again.

'Jesus!'

He plugged it into the charger, then had a quick shower and got dressed. Harry considered putting on a long-sleeved shirt. But then he'd need to put on long pants, and it was too hot for long pants.

Screw it. These are part of me now.

As soon as he thought it, it felt right. These tattoos were part of him. He didn't understand why, or how, but the thought of having them removed felt wrong.

He felt much better by the time he was sitting in his car. Mouth feeling fresh and hair slicked back with water. Then he turned the key in the ignition.

Click!

He tried again.

Click!

'For the love of…'

A third time, even though he had no right to expect a better result.

Click!

He pulled his phone out and dialled the RACQ. Eventually, Mike turned up, changed the battery. Harry explained what had been going on. Three days, three dead batteries.

Mike put a multimeter on the new battery, frowned.

'Doesn't look like there's anything drawing too much power,' he said. 'But then car electrics are tricky things.'

He said that the new battery should help things, then dropped the bonnet with a crash that reverberated under the house.

'Sometimes you can't do much for a tired old thing like this,' he said.

Mike suggested parking the car up the street, facing downhill, until he could get an auto electrician to have a look at it. That way, if the battery went flat, Harry could hill-start it.

'You do know how to hill-start, right?' he said. A rhetorical question.

'Oh yeah,' Harry said. 'Of course.' It was one of the skills Dad taught him after Mum left. They all got very good at improvising and making do. Chewing gum and bread ties were not uncommon in dad's attempts to get another hundred kays out of their ancient Holden.

Harry walked Mike back to his ute, and they looked up the steep road towards the water tower.

'Up there somewhere,' Mike said, as though Harry – despite being able to hill-start a car – might not appreciate the concept of 'downhill'.

He wondered if there was a way of hill-starting his iPhone.

* * *

Harry sat in the doctor's surgery, wishing he'd thought to bring his jumper with him. They always had the air-conditioning cranked. Whether this was to lull patients into a soporific state while they waited, or to suit the Scottish secretary, Harry wasn't sure. He'd been coming here for years. It was one of the things he and Bec shared that would become part of the unarticulated post-separation carve-up over the coming months. All their shared places – the cafes, restaurants, parks, cinemas – would go one way or the other.

Harry wanted Black Cat Books in Paddington and Avid Reader at West End. Maybe Brents restaurant over the back of Toowong, though there were so many memories associated with that place that maybe it would be better to let it go. It seemed bizarre that he and Bec would never go there again as a couple for Valentine's Day or one of their unofficial 'anniversary' dinners. And it seemed even more bizarre and unlikely that one day Harry might take someone else there and be able to not associate it with her.

His phone buzzed. A message from Christine: *Are you OK?*

He texted her back: *Yeah. Thanks.*

A brief message that in no way summed up how he was doing. He always wore long-sleeved shirts to work, so he didn't have to worry about her finding out about the latest tattoo in the short-term. He'd probably wear his suit to the end-of-year awards night. And by then, he should have some idea of what he was dealing with. Anyway, maybe she'd like this one, like she did the last one.

'Harry?'

He looked up. Dr Boyd was there, holding Harry's file, dressed in shirt and slacks, juxtaposed with worn cowboy boots. Harry had never felt comfortable asking what the deal was with the boots, whether they were the symbol of a mid-life crisis or something else. But a year or so ago Harry had to have a mole cut out of his back, and while Dr Boyd cut into his flesh – *What are we going to do with these?* – he had Johnny Cash playing on the sound system, so things came together slightly. It was a little disconcerting listening to his scalpel-wielding doctor whistling along to a tune about a guy who shot a man in Reno, just to watch him die.

Harry quelled the rising nausea as he rose to walk through to the doctor's consulting room. The appointments over the years always took the same path. Dr Boyd came out, brandishing Harry's file and calling his name as though it were the first time he'd ever said it. Harry sat down in Dr Boyd's room. Dr Boyd asked: 'So, how's it going?' Harry described his symptoms, and usually offered some apocalyptic self-diagnosis from time spent on the internet, pointing to dark options such as tumours and cancer. And then Dr Boyd, while Harry peered at the sporting memorabilia on the walls, told him it was something relatively benign. And then prescribed a cream, ointment or, if things were really bad, antibiotics.

'So, how's it going?'

Harry took a big breath. 'Not so great.'

He pulled up the sleeve of his shirt, displaying the new tattoo. 'I got this tattoo.'

Dr Boyd moved in, peering over his glasses, studying Harry's arm as though it was a rash. He took Harry's arm and gently turned it.

'Looks fairly recent. When did you get it? Yesterday? Day before?'

'I don't know. Last night, I think.'

Dr Boyd looked from the arm to Harry, then back to the arm. Harry thought he'd ask for an explanation, but instead he just sat back and waited.

'I think I'm having blackouts,' Harry said. 'In fact, I know I am.'

Harry told him the story, from waking up the night after Dave's buck's night, to the visit to West End Tattoo, finishing off with his discovery this morning. Dr Boyd sat in front of his computer, tapping notes out on the keyboard.

He took his ophthalmoscope, turned Harry's head and shone the light into each of his eyes.

'Have you been experiencing any dizziness? Anything like that?'

'No.'

'Seeing lights flashing behind your eyes? Things floating in your field of vision?'

'No.'

'Odd smells? Any strange sounds?'

Harry thought of the scratching he'd heard under the house the past three nights, just as he was waking up. But that was just rats, right?

'Smells?' Harry said.

'Yeah, often – if it's a problem with the brain – there can be what we call auras before episodes. Often visual, like blurry spots or losing your peripheral vision. But sometimes olfactory – smells, in other words. Or aural – sounds.'

'No, no smells.'

Dr Boyd put down the ophthalmoscope, turned back to his PC and clicked through some screens. 'Can't see anything here about head injuries. Is there anything from when you were younger?'

Harry thought about it. He always found himself trying to second-guess the diagnosis, provide the 'right' answers.

'No,' he said.

'How about your family? Any history of seizures, migraine, that sort of thing?'

'Well, they're all batshit crazy,' Harry said. 'But just in the usual family way. Mum went through a phase where she had a lot of migraines, but that was just before she split up with my dad, so…'

Dr Boyd nodded as though he knew what Mrs Hendrick was going through. He pulled out another piece of equipment.

'Here, give me your finger,' Dr Boyd said. 'This might hurt a bit. I need to test your blood sugar level.'

Harry offered his hand. There was a brief sting. Harry saw a smear of blood on a small piece of cardboard. The doctor slipped it into a small machine, which beeped. Dr Boyd checked the readout. He pressed a cotton wool ball against Harry's finger.

'Yeah, that's fine,' Dr Boyd said. 'How have you been sleeping?'

'Okay. But I've been having nightmares.'

'Is your bed, ah, dry in the morning?'

Harry did a double-take.

Dr Boyd cleared his throat. 'It's just that, when people have seizures or other similar episodes, they often lose bladder control.'

'No, I mean, it's wet, but it's just sweat,' Harry said. He leant forward and rapped his knuckles on the table, aiming for a levity he didn't feel.

'Uh-huh. And obviously on the first night, you were under the influence…'

'Putting it lightly.'

'How about last night. Alcohol? Drugs?'

'Just one beer. A VB.'

Dr Boyd made a note of that, as though the brand were important. He opened drawers, pulled out more equipment. Checked Harry's pulse and blood pressure. Then his reflexes.

'Ooookay, that's all fine,' Dr Boyd said. 'You're getting your money's worth today, right? If you could just pop up on the bed.'

Harry climbed up on the bed, feeling a distinct unease. This wasn't panning out like his usual doctor's visit. In and out in ten minutes. For once, he feared the diagnosis was going to be worse than he anticipated. Dr Boyd rolled a machine over. It was plugged into the wall.

'Shirt off, please,' Dr Boyd said.

Harry took off his shirt and lay down.

'Have you had an ECG reading before?'

Harry shook his head.

'It's easy. I just attach these electrodes and it reads your heartbeat. You've probably seen it in movies hundreds of times.'

'In the movies I've seen, it doesn't end well.'

'Ha! You'll be right. I just need to rule things out before I send you up to the hospital.'

'Hospital?'

Dr Boyd nodded. 'Just as a precaution. Would be good to get this sorted. It's your brain, Harry.'

He attached the electrodes. Started the machine. Peered down at Harry.

'Any trouble on the home front?' he said.

Harry laughed. 'Is it that obvious?'

Dr Boyd shrugged. 'Nah. Standard question.'

'Bec and I split up.'

To his credit, Dr Boyd didn't rush in with the shallow condolences that had been coming at him thick and fast, in person, on the phone and on Facebook.

'That's rough.'

'Yeah. We'd been together six years, so…'

Dr Boyd glanced at Harry, but seemed to look through him. 'And how have you been dealing with that? Any suicidal thoughts?'

Harry was taken aback. He laughed nervously. To be honest, there had been one. Right after the fight. He had sat in his car watching the traffic go by, thinking that if he did something stupid, drove his car into the path of an on-coming truck, she'd regret it. But it passed as quickly as it arrived. It was a mass of hurt and anger trying to find an outlet.

'No. I've been good. Considering.'

'Uh-huh.' Dr Boyd checked the machine, looked at his watch. 'Looking good, Harry.' He removed the electrodes, gave Harry a couple of tissues to wipe away the gel. 'You can put your shirt back on.

'I'm going to send you for a CT scan. It could be psychological. Sounds like you've had a rough trot of late. But we need to make sure we rule out all the physical stuff as well.

'I'm also going to give you a referral for counselling. Sometimes it can be good to talk to someone who isn't involved. Someone who doesn't have an axe to grind, you know?'

Harry nodded.

Dr Boyd looked at Harry. 'Exercise can be good for stress.'

'Yeah, I've… I've taken up running.' He wasn't quite sure if his early morning lurches through the streets were classed as 'running', but it was certainly the most sustained physical exercise he'd done in a long while.

'As for the tattoos themselves, do you know anything about looking after them?'

'No.'

Dr Boyd opened a couple of drawers, rifled through them. Then checked the bookshelf above his computer. He pulled down a glossy pamphlet.

'Here you go.' Dr Boyd handed Harry the referrals as well as a pamphlet called 'Caring for your tattoo'.

'The basics are pretty simple. No hot baths for a couple of weeks. No swimming for a couple of weeks. If it scabs up, leave the scabs alone and let them come off by themselves. Once it's healed, make sure you use sunscreen before heading out into the sun.'

'Thanks.'

Harry folded up the referrals and the pamphlet, got up out of his chair. Dr Boyd stood, removed one of his cufflinks and started rolling up his sleeve. Before Harry could question him, he'd revealed a large tattoo of Johnny Cash. It was a silhouette, with 'Walk the Line' written above it.

'Got it done twenty years ago,' Dr Boyd said. 'What do you think?'

Harry raised his eyebrows and nodded. 'Do you ever regret it?'

Dr Boyd shook his head. 'Nah. It's not like it's a tattoo of my wife, right?'

He slapped Harry on his untattooed shoulder.

'Have you got someone who can drive you up to the hospital?'

'Yeah, yeah I think so,' Harry said.

'Take care, Harry, and let me know how you get on.'

CHAPTER 8

Dave pulled out into the traffic, leaving the hospital behind them.

'Well, this wasn't exactly what I had in mind when I suggested catching up before the wedding,' he said.

Harry rubbed his face. The big yellow envelope holding his scans sat wedged between his knees. The guy who did the CT scan told Harry there wouldn't be any side effects. But he felt weird. Slightly dizzy.

'I know. I'm sorry. If it's any consolation, sitting in a neurology waiting room wasn't what I had in mind for my day off either.'

'I was kidding. Any time. You know that.' He cleared his throat. 'So?'

Harry waved it away. 'I'm fine. Normal.'

'It's normal to get tattoos and not remember it?' Dave asked. He pulled onto the Inner City Bypass, waving to a driver who had made room to let him in.

'No. My scan. They can't see anything abnormal.'

'Basically, you're nuts then?'

Harry laughed in spite of himself. 'You might need to work on your bedside manner.'

'I call it how I see it. So… you don't remember anything from last night?'

'Nope. I remember bits of the nightmare. A lot of people drowning. Fuck, it was bleak. But about the actual night, no. I went to bed, woke up with the ink.

'It's stupid, but if I'm not going out to get the tattoos, then someone's coming and giving them to me.'

'Sounds a bit David Lynch,' Dave said. 'To what end? Best prank ever?'

Harry shrugged. They drove on in silence for a while. He squinted through the dusty windscreen of Dave's sedan. Heat baked the road, turning the tarmac into a shimmering oasis. Harry wished he'd brought his sunglasses. At the top of the hill they passed St Bridget's, the gothic-style church glowing like a red brick beacon. Then the run-down row of shops that had been a mainstay of uni life until rental prices pushed the students further out of town.

'If you want me to stay, I will,' Dave said.

The car dropped down the other side of the hill, into the shadows, following the traffic out of Brisbane.

'Dave, you're getting married tomorrow. But I appreciate the offer.'

Dave shrugged. 'I'm worried about you.'

'I'm fine.'

Dave cocked his eyebrow.

'Well, not fine. But, you know.'

Dave shook his head. Sighed. Then threw a hand up. 'Okay. Okay. Just… let me know if there's anything I can do.'

The traffic ground to a halt at the charred remains of the Red Hill Skate Arena. Popular in the '80s, it went the way of pinball machines in the '90s, before closing down.

The owners wanted to sell it for redevelopment. There was talk of it being heritage listed. Then the place was torched.

Harry had driven past the place hundreds of times. Now, for some reason, in this reddish light, its charred roof beams and rusting fences brought him out in gooseflesh.

'How'd your interview with Mr Excitement go?' Dave asked.

'It was okay.'

Harry was still confused, still angry at Ron for dredging up all that stuff. *The story was good.* If he knew that, how many others did? How many others kept their mouths shut and let a uni student take the hit rather than have a scandal rock the ALP? He could have vented. But Dave would offer him a slightly bemused expression, make some quip, and that would be the end of it. They'd been friends for fifteen years, would probably be friends for another fifteen, or thirty. If Harry murdered someone, then went down for it, he could see Dave sitting on the other side of the plexiglass window, that same slightly bemused expression on his face, as Harry told him how it came to be. That's just how it was with Dave.

'Well, he didn't bore you to death, so that's one thing,' Dave said.

'So, who are you going to vote for?'

Dave shrugged. 'What's the difference? None of them have any real power.'

'That's a cop-out.'

'Point out a politician in recent years who's actually made a difference. The whole thing is a facade. We're meant to believe this is real but they do their schtick, we all trudge out on the day, in the stinking hot most likely, tick the box…'

'You number the boxes.'

'What?'

'The boxes, you number them.'

'Oh right, yeah. Whatever. And then the next guy gets in, tells us that he can't really do anything he said he'd do, because of the state of the economy or the deficit or some bullshit, and then we continue on as before.'

'Jesus. You're more cynical than I am.'

Dave shrugged. 'When you work in a hospital you quickly get a sense of what's important and what isn't.'

'In other words, it's not you speaking, it's the old people.'

'Maybe they're right. That's another thing. We think we know better. They're the ones who have been around longer – sometimes twice as long as we have. And yet we just discount everything they say. Maybe that's why we never get anywhere.'

Like Fred. Quite true. Most people thought he was just a crazy old man. And sure, there was a touch of the crazies about him, but he also knew a lot. He had a lot of connections.

They wove through the streets. The water tower appeared like a lighthouse in the afternoon sun, looking out over a sea of jacaranda trees and corrugated iron. And then Dave's car was plunging into the deep, dark waters of Croydon Road. He pulled up outside Harry's place.

'Do you want to come in for a coffee? Beer?' Harry asked.

'Nah. Gotta push on. The in-laws are doing a dinner thing. You sure you're going to be okay?'

Harry shrugged. 'I can look after myself.'

He climbed out. Dave turned the car around, then leant out the window.

'Oh. If you can avoid getting anything tattooed on your

face before tomorrow, that'd be great,' he said. 'You know where we're meeting?'

Harry nodded. 'Simmo may be a misogynistic prick, but he's an organised misogynistic prick.'

'And *that's* why he's my best man. See you tomorrow.'

Harry was about to walk up the steps when he remembered the scratching noise. He went under the house. The few packing boxes he'd finished with were folded up at the back, leaning against the wooden slats. Cardboard would make a perfect rat's nest. He strode across the cracked, oil-stained concrete slab and pulled out the boxes. He checked them out, and they looked okay.

The far side of the under-house area, away from the laundry, was bare dirt. Harry walked over and peered at the ground. He couldn't see anything that looked like paw prints, but then he wasn't an expert. Over in the far corner was a rusty possum trap, covered in cobwebs. He much preferred the thought of possums scratching around under the house, but they'd be far more likely to stick to the mango tree, or his roof.

He came out the back and saw the woman from next door, bringing in her washing. She was about his age, but clearly much fitter. Dressed in a singlet and shorts. He wasn't sure if he even wanted to talk to her. But as he was turning to go up the stairs she looked over, and he caught her eye.

'Hey,' he said.

'Hi.'

Harry stood there, not sure what to do. Then walked over to the fence. 'I'm Harry. Just moved in.'

'Hi. I'm Karen.' She dropped one of the blue uniforms

into the basket and offered her hand. Harry shook it.

'You're a nurse?'

'No, sex worker. I specialise in medical fantasies.' Beat. 'That's a joke.'

Harry laughed, embarrassed.

'Yeah, I'm an RN. At Royal Alex. You're clearly a trained observer.'

'Heh. I am actually. I work for the *Chermside Chronicle*. A friend of mine is a nurse, over at the Royal. Studying to become a doctor.'

'Aren't we all?'

'Hey, have you had any trouble with rats at your place?'

Karen unpegged another uniform. Shook her head. 'Nah. We do get bush rats around here though. They come for the mangos. You got some?'

'Ah, I don't know. Scratching under the house at night.'

'Uh-huh. I've got some traps, if you want them.'

Harry considered. Deep down, he didn't think it was rats. 'I'll see how I go, but thanks for the offer. Anyway, I'll let you get back to it.'

'No worries,' Karen said, and Harry turned back to the house.

CHAPTER 9

Harry sat in front of his laptop, eyes glazed over, barely seeing the screen. His arm throbbed. The sun was long gone, but it was still stinking hot. Sweat beaded on his chest, running down to the waistband of his shorts. The house creaked, expanding with the heat. The tin roof tick, tick, ticked. Distant thunder taunted.

He took another mouthful of beer, went to Google and typed 'phantom tattoos'. The page loaded and he laughed. The screen filled with links to photos and discussions about tattoos of the Phantom of the Opera and the Ghost Who Walks. He clicked on 'Images'. Skulls peered out at him, but they were either on the Phantom's belt buckle (where they should be) or surrounded by blood-red roses. None of them were anything like his drowning man, or the 'Arabic bingo card'.

He opened a text document and wrote down everything he could remember from the latest nightmare. A soldier called Rob. Men, women and children, drowning. UBAs, Rob had called them. He stared through the screen.

'They were trying to turn the ship around,' Harry said to himself.

Shit. Harry sat back in his chair, ran his fingers through his sweaty hair. Took another slug of VB. He could hear them screaming.

Two tattoos. Two nightmares. Was Rob the guy buried in the shallow grave? Harry thought he was.

He searched for 'asylum seeker tragedy'. The screen filled with the first page of more than a million hits. Everywhere from Australia to Africa to Afghanistan. He added 'Christmas Island'.

The top result was a news story from a week earlier: *Former minister reflects on Christmas Island tragedy.*

During the 2001 federal election campaign, Harry read, Australian forces were sent from Christmas Island to turn around an Indonesian tramp steamer that had strayed into Australian waters. The ship was full of asylum seekers, picked up after the fishing boat they were travelling on sank. The ship's captain wanted to offload them on Christmas Island.

But when the Australians neared the ship, it exploded. A report into the tragedy found that asylum seekers had tried to sabotage the engines, and accidentally ignited the ship's fuel supply.

With a storm fast approaching, the vessel sank quickly. Of the more than 400 people on board, only 45 were saved. The SAS troopers involved, who weren't named, were awarded the Medal for Gallantry.

The former immigration minister, reflecting on the 'unnecessary' loss of life, put the blame back firmly on the people smugglers, rather than the government's decision to turn the boat around. Further down the article, Labor's immigration spokesperson blamed the government for the asylum seekers' deaths. But in the next quote she promised even tougher border controls under a Cardinal Labor government.

Harry typed some more notes, then returned to Google. He finished his beer, and rose from his chair to fetch another, then stopped. On a whim, he typed in 'ghost tattoos'. Again, a heap of links to literal tattoos popped up. But on the side, in the sponsored links, a list of different results. A couple of local tattoo parlours, including West End Tattoo, but also psychics: City Psychics, Australian Psychics, Brisbane Psychics. Harry stared at the links for a long time, but didn't click.

Instead, he returned to the fridge and pulled out another beer, replacing the empty bottle in his stubby holder. He shouldn't really be drinking, given his likely psychological problems. But when you're at the point where you're going out and getting tattoos done while you're unconscious, a couple of beers couldn't hurt.

He stood in the kitchen, looking out at the house next door, and its back garden. Thinking of Karen. Of brain tumours. Of drowning men and buried men and screaming. Lots and lots of screaming.

He took his beer back to the lounge room and stretched out on the couch, watching movies in his mind. How did it all fit together? He felt like he had when he'd been at uni, working on his final assignment. In the early stages. He'd had all these pieces of seemingly unrelated information. And then, one day, they'd clicked together.

Harry sculled the rest of his beer, enjoying the buzz. He lay back and stared at the ceiling. Outside, the wind picked up. Off in the distance thunder boomed. Harry drifted to sleep, goosebumps prickling his flesh.

CHAPTER 10

It was a bad day for suits. But it was a wedding. There wasn't really a choice. Simmo, eyes slightly glazed, handed out matching ties. They'd spent a couple of hours at the Paddo Tavern, downing schooners of XXXX and eyeing off the barmaids. Simmo had tried to use the fact that it was a wedding day to acquire free beer and phone numbers. When he didn't get either, he proclaimed that the blond-haired honey behind the bar was either blind, stuck-up or a lesbian. There was toast after toast, bad joke after bad joke, until Dave put his foot down and decided that this was the absolute last round.

They retreated to the B&B Dave had booked. The place had aircon, and a fine view. From the verandah you could look out over the lush jacaranda trees and patchwork of tin roofs to the modest spires of Brisbane's CBD. Tonight, Dave and his new wife would be spending their first night as husband and wife together. While Dave was out of the room, Simmo had helpfully put a large, black dildo under one of the pillows.

They'd had the suits fitted in the city a couple of weeks before the buck's night. It was the first time Harry had seen any of the guys, other than Dave, since high school. They had a few beers (at Simmo's insistence) – it was bizarre seeing them all again. The same faces but fatter, with less hair. There were beer guts and fat arses. Wrinkles. Grey hair. Harry supposed he must look the same to them. When you saw yourself every day it wasn't such a shock. You knew you were getting older – the calendars and birthdays told you that – but in some ways the mind blocked it as an unpleasant truth.

Harry turned away from the other groomsmen and took off his t-shirt. He was hoping that no-one would notice. If he could just…

'Hey! Haz! Nice ink!' Simmo said.

Harry tried to pull on his suit shirt but Simmo grabbed it, held it down. He put his arm around Harry's neck and turned him, so the rest of the group could see. Harry saw himself grabbing Simmo's hand, just above the wrist, twisting until he heard a satisfying crack, then doubling him over so he could smash his ribcage with his knee and bring him down with a roundhouse to the back of the head.

Harry shook his head, to clear the image. *Where did that come from?*

The other groomsmen looked on with confusion, half-smiles. They were wondering if it was a wind-up. During high school, Harry's rebellion stretched no further than growing his hair slightly long. Then he got it cut when his dad, who had other things to worry about – like paying the mortgage – failed to comment. He'd gone on to have a surprisingly uneventful time at uni. There may have been drugs and sex for others, but not for him. And then he moved into a stable, safe, white-collar job.

The drowning man did not match what they knew of Harry. Hell, it didn't match what he knew of himself.

Simmo licked his finger and tried to rub it off. 'It's real!'

'Yeah. Got it last week.'

Simmo screwed up his face, peered at the picture. 'Um... interesting.'

Harry buttoned up his shirt.

Simmo pointed. 'Ah, I know what this is about. Mid-life crisis! Early mid-life crisis!'

Dave took a step forward. 'Hey, Simmo! Why don't you tell us all about *your* tattoo?'

Simmo scowled. Dave shrugged.

'What? Aren't you going to show everyone the gecko on your arse?'

General laughter.

'It disturbs me that you've seen the gecko on Simmo's arse,' Harry said, sensing the opportunity to turn things onto safer territory.

'Well, we all have our secrets. Don't we, Simmo?' Dave blew him a kiss across the room.

Simmo shook his head. 'Fucking homo.'

Harry stood at the altar of the small church in Paddington, looking back out at the family and friends. Suits and sunglasses for the guys. Chiffon and fake tans for the girls. There were no more familiar faces, thank god. All of 'the boys' were groomsmen and no-one else from school was there. No-one else to inquire about what he'd been doing these past twenty-odd years. When he got into uni, it was cool telling people he was doing journalism. It was so broad, and while the profession wasn't well regarded, it still carried an edge. People thought of trashy TV – *Today Tonight* and *A Current Affair* – but they also thought of some of the big stories that had been broken. Phil Dickie, staking out brothels in his car and bringing down the Queensland government. *Brisbane Mail* journo, Hedley Thomas, unveiling the atrocious record of a rogue doctor at a regional hospital. It was cool. Journalists shone a light on the dark places. Even now, when he met people and they asked what he did, their eyebrows went up when he told them. But the follow-up question was always: 'Oh yeah, where do you work?'. When he told them they invariably felt the need to explain that they didn't read the local paper. Christine was right when she said the local paper was important to 'some people' – but few of those people were under sixty.

The opening strains of U2's 'With or Without You' piped from the speakers. Dave turned as Ellie walked slowly into the church, holding her dad's arm. She was beautiful. Brides always were. Family and friends turned in their seats and in that moment, everyone forgot that it was boiling hot and the ceiling fans were barely stirring the tepid air. You could see the couples in the room shift closer, clutch each other's hands. For those who weren't yet married, it was something to look forward to. For those who weren't getting on, it was a reminder that sometimes things worked out. And for those who had been married a long time, like Dave's grandparents sitting up front, it was rejuvenating.

For Harry, it was pure hell. Because he couldn't help but imagine Bec walking down that aisle. He would have gladly married her, even though things were less than perfect. Even though to some extent he'd had to mould himself to her idea of who he should be. Was that necessarily a bad thing? Already, he'd noticed his drinking had picked up, back almost to the point it was before they met. He was finding it harder to control his temper. And while he hadn't actually lashed out at Simmo earlier that day, when he thought about hurting him it was as though someone else was in his head.

Simmo nudged him. Harry was still staring at the bright rectangle of light, even though Ellie wasn't there anymore. She and Dave were holding hands now, as the celebrant took them through their vows. Everything was white. The walls, the flowers, Ellie's dress. But in Harry's mind, all was dark. He saw a face, eyes and teeth almost glowing in the gloom. Harry let his eyes go slack, knowing that if he tried to focus on the face, it would disappear.

His neck burned. The old man leant forward and dipped the bamboo shoot into a clay bowl filled with black. Then he sat up straight again and Harry saw the line of the woman's shoulder. She had long, black hair. He couldn't see her face, because the only light in the room was a candle, somewhere behind him. He felt her grip his hand, and he could smell her. Cheap deodorant. Sweat. The heady musk of sex. She drew in breath as the man applied himself to her neck. She leant back, almost in ecstasy, and he caught a glimpse of her face.

'Harry!' Simmo. Nudging him again. 'Shit mate, you on the hammer? Is that part of your new biker look?'

Dave and Ellie were already on their way outside. There were tears aplenty in the crowd. The groomsmen were meant to form up with the bridesmaids, and Harry was standing there like a doped-up loser. His heart thudded heavily in his chest. He rubbed his face and moved forward, following Simmo's lead. He offered his hand to his bridesmaid – he thought her name may have been Lisa, or Leela – and they walked out into the early afternoon. There were guests waiting to throw confetti.

Shit, people still do this?

Well-wishers milled around outside. Cars slowed as they passed, some to check out the wedding, others just worried about hitting one of the kids running around on the crowded footpath. A few clouds gathered in the west, but Harry doubted there would be a storm. But something big was brewing.

He walked around the side of the chapel, to where Simmo had stationed an esky for people to grab a quick drink before heading to the reception, which was going to be at a conference centre down by the river. There were soft drinks and poppers for the kids, and Harry had to admit that while Simmo could be a real dick, he wasn't all bad. Harry reached in, pushing the imported beers aside until he fished out a VB.

Harry cracked the can, sculled deeply, then walked back up to the road. The photographer was busy with Dave and Ellie for the time being. Simmo and the other groomsmen were hanging with the bridesmaids. The best man had procured a bottle of champagne and was filling glasses, both for the bridesmaids and for his wife, who clearly wanted the bridesmaids to know that her hubby was off the market. They may have been fat and balding blowhards, but they were also accountants and engineers who'd been plying their trades for close to twenty years, while Harry was stuck on comparatively minimum wage. Money = power = sex appeal.

Out the front of the chapel was a zebra crossing, leading to a lookout that offered a great view of the city. There was a piece of quirky street art Harry had driven past countless times. It looked like a comfy lounge chair with a throw over the back. It was only when you got close you realised it was concrete, covered in small coloured tiles. It had already attracted a small gaggle of wedding guests, so Harry moved over to the stainless steel rail and looked out at the city.

He didn't see it though. He saw the woman. The way her hair fell about her face. The line of her bare shoulder. The sharp intake of breath as the old man started tattooing her. And there wasn't any doubt that *that* was what was happening. And he knew exactly what the tattoo was. A grid, filled with strange sigils.

She's out there somewhere.

Harry felt his breath quickening, his heart racing again at the thought of meeting her.

'Kyla.'

He spoke the name. He knew it came from the dreams. He didn't know who she was, or why he was dreaming about her, or what the hell it had to do with people drowning. But he knew that he had to find her.

'Hey.'

Harry turned. Dave was there. 'Hey Dave.'

'Photo time.'

Harry finished his beer. He went to move past his friend, but Dave grabbed his arms, gently but firmly.

'You okay?' Dave asked.

'Lots of people have been asking me that lately.'

'Well?'

Harry shrugged. 'Not really.'

'Is there anything I can do?'

Harry looked at the ground. Shook his head.

'Harry, we'll sort it out, okay? Just… just don't do anything rash.'

It took Harry a while to realise what Dave was talking about. And then he flushed.

'No… I wouldn't. Thanks, man.'

Together, they walked back over the crossing, where people were still milling about in front of the chapel. Simmo filled them in on the deal with the photos. Dave and Ellie just wanted some basics with family and the bridal party. Then the newlyweds and the best man and maid-of-honour were heading to New Farm Park for some arty shots, before meeting everyone at the reception venue.

Someone had their iPhone out, watching news. Harry slowed. There was a white car, a government car, Australian flag flying from the bonnet. The guy holding the phone saw Harry looking over his shoulder.

'It's the PM. On his way to Government House. He's gonna call the election. Mid-December, they reckon.'

Harry felt the sky darken, felt his limbs grow heavy. And he had no idea why.

CHAPTER 11

Harry chose the chair over the couch. Tom, the counsellor, said most people did on their first visit. The reality though was that he wanted to choose the couch, just to get some rest. There'd been no let-up in the nightmares over the past week. If anything, they'd intensified. With Dave on his honeymoon, he had no-one to talk to. And he felt as though it was all building up. *Building up to what?* He had no idea. He was exhausted.

The office was small. There was a bookcase on one side of the room, under the window, with various self-help books and also a stack of DVDs, again some self-help, but others you'd find in the 'Drama' section of the video shop. Trees thrashed around outside the window, and rain spattered against it. Another storm.

On Tom's desk was an old computer monitor, with Post-it notes tacked to the side. Behind the monitor, on the wall, there were drawings by a small child. A photo in a frame leant next to his keyboard.

'So, what's up?' Tom asked. He leant back in his chair, notebook on his lap.

Harry took a deep breath, and repeated the story. Starting with the break-up, moving into the new place. The first tattoo. The nightmares. His visit to the tattoo parlour. The second tattoo. More nightmares. With each telling, it became more like a story. Less real.

'Uh-huh. And how long were you with your girlfriend – Bec?'

'Yeah. Bec. Six years. We met at a party, mutual friends. You know the deal. I probably wouldn't have asked her out except I was half cut. God, sometimes I wonder what she saw in me that night. And why she kept going out with me when she realised I was nothing like that person.'

'I think even when we're drunk some of the good stuff shines through.'

'Maybe. Anyway, we hit it off. Had similar tastes in music, movies. Not perfectly aligned or anything, but...'

'Some common ground.'

'Yeah. She was living out at Menzies then, so it was kind of a long-distance relationship.'

He had fond and not-so-fond memories of those weekends there. An hour-and-a-half west of Brisbane, at the foot of the range. When he could swing it, he'd take off early on Friday arvo to beat the traffic, then come home bleary-eyed but happy Monday morning, sometimes driving straight to work from her place.

'She wanted to go overseas, do the London thing. To be honest, I'd never really thought about it. I didn't have anything against it, just kind of thought it wasn't my thing.

'But, you know, when you're with someone you see things in a new light. The thought of being there with her made it seem more manageable, more exciting.

'We worked there for a couple of years – she managed to get sponsored so we were allowed to stay on longer than most people. We both worked casual so we could travel a bit. Did all the usual stuff. Paris, Amsterdam, Rome. A bit of Eastern Europe.'

Tom made a few notes.

'How was travelling?' he asked. 'Some people say you never really know someone until you've travelled with them.'

'It was great. I mean, it wasn't perfect. We fought. There was one time, this disastrous camping holiday in France. I thought she was going to stab me with a butter knife…'

Cut or dig? Cut. Or dig?

'Sorry, digressing a bit.'

Tom waved it away. 'The digressions are often the good part.'

'We came back and life just sort of carried on. I went back to the *Chronicle*. She got a PR job in the city. We moved in together. We didn't even really discuss it. I mean, we'd been living together overseas. To me it meant: this is it, this is forever.'

'But not for her?'

'I broached the subject of tying the knot a couple of times. She always turned it into a joke or just changed the subject. I let it go. My parents separated when I was a kid. I don't know, I think I wanted to prove that it could be done. That there was such a thing as a happy ending. But I figured if she didn't want to marry, that was fine. Lots of couples don't marry.

'And then a couple of weeks ago I got home from work. She was sitting on the couch. She told me that she couldn't imagine spending the rest of her life with me. We had a big talk. You could call it a fight, I guess. The mother of all fights.

'I moved out. It was crazy. Wednesday morning I

thought everything was okay. By Saturday I was moving my stuff into a new house.'

Tom made a few more notes, then put his book down.

'Do you mind if I have a look at the tattoos?'

'No, that's fine.'

Harry swung around in his seat, put his chin against his chest. 'This is the first one.'

'Uh-huh.'

He felt Tom's hand at the nape of his neck, fingers running over the ink, almost as though he were checking to see if it were real.

'It looks Arabic,' Tom said.

Then Harry pulled up his sleeve, showed him the drowning man.

'Pretty full-on, hey?' Harry said.

'Mmm. I've seen more confronting tattoos. But yeah, it's not exactly rainbows and unicorns.'

Tom made a few more notes. 'Do you mind if I take photos?'

Harry shook his head. Tom opened the middle drawer of his desk, rummaged among old computer cables, notebooks and random pieces of paper, and pulled out a camera. He took a couple of photos of the arm, then the back of the neck.

'Thanks.'

He placed the camera down on the desk.

'So, am I crazy?' Harry said.

'We're all a little bit crazy. Sorry, that must sound trite. The break-up has shaken you up a bit?'

Harry looked out the window, watched the raindrops flow down the glass. He could feel the tears coming, tried to hold them back.

'Harry. If you need to cry, cry. Let it out.'

Harry thought he was going to, but then something clamped down. The tears dried up. The lump in his throat disappeared.

'No, I'm okay.'

Tom shrugged. 'You're upset. Anyone would be, right? Anyone with feelings. It's good that you're upset.'

Harry nodded.

'Harry, sometimes when people are under a lot of stress – and I mean *a lot* of stress – their mind kind of rebels. It shuts down to some extent.

'It's called a fugue state. Dissociative fugue. What happens is, on one level you keep operating, doing stuff. But when you become fully aware again, you can't remember what you did.

'The condition can be exacerbated by alcohol or other drugs. Like, maybe, having drinks at a buck's night.'

Harry nodded.

'You know Agatha Christie, the writer?' Tom asked. 'She once went missing for eleven days. Couldn't remember a thing about what had happened. Must've been a hell of a hen's night, right?

'There have been cases where people have wandered off, caught a train to a new city, started new lives – only to regain their memories years later.

'Sorry – not trying to freak you out. Most cases are short. Hours or days.'

Harry thought about just upping and leaving, starting afresh somewhere new. It almost appealed. But then a part of him, this new part of him, knew he had unfinished business here in Brisbane.

'I feel like I'm splitting in two,' Harry blurted. 'I feel

like there's someone… I don't know. I feel like I'm – losing myself.'

Tom nodded. 'In a way, you are. You've just hit a major crossroads in your life. You have to find yourself again. Maybe the tattoos are part of that?'

He shrugged. He hadn't really come to counselling for maybes. He was expecting more answers.

'You said that a friend of yours told you the first tattoo was Persian? From Afghanistan?'

'Yeah.'

'And then the second tattoo. You said you got that one…'

'It appeared…'

'Yeah, you said it appeared after talking to Fred. So, in your mind you'd made the Afghanistan connection.'

Harry shook his head. 'There were so many details in that nightmare, though. I mean, I'd heard about those asylum seekers, but I didn't know the SAS were involved.'

'You'd be surprised what your memory retains. Everything that happens to you – *everything*, right from birth – is stored in there somewhere. Even the stuff you can't remember. Accessing it is the problem. Getting those tattoos. If we work on it, they'll come back.'

Harry pictured the man, grinning in the darkness, all white teeth and bloodshot eyes.

'I don't know if I want the memories back,' he said. 'I'm just worried about what else I might do while I'm out of it.'

'Understandably. There's a range of things we can do to help. We can talk, like we have been. Do you know about cognitive therapy?'

'I've heard of it.'

'It's basically rewiring your brain. Changing dysfunctional brain patterns into more positive ones.

'You can do creative therapy – using art and music to express your feelings. Hypnosis, so we can go deep and get to those memories.'

Harry felt a weird excitement at the thought of tapping into his memories. Part of him pushed away the idea, but a deeper part of him wanted to get it all out, like lancing a boil.

'The other thing to remember is that, in many cases, people have one or two episodes and even without treatment, resume their normal lives,' Tom said. 'And maybe those memories never come back, but maybe that's no biggie.'

Harry didn't feel comfortable telling Tom, but he had a feeling this wouldn't be the case with him. That unless he did something drastic, this was going to get worse and worse.

Harry sat at his desk staring at the screen while Christine tapped away productively next to him. Another edition had come out with a front-page story about a dangerous intersection. Harry had written the story, but he barely remembered it.

At the news conference with their editor, Christine did most of the talking, while Harry zoned out, drawing doodles on his notebook. Eyes, teeth, the line of a neck and long hair, face in shadow, a drowning man, another one holding a tattoo machine, the line dripping and turning to blood.

Kyla. She was a part of the puzzle. But what puzzle? Did she have something to do with the tattoos? Was he under

her spell? Was she somehow conjuring these fugue states?
Screams. Terrified screams from a dark ocean.

Screams. But not that kind. He looked over at the
TV. Andrew Cardinal was visiting a primary school on
Brisbane's southside. The kids crowded around him, waving
pieces of paper for him to sign. Ron Vessel stood in the
background, getting pushed further away as the mob grew.

'What is it about kids and politicians?' Harry muttered.

He remembered when he was a kid, the then-premier
was mobbed by kids as he strode towards Parliament House
on George Street. Harry remembered his dad gripping his
shoulder, holding him back. Around home Harry had heard
nothing but bad things about the premier, so he didn't plan
on running for an autograph anyway.

Harry was getting the same vibe from watching Andrew
Cardinal on the TV. The newsreader was talking about new
opinion-poll figures, showing that if the election were called
today, Labor would win in a landslide. Out in the middle
of the oval, Cardinal picked up a girl and lifted her onto his
shoulder. For a moment Harry thought he was going to grab
another kid to balance himself out. Some sort of impromptu
circus act. But he didn't. He just turned slowly, girl on his
shoulder, grinning. Harry thought the act was a little odd.
These days, adults had to be careful how they were around
kids, and Harry suspected this was partly the reason why
politicians always looked slightly uncomfortable, slightly
stiff, during these kind of visits. But Cardinal didn't care.
Neither did Vessel, who stood there grinning, applauding.

'It's all over, bar the shouting,' Christine said, 'Right?'

Harry shrugged.

'Come on! This guy's a war hero.'

He was, except no-one knew much about his military

service, other than where he'd served, because he was part of military intelligence. It was all secret. But the list of deployments was impressive enough: Kosovo, Rwanda, Iraq, East Timor, Afghanistan. Upon Cardinal's retirement from the service, the chief of defence said that while much of what he'd done would remain classified for many years to come, there was no doubt that he had done a lot to make Australia a safer place. You couldn't ask for a better endorsement than that. And he'd seen enough actual action – where bullets were flying and bombs exploding – to avoid the accusation that he'd merely flown a desk. Put him up against the PM and, yeah, he looked pretty good.

'I guess the thing with election campaigns is that you never really know what's going to happen,' Harry said.

But he knew what he and Christine would be doing. Miles wanted pen-portraits of all the local candidates. Harry expected weeks of various candidates toeing the party line, pointing to improvements in local areas that were tied to government initiatives, or to problems in local areas that could be traced back to local inaction. And all the local lobby groups would be aiming to use the election to their advantage. He didn't expect much access to Cardinal or the PM – local papers tended to get shafted – but the Labor Party launch was expected to be held in Brisbane, so there'd be that. The trick on a weekly newspaper was to try and find a different angle, rather than trotting out news that people had read three or four days earlier.

The picture on the TV changed to the PM addressing a group of supporters at a nursing home in Melbourne. The images couldn't have highlighted the differences between the PM and Cardinal any better. The PM was playing it safe, going for the baby boomers who were worried about Labor squandering their retirement funds. It had worked for his predecessor for years, but it was becoming an increasingly shortsighted strategy.

Harry's phone rang. He scooped it up.

'*Chermside Chronicle*. Harry Hendrick speaking.'

'Ah, hello. This is Bill. From Save the Tower.'

'Hey, Bill. Have you been talking to Fred?'

'Ha. Yeah, you could say that. You know, we've seen so much of Brisbane's heritage just disappear over the last few years. It's not like London or Paris, where so much of the architecture is more permanent…'

No, thought Harry, it's certainly *not* like London or Paris.

'In Brisbane we've lost so much already just because our houses are wood. Easy to demolish, easy to ruin. Easy to raise them and add in an extra level below – great for families but not for the look and feel of Brisbane, so… anyway, Fred was saying you've moved in just down the road?'

'Yep.'

'Why don't you pop round after work? We can go for a walk up there and I'll show you exactly what I'm talking about.'

'Sounds great. Thanks, Bill.'

Bill gave him the address and Harry jotted it down.

'Oh, and thanks for that info on the Middle East stuff,' Harry said.

'My pleasure.'

Harry stood in the office kitchen, staring out the window towards the city. He couldn't see the CBD from here – just a thin layer of smog, soiling the blue sky. Harry thought about what Christine said about his tattoo, about how she thought it suited him. He wondered what Bec would have thought of it. Thought of *them*, he reminded himself. Two tattoos now. She thought he couldn't change. Well, he did. Just like that. Maybe she'd like the new, impulsive Harry.

He pulled out his phone, found Bec in his contacts. Stared at her photo. He missed her so much. He could do anything, right? He just got his second tattoo. Even if he didn't remember it. He could call her. What's the worst that could happen?

He dialled.

'Hello?'

It was her. And even though he initiated contact, he was lost for words. His heart slammed in his chest, his brain went into vapour-lock.

There had been a moment of lucidity at some point, just before he dialled. He had to tell her what was going on. It wasn't some random plea for attention, some vague hope that if she knew what was going on, she'd reach out to him (although that was in the back of his mind also). But as soon as she answered the phone, all of that slipped away.

'Hello?'

'Hi,' Harry croaked. 'It's me.' And then, when she didn't say anything. 'Harry.'

'Hi, Harry.' Guarded.

'Hi.'

Harry could feel the sweat beading on his brow. A drop slid down the bridge of his nose and into his eye, stinging. He rubbed it away.

'How's things?' Bec said.

Where did he even begin? There was nowhere. He could begin nowhere, and end in the same place. This was a big mistake. Bec was someone who once cared for him, loved him. She was someone who listened to whatever he had to tell her. She didn't always tell Harry what he wanted to hear but she listened, and that was important.

Harry was conscious of how long he'd been standing there, phone to ear, not saying anything.

'Yeah, okay,' he finally squeezed out. 'You?'

A pause. 'Harry…'

'I miss you, Bec. I miss you so much.'

And it was true. But he also missed *life* with Bec. The life where he wasn't plagued with bizarre nightmares. The life where he wasn't compelled to seek out tattoo artists while he was in some sort of dazed, not-really-there state. He was losing it. Fugue state or no, this was not normal behaviour. He was off the reservation.

'Harry… This isn't… I'm busy, okay. I'm sorry. I've gotta go.'

The line went dead. Harry said 'Bye' to the dial tone. He walked back to his desk, choking back tears. Slumped into his chair and stared at his screen. Community diary entries.

'Are you okay?' Christine asked. She pushed her glasses up onto her forehead. As much as Harry hated the glasses, the gesture was endearing.

'Not really.'

He unbuttoned his shirt. Christine looked away, shuffled in her seat.

'It's okay,' Harry said. 'I haven't lost it. Not totally, anyway.'

He pulled his shirt off his shoulder. Showed Christine the new tattoo.

'Holy crap!'

'Yeah, I know. I don't remember getting it.'

He shrugged the shirt back on, did the buttons back up.

'What? As in, you were wasted? Again?'

'No,' Harry said. Regretting getting into it now. 'It's like sleepwalking, except you're awake.'

'Are you…'

'I'm seeing a counsellor. Yeah. He says most people get over it. Probably something to do with the break-up.'

'Uh-huh. I'm sure it'll be okay, Harry. You know. You'll find someone.'

You'll find someone.

Christine turned back to her computer. Tapped some keys. Then she asked him about the candidate profiles she was working on. Some bland, boring question. Something she clearly already knew the answer to. She wanted to change the subject, and Harry thanked her for it. He slid over beside her, watching as she typed.

'Do you mind if I…' he gestured at the keyboard.

She shook her head. He pulled the keyboard over and made a couple of corrections.

'Hey, are you coming to the awards night?' she asked him.

He usually avoided them if he could. But this year Christine was a finalist for a piece she'd done about bed shortages at the Prince Charles Hospital. Miles, bless him, had sought approval from head office to book a table.

'Yeah, I guess.'

'You guess? Frightened I'll show you up?'

Harry laughed. No, that was the least of his worries. In fact, he hoped she'd win the award. She was up against the big guns from the *Brisbane Mail* so, to be honest, she didn't really have a hope in hell. The main reason he didn't want to be there was because it was an opportunity for all the people he went to university with, and all those who came after and heard the story at uni, to lord it over him.

'Come on,' she said. 'If I win, I'll buy you a drink.'

'Yeah, okay. It's a date.'

CHAPTER 12

Bill's place was a large Queenslander with verandahs all the way around. Tattered prayer flags hung out the front. The garden was tropical, overgrown but not messy. Harry pushed through the front gate. An aged Buddha statue peered through the foliage. He saw a ship's bell by the open front door but didn't have a chance to ring it. Bill lumbered across the threshold, big grin on his face, as though he'd been waiting for Harry to arrive.

'Harry Hendrick!' he said.

Bill was in his sixties, with a full head of grey hair, a wide-brimmed straw hat clamped down over it. He was stocky but not fat. He walked with a slight limp, one foot turned inwards, but it didn't seem to slow him down. A couple of weeks earlier, before the urge to take up running had struck, Harry would have had trouble keeping up with him.

They shook hands. Bill turned to lock up. 'Let's go see this tower then,' he said.

They walked to the end of Bill's street, sun beating down on them, then up towards the water tower, past Harry's car. Since he'd been leaving it in the street, the battery had stayed charged. He didn't know whether it was something to do with the angle – maybe it did something to the fluid

levels in the battery or caused a wire to lean a certain way –
and he didn't really care. It worked.

The tower loomed above them. If they were good
climbers they could have scaled the rock wall at the top of
Harry's street, then another ten metres of steep, grassy land,
and they would have been standing underneath it. But they
weren't, so they turned left, walking parallel to the rock
wall. An old tree leant over the road, its roots intertwined
with the stones. It looked as if one more big storm would
send it crashing across the road and into the house below.

'How are you settling in?' Bill asked.

'Yeah, not too bad,' Harry said. 'You know what it's like.
Getting used to new noises.'

He decided not to mention getting used to the phantom
tattooist. He felt there'd been enough sharing already today.

'Yeah. I know what you mean.'

They walked through a small park dominated by a
massive old fig tree. There were benches in the shade,
offering views out to the city below. As they crossed the
grass, Harry felt the first puffs of a breeze, cooling the sweat
on his shirt.

'How about yourself? Have you lived in this area long?'

Bill nodded. Because of the hat, Harry had to stoop to
see his face. 'My whole life,' Bill replied. 'Well, not here. I
grew up in Ashgrove. Lived out at The Gap for a while, after
the war. But the past ten years, I've been here.'

He gestured behind them, the way they'd come.

'It's great for the grandkids.'

Bill led Harry up the hill, into a winding street that
reminded Harry of the narrow alleyways in Athens, behind
the Parthenon. The only things missing were stray cats and
white paint.

'My whole life, the water tower has been there. If I had a dollar for every time I'd seen that water tower, I'd be able to buy that place,' Bill said.

He gestured then at an old Queenslander, imprisoned by temporary fencing. The place was deserted, windows smashed, graffiti marking its heritage pink walls. On the verandah sat a bathtub, also peppered with graffiti tags.

'Jesus. What's the deal?'

'Swenson,' Bill said. He almost spat the word. 'He wants to buy up the top of this hill. He's got that place, he's got the water tower.'

They rounded the corner, and the tower came back into view. Bulky concrete stilts ten- to fifteen-metres high. Peeling paint. Water stains. The taggers had also made their mark here, although how they'd done it Harry couldn't see. Mobile-phone towers stuck out at the top. Probably the most valuable thing about the entire structure.

The monolith was surrounded with more temporary fencing and a faded security sign: TRESPASSERS WILL BE PROSECUTED.

'That mob went out of business two years ago,' Bill said, gesturing at the logo on the sign.

The sections of fencing had been pushed and pulled until there were big gaps between them.

'Back in the '30s, this area was called "the dress circle of Paddington",' Bill said. 'And this marvellous piece of technology allowed the locals to have their own supply of running water.'

They stood, sweating, staring at the structure. The whole situation was absurd. The tower was built for rich people. People who could enjoy the views and the breezes while the plebs sweated it out in the valleys below. And now Bill – who clearly had a bit of money behind him – was trying to stop the place being redeveloped for other rich people. Harry had seen this pattern play out time and time again. Well-off 'Not in My Back Yard' activists pushing developments into poorer areas where people didn't know better or just didn't have the resources to stand up to the developers.

On the other hand, the thing was a Brisbane icon, and poor old Brisbane needed all the icons it could get.

'Come on,' Bill said. He headed for the fence, pushing two sections apart. Harry hesitated.

Bill laughed. 'It doesn't matter. The sign's just there to protect Swenson. Truth be told, they'd love it if someone fell off the tower. Swenson could couple the word "dangerous" with "eyesore" in his lobbying documents.'

Harry followed Bill through the fence. The old man scouted around the long grass under the tower until he found a lengthy steel pole with a hook on the end. He hefted it and moved over to a ladder, which had been pushed up, out of arm's reach.

'The taggers are doing their bit for the developers as well,' he said, grunting as he hooked the ladder and pulled it down with the scrape of steel on steel. 'But at least they don't leave this thing down so little kids can get up there.'

The steel groaned under Bill's weight as he climbed the ladder, the bolts that had once secured it to the concrete pylon long-since corroded. Bill climbed up onto a small walkway that ran under the water tank's base. He waved Harry up.

Bill led the way along the creaking walkway. At the far end was another set of steel rungs, up the side of the tank, to the top. Harry was panting by the time he reached the final climb. Partly through lack of fitness, but mostly due to his fear of heights. As he gripped the steel, on the outside of the structure, his palms were sweating and his hands were buzzing. Bill peered down at him from the top.

'Come on!'

Harry clutched the rungs. At least these ones were still securely attached. He started climbing, focusing on the concrete in front of his face. Halfway up there was a tag and, unlike most tags, he could read this one. TRENT! He wondered who this Trent was, and why he felt the need to express himself so exuberantly in such a precarious place.

Bill helped him up onto the top. There was nothing to protect them from the sun up here, but the wind was fresher, strong enough to whip at the collar of his shirt. There was a low railing around the edge, but it didn't look strong enough or high enough to stop anyone from falling. Just looking at it induced pins and needles in the soles of Harry's feet, and he moved to the centre.

'Not a fan of heights, hey?' Bill said. He stood near the edge, hands on hips. One hand held the hat. The wind snatched at his hair.

'Not particularly.'

'Used to be the same, a long time ago,' Bill said. 'But then after the war... ah, I dunno, war just teaches you the real meaning of fear.'

Bill took pity on Harry, and came over to where he stood. Harry felt like sitting down, but he managed to resist the urge by concentrating on his notebook. It was a ridiculous way to conduct an interview, but once he was focused, he found it easier to bear. He even risked a look out beyond the barrier, between the mobile-phone towers, and while he couldn't fully appreciate it, he had to admit that other than the lookout at Mount Coot-tha, this would have to be the best view in Brisbane. In fact, in some ways it was better. Mount Coot-tha was perched on the city's edge, whereas here they were close enough to see the undulations of the inner-city suburbs. Jacaranda trees. People sitting out on their decks enjoying the afternoon. And the flash of sunlight off the buildings in the city.

Bill skimmed through the history of the water tower, but it was barely more than the information on the flyer, and Harry doubted he'd put much of it in the story. What was more interesting were Bill's personal stories. Anecdotes about the structure's place in his life. He used to come up here with his wife when they were courting. Sometimes they'd climb it, sometimes they'd just walk the narrow laneways around Paddington. He was within sight of it when he heard about the September 11 terrorist attacks in 2001, at a cafe just down the road. Someone changed the channel and they saw a replay of the passenger jet hitting the World Trade Center.

'I walked outside, I was trying to phone my daughter and I couldn't get a line. And I saw our tower there and, I don't know, it grounded me,' he said.

Harry wasn't sure if that was how it was, or how it came to be through the retelling of the story. It didn't matter. People wrote their own history. It was true for massive events, such as world wars and depressions, as much as the tiny, seemingly insignificant details in people's lives. And there was nothing wrong with that.

Bill told him more about the social media campaign they'd started – his daughter's idea. They wanted everyone to share their stories about Paddington water tower on Twitter and Facebook. The concept was that the tower was filled with memories, even if it was decades since it carried water. And, as such, destroying it would be just as wrong as if it were still a vital part of urban infrastructure. It was a vital part of cultural infrastructure. Harry had to admit, it was a good idea. People loved to share stories. When the structure was 'full' of stories, participants would get to vote on their favourites, and the winners would get a Save the Tower coffee mug or t-shirt.

'Hey, I probably shouldn't mention this. I might jinx it,' Bill said.

Harry paused. He left the notebook down by his side. Sometimes it put people off. Sometimes, the best quotes came after the interview was over.

'Andrew Cardinal's people have been in touch,' he said.

'Oh yeah?'

'My daughter, friend of a friend, all that kinda thing. Anyway, word is, he's considering backing our cause.'

Harry nodded. Impressed. 'Well, it would certainly help.'

'He's big on heritage, apparently. Can you keep that under your hat?'

Technically, anything said *before* asking for confidentiality was fair game, but there was no story until it was confirmed.

'Sure. I'll put it in the vault. Fred said your daughter heard something about corruption, Swenson paying people off. Is that true?'

Bill nodded warily. 'Can I stay off the record? I just don't want to get sued.'

Harry hesitated. At uni he learnt to avoid letting people go off the record at all costs. You never knew what they were going to say, you never knew what axe they were trying to grind. And once someone was off the record, it was much harder to get them back on it, especially if they had something really worthwhile to say. Bill blundered on without waiting for a response.

'My daughter Shelley works in the property industry, right? She says a lot of the developers reckon Swenson is on the nose.'

'Why's that?'

'Look at him. Twenty-odd years ago he was a builder, right? Then he moved into development, grew his business. Fair enough. But that Cherry Grove deal? Come on. There's no way that area should have been allowed to be cleared for housing.

'That gave him a massive boost, right? But there was a period, after 2001, or so my daughter says, where no-one could undercut him. The blokes Shelley talks to reckon he was either paying someone to give him insider knowledge on the rival tenders, or he was getting cash from somewhere to subsidise his business.

'Now, I can't verify that, otherwise I'd go on the record. But sometimes there's just too much smoke for there not to be a fire. You know?'

A strong gust of wind swayed Harry off his feet, and he reached out to grab something to steady himself. Bill took his hand.

'Look at me,' he said. 'Look into my eyes.'

They were blue. Lines creasing the skin at the corners. The dizziness passed.

'Sorry for bringing you up here,' he said. 'I didn't realise.'

'That's okay. Really. I'm glad I saw it for myself.'

* * *

They walked back down to the park. It was darker under the boughs now, almost menacing. But at least it was cooler. Harry turned towards his street. Bill touched him on the arm.

'I'm heading this way, finish my walk,' he said.

'Wasn't that enough for you?'

He shrugged. 'I like to do forty-five minutes a day, if I can.'

'Okay. Well, it was nice to meet you,' Harry said.

He gave Bill the spiel about how he couldn't guarantee that the story would make it to the paper, and that he'd try to let him know if it did. And that if they were going to run the story, he might try to book a photographer to come and take some photos.

'Thanks, Harry. Here,' he said, handing Harry a business card: 'Save the Tower', followed by Bill's phone, email and street address.

'Thanks.'

Bill was about to turn away, then hesitated. 'Oh, I meant to say. That symbol of yours, where did you find it?'

Harry shrugged, lied. 'Saw it on the internet.'

Bill grunted. 'I'm surprised you saw that symbol on the internet. It's quite arcane.'

'Well, you know, everything's on the internet these days.'

'So you just happened upon it on the internet, and sketched it, and asked Fred about it?'

Harry felt his face burning. 'Yeah, why?'

'Magic's trendy these days, seems like everyone wants to go to Hogwarts or fuck a vampire…'

Harry jolted at the language.

'… but some magic is real, and some magic is really evil.

112

I've only seen symbols like that once before, after the war, and I don't want to see them again.'

'Oh. Okay.' Harry wondered if his hair fully covered it. Or if Bill had seen the tattoo already and was just testing him.

Bill slapped him on the arm and grinned. 'Sorry. I'm a superstitious old prick at times.'

Harry wanted to know more, but Bill turned, striding towards Paddington.

'See ya, Harry. Stay safe!'

CHAPTER 13

Harry walked through West End, dodging the itinerants begging for change outside cafes and the waiters delivering Saturday morning coffee. It was hard to believe it had been almost two weeks since the first tattoo. A week and a bit since the second. According to Tom, he wasn't crazy. According to the scan, he wasn't sick. It was something to cling to when he woke up in the middle of the night, in a cold sweat, listening to the phantom scratching under the house.

He'd been trying to get hold of Bill, but every time he phoned, it rang out. Fred said he was busy with Save the Tower stuff. The general day-to-day routine helped sustain the illusion that everything was okay. He wrote up a rough draft of the water tower story, but was waiting for an update on the Andrew Cardinal angle. That would really make it something worth writing about and, if he could use his contacts through Ron Vessel to at least schedule the announcement just before the *Chronicle* went to press, then all the better. He had to admit, it would be one of the cuter stories of the campaign trail – a rugged army type teaming up with two World War II veterans to save a worn-out Brisbane icon.

But the nightmares were getting worse, no matter how many VBs he downed before bed. The first one, the one where he was buried, had initially just been a series of flashes and sensations. Now, it was in full HD. He could see the grains of dirt on the ground, the smudge of dust on the ant's shiny body. He could smell the cigarette smoke so clearly he could almost name the brand. Thankfully, there was still no sensation when the cutting began.

The Fajar Baru nightmare was like being there. The feeling of the salt spray on his face, the rising fear when he saw the plume of fire and smoke on the horizon. The expressions of terror on the refugees' faces as the RHIBs turned back to Christmas Island. He thought again about hypnotism, freeing the memories, and his stomach filled with butterflies.

If Bill couldn't answer his questions, maybe Sian would.

Harry pushed through the door into West End Tattoo's cool air-conditioning. The place was packed. A woman had to move her backpack to one side so he could open the door. The bench seats in front of and to the side of the counter were once again full of people waiting, going through their art folders or playing with their phones. It sounded as though every tattoo machine in the place was going full-bore.

Sian nodded to him, phone cradled between her ear and her shoulder, free hand scribbling in a dog-eared appointment book. While he was waiting, a woman with a zombie waitress on one arm was called upstairs. Harry took her empty seat, then picked up the tattoo magazine she'd been reading. Old-school sailor tattoos, hearts with names, symbols with meanings.

'Harry,' Sian called.

He jumped. Smiled awkwardly, then left the magazine open on a page of birds. Everything from swallows on a buttock to an emu on someone's back.

'Hi, Sian,' Harry said as he went up to her.

'So did you solve the mystery?'

'Uh, bits of it. The symbol is from Afghanistan.'

'Of course! I knew it was from that neck of the woods.'

Behind Harry the door opened, letting more light into the front office. The tattoos on Sian's arms seemed to come alive.

'But I still don't know how I got it. And now there's this…' Harry turned and pulled his sleeve up, showing Sian the drowning man. The first tattoo was growing on Harry. This one wasn't. Every time he saw it, he felt slightly nauseous. Sian sucked air through her teeth.

'Nasty.'

'I know.'

She raised a hand to the side of her face. She had the letters LOVE tattooed on her fingers.

'Hang on. Looks familiar.' Her brow creased. 'But it can't be. Where did you get this done?'

Harry shrugged. 'Beats me. Just like the first one – I don't remember.'

'Come with me.'

She led Harry through a beaded curtain, into the room behind the counter. The space was a mashup of hair salon, doctor's surgery and motor workshop. Trays with tattoo machines, inks, sterile bandages and needles. Walls plastered with framed artwork, and more stuff on see-through paper, stuck to the wall with pieces of masking tape, alongside photos of children, presumably the tattooist's kids.

Three chairs, like those you'd find in a barber shop, all occupied. A young guy was horizontal, sweating bullets as a woman tattooed some elaborate scrollwork across his chest. As far as Harry could tell, it was his first tattoo. There was an older guy, gold chain around his neck, maybe late fifties. His shirt hung over the chair as the tattooist worked on his heavily tanned arm. Harry couldn't see what he was doing, but the artwork on that part of the studio wall was old-school stuff: hearts, swallows, scrolls and skulls.

At the back of the room, a guy with a trucker's cap was getting some work done on a full sleeve of Japanese art. As he turned his arm, the samurai warrior down by his wrist seemed to draw his sword. The artist, long hair tied back, was in his forties. Both arms covered in tattoos. One arm with Maori designs, their edges ill-defined and spreading with age.

He looked up when he saw Sian, put the machine down and flexed his gloved hand.

'Yo, Mack,' Sian said.

'What's up?'

'Check this out.'

She gestured to Harry, who pulled his sleeve up again, feeling a little like a freak-show exhibit.

'Holy crap!' Mack said.

'That's what I said.'

The guy in the trucker cap peered over.

Mack looked up at Harry. 'Where'd you get this done?'

Sian answered before Harry could. 'He doesn't remember.'

'Bullshit,' Mack said. 'Firstly, you couldn't have got this tattoo in one session. You'd get the lines done first, then go back and get the shading and colour.

'Secondly, this looks like the work of a guy named Rabs. And you'd know if he did work on you. You'd certainly remember it.'

Harry stared at Mack blankly. Mack took another look at the tattoo.

'Okay, where do I find this guy?' Harry asked.

'I don't even know if he's still alive. I went to work in London for a bit and when I came back, he was gone,' Mack said.

'He used to work at a place out at Stones Corner,' Sian added. 'A bikie-run joint. But he hasn't done any work since.'

'If I were you, I'd stay well clear. If he finds out someone's stealing his work, he's gonna want to know who it is. And if you can't tell him…' Mack snorted a laugh, shook his head. Picked up the machine, dabbed the needle into the ink and went back to work.

'Seriously, dude,' he said, 'you do not want to piss Rabs off.'

Harry sat in The Three Monkeys cafe, phone pressed to his ear.

'So what are you going to do?' Dave asked. The line dropped out. Harry fancied he could hear water splashing in the background. The chink of glasses at a bar. That's what people did in Fiji, right?

Harry turned the cup in his hands. He'd only taken a couple of sips, but the coffee was sliding around his stomach and he felt sick. He was tucked into a dimly lit nook of the Moroccan-themed cafe, away from the dusty heat of Boundary Road. A light sheathed in a brocade lampshade hung over his head. The wall beside him was papered with old posters for theatre productions and musicals that had toured Brisbane over the years. Many of them were autographed.

Harry shrugged. 'The counsellor thinks I may have actually got the tattoos done and just not remembered it,' he said. 'That doesn't explain what the tattoo guy – Mack – just told me, but what's the alternative?'

He hoped Dave would say what he'd been thinking and save him the trouble.

'So either you're going sleepwalking and getting these tatts done somewhere, or someone is breaking in and tattooing you in your sleep. Drugging you. But why?' Dave said.

'And that doesn't explain how I got a two-session tattoo in one night,' Harry added. He screwed his eyes shut. He'd just have to say it. 'There's another alternative... Fuck, I wish I had a beer... The alternative is that the tattoos are just appearing. No-one is tattooing them. There's something about the house. Some sort of, I don't know, phantom radiation.'

The line crackled, seemed to go dead. 'Hello? Dave?'

'Yeah, I'm still here. I'm just thinking. Phantom radiation. Giving you tattoos. That sounds fucking crazy.'

Harry closed his eyes again, took a deep breath. 'Yeah. You're right. Of course it is. I dunno.'

'Thanks, babe,' Dave said. 'Sorry, not you. Ellie just handed me a drink...'

'I'm sorry, I should go...'

'Nah, nah. It's fine. Seriously. Harry, maybe you just need a break from your place.' He sounded half-cut.

Harry had considered it, of course he had. But when he thought about it, he felt the same way he did when he thought about getting rid of the tattoos. It felt... wrong. That's all. Just wrong.

'Harry, you're not saying anything. Get the fuck out of Dodge. Camp at my place until we get back. It's no drama.'

'Yeah. Yeah, maybe you're right.'

'Of course I am!' Dave's voice went quiet again. 'Yeah. Sure, hon.' And then: 'Sorry, Harry, not you. There's a key under the house, in the old dryer. Okay?'

'Yeah. Okay.'

'I'll see you when I get back, all right?'

'Yeah, sure Dave. And sorry again.'

'Forget about it, Harry. I meant what I said at the wedding. Don't do anything stupid. You'll get through this.'

'Thanks.'

The line went dead. Before Harry's phone was even on the table, he knew he wasn't going to leave his place. He couldn't.

'Maybe the loneliness is getting to me,' he mumbled.

He wondered what Christine was doing. Short skirt. Crazy glasses. Wished he was a few years younger.

Harry glanced up at the TV bolted onto the wall. Andrew Cardinal was grinning, waving to fans at a rally in Sydney. He'd really got them fired up. There were placards, custom t-shirts; people had even made Andrew Cardinal masks to wear, which was a bit creepy. It vaguely reminded Harry of John Hewson back in the early '90s. Except Cardinal had real substance. Vessel was in the background, still grinning like a moron.

Harry's phone rang. He picked it up, half expecting to see Fred's name on the screen, but it wasn't. It was Bill.

'Turn on your TV,' he said.

'There's a TV here.' Harry's eyes glanced up to the TV

120

again. The footage they were showing before must've been file footage from earlier in the week, because now Cardinal was standing in front of the Paddington water tower. The camera was low, trying to catch the top of the water tower as well as frame the politician.

The volume was down. Harry got up, still holding the phone to his ear, and tried to turn up the volume.

'I can't hear what he's saying.'

'Never mind.'

Next minute, he saw Bill standing in the shot, in the media scrum, holding his phone out to catch Cardinal's speech.

'I'm here today at the Paddington water tower to announce a new initiative by a Cardinal Labor government,' he said.

'If elected, my government will move to protect areas of cultural significance. For too long, the Federal Government has stood by and let these gems disappear. And once they're gone, they're gone forever.

'Under the current government…'

He lapsed into some statistics about how heritage listing had faltered under the government, and Labor's statistics under Keating. The press pack could barely contain itself. There was already a heritage system in place, as well as state and local building codes. Cardinal was suggesting his government would streamline that process, and take control away from local governments, until the heritage minister gave projects his seal of approval.

Harry stared, mouth agape. It was bizarre that Cardinal would risk his substantial lead in the polls by pissing off local and state governments, not to mention a stack of influential and rich property developers.

Cardinal held his hands out to calm the reporters. 'Hang on, hang on. I'll answer your questions, but first I've got something to say. Where are Bill and Fred?'

The volume dropped as Bill held the phone by his side. Journalists in shot swung their heads around. Eventually Fred edged into shot. He looked extremely uncomfortable. Harry held a finger over his ear, blocking the piped music coming through the cafe.

'Bill and Fred here are heroes of the Australian suburbs. They are taking on these developers because they want to save our architectural heritage for future generations. They understand that we can't truly move forward without understanding our past.

'As part of their campaign to save the tower, they've been asking for people to share their stories. And I've got a story for them. When I was a kid, we used to drive past the tower, along Latrobe Terrace down there, on our monthly trek to the grandparents'.

'As a five or six-year-old, that was a huge journey, all the way from the southside. But I didn't care. Because I wanted to see the spaceship. Yep, for some reason I'd decided the Paddington water tower was a spaceship…'

He paused for the laughter to die down.

'I can't tell you how disappointed I was when I found out it was a boring old water tower…'

More laughter.

'But by then my obsession with space travel was well and truly established. I was going to be an astronaut, and then when I got older and realised my maths and physics grades weren't quite up to scratch, I settled on the military.

'So you could say that if it wasn't for that water tower, I never would have joined the army. And if it wasn't for the army, I don't know if I'd be doing what I'm doing now.

'Point is, we all have connections with our geography. With the buildings that we grew up with. The places that are part of us.'

Harry felt the hairs on the back of his neck stand up. He was thinking of Mount Coot-tha, where he and Bec used to go when they were first seeing each other.

'I know there are people who don't believe politicians. They think we're all talk, and rightly so after so many years of the current government…'

There was a cheer from somewhere back in the crowd.

'That's why I'm going to put my money where my mouth is. I'm confident we're going to win the election. I'm confident Bill and Fred here are going to win their battle, too. So in cooperation with the current owners of this land, I'm going to put up new security fences. Proper security fences that will actually keep the kids out, so this place can be saved and can be enjoyed by future generations.

'And not just here. Right around Brisbane's western suburbs, we're moving to protect icons that have been allowed to rot for too long.

'Thank you, Fred. Thank you, Bill. You might like to take a step back before these guys eat me alive.'

A polite laugh from the press pack. Applause.

'I'll now take your questions…'

Harry turned away from the TV.

'Well?' Bill said, back on the phone.

'Unbelievable!'

'I know! Look I've gotta go. I'm sorry I couldn't give you a heads-up.'

'No, that's okay. I understand.'

He hung up the phone. He should have been angrier. But he was happy for Fred, after all his years battling Swenson and other developers. Besides, there would be plenty of local follow-up stories to this bombshell.

CHAPTER 14

Heat shimmered off rocks the colour of dried bones. In the valley below, the bright red and green of the poppies provided stark contrast to the deathly pale landscape. Women, dressed in black, moved between the rows like wraiths. The troopers saw the dust rise from a couple of kays out, watching through binoculars as the armoured vehicles approached the plantation.

'They ours?' Rob said, but he already knew the answer.

'Looks like it. Bushmasters.'

'What the fuck are they doing out here?'

'Dunno.'

There was nothing they could do but watch. The guards at the plantation must have seen the clouds of dust rising almost as soon as Rob and Tim had, but they didn't seem concerned. They ambled up and down, out of the mud-brick compound, AK-47s on their shoulders. There was another guy up on the roof, back against the wall, rocket-propelled grenade next to him, ready to go.

Rob lined him up in his reticle. Eight hundred metres. From the way his kameez rippled, there was a slight wind coming from east to west. A relatively easy shot. Beside Rob, Tim shuffled, watching the incoming convoy.

'Reconstruction Taskforce?'

'If they are, their satnav has let them down badly.'

Heat baked off the rocks. The men below continued to patrol. Three of them moved to the front of the compound as the Bushmasters neared. Dust soiled the clear blue sky.

Tim listened to the stolen Taliban radio. Spotters were watching the convoy come in.

'There's some chatter. Nothing suggesting the bad guys are going to light up some of those RPGs.'

Rob grunted. So far, the Taliban hadn't decided to blow the convoy to kingdom come with one of the IEDs that peppered the rugged track between here and Camp Rhino.

'Get onto the others. Tell them what's going down.'

With his scope, Rob would have been able to make out Geoff and John on the other side of the valley, but only because he knew where they were. They were atop a low ridgeline, closer to the plantation but almost invisible. Tim got on the radio and relayed the information. Their mission was simply to observe the plantation, gather intelligence about Taliban players. The US had provided some intel that a Taliban commander was heavily involved with moving opium out of the place. He liked to micro-manage, apparently.

The plan was to watch the place for a few weeks, gather intel on his movements and then, next time he stayed the night, move in and secure him.

But this, this was something else.

The lead Bushmaster pulled up outside the compound. The second one stopped short, and half-a-dozen soldiers piled out, brandishing F88 Austeyr assault rifles. They fanned out, forming a rough line, giving them line of sight around the sides of the compound, far enough apart from each other that they wouldn't make an easy target.

'Contractors,' Rob said.

'Hmm… some of them.'

From the lead truck, another soldier climbed out. Unlike the other guys, he was in Australian uniform and only had minimal gear. No rifle, just a service pistol strapped to his hip. His silver crewcut shone in the sun. He reached back into the cab, grabbed his slouch hat and pulled it onto his head.

The driver also climbed out of the first truck. He was tall and skinny. The door on the second truck opened and another Australian soldier climbed out. This one was stocky. Almost overweight.

'Three Australians,' Tim said. 'The rest contractors. Looks dodgy.'

From within the complex of mud huts, men shouted. The women in the fields ran back to the compound, scooping up their children as they went.

Moments later, a man emerged from a darkened doorway, his tribal dress billowing in the wind. He was flanked by two men with AK-47s and RPGs slung over their shoulders.

'Is that our guy?' Rob asked.

'Nah. I think it's his second. Fazlullah.'

'You think?'

A pause. 'Yeah. Fazlullah.'

The RPGs would be useless at this range, they were just there for show. But it was bizarre. Usually, the Taliban would do everything they could to hide their weaponry. The only time you saw an RPG was through your reticle while you were taking out the bad guy trying to fire it, or, if things didn't go to plan, as it was zooming towards you.

Here, it was all hanging out.

'It's like a fucking dick-measuring contest,' Tim muttered.

'Yeah, and guess who's gonna get fucked up the arse?'

The men in the valley talked, but it was impossible to hear what they were saying or even to read their lips from this distance. At one point Old Silver laughed, throwing his head back at something Fazlullah said.

'The silver fox down there,' Tim said. 'I've seen him before.'

'Yeah. Me too. And he's definitely not Reconstruction.'

'What about the other two?'

'Dunno. Just grunts.'

Old Silver turned and spoke to the tall guy, who then ran back to the truck and pulled something off the front seat. A large suitcase. One of Fazlullah's offsiders slung his AK and moved to take the suitcase. Then Old Silver said something. Fazlullah raised both his hands in a *what?* gesture, then shook his head. He turned, moved inside the compound. Old Silver followed, and then the driver, still lugging the suitcase. It was heavy, and there were no prizes for guessing what was inside it. Fazlullah's bodyguards were next to move inside. The guys in the second truck maintained their position, as did the Taliban guards on the roof.

'You know what this is, don't you?' Tim said.

'I know what it looks like. A drug deal.'

'What should we do?'

Rob considered. It would be pointless compromising their cover, given they had no idea what was going on down there.

'Could be an AUSTINT gig,' Rob said.

'And we're not told?'

Rob shrugged. 'This is bullshit.'

'Same shit, different day. Right?'

Rob and Tim lay on the hot stones. Flies buzzed around their faces, settled on their lips. The guards walked up and down the roof while whatever business was being done continued inside. A drug deal. A suitcase of money. Australian Defence Force involvement. Rob seriously hoped it was what he thought it was – a communications snafu. This one, given the circumstances, was potentially very dangerous. But the alternative, that members of the ADF were knowingly engaged in drug smuggling, was much, much worse. Worse, but not impossible. Sometimes the temptation was just too much.

Gunfire. The pop of small calibre rounds. An automatic handgun. Then something heavier. A sustained burst of an F88. Screams.

'Fuck me,' Tim said. He got on the radio. 'Muzzle flash from the windows.'

'Hold,' Rob said. 'Tell them to hold for now. We don't know what the fuck's going on.'

The soldiers outside the compound took cover. One of the guards fell. Through the scope Rob saw a spray of blood as the rounds took him across the chest. The other guard dropped too, taking up a defensive position on the top of the roof. The soldiers below took cover behind the Bushmasters.

Gunfire continued inside the compound. There was the low *krump* of a grenade detonating.

Rob let his reticle settle on the guard on the roof. Yeah, he didn't know what was going on, but he wasn't going to let this doofus take pot-shots at coalition soldiers, even if they were contractors.

He adjusted for wind. He began his breathing cycle,

steadying his hands for the shot. The guy was still huddled behind the low wall, AK-47 poking over the top. Shots plinked off the wall, dusting him with shards of mud brick.

Three… two… one…

Rob took the shot. The guy rocked back as the round tore through his chest.

'Bullseye,' Tim said.

A couple of the soldiers looked around. They'd heard the shot but Rob had chosen his firing position well, the geography making it sound as though the gun had been fired from further down the hill. He searched for other immediate targets, but none presented themselves.

'We'd better move,' Rob said.

'Wait.'

More screams. Women wailing. A baby screaming. The soldiers from the second Bushmaster now formed a phalanx across the front of the compound. A woman ran out the front door, her niqab ballooning in the wind. She stopped still when she saw the soldiers shouting at her to get down.

Gunshot. She slumped forward, pushing up a cloud of dust where she fell.

'Shot came from inside,' Rob said. 'Pretty fucking stupid with those guys out front.'

He watched her. At first he thought it was a one-shot kill. Then she struggled to her hands and knees. Blood bubbled from her mouth. She slumped down again.

'Out back,' Tim said.

Rob pulled back from the scope. A woman ran between the poppies. Old Silver chased her, handgun out. He yelled at her in Dari, then Pashto: *Stop! Stop!* Rob waited for the shot.

The woman staggered, fell. Old Silver grabbed her,

dragged her back inside the building. Her hijab fell away from her head, onto the ground. Through the scope, Rob saw the terror on her face.

'Fuck me. Call this shit in. Find out what the deal is.'

Tim got on the field radio. He spoke for a few minutes, checking his map and calling in the coordinates. Rob gathered enough of the conversation to know what the verdict was.

'They don't know anything about it. They want us to maintain position, while they find out what's going on.'

'Shit! Fucking spooks.'

So they waited. The sun tracked across the sky. The screams continued. The worst was the baby. For hours the baby screamed until suddenly the cries stopped. Rob found that even more disturbing. Gradually, the soldiers outside moved inside, two guards rotating in and out of the compound.

Tim called in again. Same message. As dusk fell, soldiers emerged carrying what looked like ammunition crates, twenty of them. They loaded them onto the first Bushmaster. Old Silver and his driver emerged, had a brief chat with Fatty. Rob settled his reticle on him. Yeah, he'd seen him around. Now he knew why he didn't know his name. Because it was Old Silver's job for people to not know his name.

Old Silver took a look around, climbed into the Bushmaster. They fired up and rolled out, chasing their shadows back down the valley.

'Come on,' Rob said. 'Let's check this out.'

Rob expected to find dead men. He expected to find the women cowering in one room. He expected another room to be littered with cable ties, knives, engine oil, electric cables – tools of trade for the interrogators. Not officially of course, but from the screams he'd heard that afternoon, this clearly wasn't an official mission.

But he wasn't prepared for what he found. The death room. Caked in blood. A man still tied to a chair, naked body covered in cuts of all shapes, sizes and depths. The last one, presumably the last one, across his neck. He'd shat himself when he died. Flies buzzed around the room, landing on his filth and on his mouth.

Rob grabbed a handful of hair and lifted the dead man's head up, so he could see his face. It was barely recognisable.

'Fazlullah,' he said.

Lying on the floor just inside the doorway were two once-white forensics suits, now stiff with dried blood.

'They wanted to do the dirty work, but not get dirty,' Tim said.

Geoff and John were still outside, keeping guard. The last light was fading from the sky, but they had night vision goggles. Rob pulled a camera from his pack and started taking photos. The gaping neck wound. The car battery in the corner of the room. Fazlullah's left hand was missing its fingers. Rob searched the room, couldn't find them.

'We've got company,' Tim said, holding one hand to the earbud. 'ETA half an hour. Looks like locals.'

'Well, we better make this quick then.'

They moved through the compound, documenting the atrocity. It was clear that while there may have been some intel gathering going on, it was secondary to Old Silver's sick games. Most of the guards had died quickly, chests and heads torn open by the F88s and, in one instance, a shotgun. One man by the doorway to the second big room had his throat slit.

They pushed inside the room. Saw the women and children.

'Oh, fuck me. Fuck me,' Rob said.

The women had tried to protect their kids. The kids were in the corner of the room. The women over them. A mass of broken bodies, blood, flesh and bones. Tim had a quick look. They were all dead. One of the women had been dragged to face into the middle of the room, hands tied over her head and secured to an eye bolt on the wall.

Her traditional robes were pushed up, revealing bruised and bloodied legs, still spread.

'This is fucked up,' Rob said. 'This is really fucked up.'

Her hijab was missing. At first he thought it was because it had been souvenired. And then Rob recognised the robes. He took photos. The bastards wouldn't get away with this. He'd make sure of it, if it was the last thing he did.

'Out this way,' Rob said, leading Tim out the back of the compound. They cleared each of the rooms, taking photos of the dead. It seemed odd to him that Old Silver had left the scene of the crime intact. It would have made more sense to burn the place to the ground. Maybe they were planning on coming back. Maybe they wanted locals to find the bodies. Maybe it was part of a plan to expand their operation, encroach on the warlords in surrounding fiefdoms.

Only once they were back out in the fresh air did Rob fully appreciate how badly the compound stank. The rows of poppies glowed in the last light. Tim made straight for the low rise off to the left. Geoff and John were up there. Rob detoured via the plantation. It was still there, lying in the dirt, the woman's hijab. He picked it up, stuffed it into his pack, and followed Tim into the gathering darkness.

CHAPTER 15

Harry's eyes shot open.

Fuck, fuck, fuck! Where am I?

He reached under his pillow for his Glock 19, trying to control his breathing and get his heart rate steady. The gun was gone. He scanned the room, trying to make sense of what he was seeing.

'Tim? Tim!'

He sat up in bed, crying out as the sheet peeled away from his back. It was sticky with blood. He fell to the floor, dizzy.

'Fuck! Tim!'

Harry closed his eyes. Took a deep breath. Opened his eyes. It was like adjusting to a 3D movie, or pulling yourself out of a really good book. He got up onto his knees, let his eyes drop closed then opened them again.

'There is no Tim,' he said, under his breath. *A lie.*

'There is no Rob.' *Another lie.* But it helped. 'I'm Harry Hendrick.'

His breathing slowed. He sat on the mat. 'This mat. Dave gave me this mat when we were still working at the pizza joint.'

He stared at the pattern. It wasn't anything like mats

they had in Afghanistan. He'd never been to Afghanistan. But he just knew. He turned, rested his head on the edge of the bed. Closed his eyes.

'Bec hated it. It stayed in storage most of the six years we lived together,' he muttered.

Opened his eyes. Afghanistan wasn't real. Afghanistan wasn't real. A third lie. Just a nightmare. Just a nightmare. He looked at the blood.

But that's *real*.

Seeing the blood, realising it was his own, sparked a connection and suddenly he felt a long, pulsing throb across his shoulders. A burning sensation. Severe bruising and severe gravel rash, both at the same time, but much, much worse.

Harry reached back and gently touched his skin. His fingers came away red. He gingerly carried himself to the bathroom. He turned, prompting a new wave of agony, and twisted his head to see his back in the mirror. Harry moaned. The top third of his back was covered in blood. In some places deep red, in others purple and black as it started to dry. There was a tattoo underneath, but he couldn't see it through the blood. Just lots of lines, circles maybe.

Harry leant over the sink and sucked in deep breaths, trying to decide what to do. Sweat dripped off his forehead. He felt sick. Feverish. He could try and wipe his back down with a washer, or he could climb in the shower. Neither option appealed. He considered going next door for help, but shied away from it. He hunkered down on the balls of his feet, placed his hands against the cool tiles. He felt violated, that was the long and short of it. He wasn't doing this to himself. He knew that now. So someone or something was doing it to him. All he wanted to do was get clean.

He climbed into the shower, turned the water on to almost fully cold, and gradually stepped under the jet. The cool water ran down the front of his body. He dipped his head under and the first rivulets ran down his back. He steadied himself against the wall, gritting his teeth. Groaned. He watched the water turn red around his feet. Eased himself under a bit more, until he could rest his forehead against the tiles. The water hammered his abused flesh. He shoved two knuckles into his mouth and bit down to stop himself greying out, and soon blood was oozing from his hand as well, running down his arm and off his elbow.

He had no idea how long he stood like that, under the water. When numbness replaced pain, he turned off the taps and sat down in the tub, leaning over his crossed legs. Within seconds the oppressive heat was on him again. He cried, in anguish this time.

'You fuck. You fucking fuck! You're gonna pay.'

But he didn't know who he was talking to. He wasn't even sure if it was him talking.

Harry looked at the picture on his iPhone. It wasn't the best photo ever taken. It wouldn't win any awards. It wouldn't appear in any tattooing magazines, but that was nothing to do with the artwork. Even in pain, even in anger, Harry could see that this tattoo was a masterpiece.

Bright red poppies covered his shoulders, each one pretty much life-size. That was part of the reason he hadn't been able to see the design. He thought his flesh had been stripped away but it was just the blood blending in with the ink. As the poppies drifted down his shoulder blades, they changed to pale skulls. And then the skulls faded, blending back into his skin. It reminded Harry of an Escher drawing: ducks turning into fish.

He went to the fridge and got himself a beer. He didn't care if it was ten on a Sunday morning. It was hot enough to be lunchtime and if this latest invasion didn't warrant a beer then he didn't know what did. His hands shook as he broke it free of the six-pack and twisted off the lid. He slumped in his chair and took a long drink, enjoying the harsh bitter taste.

He couldn't think of what happened in Afghanistan as a nightmare. It was a memory. It was the sort of thing that veterans were plagued by when they returned from a war zone. A flashback. He was having someone else's flashbacks. He guessed the tattoos went with that.

He pulled his notebook over to him and jotted down some notes, pausing every now and then to drink. The man's name was Rob. A military man. Probably special forces. Australian accent so that probably meant SAS, although he could have been a commando. Involved in the Fajar Baru debacle. Deployed to Afghanistan. Harry didn't know what date. Post-2001 was as good as it got at the moment.

Did he live here? Harry added a couple of extra question marks, underlined the query. Ghosts usually inhabited places that were significant to them. Ghosts? Harry laughed. Here was his notebook. Full of shorthand accounts of accidents waiting to happen and morning-tea fundraisers and wedding anniversaries, and now he was writing about ghosts and it wasn't the story of some crazy man – Harry taking notes just to appease him – it was his own story.

There were aspects of this mystery Harry could tackle with the skills he'd honed over the years at the *Chronicle*. Asking questions. He could find out about the history of the house. That was a piece of piss. He could start right now, with the neighbours. A nurse, coming and going at all hours of the day and night; she'd have plenty of information on previous tenants. He could do some database research, go through the newspaper archive and see if anything significant had happened on this street. Harry felt a bit better, knowing that he was starting to gather enough information to take action.

But he was going to have to go even further off the reservation on this one, employ techniques that were foreign to him. He finished the beer, got another one and then went to the study and grabbed his laptop. He had a quick scout around the news and his email before he got started – a bad habit, ingrained procrastination. Then he went to Google and typed in 'Brisbane psychics'. Thousands of results popped up. Most of them looked dodgy. The readings were done over the phone or via email. The websites were all pastels and soft focus. The names seemed made up. About halfway down the first page, there was a news result.

Psychic finds wrong body.

Harry scanned the article. The psychic, Sandy Flores, had been given information from the spirit world about the disappearance of a teenager from the Sunshine Coast three years before. Every night for a week she had dreamt about finding the body, in bushland near the Mooloolah General Cemetery, in the shade of the Glasshouse Mountains.

She informed police, and took them to the spot. They didn't find the body, but they found *a* body. A man's torso. Police dogs were brought in. They located a head, arms and legs three-hundred metres deeper into the bushland, in an old suitcase. They were still trying to identify the man.

Harry googled the woman's name. There was no website.

Nothing at all, certainly nothing with soft focus and pastels. Instead, there was a White Pages listing. Harry jotted down the name and number.

There was something about the story. Harry wasn't put off by the fact that she'd found the 'wrong corpse'. Instead, he found it comforting. It meant that something was going on with her, unless she was involved with the man's death.

He scanned further down the search results. She had a blog, last updated two years ago. At that point she was offering her services, doing readings. But then something happened and she gave it all away.

Harry picked up his phone and dialled her number. While it rang, he doodled in the margins of his notebook. Poppies, skulls, a tattoo machine.

'Hello?' Wary.

'Hello, is this Sandy Flores?'

'Yeah.'

'Hi. My name's Harry Hendrick, I'm a journalist with…'

'Look, I'm not talking to anyone else. That last bastard told me it was off the record and…'

'I'm sorry, I'm not calling about the body.'

'I don't care what you're calling about. Goodbye.'

'Wait!'

Something about the tone of his voice gave her pause. She didn't hang up.

'Look. I am a journalist. But that's not why I'm calling. It's sort of a habit to introduce myself like that.

'Something weird is going on. I think I might be haunted… or possessed, or something.'

Silence. For a long while, he thought she was going to hang up. He could hear her breathing. He could hear magpies calling in the background.

'You think *you* might be haunted? I don't do readings anymore,' she said.

'I know. That's why I called you.'

'What do you mean?'

'The people who *are* doing readings – they look, I don't know, they look kinda dodgy.'

Another pause. Shorter this time. 'So, what's been happening?'

Harry took a deep breath, closed his eyes. With his free hand he massaged his temples. He would've thought that with each telling, it would get easier. But it was the opposite, as if each revision of the story made it more real and, thus, more terrifying.

He started with the night out, the buck's night, and the tattoo the following morning. Then the nightmares. The tattoo parlour visit. The second tattoo, and the revelation that it was the design of someone who'd apparently just dropped off the scene. He finished up with the tattoo that arrived overnight, the blood on the sheets, and the strong feeling that he wasn't having nightmares, he was having memories, delivered by the tattoos' DNA.

By the end of the story he was shaking, he'd downed another beer, and the poppies on his back were throbbing. He felt dizzy again, and forced himself to take a deep breath. He waited for Sandy to say something. There was nothing, not even the breathing. For a moment Harry thought the line had cut out. Wouldn't that be a laugh, having to go through it all again. Then she cleared her throat.

'I'm not bullshitting you,' Harry said. 'I know this sounds like some sort of schizo…'

'No, I know you're not lying,' she said. 'I've never heard of a spirit manifesting like this. I'm picking up some odd vibrations, just talking to you. It's… it's all jumbled up…

'I… I don't do readings anymore. I told you that, right?'

'Yeah.'

'But… there's definitely something going on. I'd need to meet you.'

'That's fine. Of course.'

Another pause. A sigh. Harry could sense her reluctance. He dealt with this a lot, as a journalist. People who wanted to commit, but had trouble actually going through with it.

'Whenever is convenient,' Harry said. 'And wherever. We could meet at a coffee shop or something if…'

'No. No. I'd prefer if we met here. This person, this spirit, do you have anything of his?'

'No. Well, the tattoos,' Harry said.

'The tattoos. Yes, that'll do.'

'Okay. When?'

'Friday?' she suggested.

'Okay,' Harry said. Then he remembered the awards night. This was more important. But he couldn't explain it to Christine, and she'd be livid if he missed it. 'Hang on. Sorry, I've got a thing on Friday. Saturday?'

'Sure.'

She gave him the address. It was up the coast, at least an hour's drive away. Near the Glasshouse Mountains. The thought of his new tattoo rubbing against a sweaty car seat for an hour made him feel sick.

'Thanks, Sandy. Thank you.'

'Hmm. I'll see you Saturday.'

Harry scouted around on the web, looking up information about Afghanistan in general and the drug trade in particular. He read up about Australia's involvement in the war over there. Australian troops went to Afghanistan in the wake of the terrorist attacks in 2001. The first phase, involving special forces and the RAAF, lasted about a year. Then Australians all but withdrew from Afghanistan until 2005, when the Special Forces Task Group returned.

In late 2006 the focus shifted to reconstruction, with an engineering regiment deployed along with protective elements. In 2009 Operational Mentoring and Liaison Teams were embedded within elements of the Afghan National Army, to pave the way for the withdrawal of Australian soldiers.

Harry had a vision of a bleak valley. He felt the sun on his back and the dry wind in his face.

Reconstruction Taskforce?

If Rob was special forces, and Harry suspected he was, then it must've been 2006 at the earliest.

He opened a new browser tab, loaded ABC News 24. He wanted to look at something totally unrelated while he processed the information. There was a piece on funding for private schools. Harry zoned out, eyes blurring.

'Meanwhile, Labor leader Andrew Cardinal has vowed to maintain funding to private schools if he is elected,' the voice said.

There was a shot of Cardinal walking away from the camera, with school kids bunching around him. He was in the shadow of an old, red-brick building. He stepped out into the sunshine.

And the sun caught his hair. Harry was back in the nightmare, back in Afghanistan, watching through his scope as the guy with the silver crewcut faced off against the men at the poppy plantation. Old Silver. Andrew Cardinal.

'Oh shit,' Harry said. 'It can't be. It can't be.'

But he knew it could. He knew it was.

Harry heard heavy footsteps coming up the front steps. He looked up from the screen, blinked. His tattoo throbbed dully. Dave. He looked tanned and was wearing a flowery shirt Harry hadn't seen before. He should have looked relaxed, but as he pushed his sunglasses up on his head, Harry saw the worry lines around his eyes.

He stood in the sunroom, backlit, hands out.

'You okay, Haz?' he asked.

'Welcome home!' Harry replied, trying for a light tone but not quite nailing it.

Dave walked over to the table and laid down his sunglasses. He was breathing heavily.

'Do you remember our last conversation?' he said.

Harry nodded.

Dave shrugged. 'Well?'

Harry closed his MacBook. 'I decided you're right. Phantom radiation? Pfft.'

He remembered the feeling of relief when Dave suggested he stay at his place. He remembered the feeling that followed right after that, one of unease at the thought of leaving. Dave was going to explode when he saw the latest addition.

'I'm going to show you something, but I want you to promise me that you're not going to lose it,' Harry said.

'Mm-kay.' Dave reached for his sunglasses, then put them down again. Clenched one fist.

'I mean it,' Harry said.

'Can we go outside, at least?' Dave looked around the room. 'This place creeps me out.'

Harry walked towards the back door. He could understand Dave wanting to get out of the house, but he also didn't want to be like some sort of public freak show in the back garden. When he heard Dave following him down the hallway, past the kitchen, he pulled his shirt off, wincing as his shoulder muscles bunched.

'Whoa,' Dave said.

Harry stopped on the small back porch, at the top of the stairs that led down into the garden. He hoped Dave wouldn't touch it. When he turned around, he saw Dave standing a good couple of metres back.

'Are you scared you'll catch it?'

Dave shrugged. 'Maybe.'

Harry pulled his shirt back on. 'Come on. Let's talk.'

They sat on the grass, under the shade of the mango tree, looking back at the house.

'When I told you I was going to hang at yours, I meant it,' Harry said. 'But then it didn't feel right.'

'Didn't *feel* right? How does it feel now, after that?' Dave gestured at Harry's shoulders.

'I felt like shit this morning. When I woke up I didn't know where I was. I didn't know who I was. But now...'

He held his hands out. They shook.

'You want to see this thing out?' Dave said.

Harry nodded. 'I don't know what is going on. I'm pretty sure I'm not "getting" the tattoos. I guess, theoretically, someone could be breaking in, drugging me, tattooing me. But that doesn't explain the nightmares.'

Dave sighed. 'What do you remember about them?'

'The first one was about being buried. I thought buried alive at first, but now I think he was dead.

'The drowning man. There was a sea full of screaming people. They were asylum seekers.'

He gave Dave a rough outline of the Fajar Baru disaster.

'Yeah, I remember that. The government tried to cover it up. What about the poppies?'

Harry closed his eyes. When he'd awoken, it was all there, so real that he had trouble remembering it was a nightmare. But now, already, it had faded. He could only remember vague details.

'It was Afghanistan… Red poppies in a bone-white valley… I can remember soldiers…'

'Australian soldiers?'

'Yeah. And Afghans. And… I don't know… You know those guys… mercenaries…'

'They call them security contractors these days.'

'Yeah. That's it… Something awful happened there. I remember a… what do you call it… the thing Afghan women wear on their heads…'

'Hijab?'

'That's it. It was on the ground, blowing between the rows of poppies.'

Harry shuddered.

'That's it?'

Harry nodded. He couldn't tell Dave about Cardinal. Not yet. It would be too much. 'Yeah, but the first time, it's always a bit vague. After a few nights, it becomes clearer.'

'Come and stay with Ellie and me. Just for a bit.'

Harry looked at him. Dave looked back. He had his sunglasses back on. Harry saw himself reflected back. He looked different.

'Why?' Harry asked.

'Harry. We've known each other our whole lives. I've

been with you through thick and thin. Whatever is going on, it's seriously fucked up.'

'I feel like I need to be here.'

Dave pulled off his sunglasses. 'Just have a breather. Get some perspective. You can crash on our couch.'

'I'm sure Ellie would love that. Great start to your married life.'

'If you're not there, it'll just be the usual hungover medical students. Come on, Harry. I'm worried about you.'

Harry looked into the house. He should have been scared. He had no idea how far this was going to go.

'No. I can't.'

Dave shook his head. Hissed.

'I can figure this out,' Harry said. 'I can't give up on it. I just can't.'

CHAPTER 16

Harry was in the spare room sorting through boxes when his phone rang. He ran back to the bedroom, where the phone was plugged into the wall. Christine.

'Hi, Chris,' he said. 'Yeah, I'm still not feeling the best. I'm going to take things easy at home again today.'

He didn't have to fake the sniffles; the dust from the boxes had set him off. Christine said she hoped he was feeling better soon.

Harry returned to the spare room. At the bottom of the box was a manila folder, bursting at the seams, held shut with old rubber bands. He took it out to the dining room table and set it down. He was already sweating, but seeing the folder after all these years gave him heart palpitations. It brought back so many memories.

SWENSON was scrawled across the front in red pen. He remembered the day he wrote it. Things were going well, not just with study but in general. Boozy afternoons at the rec club, reinforcing the illusion that he and his classmates were 'real' journalists. There was a sense of camaraderie with the rest of the students in his year – Redwood aside. The Swenson story had taken on a life of its own. The documents associated with it had multiplied until the story needed its own folder. He shook his head.

The story was good.

Maybe, but Harry couldn't deal with it right now.

On impulse, he grabbed his notebook and keys and headed out the door. In a few minutes he was standing outside Bill's house. He pushed through the gate, waded through the overgrown garden and into the cool shade under the verandah.

The front door was open. Harry could see bookcases inside, filled with old, dusty tomes. Ornate rugs covered the floorboards. On the Balinese-style coffee table was a stack of Save the Tower pamphlets, weighed down with a small brass Buddha. The wind blew through the central hallway, bringing with it the scent of joss sticks.

'Hello?' Harry called out.

At the back of the house, someone stirred. Then Bill's silhouette bobbed down the hallway.

'Mr Hendrick, I presume.'

'Hi, Bill. Congratulations.'

They shook hands. 'Come in, come in,' Bill said.

Bill placed a hand at Harry's back and guided him through the house.

'No need for all those pamphlets now, I guess,' Harry said.

'Ah. I dunno about that. You know what politicians are like. What Cardinal says now and what he does when he gets in are two different things. But we're in a better position now than a week ago. Drink?'

'Ah yeah, just water thanks.'

'Take a seat outside, I'll bring it out.'

The back verandah looked out over a garden no less unkempt than the front. But unlike some of the houses around here, this one looked like the ground was being reclaimed by the sub-tropical rainforest that once dominated this area. Harry took a seat on a cane chair next to the one Bill had evidently been sitting in. His glasses were on the coffee table, sitting atop the half-finished *Brisbane Mail* cryptic crossword.

Bill emerged with two glasses of water, condensation already beading their sides.

'Here you go.'

Harry took the glass. Bill sat down with a small grunt of satisfaction.

'So, working on a follow-up?' Bill said, nodding at Harry's notebook.

'Kinda. I've been thinking about what you said about Swenson. Wondering if it's worth chasing.'

Bill sipped his water. Shrugged. 'It's all about getting the evidence. I'm sure he's dirty, but he's also cunning. You don't get away with it for as long as he has without being cunning.'

'Hmm.' Harry gulped some water. He stared out into the garden. 'Actually, that's not the main reason I'm here,' he said.

'Oh?'

'No. You know that symbol I passed to Fred?'

'Yeah?'

For a moment Harry thought he'd chicken out. Then he turned in his seat, pulled the hair up from the back of his neck. Bill gasped. Harry waited for more. He could hear Bill breathing heavily. He turned back. Bill's face was pale.

'How?' he said.

Harry recounted the story about the first tattoo. He was getting good at it now. He stopped there, wanting to see what Bill had to say without giving him any more information.

'Where are you living?' Bill said.

Harry told him.

'Oh shit. A couple of years back. There was an old guy, living at your place. People thought he went bonkers. Started getting tattoos. Hanged himself, in the end.'

Harry shook his head.

'Yeah, Harry. He had the tattoo. *That* tattoo.'

Harry climbed up out of the seat. Bill grabbed his arm. Bill's hand was hot and sweaty.

'Harry – it was Andrew Cardinal's dad.'

'What?'

'Yeah, caused a big stir at the time. It was all hushed up. I figured Cardinal's dad had pissed off the wrong person. Someone versed in the dark arts. But if it's happening to you as well, it's worse than that. This is deep shit.'

The old man rubbed his face. Harry had left his house wanting to find answers. But looking at Bill, he wasn't so sure anymore.

'Look, I've told Fred this story,' he said. 'Haven't told anyone else. Not even my wife.

'I did a bit of travelling after the war. Fred and I, we saw some fucked up shit in the desert. Did some fucked up shit. All credit to Fred – he came back, got things right with his sweetheart and settled down.

'But me, I just couldn't do it. Needed to depressurise, you know? I came back from London the slow way, through Europe, down through Afghanistan, India. South-East Asia. Home to Brisbane via a tramp steamer, if you can believe it.'

Harry sipped his drink. Bill looked past the verandah

into the yard, although Harry doubted he was seeing anything out there.

'I was staying with a family outside Kabul. They lived in a mud hut, plonked on a vast, sparsely vegetated plain where they tended their goats. Living as their parents had done, and their parents' parents.

'I'd been there about a week. I helped them out with their goats. They seemed happy to let me stay. Then one night, we'd just had dinner. We were sitting around, listening to the wind whistling through the cracks in the roof. All of a sudden their oldest son bursts into the room, jabbering.

'I'd picked up a little Pashto, but this was beyond me. But you didn't need to speak the lingo to know he was scared. Terrified. It was that sort of fear that spreads like a virus. The father said something to the wife and the other kids, grabbed his rifle and headed out into the night.

'I followed. I wanted to help, if I could. There were screams coming from the village. An open fire was the only light. On the way down, the father tried to explain in his broken English, with a bit of Pashto mixed in.

'I didn't really get it. Something about someone having crossed the local Mullah Sensee – the local medicine man, if you will. There had been a disagreement over money for services. You know the deal. A curse was laid. The man's goats started dying. The man retaliated, smacked the Mullah Sensee's head open with a shovel, buried him while he was still bleeding to death.

'It seemed like that was the end of it. But judging by the screams, that wasn't the end of it.

'We found the man, in the light of the fire, naked. His body was covered in tattoos. I thought he was on fire, at first. Then I realised he was trying to burn the tattoos off his body. His legs were a charred mess, blisters already rising on his skin. He was using a shovel-blade, heating it up and pressing it against his body.

'He was screaming, over and over again. The father told me later he was saying, "He's inside me. He's inside me." The father struggled with him, wrestled the red-hot shovel-head off him. Held him to the ground. The man's eyes rolled up in his head as he lost consciousness.

'As he lay there in the light of the fire I saw the tattoos. And there was one like that, like yours, on the back of his neck.'

Bill put his clammy hand on Harry's arm again.

'That night, the father whisked me away, told me I shouldn't get involved. Urged me to leave at dawn. He refused to answer my questions. The next morning, he pretended none of it happened.'

Harry took a sip of water. 'What do you know about it?'

'The tattoo on your neck? It's a protection sigil. It was actually widely used but usually people would scratch it on a bit of paper, fold the paper up and carry it around with them.

'What I saw that night was different. The Mullah Sensees had the ability to apply the symbol as a tattoo, and it went from just a protective sigil to something that had the ability to wreak vengeance on people, if the protective aspect failed.

'And this thing has latched on to you, although I'm guessing if you're not the first one, then you're probably not the intended target. Stating the obvious, you need to figure out what those tattoos mean, before it's too late.'

CHAPTER 17

Rob sat at a corner table in the Shelter Bar, nursing his beer, as the Friday evening crowd heaved around him. He popped a couple of tablets from the foil sitting on the table and swallowed them with a mouthful of VB. He wasn't supposed to take them with alcohol. He pretty much wasn't supposed to drink anymore. The doc reckoned the grog, along with the heavy-duty painkillers, was killing his liver. But lately Rob had a feeling that his liver was the least of his worries.

Chucky Cheese and the Misfits fired up in the corner, bathed in weak gels that had trouble competing with the evening light filtering through the windows in the front. The Shelter was meant to be a temporary building, pre-fab and down and dirty, much like the riff Chucky was belting out right now, while the neighbouring Story Bridge Hotel was being refurbished. But once the upgrade was completed, many of the old bar flies didn't feel at home among the shining brass, polished wood bar, the up-market menu and the imported beers. So the Shelter stayed. It suited everyone. The bar flies and students still had somewhere to down cheap jugs of VB, and the yuppies could sip their organic low-carb shit without feeling threatened by real people.

As the riff cranked, the painkillers kicked in. Rob both loved and hated the sensation. He hated it because the slightly dopey feeling was about a million miles from what he would consider acceptable in a threatening environment back in his SAS days, and he considered the whole Brisbane sprawl a threatening environment these days. But he loved it because it dulled the chronic pain in his lower back, and it turned down the volume on the screams he seemed to hear all the time now. Terrified screams from the poor souls escaping the burning wreck of the Fajar Baru, screams reverberating off the mud walls of the compound in Afghanistan. The screams of his mates, as the Black Hawk they were in spun out of control off the coast of Fiji.

There were a couple of people dancing now, if you could call it dancing. One woman, maybe late fifties, was jiggling up and down. Her limp grey hair bounced around her head. She was skinny, almost anorexic – except women that age didn't get anorexic, right? It reminded him of a spirit taking a body and shaking it like a rag doll. But he didn't want to follow that train of thought, so he sculled the rest of his beer. He scratched at his neck.

Kyla pushed through the crowd with a fresh jug, condensation beading on its sides. She was beautiful. Worry lines were the only blemish. She offered him a crooked smile. It was subtle. No-one else in the place, even if they'd been looking at her, would have noticed it. And in that moment Rob felt compelled to get a gun somewhere and just go and finish this thing. Or, if he couldn't do that, throw himself off the Story Bridge. Cardinal wouldn't worry about her. She wouldn't be considered a threat. And she would move on, she could leave this life behind.

'What you thinking about?' she said.

155

'Taking you home and making an honest woman of you.'

She put the jug down and sat across from him. He took her hand.

'Too late for that,' she said.

She poured herself a drink. Pulled a cigarette from the pack on the table and lit up. His hand slipped under the table to where her leg jittered up and down, as though the electric current from Chucky's solo was running straight through her body.

He couldn't really believe she'd stuck with him. This wasn't how he'd imagined things panning out for them. By now they were meant to have kids. He was meant to have one of these cushy security consultant jobs in the Middle East that all of his mates – the ones still alive – kept telling him about. Instead he was still stuck in this shit-hole, the shit-hole that had inspired him to join the army to get away from the place. And now he had enemies.

Kyla blew smoke in his eyes. 'Seriously, what are you thinking about?'

He drank some more beer. It didn't help. He leant closer.

'You know, when I was in, they used to tell us to minimise risks. It's a pretty fucking dangerous job, but you do what you can to minimise risks,' he said. 'But what about you? How can I protect you?'

She pulled his head to hers and kissed him, hard on the lips.

'Don't worry about me. It's us. Okay? Cardinal is going to pay for what he did, all right?'

Chucky finished one song and started a new one. He howled into the microphone. Someone turned up the amp and they couldn't talk anymore. Rob stared into Kyla's eyes and that was okay. One song led into another. The dance floor filled up but it was just light and movement. The volume cranked again. A glass broke and someone cheered.

'Rob!'

He could barely answer, barely tell where the voice had come from. He'd nodded off. Fucking painkillers.

'Rob!'

He jerked, saw Kyla rising from her seat. The revellers parted when they saw the bikies striding through the bar, and were even keener to get out of their way when they saw the grimy Dreadnorts patches on their backs. Crow, with his flabby gut hanging down over his belt buckle. Heathy with his greasy blond hair hanging down around his shoulders, a tear tattooed under one eye. Cardinal's henchmen. Crow had a pool cue, snapped in half. Heathy looked unarmed, which meant he probably had a gun or a knife hidden somewhere. Heathy flexed his shoulders and the Celtic bands writhed on his neck.

Rob tried to reach over the table to push Kyla to one side but she was too far away, he was too groggy and he only succeeded in knocking the table over.

Drunken patrons stumbled over each other to clear out. Crow helped one on his way, planting a hand in his face and pushing, hard. The man staggered backwards, flipping over a table with Chaplin-like grace and landing on his feet. He looked around, as though waiting for applause, and was barrelled into by a woman in a tight white dress, who cursed as her cocktail went down her front. Someone laughed.

The band played on. Kyla blocked the Dreadnorts' path to Rob, bum resting on the edge of a table. Heathy sneered, leant over to push her away. Kyla reached behind her, then whipped her arm around too fast to see. A tinkling smash. Shards of glass fell to the ground. Heathy staggered backwards, eyes wide, pawing at the holes in his grubby black t-shirt. Blood oozed down his front, blackening his jeans.

'Fucking bitch!'

She brandished the bloodied, broken schooner glass at Crow, who laughed and smacked down with the pool cue, catching her knuckles. She screamed and the remains of the glass fell and shattered.

Rob shuffled forwards, still trying to clear his head. Crow advanced like a tank, pushing the table out of the way. He lashed out with the cue. Rob ducked, but not quite fast enough. The cue glanced off his head, sending a wave of black stars skating across his vision.

Despite the beer and the drugs, the training took over. Rob slipped under Crow's cue, grabbed it and twisted, pulling the bikie past his balance point so he speared head-first into the floor. He'd be lucky if he'd be able to turn his head in the morning.

Rob lifted the pool cue and went for Heathy, who was advancing on Kyla with a hunting knife. As Heathy lashed out Kyla ducked back towards the band, who were only now starting to realise the gravity of the situation. The bass guitarist fumbled, the drummer fell silent.

Rob moved into Heathy's blind spot. Kyla backed right up to the low riser the band were set up on and Chucky stepped forward, trying to put himself between Kyla and the bikie.

Rob slammed the pool cue down on Heathy's head, hearing the crack and feeling it down his arms, all the way to his damaged spine. The pool cue split with the force of the impact. The bikie dropped, a bag of meat and bones.

Kyla kicked him in the face, once, then again. Now that the band had fallen silent, Rob could hear the sirens in the distance. Chucky was still reaching out, backlit by a golden light that made him look almost beatific.

Rob grabbed Kyla, pulled her away. 'Come on, we've got to go.'

He glanced over at Crow, who was starting to lift himself off the beer-soaked carpet. As he pulled his head up, he left a couple of teeth behind.

'Kyla. Come on!'

Chucky raised a hand. 'Godspeed, dude. Godspeed.'

Rob felt a ridiculous amount of affection for the beefy blues player. He yanked Kyla through the mob of rubberneckers, out the front doors and down the steps onto the pavement. Rob surveyed the scene, looking for further threats. The Harleys waited at the curb. The Story Bridge towered above them. The sirens were louder out here and as he watched he saw flashers gliding over the bridge.

At the bottom of the steps Kyla gravitated towards the bikes. Rob tightened his grip on her hand. As she turned to follow him she spat at them.

They ran towards the river. Rob's back hummed with pain. Beside him, Kyla spewed an endless string of expletives.

At the riverbank there was an old jetty, a weak light illuminating the sign: Holman St Ferry. Rob's face was drenched in sweat. He'd left his painkillers on the table.

'Those fucking cocksuckers,' Kyla said. 'Why can't they leave us alone?'

The sirens drew near, then cut out. He looked out over the dark mass of the Brisbane River, and the buildings beyond, lit up and reflected in the water. A ferry chugged towards the jetty.

'They're never going to leave us alone,' Rob said.

'Why can't we just go to the police with what we've got?'

Rob shook his head. 'Because it's pointless, unless we take them down completely. The whole lot. From Cardinal down to those fuckers.'

He nodded towards the Shelter Bar. He pulled Kyla close to him.

'It won't be long. Redwood's putting together a few things. And when it's done, we're going to blow the lid off this thing and they're all going down.'

The ferry pulled in. In the golden light from its cabin, Rob could see the tears rolling down Kyla's face.

'I think we should visit Ahmed,' Rob said.

Kyla pulled away from him. Her eyes twinkled in the gloom. 'Are you serious?'

Rob shrugged. 'I know you don't believe in it. And I'm skeptical myself. But we need all the help we can get.'

She rested her head against his chest.

'Come on, it'll all be over soon,' he said.

'I hope so,' Kyla said. Barely a whisper. 'I hope so.'

'Hey, Johnsons don't quit, right? Isn't that what I told you when we first started going out?' Rob said.

'I think it was after you first asked me out. After I said no,' Kyla said, a fragile smile touching her lips.

'Whatever,' he said, and she laughed.

CHAPTER 18

Harry opened his eyes. Grey light filtered through the windows. He felt dizzy, could taste beer and blood at the back of his mouth. Could smell smoke on his clothes, undercut by Kyla's perfume. In that moment, he knew it all. He knew all about Rob's past, his present, his future. He knew the answer. He knew what to do. But as he rose to full wakefulness, it slipped away.

He felt the now familiar burn, this time high up on his left arm. Ignored it for a second, looking for a way to get back into the dream.

Hey, Johnsons don't quit, right?

He grabbed his notebook, scribbled down the name: Rob Johnson.

'Shit, I'm getting used to this,' he croaked, then got up and looked at the new tattoo in the mirror on his wardrobe. At first he thought it was another version of the drowning man. A churning sea. Dark, stormy clouds above. But then, a break, a golden shaft of sunlight. And in the light, two swallows.

His granddad had a swallow on the back of his hand. It was part of the reason Harry had thought about getting one. They were a symbol of fidelity, and also a talisman of good

161

luck. Swallows always returned to the same nest, the same mate. Sailors used to get them tattooed before they went away, to increase their chances of returning home safely.

Despite the ominous blues and greys that dominated the image, the sunbeam gave it an optimistic feel. He figured that's what Rob wanted, and that's what Rabs delivered. And he had a feeling, it wasn't a memory as such, just a feeling that Kyla had this same tattoo. Was there someone else out there, going through what Harry was going through? He thought there was.

Harry rubbed his face. He slipped out of his pyjamas, pulled on his shorts and a singlet, groped under his bed for his running shoes. Grabbed a house key and was out the door.

Harry knew his plan had backfired the moment he pushed through the door to Swenson Constructions. He'd assumed that Brian Swenson wouldn't spend much time at the Chermside office. Harry had been hoping to talk to Nick Swenson, Brian's son and the general manager of Swenson Constructions. But there was no mistaking that voice, loud enough that the whole office reverberated with it.

The receptionist looked up. She seemed flustered to start with, and visibly paled when she saw Harry. Brian Swenson had a long memory, and he apparently made sure his staff did too. At one time, Harry would have turned around and run. But he stayed. Took a deep breath. What was the worst that could happen? He stepped further into the reception area and surveyed the office. Grey walls, venetian blinds and fake pot plants. Faded leather couches and dusty brochures.

It was a far cry from the flash website Harry had been

mining for information an hour earlier. The website was still putting on a brave face.

'What the fuck! What the fuck are you telling me, Nick! That we have to bend over and take this?'

Harry didn't want to talk to the receptionist yet, even though it looked like she wanted the distraction, and maybe an excuse to interrupt Brian before he really got going. Harry quickly turned and picked up one of the brochures. It was for a housing estate called Pine Lakes, west of Brisbane. Judging by the stack of dusty pamphlets, it hadn't been a big hit.

After Harry's failed exposé, Swenson Constructions went from strength to strength. Cherry Grove – the very development that Harry had uncovered corruption on – had been a wild success, in part because of the attention the lawsuit attracted. No such thing as bad publicity, it seemed.

Swenson's next target was farming land in the Redlands – what used to be known as 'Brisbane's salad bowl' until the farmers got sick of trying to compete with the supermarkets, and their kids decided working the land was a mug's game.

The property developer made a mint, so he did it again on the northside, buying up old cattle-grazing land and building a 'mortgage belt' as Brisbane's population exploded and the price of property in inner-city suburbs went through the roof.

Then Swenson Constructions won a major tender to redevelop the city's main sports stadium in 2008, turning Lang Park with its quaint grassy 'outer' into a world-class 60,000-seat sporting and entertainment venue.

And then the GFC hit. Judging by the articles Harry had been able to dig up online, 2008 was the turning point. In one article – the *only* article Harry could find that suggested a possible chink in the armour – Nick hinted that his dad had over-extended to win the Lang Park tender. After that, Swenson's son toed the company line. Listening to the diatribe of which Nick was now on the receiving end, Harry could well understand why.

A mumbling voice. Nick, Harry assumed.

'The guy is a fucking psychopath! Buying up his little heritage projects here and there, and now he wants to steal mine too! Fuck him! Fuck! Him! Listen to me. We *need* that fucking water tower. We need to tear that fucker down and replace it with some prime real estate.'

Harry felt as much as saw his approach. A giant shadow emerged from a corridor behind the receptionist's desk. She flinched when he burst into the room.

Brian Swenson was in his early sixties, overweight, with a ruddy complexion suggesting he needed to watch his cholesterol and stay off the grog and smokes, although maybe he struggled to do that. Shirt and tie, pants that were tight around the waist but billowed around his skinny legs. One hand clutched his briefcase, the other a copy of the *Chronicle*.

He looked at Harry, dismissed him, then looked again. He stopped halfway across the room. A wave of body odour washed over Harry. He was instantly transported to that day in the Vice Chancellor's office, flanked by his lecturer and a UQ lawyer. That day, Swenson accepted Harry's apology, then delivered a forty-minute rant on defamation law and the importance of the property sector.

'I don't believe it,' Swenson said. He tapped the newspaper against his leg. 'Harry fucking Hendrick. Your timing is impeccable.'

He switched the newspaper to his briefcase hand, offered the other. Harry shook it. Felt like he was going to be sick. The backache he'd woken up with intensified, sending waves of pain up his spine and through his tattoos.

Brian put down his briefcase and unfolded the newspaper. 'Water fight', in big black letters, and a picture of Bill and Fred clinking champagne glasses under the Paddington water tower.

'I was, ah, I was just looking at this article you've written,' Swenson said. 'I was quite surprised to see your byline on that story, Harry. Quite surprised.'

Harry rolled his eyes. 'Come off it, Brian. It was massive news. Covered by the *Brisbane Mail*. *The Oz*. ABC. The whole deal. Why are you surprised we covered it?'

'I thought you might have learnt your lesson.'

Harry's fear turned to anger. He pulled out his phone, opened the voice recorder app, held it out in front of him.

'Do you want an interview? Because there are some questions I'm dying to ask you. I'm working on a follow-up, about the Cherry Grove deal.'

Swenson swatted the iPhone away. 'Don't fuck with me, Harry. I've got lawyers poring over everything you've written about The Towers project.'

'Is that a threat, Brian? Are you threatening me?'

Swenson's face turned bright red. He bared his teeth. Then stopped himself. He took a deep breath. Forced out a laugh.

'Of course not, Harry! Of course not! But here's a word of advice. If you're planning on doing any more stories on The Towers, give my son a call – he'll get our girl to whip up a press release for you. Okay?'

He didn't wait for an answer, instead retrieving the briefcase and pushing through the door. Heat and the stench of pollution wafted inside.

Harry opened and closed his fists, breathing deeply. The receptionist was trying hard not to notice. He put his phone away and opened his notebook, jotted down a quick note: *Cardinal buying up heritage sites?*

'Is Nick in?' Harry asked.

The receptionist looked up. 'I'll just check for you. One moment. Your name?'

Harry laughed. 'Harry. Harry Hendrick.'

But before she could buzz Nick, he was in the room. Young, tanned, black hair combed back. His smart white shirt and dark pants were simple yet well cut, but the gold chain around his neck seemed a bit much.

'Mr Hendrick, I presume.' He offered his hand, and Harry shook it.

Nick's office was basic. Black desk. Abysmal modern art print on the wall behind his head. Bookshelves with business manuals and property magazines. Harry scanned his desk, saw reports with lots of red writing in the margins.

'So, Harry, where do you stand on this water tower business?'

'I'm an objective observ…'

'Bullshit. Come on. Where do you stand?'

Harry chose his words very carefully. 'I was surprised that the locals were mobilising to save the tower… and I was really surprised that Andrew Cardinal put himself out on a limb over it. I think everyone was. People have to live somewhere, right?'

Nick held one hand to his mouth. Peered at Harry for a moment. 'I can't go on the record, okay? I'll email you the press release.'

'Okay.'

'Off the record now…'

'Yeah, off the record,' Harry said. He tried to look relaxed. Every journalistic nerve in his body was telling him this was a man he could not afford to go off the record with, but he needed information.

'Off the record, this thing Cardinal is trying to pull is going to completely fuck us over. I mean, we've put a lot of money into The Towers. A lot. And, you know, with the GFC and shit, we can't afford to lose this project.

'Dad's angry. He and Cardinal go back a ways. But fuck me – I've got a lot more to lose from this than he does, if you get what I mean.'

Harry nodded.

Outside, lightning cracked through the sky. Nick flinched, rubbed his face.

'Look, I know it's nothing to you, one way or the other,' Nick said. 'The tower goes, the tower stays. You get a bunch of stories either way. But I'm telling you, Cardinal is holding a knife to our fucking necks.'

'What do you think his angle is?'

Nick shrugged. 'Property developers – easy target, right? His spin doctors have probably told him he looks like too much of a hard-arse, with his military super-spy background. They want him to look like he gives a shit.

'Cardinal never cared about heritage. Then a few years ago he starts buying up all these quirky properties around Brisbane, lending his support to these fucking NIMBY arseholes.'

Nick shook his head.

'What was that you were saying, about your dad and Cardinal going back?' Harry said.

167

'Ah, you know. They did some business deals a while back. Cardinal had some money he wanted to invest. Dad showed him how to do it right. Cardinal made a packet. I reckon that's how he got into politics, you know? Using that nest egg that Dad helped him build.

'And then, after that, Dad used to call Cardinal when he was about to redevelop some old dump. Dad would let him have a snoop around before the wreckers moved in.'

'Why?'

Nick shrugged. 'Dunno. Like I said, he became a nostalgia geek all of a sudden. Saw him one time, coming out of the old Regent site clutching some old movie posters and a brass light fitting. Weird.'

Harry nodded. So far, just about everything Nick had told Harry was on the public record. But it was interesting to hear it from Nick. The one thing that wasn't widely known was how close Swenson Constructions was to the precipice. And Cardinal's bizarre interest in old buildings may not have been criminal but it was, as Nick noted, weird.

'So what exactly do you want me to do?' Harry said.

Nick held out his hands. 'If people knew how close we are to going broke…'

'You could win a lot of sympathy. Your dad, for all his faults and failings, is an icon around here. And, you know, coming from me that's saying something. But you need to go on the record.'

'I can't. Dad would kill me.'

Harry considered. 'Well, you need to help me out. You need to give me something to get me started.'

Nick looked up from his desk. 'Okay. I'll think about it.'

* * *

Back at the office Harry sat in front of his computer, opened Google and typed 'Register of Member's Interests Andrew Cardinal'. Hit 'Enter'. It brought up the Australian Parliament House website, with links to every MP's Register of Interests form.

He clicked on the link.

Cardinal had listed their home on the southside as a residence. Half a dozen other addresses as 'investment properties'. A similar number were listed for his wife. He printed out the form. The register only required the MPs to list the suburb, so he had more work to do. But it was a start.

He glanced down at his notebook, and saw the note he'd scrawled this morning, just after he woke. Rob Johnson. He picked up the phone, dialled a number.

'Queensland Police Media. Phil speaking.'

'Hey, Phil, it's Harry.'

'Hazza! How's things? How was the wedding?'

Harry tried to remember. It seemed so long ago now. He was on the head table. He danced with Leela. Despite Simmo's attempts to get him drunk and set him up with her, he left the reception relatively early.

'Yeah, it was okay.'

'You get your end away?' Phil laughed.

'I don't kiss and tell,' Harry said, thinking about coming home to his pitch-black house, cursing himself for not leaving a light on. Somehow that made it worse. The darkness. It seemed to radiate from under the house, like fire in reverse. He had stood on the doorstep, key in lock. Listening to the night. Music blared from a party down the road. Powderfinger. Harry experienced a moment of deja vu, then shook it off and went inside.

'Wasn't expecting your call,' Phil said.

Every week, Harry did his police rounds call on a Wednesday. Unless something big happened, which was never.

'Yeah, something's come up. It's a bit left-field.'

'I can do left-field.'

'Can you see if there's an ongoing investigation into the murder of someone called Rob Johnson,' Harry said. He spelled out the name, then realised he didn't know for sure if that was the name. 'Could be Johnston. Something like that.'

'Rob Johnson or Johnston. Right. Whereabouts. Chermside?'

'I don't think so, maybe Paddington, around there. Inner West.'

'Uh-huh. When was this?'

Harry rubbed his face. 'I don't know, to be honest. Recent. Past ten years. Definitely after 2001.'

'Sounds shaky, Harry.'

'I know. Humour me.'

'Okay. But you owe me.'

'I'll buy you a drink at the Christmas party.'

'Ha! You're on.'

Harry hung up. He typed in 'Andrew Cardinal urban exploring'. He wasn't expecting a hit, but he got one. There was a photo of Cardinal in a tunnel, with a hard hat and high-vis vest. If Harry had a dollar for every time Cardinal had been photographed like this, or with his shirt off, he'd be a rich man.

Cardinal gets down and dirty, the headline read.

The story was a feature, written just after Cardinal won preselection for the seat he went on to win.

Don't be surprised if you see a rising Labor star digging

the dirt, or prowling around some of Brisbane's derelict landmarks, the story kicked off, and went on to explain how Cardinal had discovered his love of urban exploring after returning from the rough and tumble of Afghanistan.

While not condoning illegal entry to private property, Cardinal said he could well understand the buzz urban explorers got, and had even started buying up some properties around Brisbane so he could preserve some of Brisbane's crumbling icons.

Harry jotted down some notes, stared out the window.

When Harry got home the old yellowing folder still sat there on the table.

'Ah, fuck it,' he said.

The rubber bands came away in his hands, and the folder flipped open. The legal letters from Swenson's lawyers were on top, as well as the responses from the university's legal team. He set them to one side. Print-outs of his drafts followed. One was covered in red pen: his lecturer, marking the points at which Harry needed to provide evidence to back his claims. There were two copies of the front page. One was his. He remembered looking at it the day it came out. His first front-page lead. He'd intended to get it framed. There was one more in there, from his dad. He'd posted Harry the article. There was a Post-it note stuck to the front: 'Go get 'em, Scoops!' Seeing it dropped a great weight on his chest. His dad had been supportive, but in his eyes, the lawyers were always right. He thought Harry must've done something wrong.

He set copies of the front page to one side. Tunnelled back through time. The company searches. Media releases on the Cherry Grove development. Articles in the *Brisbane*

Mail. Transcripts from a report on the ABC's *AM* radio current affairs program. Harry laid out every piece of paper on the desk, and looked at them all. There was pain associated with each one, but over time he became desensitised. Numb.

The thing that had intrigued Harry most about the story were the front companies. Feeder companies that had directed the money to the councillor, so that there was never any link from Swenson to the money the councillor received. Bright Wing Holdings. Orange Water Pty Ltd. Circle Diagnostics Inc. It seemed overly elaborate for the sums of money involved.

But maybe, if what Bill was saying was true, Cherry Grove wasn't just a one-off.

CHAPTER 19

The taxi glided through the suburban streets, a light rain pattering down, just enough to piss off the driver and make the streets extra steamy. Harry sat in the back seat, sweaty, feeling sick. The houses they passed looked old and stale, dusty in spite of the rain. Overgrown lawns, broken letterboxes, flaking paint. The property boom hadn't touched this area. On their right, a glowing beacon loomed out out of the darkness: Christmas lights hanging from the fence and the house; a light-up Santa in the middle of the lawn, tending his light-up reindeer and sleigh. The taxi driver shook his head.

Harry had spent all afternoon staring at his screen, watching Twitter status updates, opening and closing documents, not really seeing anything. Replaying the encounter with Brian Swenson, and then with his son. Christine prodded him about the election bios he was meant to be helping with. He opened the list but couldn't motivate himself to do any more on it.

At some point he snapped out of the trance, aware that the light had faded outside. He vaguely remembered Christine reminding him to pick her up on the way through, but it was like something that had happened to someone else. He checked his watch.

As he headed home the tension started to build. As he dressed, it got worse, despite downing a stubby of VB. If anything, the beer made it worse. And as the taxi weaved its way through the Friday night traffic, his legs were jiggling with it, his hands tapping.

He pulled out his phone, dialled Christine's number.

'Hi, Christine, it's Harry,' he said.

'Harry!' There was music on in the background. Something heavy.

'Um, I'm not feeling too good. I might…'

'Whoa! You're not going to pike on me, are you?'

'Maybe, I…'

'Where are you?'

'I'm in the cab, but I might just get him to turn around…'

'No! No way, Harry! Come on – you need a night out. You need to let your hair down!'

Outside, a man stood on the side of the road, holding an umbrella. Three of its panels were missing. The man watched the taxi go past, made no effort to cross the road.

'Harry – at least come over here. There's no way I'm going to be able to get a taxi at this time of night. Come on! If you still feel crook, you can crash at my place.'

Harry had seen inside Christine's house once. The thought of crashing on a couch at a normal house, with normal people, with no ghosts, now appealed. He recalled Dave's plea to take a break.

'Yeah. Okay then.'

The taxi wove deeper into the suburbs, away from the main road. The rain picked up a bit. The driver's phone rang and he took the call, speaking a language Harry couldn't understand. He thought about death. And life after death. And whatever came after that. Peace?

The cab driver pulled up outside a low, brick apartment building.

'Can you wait here for a sec?'

'Sure thing, buddy.'

Harry stepped out into the rain, running across the driveway and through the carport. Up the concrete stairwell. The door was ajar. Christine's iPod was still docked, but the volume was down.

'Come in,' she called out.

She emerged from her room, pulled the door shut behind her. Harry's breath caught in his throat. She wore a deep-blue dress. High neckline. Sleeveless. Harry had no idea what it was made of, but it was sheer, and shiny.

'Wow,' Harry said. He cleared his throat.

She smiled. 'You're not too bad yourself.'

When she had turned to pull her bedroom door shut, he'd seen the tattoo on her left shoulder. A fairy. On a leaf.

'I didn't know you had a tattoo,' Harry said.

She shrugged. 'I'm kinda embarrassed about it. Got it when I was drunk. I wanted to get a tattoo, but I always said I'd get something with meaning. You know?'

Harry almost laughed. Tattoos with meaning. Yeah, he could grasp that concept. She had a tattoo without meaning. He had meaningful tattoos he didn't understand. He self-consciously rubbed his upper arm, where the swallows flew.

'Right, Harry Hendrick – sit,' she said.

'The cab's outside…'

'It'll wait. Plant your arse and tell me what's going on.'

Harry sat. Christine sat down next to him. Her perfume wafted over him. Her knee brushed against his. He didn't want to go to any awards ceremony. He wanted to stay right here with Christine and drink bourbon. And he didn't even like bourbon.

'It's just… there's going to be a lot of people who I went to uni with, or have crossed paths with over the years,' he said. 'You know, people who have done something worthwhile with their lives.'

'So what? Do any of them have a date as hot as me?' She turned her head to profile, batted her eyelids.

'Heh… no.' He stared at the carpet, worried his eyes would betray him. In his peripheral vision he watched as she crossed her legs.

'Well then, fuck them. Harry, there's no right or wrong way to live your life.

'Your life isn't over, is it? You're going through a rough patch, but you'll get through it. And let's face it, it's only the Community Media Awards. It's not the Walkleys. Or the Pulitzers.'

Harry stared at the dark TV screen.

'Come on. Let's go.'

Christine grabbed his hand. She felt warm.

They climbed into the back of the taxi. Christine kept his hand, holding it against her thigh.

'You need to trust me more, okay?' she said.

The taxi pulled away. The rain came down heavier, and the driver wound his window up. Harry was intoxicated by Christine's perfume. He squeezed her hand and she squeezed back. Outside, the world passed by in a mish-mash of abstract colours and shapes. People ran for cover under shop awnings and bus shelters. Harry watched for the man with the broken umbrella, but he was gone.

The Chermside RSL was like a beacon in the night, spotlights and gaudy neon. The taxi pulled up under the portico out front. Harry passed his card through, and Christine opened her clutch.

'Don't worry about it,' Harry said.

'You sure?'

'Trust me. I owe you.'

'Okay.'

They stepped out onto grimy red carpet, pockmarked with cigarette burns and lumps of blackened chewing gum. People milled around outside smoking. The media award attendees all stood out – the men were in suits, the women in dresses that really had no place at the Chermside RSL. Harry scanned the crowd, half-expecting to see Brian Swenson or Ron Vessel lumbering towards him. Or, at the very least, Terry Redwood. But no. None of them. They were probably waiting inside for him with meat axes and a chainsaw.

'What are you grinning about?' Christine asked.

'Nah. Nothing. I think I may have found my mojo again. Take me to the bar.'

Christine led him inside. They walked through the automatic doors and there was a bearded photographer waiting. He smiled.

'Hey, Stal,' Harry said.

'Quick photo?'

'Sure,' Christine said.

Harry stepped to one side. Stal raised an eyebrow. 'Uh. I meant both of you.'

Christine pulled him towards her, put one hand around

his waist, leant her head against his shoulder. The flash went off. Harry could smell her hair.

'Um, can we try one where you don't look like you've just been poleaxed, Harry?'

'Ah. Yeah, sure.'

Harry put his arm around Christine. Smiled. The camera flashed. Stal adjusted the settings on his camera, took a few more shots.

'Luvverly,' he said. 'Have a great night.'

They found the conference room. People milled around tables set with cutlery, white linen and bottles of wine. At the front of the room there was a low stage, with a lectern on it. To one side there was a small bar, and this seemed to have attracted the majority of the attendees, despite the wine on the tables and the waiters hovering with drinks on trays.

'I'm starting to feel better,' Harry said.

Christine smiled. 'Good.'

'Harry Hendrick! Well, I never thought I'd see the day!'

'Maybe I spoke too soon,' Harry muttered, and turned to greet Terry Redwood.

Redwood clutched a stubby of XXXX in one hand, grabbed Harry's hand with the other and shook it vigorously, only letting go when Harry pulled away.

'You coming out of retirement?'

Harry felt dark clouds gathering. He forced a smile. 'Nah, just here to support Christine.'

Redwood's eyes shifted focus, devoured Christine. When he shook her hand he once again held on too long, but Harry suspected his motives were different.

'Christine, is it?'

'Yeah. Christine King. I work with Harry.'

'Oh well, don't worry, that won't last forever.' He bellowed laughter, gave Harry a playful jab in the upper arm. Then his eyes lit up.

'Christine King! Right – you're one of the finalists in my category!' He took a swig of beer, eyes never leaving her for a second. 'Oh well, you can't win 'em all, right?'

'I only graduated last year, so it's an honour just to be nominated.'

'That's right. That's right. Plenty of time for you. Unlike Harry here. How's that scoop coming along, Hazza?'

Every time they met, Redwood asked him about 'the scoop'. Harry saw himself grabbing Redwood in a headlock, squeezing until he fell unconscious.

'Yeah, it's coming. I'm just lulling you into a sense of false security.'

Redwood leant in. The stench of stale sweat and alcohol washed over Harry.

'Let me know if you want me to help you out. You know, save you from some embarrassment.'

Harry's throat locked. Redwood grinned. Harry would have liked nothing better than to ram his teeth in. He felt a tug at his elbow.

'Well, Terry,' Christine said. 'We're going to grab a drink. Nice meeting you.'

'You too, love. If you ever get bored at the *Chronicle*, I can help you get a real job, okay.'

Christine ignored him. 'Arrogant prick.'

Terry turned. 'What's that?'

'I said, "Good luck!"'

'Yeah. You too.'

Christine led Harry through the crowd. He saw familiar faces. Some he could put names to – he'd seen their photo bylines – others he couldn't, but was fairly sure he'd studied with some of them at uni. The lights dimmed slightly. As they neared the front of the queue at the bar Christine tapped a young guy on the shoulder. He turned, and his eyes lit up when he saw her.

'Chris!' he said.

'Hi, Darryl! How's things?'

'Good. Good. Doing the *Brisbane Mail* cadetship thing. Hey, congrats on your award nomination!'

'Thanks.'

She let go of Harry's arm. He felt a ridiculous burst of jealousy.

'How's the cadetship going? We just met one of your colleagues. Terry Redwood.'

'Ah. He's a character. It's okay. Still haven't worked up the courage to tell Dad I'm working for the Evil Empire.'

He did a quick impersonation of Darth Vader. Harry had to admit, it was pretty good. They chatted some more. Harry moved forward in the queue, leaving them to it. Earlier, he'd had this stupid feeling that Christine was coming onto him. But seeing her with someone her own age set him straight. He ordered two beers and a gin and tonic, brought the drinks back to them.

'Cheers, everyone,' Harry said.

'Thanks, man,' Darryl replied.

'You remembered!' Christine said, gesturing with the glass.

Harry shrugged. 'It's a G&T. The galaxy's universal drink, right?'

By the time the ceremony started, Harry had two drinks under his belt. He and Christine found their table. Harry wasn't particularly surprised to find Redwood sitting with them, along with a bunch of his *Brisbane Mail* mates. At first, Harry didn't really care. He claimed a bottle of red and proceeded to demolish it, occasionally topping up Christine's glass.

He didn't hear any of the speeches. He saw they were flashing up headlines and pieces of audio and video. He heard music, and people laughing occasionally. He knew there was meaning behind it all, but couldn't put it together in his head.

The tattoos burned on his skin. He scratched his back, thinking of Afghanistan. He could almost taste the dust. Rob was pushing, asserting himself. What would happen if Harry let him out? He had a fair idea. He knew what Rob was good at. And it wasn't writing newspaper articles. Harry didn't know for sure, but he thought the SAS sniper didn't lose any sleep over killing. When he woke up screaming, it was to visions of that poor woman, spread-eagled on a cold, bloodstained concrete floor.

The drinks kept coming. Someone put money on the bar so that when the wine was gone, spirits were the go. Harry ordered bourbon and Cokes, even though he'd always hated bourbon. The world lost its focus.

Christine squeezed his leg under the table.

'I'm up,' she said.

He looked at her and for the first time since zoning out he saw something real. God, she was beautiful. And young. So full of enthusiasm and hope. And she deserved to be. She had a lot going for her.

On stage, some guy in a tuxedo was reading out the names, the story titles, and a short spiel from the judging panel. On the screen behind the emcee, photographs of the articles popped up. Harry remembered seeing Christine's face when she got her hands on a copy of it. Her first front-page lead. And it was a doozie. Uncovering incompetence at one of the local hospitals.

The *Brisbane Mail* crowd cheered when Terry Redwood's story replaced Christine's on the screen. He'd gone up north to report on the situation at Palm Island, where residents of the Aboriginal community there were in conflict with police over the death in custody of a young Aboriginal man. It was a good story. But in Harry's mind it was nothing earth-shattering. It was a colour piece – nothing that new in it other than the fact that a Brisbane-based journo had bothered to make the trek to Palm Island.

'And the winner is… Terry Redwood!'

'Bullshit!' Harry said.

He was drowned out by cheers from the other side of the table. Harry didn't realise he was squeezing his glass until it burst in his grip, showering him in wine and shards of glass. This prompted more laughter from the *Brisbane Mail* crew. Harry felt Rob pushing. He suppressed it. He focused instead on Christine, who had reached for a serviette and was brushing the worst of the mess off Harry's shirt and pants.

'While you're down there, love…' one of the faceless journos said.

'Fuck off, dickhead!' Harry spat.

Terry was on his way to the podium. Harry made to rise out of his chair, but Christine grabbed his arm, holding him.

'Don't, Harry,' she said. 'It's fine. I meant what I said earlier. I was honoured just to just nominated. You know how these things go. Ever watched the Oscars?'

Terry climbed up onto the stage and accepted his

award. He held it up, looked at it, and approached the microphone.

'Well, it's not a Walkley, but still…'

Raucous laughter from the table.

'Seriously. I'd like to thank the judges for the award. You know, it was a hard story to write…'

It won't be long. Redwood's putting together a few things.

But the story never came out. Because Redwood deep-sixed it.

Harry shrugged out of Christine's grip and headed for the podium.

'Harry? Harry!'

She followed him a few steps, grabbed his arm. He pulled away again. Terry saw him coming.

'I think me old mate Harry Hendrick is coming to give me a kiss,' Terry said.

More laughter. Harry's world swum around him. He was striding across the barren flatlands of Afghanistan, striding across the sticky carpet of the Shelter Bar. He staggered slightly, reached out for the back of a chair to steady himself but his hand landed on a woman's bare shoulder. More laughter.

The light was too bright on stage. He held up one hand to block it out. Headed for Redwood. They grappled. Arms on arms, face to face. A combative waltz.

'Why did you bury it?' Harry hissed.

A moment of blankness in Redwood's eyes, before the anger returned. 'What the fuck are you talking about?'

'Rob. The massacre in Afghanistan. You buried it!'

A flash of something – bewilderment? Shock? Disbelief? – then the shutters came down.

'The only thing I'm going to bury… is you.'

183

With that he shoved. Harry caught his balance and returned with a fist. Terry blocked the clumsy strike and responded in kind. Harry was ready for it but too drunk to move fast enough. He ducked, but Terry's meaty fist deflected off the top of his head, sending him staggering backwards. If he'd been sober he would have stayed on his feet, but he wasn't sober. It was a miracle he was standing at all, without trying to dodge punches. He fell on his arse, bounced.

Terry came after him. Harry bunched up his legs, protecting himself. Redwood loomed over him, jabbed a finger down at him.

'Get yourself a lawyer, you crazy prick,' he said.

He walked back to the microphone, forcing a laugh. 'Ladies and gentlemen, Harry Hendrick. Former journalist.'

Christine and Darryl were waiting outside on the red carpet when he emerged. The top of his head throbbed. He probed with his fingers and felt a lump there. His neck ached. Redwood got more contact on him than he'd initially thought. The adrenaline was still coursing through his system. He didn't feel drunk anymore.

'Sorry,' Harry said.

Christine ignored him, mumbled something to Darryl. Harry touched her arm and she shrugged away from him.

A taxi pulled up. 'Can I make it up to you?' Harry said. 'Buy you a drink?'

'You really want more to drink?'

'I'll drink lemonade.'

'Yeah, right. I'll believe that when I see it.'

She climbed into the back of the cab. Harry advanced. Darryl stood at the door of the taxi, blocking him. He looked embarrassed. Harry peered around him. 'Well, I told you I'd buy you a drink, right?'

Christine peered out of the taxi. She sighed. 'Fine.'

She shuffled over. Darryl climbed in beside her, leaving Harry to sit in the front next to the driver.

Christine gave the cab driver directions. Red Hill, via the bottle shop. They skirted the city. Even at night, it was hard to miss the cranes everywhere, highlighting Brisbane's recovery from the global financial crisis. It was hard to believe the Swensons were really struggling to make a buck out of it.

At the Paddo Tavern, Christine opened one of the fridge doors and reached for a bottle of cheap-ish sparkling wine. Harry made her put it back, and took down a bottle from the top shelf.

'Are you crazy?' she said.

Harry shrugged. 'What else am I going to do with my money?'

'Thanks,' she said. But she looked at the ground when she said it.

He grabbed a bottle of bourbon and a bottle of Coke for himself, ignoring Christine when she cleared her throat and raised her eyebrows. Darryl bought a six-pack of beer. They paid for their drinks and climbed back into the cab.

When the taxi finally stopped, Harry thought the driver had got the directions wrong. They were sitting at the top of Red Hill. On the other side of the road, a row of shops – only the chemist and No-No's Lebanese takeaway were open. On this side of the road, a party shop, tyre fitter, laundromat. All closed.

Darryl paid the driver with his card. When Harry opened the door, he heard the music. The discordant clash of guitars, a crazy rockabilly beat, double-bass. A low, resonant voice bellowing over the top. Harry climbed out of the cab, still looking for the source of the noise. People milled in front of the laundromat. Jaunty hats, striped tights, the dim glow of iPhones.

'Come on,' she said. She led them down the side of the laundromat, through the gaggle. 'Have you got any cash on you?'

Harry checked his wallet. 'Yeah.'

At a small desk, two guys manned a cash register. The sign tacked to it read: The Hangar. $10 cover charge.

'Ten bucks? To drink our own piss?'

Christine nudged him. He paid. She and Darryl led the way down the side of the building. At the back there was a small courtyard, packed with people. Under the building, an even smaller room, pulsing with red light. The band was so much louder down here.

Harry, Christine and Darryl stood together in the courtyard. Around them people shuffled about, yelling to be heard over the music. Over in the corner a guy with a jester's hat pirouetted, lost in his own world.

Christine cracked open her bubbly. She looked at the label, shook her head.

'I really shouldn't be doing this but… cheers,' she said, and swigged out of the bottle.

Harry looked around, realised he'd left his Coke in the cab.

'Fuck it,' he said. He twisted the top off the bourbon bottle, took a swig. 'Cheers.'

He turned the bottle cap over in his fingers a couple of times before cursing again and casting it into the weeds by the rusty chain-link fence.

'I'm sorry about the awards,' Harry said.

Christine shrugged. 'Forget about it. Seriously. Probably wouldn't have hung around much longer anyway. You can bet Redwood's not done throwing punches. By morning no-one will remember.'

No. Harry thought that no matter how drunk Redwood got, he would remember. He'd been goading Harry for years, trying to elicit this exact response. And Harry had always turned the other cheek. He shook his head, angry at himself. Redwood had let Rob down, and maybe Rob had died as a result. But Harry couldn't let himself lose control like that.

'... isn't going to last long,' Darryl said.

'Sorry?' Harry said.

'I said this place. It's not going to last long.'

'Really?' Harry replied. He took a big mouthful of bourbon. It burned inside him.

'They're developing this site. They're going to build apartments here. Like Brisbane needs more apartments.'

'Who's doing it?' Harry asked.

Darryl pointed. Up on the chain-link fence was a faded Swenson Constructions sign. Harry thought about what Nick had told him. Without the water tower project, the company was dead.

'Well, maybe it won't happen.'

Christine didn't look convinced. 'They're not even meant to be here tonight. Let's make the most of it.'

Christine dragged Darryl over to the doorway, leaving Harry by himself. People pushed in and out of the room where the band hammered out their tunes. It reminded Harry of the parties he went to when he was at uni. People roaming about, usually out the front of some run-down old

Queenslander. No method to the madness, just the need to keep moving. Harry felt older than ever.

Harry followed Christine and Darryl, shuffling into the room. The double bass thumped through his body, resonating with his tattoos. The heat hit him hard. His mind flashed on his days labouring, digging holes on a housing estate – the first job he had out of school. Then Afghanistan, lying on the ground in the heat, peering through the sight of his sniper rifle.

He drank some more bourbon, felt the buzz coming back.

The lead singer was leaning on the mic stand, like Jim Morrison. The posturing was where the similarity began and ended. Both arms were covered in tattoos. Bits and pieces of everything: skulls, a zombie nurse, a dragon. It shouldn't have worked but it did.

The singer wore a battered pork-pie hat. A red t-shirt with a black vest over the top. As he threw his arms wide the vest opened, revealing the t-shirt design: SATAN CLAWS, above a picture of a zombified Santa leering over sleeping children.

There was a woman on the double bass, fake eyelashes and heavy eye make-up, tattooed werewolf lurching from her bare upper arm. A small guy on the drums. Another on the slide guitar, with a thick swathe of dark, unkempt hair and a fairly restrained goatee. He had laughter in his eyes.

The band amped up. The music pulsed through the room and the people cramped in there moved as one. Christine dragged Darryl into the middle of the throng. They danced. Harry felt sullen jealousy building.

Darryl smiled and Christine laughed. The song ended and the next one began. Harry couldn't watch anymore. He retreated to the relative cool of the courtyard, peering from the shadows, feeling more like an outsider than ever. When they finally emerged, Harry had worked his way through half his bourbon. Darryl's hand was on Christine's waist, guiding her through the crowd.

Harry strode over.

Darryl cocked his head. 'I'm going to the…' Christine smiled as he disappeared back inside.

'I thought you'd gone home,' she said to Harry.

He stared at her. 'You're beautiful.'

She looked away. He felt a twinge of annoyance. The band cranked up again, slide guitar leading the way this time. He took her hand.

'I'm serious, Chris.'

'Harry…'

He gripped her hands tighter. She was shaking slightly. He let go, raising his free hand to the side of her face.

'I think I'm in love with you,' he said. He leant forward to kiss her.

She pulled away. 'What?'

'I said…' but he looked into her eyes and saw only anger.

She pulled free. 'Go home and get some sleep, Harry.'

His own anger flared. He threw the bottle of bourbon. It smashed against the concrete. Someone cheered. There was always someone around to cheer. He strode out of the courtyard, up along the side of the building, pushing his way through the crowd. What were they? Fucking Gen Y pukes playing dress-up! Fucking country music!

'Harry!'

He ignored her. First Bec. Now this. As he walked home, the ground threatening to spin from under his feet, the thoughts came faster. Every moment with Christine over the past month. Assessing. Every moment. He wanted to believe that she'd led him on but the more he looked at it, the only deception was on his part. He'd been lying to himself.

CHAPTER 20

Harry walked across the petrol-station forecourt, sun baking down on his head. Cars edged past and out onto the highway, heading north. It was a perfect day for a quick trip up the coast.

He slipped into his car, not for the first time wishing that he had a decent ride with air-conditioning. The hangover wasn't anywhere near as bad as he deserved. He'd woken up a little later than usual, but still forced himself out for his run. After a shower, some paracetamol and breakfast, he felt almost normal. Harry popped out the Counting Crows tape. The time for crying was over. He opened his glovebox and pawed through it until he found was he was looking for. He slid the tape in.

The opening guitar riff of Rage Against the Machine's 'Bombtrack' pulsed through the speakers, and Harry grinned.

He flashed back to the night before, and shook his head. It wasn't like him. He was usually a melancholic drunk. Not angry, or aggressive. And certainly not sleazy. Redwood was going to be a big problem now, particularly if it turned out that he did indeed have something to do with Rob's fate. And Christine… She showed a bit of interest in him in the wake of the break-up, and this was how he repaid her? He'd texted her an apology, but she hadn't responded.

Harry pulled out onto the highway, the Corolla struggling to get up to the 100 kays-per-hour speed limit. Big, shiny four-wheel-drives roared past, most likely forgoing off-road adventures in favour of braving the speed bumps on Noosa's glitzy shopping strip, an hour or so north of Brisbane. Like members of a secret clan, drivers' had plastered their rear windows with stickers proclaiming membership of elite schools, and 'My Family' decals – stickmen playing golf, women going shopping – masking the reality of overwork and mortgage stress.

The highway threaded through endless suburbs packed with low-set brick homes on small blocks, huddling behind concrete noise barriers. Meagre farmland, two giant radio masts towering over dusty cattle. Eucalypt scrubland looking dry and diseased despite the recent rain.

Then more houses, orange and grey under the sun. Satellite suburbs for the wage slaves. Estates with posh-sounding names that would be forgotten before the houses needed a fresh coat of paint. Crystal Waters. Freshwater Lakes. Paradise Grove. Streets that curled in on themselves like fractals, lined with McMansions and postage-stamp gardens.

Harry passed a billboard for 'Eden Valley', a new estate somewhere to the north-west. A nuclear family and a dog, walking in a luminous green rainforest. The Swenson Constructions logo stamped in the bottom right. He wondered again about Nick's revelation. If the company really was on the brink, and Cardinal killed The Towers, it looked as though there were a lot of projects that would go unfinished.

After about half an hour the suburbs gave way to pine forests – hectare after hectare of plantation timber. A few years earlier a man broke down in one of the plantations. He left his car, got lost, died of thirst. Looking along the rows of identical trees, it wasn't hard to see how easily that could happen.

Harry pulled off onto Steve Irwin Way, leaving the state forests behind him. Mount Tibragargan loomed over the road – it had always amazed Harry how a geological formation could look so much like a giant face, staring out to sea. At Landsborough he cut across the rail line, then passed a small block of shops and a cricket oval.

Harry checked the street directory on the passenger seat. He loved his iPhone, but there were some things he still liked to do the old-fashioned way. He turned down the volume on the music, concentrating on finding the right street. Lots of low-set houses, established but by no means old. A couple of girls pushed their bikes along the side of the road. He followed the streets back from the highway, towards the mountain. The trees on the sides of the road got bigger, the scrub thicker. The standard house blocks stretched to half an acre and then a full acre.

Harry was struggling to read the numbers on the mail boxes when he saw the woman waiting on the side of the road. She was dressed in old jeans and a t-shirt, with a broad-brimmed straw hat casting her face in shadow. She looked like she'd been doing some gardening. She waved. He pulled over.

'Harry!' Not a question. She hurried around the side of the car, opening the passenger door. Harry picked up the street directory and threw it on the floor, just before she dropped into the seat.

She thrust a hand at him. 'Sorry. Sandy. Sandy Flores.'

'Harry Hendrick.'

He took her hand. She felt fevered. She was about his Mum's age, but had clearly spent a lot of time outside in the sun. Deep lines spread out from the corners of her eyes and her mouth. They struck Harry as the sort of lines one got from smiling a lot. But she wasn't smiling now.

'Turn around,' she said.

Harry stared at her.

'Quickly. The spirits sent me a message last night. About you.'

Harry got the car moving, pulling into Sandy's driveway so he could turn the car around.

'A message?'

'Well, not so much a message. A vision. A place. It's important.'

'Important how?'

'I don't know! It was like this with the boy. That poor boy. The spirits gave me a vision, showed me where he was. Quick. It's fading.'

Harry pulled back out onto the street and switched the stereo off. He remembered the article he'd found online. She found a body, just the wrong one. A body. She knew where Rob's body was buried. Or the spirits knew, and had passed on the information to her. Where would it be? All the way back in Brisbane? Or somewhere up here, in the state forests he'd just motored past? Row after row of pine trees, tombstones stabbing up at the sky.

She directed him to Landsborough, back the way he'd come.

'You used to do readings? Why not anymore?'

'Shh!'

She laid a hand on his arm. 'I'm sorry. Sometimes these messages are strong. Sometimes they're barely audible or visible. This is the latter. We can talk later.'

When they got to the highway, Sandy sat there, head pivoting left and right as cars zoomed past. He could feel the stress radiating off her, smell her sweat.

'Which way?' he asked.

The car behind beeped. Harry raised a hand. A couple of Harleys boomed past, heading north. The car beeped again.

'Sandy?'

'North. No… south! South!'

Harry pulled out, wheels spinning slightly. Heading towards Brisbane. As they pulled into the traffic, Sandy looked behind her, then ahead, then behind her again.

'No, no, this looks right,' she said.

Harry offered her a doubtful look. All the enthusiasm he'd felt this morning, the sense that he was finally going to get some answers, was evaporating. He could feel heat rising up his neck, his scalp prickling with sweat. Panic threatened to take over. What if this was it? What was the next step if this turned out to be as fruitless as it appeared it was going to be? Another trip to the counsellor? A visit to a psychiatric hospital, where they could lock him up so there could be no more nocturnal visits to the tattooist?

He felt so stupid. It was clear they were all in on it. Sian, lying through her teeth. And then laughing about it behind his back with Mack and the rest of them.

No.

The cacophony cut off in his head, just like that. One word. Did he speak it or did someone else? It didn't matter. He could feel calm returning. His heart rate dropped. The sweat evaporated. He breathed deeply. He was in control of this situation. He was staring down the scope, target firmly within the reticle. He saw the man with the silver hair walking towards the compound. But this time he took the shot. The round opened his target's head like a melon, blood fanning out on the mud-brick wall. And he felt no remorse. No sadness. No guilt. He felt like a soldier who'd just done the world a favour.

'… housing estate.'

'Huh?' For a moment Harry remained in Afghanistan. Then he saw the truck looming large in front of him and wondered how the hell he'd kept the car on the road. What was it the counsellor had called it? Dissociative fugue.

'The place. It's in a housing estate.'

'Are they talking to you?'

'No. Yes.'

She turned away from him, staring out at the rows of pine trees. 'It's as though someone is trying to talk to me. But they're a long way away, so all I get is the image.'

'A long way away? Like Brisbane?'

She laughed, placed a warm hand on his arm. 'No, not in that way.'

She kept her hand on his arm. 'That's one of the tattoos, I take it?'

Harry glanced down, as though he'd forgotten it was there. 'Yeah. That's the Fajar Baru one. Will touching it give you anything?'

She shrugged, and drew away. 'Maybe. Probably. I don't know. Usually it's jewellery. Clothing. But I need to stay clear.'

'Won't touching the tattoo help?'

She shook her head. A cattle truck roared past in the overtaking lane. Harry glanced over and saw rolling eyes peering at him between wooden slats. The truck stank of shit and death.

'No. This is… this is something else.'

Harry was starting to think he really would end up driving all the way back to Brisbane when she spoke again.

'Look for a low brick wall out the front, and green grass,' she said.

Sandy stared out the side window. Again, Harry felt like this was going to be a waste of time. She'd seen the Eden Valley billboard from the highway, he imagined, absorbed it subconsciously and then regurgitated it as a vision. Except, he recalled, the sign didn't feature a low brick wall and green grass, it featured an advertising family. Mum, dad, boy, girl.

They rounded the corner, and Harry saw the low brick wall with the green grass. There were also a few weeds. The wall carried a sign: Cedar Falls. There was no cedar to be seen, no waterfalls either.

'Can you feel it?' she asked.

Harry nodded. Tension, in his shoulders.

They entered the labyrinth. Curving streets, houses that weren't identical but clearly siblings. Generated by a computer at a glitzy showroom somewhere. One-storey, two-storey. Single garage, double garage. Some took up their entire allotment of land, some left enough space for a small lawn out the front, cowering behind the faux stone letterbox. This was a housing estate in the prime of its life. All the blocks had been sold, built on and had the landscaping done. But none of the houses had got to the point where they'd started to look dated or seedy. A few had Christmas lights out the front, or a tree positioned so it was visible through the front window.

At every intersection, Sandy asked Harry to wait. Occasionally a four-wheel-drive would roar past, but mostly the only cars he could see were parked in driveways, some being washed. Left. Right. Right. Left. They reached the end of another cul-de-sac, turned around. Sandy asked Harry to pull over. She stared up at the house. A small girl – probably five or six – stared back at her from the garden, then ran into the open garage.

The sun was high in the sky. The car was hot. Harry's back was sweating and the tattoo there started to ache again. He was irritable.

'No, not here,' she said.

Harry pulled out. Repressed the urge to sigh. Up and down streets. They were starting to retrace their steps now, or at least that's how it felt. Here or there a curtain flicked. The men washing cars stared at Harry's battered Corolla, rather than ignoring it as they had the first time past.

'Here,' Sandy said.

Harry pulled over to the curb. The house was one of the low-set variety.

'Didn't we just go past this place?' Harry said.

Sandy ignored him. Harry peered out at the letterbox, the small lawn. This one looked like it had been put down fairly recently. The garage door was open, but empty. The front door ajar. Harry switched off the engine.

'Here, what?'

'Here.' She gestured with her hands, as though this would make it clearer. 'This is the place.'

'And what does it have to do with me?'

A curtain twitched. The hairs on the back of Harry's neck stood up. Sandy grabbed his hand, squeezed it. She was sweating. The warmth of her hand told him his was cold.

'I don't know, sweetie,' she said. 'But I don't sense danger. Not anymore.'

Harry's pulse throbbed in his ears. He wished he'd bought a bottle of water at the servo. His stomach felt light, insubstantial. The last time he could remember feeling quite like this was as he leant in for his first kiss, on Peregian Beach back in the '90s. An equal mix of fear and excitement.

He climbed out of the car. His legs felt weak, but it was good to stretch them. While he'd been sitting in the car he hadn't realised how badly they'd been shaking. He took a deep breath. Looked again at the house.

He walked behind the car and saw the screen door open. Someone stepped out from the shade into the sunlight. He saw everything at once. Her rumpled white blouse, hanging loose at the unbuttoned cuffs and around the neckline. The trendy jeans, custom frayed before they reached the store. Big Jackie O sunglasses, masking the apprehension that still showed around her mouth and in her stiff-legged gait.

But most of all, he noticed the tattoos. And that was funny, because she'd gone some way to hide them. But since Dave's buck's night he saw them everywhere. Young women, old men, Sailor Jerry rip-offs on kids' arms. This woman had a tattoo on the inside of her forearm, poking out from under the shirt sleeve. Another only visible between the bottom of her singlet and the top of her jeans. Her long brown hair was tied up in a bun, a pencil holding it in place, and he knew that if she turned he would see the grid there, in the same place as his.

Her shirt glowed in the sunlight. Harry squinted and held a hand over his eyes in a bad TV salute.

She stopped just behind the letterbox, resting one hand on it. Using it as a shield. Wedding band. Whopper of an engagement ring. Harry walked up to her, then realised he didn't know what to say.

'I… ah, I'm here… I'm here about Rob and Kyla,' he said.

'No,' she said, and started backing up the path.

Harry ducked around the letterbox, trying to catch up with her. 'Yes. I'm Harry. Harry Hendrick.'

She flinched at the words. Turned and wrenched the flyscreen door open. 'No! This isn't real. This isn't real.'

Her legs buckled. Harry pushed through the doorway and caught her. She wasn't heavy but he was having trouble keeping upright himself. Even in the house it seemed too bright. He could taste dust in the air. It was as if electricity was surging through the ground, into their bodies.

When he touched her he felt something big and heavy drop into place. Some dark machine somewhere cranked up a gear, and cogwheels churned away, opening a doorway to a terrible place. He didn't care. He could feel her body against his, this woman he knew nothing about. She carried secrets. And maybe together they could work this thing out.

The woman regained her footing. 'No!' she said, slapping his chest. 'No! No! No!' Turning her open hand into a fist.

He pulled her closer, protecting her. Thinking of Rob and Kyla. He didn't have the full story, but he knew it didn't end well.

You used a shottie. Half his fucking chest is gone.

CHAPTER 21

She didn't want to believe him, but when she saw the tattoos she had no choice. They only shared one. The grid at the back of the neck. And it was the one she didn't seem ready to tell Harry about.

She showed him the two swallows on her midriff, off to the left-hand side. When they compared the tattoos, it was clear the birds were the same. One tattoo was based on the other. But she didn't dream of the night at the Shelter Bar, under the Story Bridge. Instead, she dreamt of a little yellow worker's cottage with an overgrown garden. A small verandah at the front. Fireworks. All the lights were off, and Kyla and Rob held each other, watching the explosions of colour, smoking pot and drinking bourbon.

'That was the moment that she knew they'd be together forever,' she said. In the light coming through the kitchen window, Harry could see goosebumps on her bare arms.

When she was calm, she sat at the kitchen table, shaking her head, while Sandy made tea in the kitchen.

'Sorry,' she said. 'I'm Jess. Jessica McGrath.' She offered Harry her hand. It seemed too formal but he took it. Her fingers were cold.

When the tea was made, the psychic brought it to the

table, taking her own cup to the patio setting outside.

'I don't mind if you sit with us,' Jess said. But Sandy waved it away.

'I don't need to hear your stories,' she said. 'I can feel them.'

On Jess's left arm, a demented Raggedy Anne doll, one eye pulled from its head.

'She was abused, when she was 14, by her swim coach,' Jess said. 'She never confided in anyone, she never felt safe with anyone, until she met Rob. When Kyla told him about what happened, he went round to the swim coach's house and beat the shit out of him. Even though it all happened years earlier.

'Rob was in the army, wasn't he?' she asked.

Harry nodded. 'SAS, I think. Special forces, anyway.'

He told her about the drowning man, showed her the tattoo. Jess reached out towards the tattoo, then hesitated as though she were scared the man might spring from Harry's flesh and drag her under. Her fingers felt cool on his skin.

Harry pulled his shirt off to show her the poppies. Outside, Sandy left her tea on the table and took herself on a tour of the garden. Wind rattled the windows.

'Holy crap!' Jess said.

He hoped she would touch his skin again, but she didn't. Maybe she was scared of the tattoo, or scared of what might happen if she touched him again.

Harry felt the heat rising in his cheeks. 'Rob saw something horrible. He saw Australian soldiers – or maybe contractors, working for an Australian – massacre a group of Afghans. At least one of the women was raped. And then...'

He pulled his shirt back on. Shrugged.

'I don't know what happened then. The memory… the memory I have is that there was no way he was going to let them get away with it. He felt like shit, watching it unfold through the scope on his rifle.'

'I think he came home, tried to get some sort of justice on his own terms,' she said. 'I think that's what this one is about.'

She turned, so that he could see the tattoo on her right arm. A sexy, zombie librarian. Leg up on a stepladder, revealing stocking top and suspender. Hair pinned back with bloody throwing knives. She was holding a manila folder, the pages tumbling to the ground.

'She helped Rob. When he hit the roadblocks, she went in and helped him out,' Jess said.

'Helped him out?'

'Mata Hari-style. I didn't… I can't remember it all. I remember her staring at the ceiling while this hairy-backed brute fucked her. I can remember Kyla leaving, slipping some documents into her bag while he was still asleep in the bedroom. His uniform was strewn across the floor.'

'Uniform?'

'Army uniform.'

Harry considered this new piece of information. 'Wow. Just… wow.'

'Yep.' Jess drank some tea. 'I guess… I don't know… she was sexualised young. Abused. Maybe she decided she wanted to use sex to help Rob.'

Harry thought about it, stared out at Sandy, who was leaning over a flower bed at the bottom of the garden, smelling a white rose. He sipped his tea, listened to the gum trees rustling in the wind. Harry looked up at Jess. She stared at him with dark eyes. She pushed the hair back off her face, tucked a curl behind one ear. He'd only just met her, but it was a gesture he was sure he'd see a lot of.

'You're married?' he said.

She held up the finger, flashed the ring. 'Yes. Just.'

Harry imagined what it must have been like for her. It was bad enough having to deal with it by himself. But if he'd still been with Bec, well, he wasn't sure the relationship would have withstood the stress. *Well, duh.*

She nodded, reading his mind. 'Yeah, Darren thinks I'm crazy.

'The neck tattoo... What did you say it was?'

'It's from Afghanistan,' Harry said. He considered elaborating, passing on the information Bill had given him. But he didn't want to freak her out. Not yet.

'Right. That one appeared while he was at a conference. So I had the shock of it to deal with, and then I had to try and explain it to him. I'd had a couple of wines, but it wasn't blackout material.

'And he didn't believe me, when I told him it had just appeared. Well, why would he... Would you?'

Harry shook his head.

'I think he thought, you know, early mid-life crisis. Night out with the girls. Bad Boys Afloat. Too many margaritas. Tattoo.

'And the funny thing was, he seemed to accept that. If I had told him that's what had happened, he would have thought it was funny. A great story to tell. He's no prude. He's got a couple of tatts himself. And now...'

She got up, took her cup to the kitchen. Filled herself a glass of water from the tap. Stared out into the garden. Harry could see she was struggling to keep it together.

'Now... I don't know. I think he thinks I'm someone

else. Maybe I am. Do you know what I mean?'

Harry did. He wanted to get up and comfort her. He wanted to do a hell of a lot more than comfort her. But that wasn't him. That was Rob. And he didn't want to do it to – with – her. Not that there was anything wrong with Jess. But this was Rob, reaching out to Kyla. He nodded, but she was still staring out the window.

'Jess, I know exactly what you're talking about. They're growing. They're real people. Or the spirits of real people. Inside us. And as the tattoos appear, their influence on us is growing.'

She returned to the table, wiping her eyes. Forced a smile.

'The neck tattoo,' Harry said. 'I know you don't want to talk about the memory that it had attached to it but... I can remember a dark room, a man's face. I think it's the guy who did the tattoo, the guy Rob pulled from the sea.

'It all seems to be linked to him, to what he did. I thought if we could...'

'Ahmed,' she said.

Harry gasped. As soon as she said the name, it locked into place. He wanted to speak but Jess had her eyes squeezed shut, hands out as though feeling for something in the dark.

'He had a wife... and a boy... I can see him in a high chair. Afsoon. The wife's name was Afsoon.'

She opened her eyes. 'I thought it was just some random dream. A kitchen.'

'If we can find them, maybe...'

Jess nodded. 'Yeah. Maybe...'

Harry checked his watch. 'Is Darren going to freak if he finds Sandy and me here?'

She tilted her head to one side, screwed her face up. 'It's not going to help.'

'I'll get Sandy. I don't want to cause you any more problems, but we do need to talk about this some more.'

He finished his tea, got up, and opened the door to the patio. Sandy turned, smiling. But there was a haunted look in her eyes.

'Ready?' she said.

'Not really, but…'

'Yeah.'

Harry and Jess swapped phone numbers. She asked him to text rather than call.

'You know, because of…' She gestured in the direction of the garage, where the car was missing.

She walked them out. At the bottom of the driveway Harry turned, looked into the vacant garage. This time he noticed the empty packing crates stacked there.

'How long have you been here?' he asked.

'Oh, not long. A month or so.'

'Who lived here before you?'

Jess shrugged. 'No-one. This was the last block on the estate. They dropped the price to get rid of it. Put the house on it. We moved in.'

Harry scratched his head. Sandy climbed into the car, leaving him alone with Jess. He was never good at goodbyes, even at the best of times.

'Thanks,' he said. He held out his hand.

She sidestepped the outstretched hand, and wrapped her arms around his waist. She planted a kiss on his jaw. He breathed in the scent of her hair. He could feel her heart beating against his chest. Goosebumps rose on his arms. Since splitting up with Bec, this was the loneliest he'd ever felt.

'You know who did it, don't you?' Jess said.

Harry thought of the silver-haired man, striding into the compound in Afghanistan.

'Yeah, I do. You?'

She nodded, squeezed him tighter, then let go. 'We're going to have to be careful,' she said.

Jess turned and walked up the path. She sniffed back tears. 'Talk soon.'

Harry watched her go, then climbed into the car. Sandy reached around to get her seatbelt. He saw her hands were shaking so badly it took her three attempts to click it in place.

Harry looked at her, but she wouldn't return his gaze. 'Drive.'

He drove. Back through the labyrinth of landscaped suburbia, past kids playing street cricket. As they left Cedar Falls, with the comforting roar of the highway growing louder by the second, Sandy took a deep breath, cleared her throat and finally spoke.

'Something really bad happened there. She's buried there.'

Harry felt the hairs on the back of his neck stand up. 'Kyla?'

'If that's her name. Long dark hair. Feisty. Tattoos.'

'That's Kyla.' Harry looked out the window. 'Holy shit!'

'What?' Sandy said, following his eyes as though he'd seen something out the window.

Harry's mind reeled. The ant walking in slow circles.

Well, we are concreting his driveway.

Floorboards.

Scratching.

Dead batteries.

'I've been such an idiot. I know where Rob's buried.'

Sandy was quiet. He looked across at her. Saw the tear rolling down her cheek. She hitched a breath, trying to hold it in.

'Sandy? Are you okay?'

'Of course I'm not! Jesus. This is why I don't do this shit anymore!'

CHAPTER 22

Harry sat underneath the house, peering through the darkness, shivering. He'd never felt so cold. He supposed at least some of it was shock. But it was far colder than it should have been in summer. He was cold but he couldn't do anything but sit there shivering.

'They can't hurt you anymore, Rob,' he whispered.

Harry rubbed his arms.

Do you want to cut, or dig?

He should have called the police. Before he dropped Sandy back home. He should have called the police and told them there was a body under his house, then given them Jess's address and told them there was a body there, too.

And then what? Get out, like Dave thought he should? Let the police take over?

'Yeah, why not?' Harry spoke out loud.

The same reason he wouldn't leave the house. The same reason Jess wouldn't either, even once he told her that Kyla was buried there. The tattoo was his. Rightly or wrongly, it was his. He had to be the one who delivered the justice. Or he'd end up like the guy in Afghanistan. Insane, trying to burn the tattoos off his body.

He slumped back onto the concrete, staring at the dark

floorboards above his head. Cold bit into his shoulders and back. He ignored it. He thought of Rob, lying in icy lay-ups, waiting for his perfect shot. He thought about Andrew Cardinal, poised to romp to victory in the election. He thought about what he knew, and what he could prove. The difference between the two was a chasm, possibly wider than that between life and death.

Do you want to cut, or dig?

You used a shottie. Half his fucking chest is gone.

Jeez. Lotta ink.

Harry's world spun. He rolled on his side just in time, as his lunch and the Mars Bar he'd bought on the way back from Sandy's shot out of his mouth, onto the concrete. He lay there for a moment, panting, his chest throbbing. Then climbed shakily to his feet, wiped one hand across his face.

He stared at the cracked concrete slab. He saw the cement mixer backing up, saw the bikies doing a bit of concreting. Crow, beergut poking out from underneath his shirt. Heathy, with his blond hair and tear tattoo. Cardinal's dad, who went and got himself some tatts and strung himself up under the house. Harry shook his head.

'It won't be long, Rob,' he said. 'I promise.'

Harry climbed the back steps. He let himself inside and went straight to the bathroom, where he turned the shower on as hot as he could stand it. He stood there until the water ran cold. Got out, dried himself and climbed into bed.

CHAPTER 23

Monday morning traffic droned past as Harry sat at his computer, in a daze, staring at the screen. Saturday felt like a dream. Sunday he'd awoken fresh, after the best night's sleep he'd had since the first tattoo appeared. He'd somehow slept through a massive thunderstorm. Sitting up in bed, he'd checked his phone. Jess's number was there. He wanted to text her but resisted the urge, instead calling Sandy to make sure she was okay. He'd decided not to go for a run, opting for a leisurely walk. On his way back home, he noticed the graffiti on the water tower had been painted over.

'Harry!'

Harry turned towards Miles's office, glancing over at Christine. She hadn't looked at him all day. On Sunday he'd tried phoning her, but she hadn't answered. He felt a stab of unease. Had she told Miles about what had happened? He was genuinely ashamed about how he'd behaved and, although he probably deserved a sexual harassment lecture, he didn't feel like he could deal with one right now.

Harry got up and walked into Miles's office. Miles shut the door, and that was the first sign that something was up. Harry could only recall four occasions in all the years he'd been at the *Chronicle* that Miles had bothered. One was when the general manager had visited, one was when Miles's wife had called him at work to tell him about the results of her scan (at one point it looked like she had lung cancer, but the tumour turned out to be benign) and the other two were when he'd had to let staff go.

'Harry. Take a seat.'

Miles sat down and started rearranging the pens on his desk. He glanced up at his computer screen as though hoping to find answers there, then back at Harry.

'Harry, what's going on?'

'I... What has Christine told you?'

'Christine? She's being ridiculously loyal. But I heard about what happened on Friday night.'

'I can explain.'

'You'd better, because I've had the *Brisbane Mail* editor on the phone this morning, demanding an apology.'

Brisbane Mail? *Shit.*

'I lost my cool. You know Redwood and I go back. We've had run-ins. I thought Christine really deserved that award... I'm sorry. I'll call Redwood myself and apologise.'

Miles nodded. Harry started to rise out of his seat.

'It's more than that, Harry,' he said.

Miles arranged the pens on his blotter, then moved them to the other side.

'I'm concerned that you've...' he frowned, but wouldn't look Harry in the eye, 'lost your focus.'

Harry nodded, brain reeling. Trying to find a defence. He needed more time to think, so he let Miles carry on.

'I know that things have been tough for you. I heard you've got tattoos?' And now he did glance up at Harry, then back down at the page.

Harry nodded. 'Yeah.' He didn't elaborate.

Miles cleared his throat. 'I wanted to remind you that I'm here for you. How long have we known each other? I know that we don't socialise, but I just wanted to tell you that you're a vital part of the team here. It wouldn't be the same without you.'

Harry blinked. It was like he was hearing his eulogy. The hairs on the back of his neck stood up. He remembered the sound of a spade thunking against stony ground as the man he now remembered as being called Crow dug his grave. The heavy sensation of dirt pressing down on him. What had Kyla gone through? The same? Worse, judging by Jess's response.

'And I wanted to remind you that we can get you counselling, if you need it,' he said, then cleared his throat again.

Shit! Harry thought, remembering the follow-up appointment he'd missed.

'Thanks. Thanks, Miles. And I'm sorry. I know Christine has been doing more than her share. I figured that it would be good for her, you know, bearing more of the load. Toughen her up.'

He realised how stupid it sounded the moment he said it. 'And I know it seems like I've been doing nothing, but I am actually working on a story.'

'Oh? Really?' He sounded as though he didn't believe it.

'Yeah. But I can't really go into it at the moment.'

Miles nodded, grabbing onto anything that could be interpreted as a positive in this grim situation.

'And the counselling?'

'I'm seeing someone.'

Miles nodded frantically, still moving the pens backwards and forwards on his blotter.

'Great! That's great! Sometimes the best thing you can do is talk to someone, right?'

Harry nodded. Miles stood. The meeting was over.

'Thanks for your support, Miles. And I really am trying.'

'I know you are, mate. I know you are.'

Miles watched Harry as he got up and left the office. Christine made a point of not looking at him. He sat down and swung his chair towards her until she looked at him.

'Christine,' he said. 'I'm really sorry.'

She nodded stiffly.

'I feel like a total goose,' he said. 'I shudder when I think about Friday night. I know there's nothing I can do. I just wanted you to know that I'm basically a good guy. I'm just going through a rough patch.'

'Thanks, Harry.' A tiny smile touched her lips, before she turned back to the computer.

CHAPTER 24

Black Hawk 230 lifted off the deck of the HMAS *Kanimbla*, engines roaring above the soldiers' heads as they hunkered down in the helicopter's load bay. In seconds they were half a kilometre over the deep blue ocean. Somewhere out there was Fiji, where Commander Bainimarama was threatening to declare martial law. In case things got out of hand, 1 Squadron was moved in off the coast to facilitate the evacuation of Australian citizens. Rob checked the strap holding him to the deck, looked around at the other guys in the packed load bay.

Rob shook his head. It didn't feel right, without Laney and Birmo. Since returning from Afghanistan, much of his time had been spent trying to find out what happened over there. Every avenue he tried, he found brick walls. Until eventually his CO made it clear it would be in his best interests to let it go. But he still woke up at night, sweating, seeing the woman lying spread-eagled on that cold floor. Except in his nightmares she was still alive, begging him to help her. To avenge her.

He still had her hijab. Kyla thought it was ghoulish, wanted him to throw it out. But he couldn't part with it, couldn't let it go.

And now Laney and Birmo were gone. An IED, as usual. Tore the Bushmaster apart. He was beginning to think they were cursed. That the mission had been cursed. He thought about the crazy guy, the one they'd saved after the Fajar Baru went down all those years ago. Ahmed. Covered head to foot in tattoos. Screaming about blessings and curses. Magic. He sure could use some of that right now.

The Black Hawk banked, the view from his doorway filled with the seemingly endless Pacific Ocean. He longed to be down there, swimming free. Then the *Kanimbla* swung into view, looking like a kid's bathtub toy.

'Okay, here we go,' he said.

They wouldn't actually be fast-roping on this run. This was for the pilot and payload master to work on their signals. All the same, Rob felt his heart rate jack.

The plan was for Midsy to bring the Black Hawk around, flare the nose to bring the speed down, then level off over the *Kanimbla*'s deck. Below them, the *Kanimbla* rushed past, and for the first time Rob got a sense of the speed at which they were travelling. Sailors on the deck below looked up, holding their hands over their eyes to block the sun.

As the Black Hawk swung over the deck, a heavy *thunk* sounded over their heads and the engine screamed. Smoke filled the cabin, then was swept away. It all happened in a matter of seconds, and yet Rob saw and felt every detail. The pitch of the engines rose until a metallic crunch silenced them. Over his headphones, someone let out a string of expletives.

The helicopter spun, the centrifugal force trying to tear Rob and the other soldiers out of the Black Hawk, the quick-release straps holding them tight. The deck loomed large, in high definition, a large X marking the centre of the landing pad.

Well, at least he's on target.

Smash.

Darkness.

Silence.

Rob tried to draw breath, got sea water instead. Tried to cough it away and then realised where he was. Bubbles drifted around him, out of the Black Hawk's submerged cabin. It turned on its side and the *Kanimbla*'s hull presented itself, wrapped in a corona of sunlight. Dark forms writhed in the glow, kicked for the surface.

He grabbed the release on his harness and pulled himself free, pushed himself out of the Black Hawk's open doorway. He saw Tim's outstretched hand and grabbed it. It was limp. Blood bloomed from a gaping wound at the back of Tim's head. Rob tried for his harness but it was stuck. The button depressed but the straps wouldn't let go.

He jammed his boots against the edge of the doorway and pulled with all his strength. Something in his back gave way and new pain blossomed through the darkness. Black spots bloomed at the edges of his vision. His lungs screamed.

Rob let go. Kicked away. The Black Hawk dropped into the darkness. He pulled the cord on his life jacket. The cylinder hissed but the jacket remained flaccid. He kicked for the surface. Every part of his body throbbed, especially his back. He thought of Kyla, back in Perth, waiting for him, and kicked one last time. His strength gave out. The life jacket finally filled with CO_2, and dragged him the rest of the way to the surface.

* * *

Harry surged out of sleep, fell off the bed. He writhed on the floor in the half-dark, clutching his back, then curled up in a ball, panting, listening to the crows cawing from the trees. His lungs were fine. His back – that was a different issue.

He pulled himself to his feet, trying to ignore the pins and needles coursing through his fingers and toes.

I'm okay. I'm okay. I'm okay.

If he kept telling himself that, it might become true. He limped around his bedroom, hands to his head, trying to get a grip.

Eventually, he'd calmed down enough to recognise the pain of the new tattoo. Above his right hip, on his back. He gingerly pressed a hand against it, and it came away bloody. Not as bad as the poppies, but little lines of blood, printed against his hand. He took himself to the bathroom, found a damp washer, and dabbed it against the tattoo.

He twisted, sending a new spasm of pain across his back, and caught a glimpse of it in the mirror. A hand, crushing something. A bird? Insect? Underneath, some writing.

He returned to his bedroom, picked up his iPhone and snapped a photo, as close as he could get without the picture blurring. No, not a bird. A Black Hawk. He shuddered, remembering the moment when the engines screamed. The tattoo was really well done. You could see the tendons on the arm, jutting out as the hand squeezed the life out of the Black Hawk. The rotors resembled insect wings. Light shining off the canopy gave it the look of eyes, seeing their last.

The writing underneath held names. He recognised one of them. Tim Daniels. The other name was Justin Middleton. It rang a bell.

He fired up his laptop and googled. The top result was a news article, titled: 'Chopper pilot blamed for fatal Fiji crash.'

He scanned the story. Two men had died in the crash – Tim Daniels and the pilot, Justin Middleton. Midsy. Six others were injured.

A report found no mechanical fault with the Black Hawk, which had to be recovered from two-and-a-half thousand metres. There were, however, faults in the life jackets, which had trouble inflating at depths of five metres or more. Harry closed his eyes, saw deep blue. The sun a pale disc a long way above him.

The news report quoted SAS soldiers who had been interviewed as part of the inquiry, telling of how they heard the engines screaming just before the accident.

Later on in the article, an SAS trooper, speaking off the record, said he could not believe that Middleton was responsible for the accident, describing him as the 'Valentino Rossi of Black Hawk pilots'.

On a whim, Harry googled 'Fiji Black Hawk conspiracy'. It threw up the same bunch of news articles and then, further down, a post on an unofficial Australian Defence Force forum. The title of the thread: 'Silenced for speaking out', by SASmate.

'I gave evidence to the inquiry, they ignored me. I spoke to the press, and was discharged when someone dobbed me in. To make matters worse, the press misquoted me. I didn't just say I couldn't believe Midsy was responsible. I said he *wasn't* responsible.'

The post was followed by a random selection of comments. Some of them backing SASmate, others accusing him of being a conspiracy theorist. SASmate dived into the thread a couple of times to defend himself, but was very coy about what exactly he knew. Harry noted his username, and then moved on.

He stared through the screen. Names. He closed his eyes, trying to capture the memory before it escaped. Birmo and Laney. Rob thought they were cursed.

Harry considered.

Googled 'Birmingham Lane IED 2008'.

Another news hit: 'Defence names Afghan dead'.

Geoff Lane and John Birmingham were killed in Helmand province when the Bushmaster they were riding in drove over an improvised explosive device. Two other men were injured.

He scanned down. A defence analyst said although major roads were frequently cleared, it was impossible to make them 100 per cent safe. He said Taliban insurgents often chose parts of the road that International Security Assistance Force troops had no choice but to drive over.

The tattoos throbbed. He knew that Tim was with Rob when they witnessed the massacre. And now, reading the names on the screen, he remembered the other two as well.

Get onto the others. Tell them what's going down.

They were on the other side of the valley when the massacre happened.

Harry sat there, fidgeting. *I need a run.* Outside, the kookaburras were calling. The sun was up but hadn't reached his place. He checked his watch. Plenty of time.

He pulled on an old pair of shorts and a singlet, and headed out. He stretched, ignoring the weight of the humid air on his skin. He'd be much hotter soon. He avoided the steep incline of his street, instead heading down a side road. He wound his way through the dark streets, concentrating on the refreshing burn of air in and out of his lungs.

On one level he was thinking about the tattoos, and Jess, and Christine, and Cardinal. On another level he was watching his surroundings, noticing the little details. A man in green overalls munching on a piece of toast by the window. A mangy old cat, yellow-eyed in the shadows. A possum, inching its way along a powerline. A young guy buzzing past on a black scooter.

Time to crank this up a notch.

Harry put on some speed, pumping his arms, relishing the pain. He took a right, heading up the hill, in the shadow of the water tower. His muscles screamed at him to stop, his back throbbed, but he kept up the pace, leaning into the steep incline, still maintaining total awareness of his surroundings. Was this what it was like in Afghanistan? Always watching, always waiting?

Harry lost himself in the streets, taking turns at random, up and down hills. Past renovated Queenslanders built in underneath and old ones with mossy gates and rusting roofs. Into the sunlight as he rose to the tops of hills, and then down into the shadows again as jacarandas threw their lush green arms over the narrow streets.

Still Harry pushed himself, tasting blood at the back of his throat. At the top of the hill he turned left, then around into the grassy park, under the boughs of the old fig tree. He stopped at the benches, gasping lungfuls of air, walking around in a circle so he could look out at the city. The run had cleared his mind. In those last few minutes all his concentration was taken up with just blocking out the pain, refusing to give in to the body's frantic demands to stop.

Walking, hands on hips, still sucking in great mouthfuls of air, he looked out to the north. Towards Jess. He wanted to call her. It was just as well he'd left his phone at home. Not a good look, calling her up after only meeting her once, panting down the line like a pervert.

He turned away, walked up the hill, into the narrow alley that led to the water tower. The sun warmed his skin as the sweat dried on his body. It was going to be a hot one today. Around him, morning sounds filled the air. Showers. A coffee machine. Cutlery tinkling on crockery. As he passed the abandoned house he heard a splash as someone dived into their pool for an early morning swim.

Harry rounded the corner. He'd pretty much caught his breath now, and the only pain he felt was a steady throbbing in his lower spine.

The water tower looked like a new place. The old temporary fence was gone. In its place was a twelve-foot monster, topped with razor wire and... Harry blinked. He couldn't quite believe it. Inside the ring of razor wire were three strands of plain wire, guided by insulators. Sure enough, on the fence was a sign, featuring a man getting zapped by a lightning bolt. WARNING! ELECTRIFIED FENCE – for those who didn't get the pictogram.

The scent of cut grass hung in the air. Harry walked closer. The gate in the fence was secured by a deadbolt. From one of the water tower's legs, the glass eye of a security camera stared down. All mention of Swenson Constructions was gone.

As far as Andrew Cardinal was concerned, it was game over.

Harry stared through the links. On the other side of the tower, he could see Croydon Street. Now that the sun had crept higher, he could even see his car.

And someone walking away from his front door. Dark

suit. Sunglasses. He craned his neck to see who it was, but they disappeared down Ozanne Street.

When he got back home he found a small beige envelope, sitting just inside the door. He turned it over. There was no writing, but the envelope bore the familiar SC logo of Swenson Constructions. Harry ripped it open and peered inside. A memory stick. No note.

Harry slotted it into his Mac, stripping out of his running clothes while he waited for it to boot. He double-clicked on the drive. His breath caught in his throat.

A folder, with a bunch of spreadsheets inside it. 'SC accounts – 2005–current'.

'Bingo,' Harry said.

CHAPTER 25

Harry got into work early, set his cup of coffee beside his keyboard and logged in. His morning run was becoming pleasurable, an antidote to the nightmares. He sipped his drink, thinking about Nick Swenson, wondering if he could be trusted. His motives seemed genuine, even if Harry's were slightly concealed. Nick was right – land developers were an easy target. They were never popular when they moved into inner-city areas and started throwing their weight around. The people who lived in those areas had carved out a niche, in many cases mortgaging themselves up to the hilt to do so, and they didn't appreciate someone coming in and downgrading their investment.

Harry slotted the memory stick in. He opened the files and copied them onto his hard drive, emailed them to his private account, and uploaded them onto his storage space in the cloud. He didn't want this evidence to go missing, as had happened at uni. Harry scrolled through pages and pages of spreadsheets, not really looking for anything in particular, just trying to get a sense of the task ahead of him. It was monumental. It was beyond him, to be honest. He wished he'd taken his mum's advice and done a business major at uni, instead of double journalism.

He looked back over the notes he'd jotted down while going through his Cherry Grove folder. Searched for the names of the front companies he'd located: Bright Wing Holdings, Orange Water Pty Ltd, Circle Diagnostics Inc. Nothing. That made sense. Harry had had to apologise for the story and retract it, but it was still published. Other journalists would have checked out the accusations and Swenson would've known he had to shut down those front companies, just in case. Harry searched again, this time breaking down the front companies into their component parts: Bright; Wing; Orange; Water; Circle; Diagnostics. Plenty of hits on those words, but there was no pattern he could see. Harry shook his head.

The one thing that was blatantly obvious, even without a business degree, was the company's rapid decline in 2008. The company dropped into the red that year, and its condition worsened each year since. Harry didn't know how much they were hoping to make off The Towers, but it would need to be a lot to turn the company's fortunes around.

He spun in his chair, saw Christine come through the front door. She looked at her reflection and checked her hair. Harry watched her for a moment, then turned away.

The year 2008. Swenson Constructions heads south. Geoff Lane and John Birmingham killed in Afghanistan. Tim Daniels and Justin Middleton die in a Black Hawk crash off Fiji. Rob Johnson survives – just. Andrew Cardinal wins preselection for the Labor Party after leaving the military. Coincidence? Harry didn't believe in such a thing anymore.

Harry checked his bookmarks and found the conspiracy theory forum. He scrolled to SASmate's post, then clicked on his name and checked his general stats. He'd last posted on the forum a couple of weeks earlier, on a thread about the continuing troubles in Afghanistan. Harry couldn't send him a message without joining the forum, so he signed up. He thought about his username. He didn't want to use his real name. But he didn't want anything too flippant either. Tainted Scribe. He smiled to himself. He wrote a quick email to SASmate, telling him he was working on a follow-up on the Black Hawk crash – would he be interested in commenting?

He hit 'Send' just as Christine sat down next to him.

'Morning,' she said.

'Morning, Chris.'

She sipped her coffee. 'What're you working on?'

Harry paused, considering. She was right, he needed to open up to her more. He moved his chair closer to hers.

'I think Swenson has been up to his old tricks,' he said.

'Huh?'

'Or rather, he hasn't been up to his old tricks. And the lack of the tricks means the company's about to go down the gurgler.'

'What!'

'Yep. Now, I've just got to prove it,' Harry said. 'I don't have enough to go to print yet, so just keep it under your hat, okay?'

'Sure thing. And, Harry?'

'Yeah?'

'Be careful.'

'Don't you start.'

Harry got back to work. He opened a stack of text documents, one for each aspect of the story, and wrote down everything he knew, everything he could prove, and everything he suspected. He lost himself in his work. He could see a story, or maybe a couple of stories, coming together. It sounded wanky, so he never told anyone, but sometimes when he wrote he felt like a sculptor. He started with big chunks of marble and then gradually chipped away, following the lines in the stone, bringing the shape out and refining it.

Harry's phone rang. He picked it up.

'Harry?'

'Jess.'

'I've got something exciting to tell you,' she said. 'Well, it's not so much to tell you, as to show you.'

Harry could hear the emotion in her voice.

'Actually, so have I,' he said, thinking of the new tattoo. 'Do you want to come over after work?'

'Sure thing.'

He gave her his address, and they decided on a time.

'Great, Harry. I'll see you then.'

CHAPTER 26

Harry stood at the front window, watching as Jess climbed out of the car. She looked beautiful, dressed in her white blouse and black skirt. There was someone else in the car.

Jess walked around the car and opened the passenger door. Harry caught a flash of white, but Jess was blocking the view. Then Jess stepped back and he saw the woman. Her face looked so dark, framed by the white hijab.

Harry moved to the front steps and watched, silent, as they walked through the front gate. Jess saw Harry's expression and smiled.

'You're not the only investigative journalist around here,' she said.

The other woman smiled, but Harry thought it was more through politeness. At the bottom of the steps she stopped and looked up at Harry.

'This is Afsoon,' Jess said. 'Ahmed's wife.'

Harry stood there, stunned. Then Afsoon crossed the distance between them and wrapped her arms around him. She released him, and they shook hands. He stood back, looked at her.

'Please, come in,' he said.

As she walked past him, into the house, he shook his head. Afsoon. Ahmed's wife. He pulled Jess to one side and spoke into her ear.

'How?' Harry said. 'How did you find her?'

'You know that dream I told you about? The one in the kitchen?'

Harry nodded.

'It must've been when they went to get the tattoo, after the run-in at the Shelter Bar. I had the dream again, and this time I saw a bill on the fridge. With their full name.'

He ushered them through to the kitchen, doing a quick clean-up on the way, mumbling apologies for the state of the house. He didn't really know what he was saying, just couldn't keep quiet. He put the kettle on, rummaging around in the cupboards for three cups.

'I can see Rob in you,' Afsoon said.

'You should see me with my shirt off.'

He realised how that must've sounded. Blushed. 'I mean, the tattoos.'

Afsoon laughed. They sat down together at the table. Outside, the light was fading from the sky. Afsoon's hijab glowed in the gloom.

'How is Ahmed? Is he working tonight?' Harry said. Then stopped, realising why Afsoon's husband wasn't with them.

'He was killed,' Afsoon said. 'Shot, like a dog.'

She folded her hands on the table in front of her, stared at them.

'I'm sorry for your loss.'

Afsoon and Jess sat at the table in silence, while Harry finished making the tea and brought it over.

'Rob was a great man,' Afsoon said. 'I can remember

when Ahmed phoned me from Christmas Island. This was many months after he left. I had thought he was dead.

'He told me the story. He told he about how Rob pulled him out of the clutches of that cold, angry sea.

'He told me how the soldiers could have stayed away. Should have stayed away. But they came anyway. And they saved as many as they could. Brave, brave men.'

Harry shivered, remembering the nightmare. Afsoon sipped her tea.

'When they got back to Christmas Island they were checking the survivors, deciding which needed to go to hospital and which straight to detention. Rob asked about the tattoos. And Ahmed told him.'

Harry nodded. He felt humbled. He gestured to the tattoo on his neck.

'What does this do, exactly?'

'It's an old symbol. Older than any of the tribes in Afghanistan. It will protect you from your enemies. The symbol itself is only part of it. My husband had... skills.

'That was part of the reason he had to flee our homeland.'

Afsoon pulled up her sleeve, revealing an arm covered in ink. Harry recognised one set of symbols – the same as on his and Jess's necks. The rest were in a similar style.

'These were no trouble for me,' she said. 'I was covered all of the time. From head to foot. You know, the full burqa.

'But the men, they were not so lucky.'

She circled a symbol with her finger, over and over again.

'This symbol, like all these symbols, has been handed down from generation to generation. Like any sigil, its strength derives not just from the lines but from the way they are applied. Only the Mullah Sensees – magical healers, magicians like my husband – know how to apply them properly.

'This symbol is a curse and a blessing. It seeks to protect the wearer. If this is not possible, it seeks vengeance on those responsible for harming the wearer.'

'What do you remember of that night? The night they came for Ahmed?' he asked.

Afsoon looked taken aback by the question.

'I know it's painful, but I think I can bring these men to justice, and I think I can do it without shedding blood.'

Afsoon nodded. A stiff up-and-down motion. 'I understand.'

'Can I talk to you on the record?'

Afsoon shrugged. 'I told the police everything. There were stories in the newspapers at the time, on TV. I don't understand…'

'Please,' Harry said. This time Afsoon nodded, and swallowed. Harry got his notebook and phone and returned to the table. He set his phone up to record.

'Can you talk me through that night?'

'It was dinner time,' Afsoon said, glancing down. 'Little Wasim was in his high chair, throwing food off his fork. Ahmed was driving taxis then, but he had the night off. It wasn't his choice. Work phoned him and told him the car was in getting fixed.

'So he was home, and I was dishing up dinner. It was nice, you know? Most nights, he worked. And then there was a knock at the front door. Ahmed had nothing to fear. We had nothing to fear. Occasionally some kids would throw stones on our roof, tell us to go home…'

She shrugged, as though this was nothing, given what they'd gone through to get to Australia.

'Even after Rob confided in him and he marked Rob and Kyla, he had no reason to fear anybody.

'And yet… I had that feeling. In that moment when he walked to the door, I knew.

'Does that make sense?'

She clutched a tissue in one hand, then dabbed her eyes with it. It did make sense. It made perfect sense. Even before all this, Harry had been in situations where something, some force, had tried to warn him of impending calamity. He thought, deep down, that he knew Bec was going to break up with him as he walked up to the apartment that day.

'I knew. And I pushed it away. I had a saucepan in my hands, you know? I was busy.'

She threw her hands up, pushed the air out of her mouth with a sharp hiss. 'How many times have I wished I could take that back? But you can't take those moments back, can you?'

Jess held Afsoon's hand.

'The screen door opened. There was a massive bang and I knew what it was. I knew from back home what a gun sounds like. A shotgun. And my first thought…'

You used a shottie.

She was crying openly now. Hands over her eyes as though she should be ashamed of it.

'My first thought was of little Wasim! I ran to him and he was crying but he was okay. Just scared. And then I turned…

'Ahmed was on the floor. The blast had thrown him across the lounge. There was blood on the floor. A lot of blood. I ran to the door. I don't know why but I ran to the door.

'I don't know what I thought I could do. Get myself killed too!'

'What did you see?' Harry said. He was prepared for her to say 'nothing'. But his premonition was wrong.

'I saw a man running away. There was a car out front. As he ran under the streetlight he turned. I flinched. I thought if he saw me there he'd come back.'

'What did he look like?' Harry said.

'Dirty jeans. Black t-shirt. I noticed the tattoos,' Afsoon said, holding up her arms. 'I always notice the tattoos. He had those European designs, interweaving bands…'

'Celtic bands?' Jess said.

'Yes! And a tear. Tattooed under one eye.'

Harry didn't make a big show of it, but he felt like punching the air. It was shaky, but it was coming together. He thought he could write a story about this.

Jess shook her head.

'You said that your son is living with you – Ahmed was murdered there. Why hasn't the tattoo manifested?'

'I don't know,' Afsoon said. 'I have seen this tattoo work. One time, back in Afghanistan, Ahmed was out tending the goats and he trod on a land mine. But it didn't explode until he was safely out of range.

'Another time – just before he escaped into Pakistan – the Taliban came to collect him. To take him away. They drove over one of their own bombs. All dead.

'But this,' she gestured to the tattoos on Harry's body, even though she couldn't see them. 'This is a mystery to me. Something is different.'

Harry thought about Rob's body, under the house. And about Kyla's, under Jess's. He held his tongue. He didn't want Jess finding out like this.

233

'Is there any way we can reverse the spell?' Jess asked.

Afsoon shook her head.

'No. This is old magic. Older than the American invaders. Older than the Taliban. Older than the Russians, and the British who came before them. Older than the Mongols. This magic is as old as the mountains themselves and, like the mountains, eternal.

'This will only end when justice has been done.'

'Justice?'

'Justice. If the people who did this are brought to justice, it will end.'

'As in, courts? Jail?' Harry said.

Afsoon shrugged. 'Harry, I could be wrong. But the magic is borne of blood. I would say this magic would require blood to satisfy it.'

CHAPTER 27

Afternoon rush-hour traffic clogged the Stones Corner roundabout. Irate commuters hunched in their cars, windows up, everyone cocooned in their own world of talk radio or music or podcasts – whatever it was that got them through.

Harry had spent the day in a daze. Partly from the lack of sleep. Partly from Afsoon's revelations. And partly just from being with Jess.

It was past midnight when she returned to Harry's after dropping Afsoon home. While she was out, Harry went over his notes and played back the interview. Ahmed had confided in his wife some of Rob's concerns leading up to his death. Magic was a big deal for them. Ahmed had not performed any since arriving in Australia. He said that was part of his old life. He was leaving it all behind. Afsoon had trouble enough getting him to speak Pashto around the house.

That all changed when Rob turned up on his doorstep, wanting to quiz him about the 'protection' tattoo Ahmed wore. After all these years, Rob had remembered the story Ahmed had told him in the aftermath of the Fajar Baru incident. A story about a special tattoo that would protect the wearer from harm or, failing that, wreak vengeance on the wearer's enemies.

Harry shook his head. *Shit – Rob must've been desperate.*

Ahmed tried to tell Rob that all that was in the past, but then Rob spilled his guts. Telling Ahmed about the drug deal, the massacre in Afghanistan, the rape. About how Andrew Cardinal had tried to cover his tracks. Bury the story so deep it would never see the light of day.

When Jess got back, he poured two big glasses of red wine and they sat out in the back garden, listening to the possums scratching about in the mango tree. Harry filled her in on all the latest on the Swenson story, and how it seemed to tie in with Cardinal. Harry copied the Swenson Construction documents for Jess. She was going to turn her eye for shonky deals onto it.

Harry felt as though he had a future with Jess. It was stupid. She was married. And he'd only been away from Bec a matter of weeks. Less than a month ago, they'd had their routine. Monday night watching the ABC. Late-night shopping on Thursday. Sleep-in on Saturday. Sunday morning at the New Farm markets. He thought he was so in love with her. And now…

Things just felt so easy with Jess. He'd never believed in soul mates. But now he wasn't so sure. Jess slept in his bed, while he took the couch. He wanted more. And he felt she wanted more. But Christine had shown his radar wasn't really working that well right now. Was this another rebound? Or was Rob asserting himself, projecting his feelings for Kyla?

Harry stood now on the pavement for a moment, staring at Stones Corner Tattoo. The building sagged with the weight of existence. The front windows were painted –

Stones Corner Tattoo, and then underneath, 'Brisbane's first, Brisbane's best' – so it was impossible to see inside. A thick coating of grime covered the glass.

Harry walked past the front door, scoping the place out. *Always have an escape plan.* The thought came from nowhere, but it made sense. He was scared. He didn't know why. He'd visited West End Tattoo a couple of times, but this place had a different vibe.

He kept walking and saw the Harleys parked out the back. Saddlebags proclaiming the Dreadnorts Motorcycle Club. Harry felt the adrenaline drop into his system. He clutched his notebook like a shield and crossed the road.

A bell rang when he pushed the door open. There was a low counter, panelled in fake wood, with a mock granite top. Behind that, a doorway that presumably led through to the studio out the back. Harry could hear a tattoo machine buzzing.

The walls were covered with designs: grinning skulls, naked babes, dragons and arcane scrollwork. A man pushed through the plastic strips. He was in his forties, arms covered in tattoos blotchy with age.

Harry felt self-conscious in his shirt and tie, but he imagined he'd feel self-conscious no matter what he was wearing. The man looked him up and down, seemed to decide Harry wasn't here for a tatt.

'Yeah?'

Harry cleared his throat. 'Hi, I'm a reporter with the *Chermside Chronicle*. I'm looking for a guy called Rabs. I understand he used to work here a while back.'

The guy stared at him for a couple of seconds before turning to the doorway.

'Hey, Pablo! Got a guy here lookin' for Rabs.'

The buzzing stopped.

'Oh yeah? Send him through.'

The guy at the counter held a hand out, gesturing towards the curtain. Harry walked around the counter, trying to see through the strips. He could see people back there, but not who or how many.

Harry had a vision of walking through there and seeing Cardinal's henchmen waiting for him: Heathy running his fingers through his bedraggled blond hair, and Crow with his thumbs hooked in his belt, arms framing his sizeable gut. *Ah, Harry, we've been waiting for you.* He pushed through, ready to run, conscious of the counter guy following him through. He remembered the fight at the Shelter Bar, wishing he had some of Rob's SAS training.

There were four chairs out the back, but only one of them was being used. Like West End Tattoo, the space here was a strange mix of hair salon, dentist's surgery and mechanic's shop. Like West End there were pieces of art all over the walls, only here there were also a couple of calendars with bare-breasted women leering out. At the back of the room there was another doorway. This one was closed. There were no locks on it so presumably it led to another room, rather than outside.

The guy in the chair had his shirt off. With his big beard and hairy chest he reminded Harry of a bear. Most of his skin was covered in tattoos. The tattooist was younger than Harry expected. Scrawny-looking, with a goatee and crazy hair. Harry thought the man was going to stop his work while he talked, but he changed the needle in the machine and carried on.

'Rabs, hey?' the tattooist said. 'And what would a nice-looking guy like you want with Rabs?'

'I'm a reporter with the *Chermside Chronicle*,' Harry said.
'Sorry, Harry. Harry Hendrick.' Harry held out his hand.

The tattoo machine buzzed away. Ink mixed with blood.
Pablo wiped it away with a paper towel scrunched up into
a ball in his hand. He ignored Harry's hand. The guy in
the chair seemed not to have noticed Harry at all. Harry
dropped his hand.

'I'm working on a story about Brisbane tattooists. I hear
Rabs was a bit of a legend.'

'The *Chermside Chronicle*, hey? Stones Corner seems a
bit out of your patch.'

'Well, the scope is a bit bigger than Chermside.'

'Got a lot of tattoo fans up there?'

Now Pablo did look up. His eyes were pale blue, and
they seemed to stare right through Harry, right through the
lie. Harry looked away. The tattooist looked back down at
his work.

'It's just funny, you coming here and asking about Rabs,'
he said. He turned to the trolley and dipped the needle into
a small pot of ink, ran the machine, then turned it off again
with the foot pedal. 'Because I hear tell of some prick who's
been stealing old Rabsy's designs. You wouldn't happen to
know anything about that, would you?'

Harry had a split-second to consider his options. Telling
the truth wasn't one of them. Even trying to tell part of the
truth would lead down a rabbit warren from which no sane
person would think Harry was telling the truth.

Harry shook his head. 'No.'

'Interesting,' Pablo said.

Outside, a Harley burst into life. Harry jumped.

'As it happens, Harry Hendrick, I do know where Rabs
is. And I'm happy to give you the address.'

The light was failing by the time Harry was shown into his room. Mack at West End Tattoo had warned him that Rabs was not the sort of bloke who bore fucking with, but the Rabs Harry was looking at was barely a man at all.

His head lolled to one side, drool staining the pillow under his head. White hair stood up in tufts. Tattoos peeked out from under his grey pyjamas. His hands rested on top of the blue blanket, letters on his knuckles proclaiming STAY and TRUE.

Harry was so transfixed he didn't see the woman sitting beside his bed until she stood up. She was in her sixties. Dressed smartly. A weak smile touched her face when Harry entered the room.

'Hello. You must be Harry. Pablo told me you were coming.' A Scottish accent.

'Hi.'

Harry crept in. A nurse squeaked past outside. Somewhere further down the ward, someone broke into a hacking cough.

'I'm Liz. Rabs' wife.' She took his hand and led him to a chair by Rabs' bed.

'Please, sit. So what is this you're working on?'

Harry felt awful, but lied anyway. 'I'm doing some research on tattooing. Brisbane tattooists. I asked around. Rabs was a legend, or so I'm told.'

Liz smiled. 'Yes, he had his good days. Won a few competitions.'

Thunder boomed in the distance.

'I'm sorry,' Harry said. 'But Pablo didn't really explain. What happened?'

'It was a few years ago now... 2008. We were doing some early Christmas shopping. Rabs hated it. Hated the shops. But I always made him come at Christmas-time. Presents for the kids – even though they're all grown up these days.

'We were at Indooroopilly, you know, the big shopping centre there. We'd finished and Rabs was pushing the trolley out into the car park. It was really busy. Cars everywhere. If we'd parked somewhere else…'

She was finding it hard to hold it together.

'Someone was waiting a couple of storeys up, the police said. Our level sort of jutted out, so they were right above us. They put a besser brick in a shopping bag. Dropped it.'

She pressed a hand against her mouth. 'Police found cigarette butts up there. Another brick. Presumably in case the first one missed.

'It didn't miss. Doctors said he was lucky not to be killed. Some days, I'm not sure about that.'

She patted his hand.

'Did they catch who did it?'

She shook her head. 'No. Security footage wasn't much help. Because it was outside. The lighting wasn't very good. He was big. Big gut. Jeans, denim vest. Police said it was to do with some feud between rival bikie gangs.'

Harry nodded. He held up his notebook. 'Sorry, do you mind?'

She waved it away. Harry scribbled some notes.

'And what do you think?'

'This isn't just about tattooists, is it?'

Harry wanted to remove his shirt, or roll up his sleeves and show her the tattoos. He suppressed the urge. Yeah, she looked harmless. She looked like someone who had been well and truly fucked over. But it would be just as hard for her to accept the provenance of the tattoos as it would anyone other than Jess, and possibly Sandy. He shook his head.

'Are you interviewing me?' Liz asked.

'We can call this background. It means that I won't attribute anything to you. In fact, I won't publish any of this stuff unless I can get it confirmed by at least two other sources. And, of course, I won't name you when I'm seeking that confirmation,' he said.

She looked at him warily.

'To be honest, Liz. I don't know if I've got a story. There are just pieces of information at the moment. Possibly unrelated. But I've got a feeling there's something in it.'

She nodded, looked down at her hands, entwined in her lap.

'Okay,' she said. 'I don't think it was to do with any rivalry between the clubs. Rabs was never directly involved with the clubs. We hung out with a lot of bikies, and the shop was owned – is still owned – by the Dreadnorts.

'We would have known if there was something going on. If the boss had known that someone was out to get Rabs, he would have told him.'

She reached up and held Rabs' hand. It was almost pitch black outside now, a storm rolling in and blocking out the last vestiges of sunset. Wind rattled the window.

'The other thing is, why attack Rabs? He was good, sure. But you've seen what bikies do when they want to close down a tattoo parlour. They firebomb it. Or they bust in and trash it, give the tattooists a bit of a rough-up. Happens all the time.

'This was just Rabs.'

Other than the subtle rise and fall of his chest, Rabs hadn't moved. He couldn't move. Harry wondered if the tattooist was taking all this in, desperately trying to speak. If he could talk through his tattoos, what would he say?

'So, what do you think happened?'

'Rabs knew something. Someone didn't want it coming out.'

'Do you have any idea what it was about?'

Liz shrugged. 'Drugs, presumably. I warned Rabs about it. They used to cut drugs out in that back room at Stones Corner. Rabs said they always made sure it was after hours.

'That would explain why the cops didn't chase it. As far as they were concerned, anyone connected with the Dreadnorts, in any way, deserved what they got.

'I called the police every week after it happened. Every week. Got the run-around. Eventually they told me, point-blank: "Forget about it, love. It's over." Pricks.'

She squeezed Rabs' hand again. In her eyes was a glimmer of hope that one day he might squeeze back.

'Oh, and there was that guy, the one who went missing. Got Rabs to do a lot of tattoos on him. Rabs got home quite late one night, said that this guy had come in just as he was packing up. Rabs did the job anyway.

'A couple of days later, the guy disappeared, and then this happened.'

'Do you remember his name?'

She rolled her eyes to the ceiling, trying to remember.

'Yeah, it was that army guy. Rob someone.'

CHAPTER 28

Sweat dripped down the back of Rob's neck. Cars churned up the thick night air. He felt sick. He felt dirty. Kyla stood in front of him, holding his hands. In the light from the streetlamp she looked yellow, dead already.

'This is stupid,' she said.

'It's not.'

'That place is where they hang out,' she said.

He didn't need to look. He had seen Stones Corner Tattoo a thousand times. It looked the same tonight as it always did.

'Can you see any Harleys?'

'Jesus, Rob! He wants to kill us! Ahmed is dead. We're next.'

'Rabs is in there. Rabs is okay.'

'But he can't protect you from the Dreadnorts, okay?'

'It's not all of them. It's not like the whole club wants to hand me over.'

Kyla shook her head. Hair stuck to her sweaty face. Rob went to push it away but she swatted his hand.

'Don't,' she said.

'I have to do this.'

'Rob. Your mate at the paper has done the dirty on us.

You know what I had to do to get some of that information?'

Rob couldn't look her in the eye. She hadn't told him everything, and he didn't want to know.

'Ahmed is dead. With all his tattoos, he's *dead*. Having another one on your body won't make a difference. We have to get the fuck out of here.'

A semi-trailer hit the air brakes coming down to the roundabout. Rob jumped and reached for the gun tucked into the holster at the small of his back.

'And we will. But first I have to do this.'

She shook her head. 'I can't believe you believe that shit.'

'You let Ahmed tattoo you as well.'

'Well, why the fuck not? But it didn't save him from that shottie, you know?'

Rob squeezed Kyla's hands. 'It'll only take an hour or so. I'll get the names first. Leave it at that, if I have to.'

'Rob. Listen to me. Please. If we can get down to New South Wales we can fight from there. Cardinal hasn't won. He just thinks he has. But he's got this place locked up tight.'

'I know. But... I don't think we're going to make it. And I want an insurance policy.'

'Well, I'm not waiting here for you. I'm a sitting duck.'

He pulled her close. She smelt of sweat and dirt. She smelt wonderful.

'I love you,' he said.

Kyla pushed away from him. 'Just... just be safe, okay?'

It was what she'd always said before he went away. Not be careful, because she knew that in his line of work he couldn't be careful. In fact, in Afghanistan, being careful was a good way of getting killed. But be safe. Do everything you can to not get yourself killed.

She turned and walked back towards the bus station. Rob took one last look at her and headed for the tattoo parlour.

There was no-one on the front desk at this time of night. But he could hear someone shuffling around out the back.

'Rabs?'

'Is that who I think it is?'

When Rob first met Rabs, at Dooley's over in the Valley, he almost got into a fight with him because he couldn't understand his thick Glaswegian accent.

'Yeah. Rob.'

The giant Scotsman pushed through the beaded curtains. He reminded Rob of Billy Connolly, but twice the size, and of course covered in tattoos. A naked woman, anchors, names, dragons, cards, dice and skulls intertwined up his arms. Rob held out his hand, but Rabs engulfed him in a big, sweaty bear hug.

'You fuckin' mad bastard. You're not safe around here, you know.'

'Don't you start. I've just copped an earful from Kyla.'

He pushed Rob away and looked over his shoulder. 'Smart woman. Those fuckers have put a mark on your head.'

'Yeah, I know,' Rob said. 'We're going to make ourselves scarce. Just need to get one more tattoo.'

'I wouldn't be worried about tattoos, Robby. I'd be worried about getting the fuck outta Dodge.'

'Just one more. It's important.'

Rabs dragged him out the back. There was no-one else out there.

'I was just packing up, but I suppose I can squeeze one more in,' Rabs said. He pulled over one of the rolling trolleys, started getting inks set up. 'What are you after? A butterfly? A nice Celtic band, perhaps.'

'Hardy-fucking-har-har, you Scots cunt.'

Rob pulled his shirt over his head. Rabs' eyes flicked to the holster, but he didn't say anything. Rob knew Rabs had seen plenty of guns, and he knew to keep his mouth shut. Rob explained what he wanted, and wrote down the names. To his credit, Rabs just nodded and got his gear ready.

Rabs took a needle out of its sterile wrapping, slotted it into the machine. Fired it up with the foot pedal. The needle flashed in and out, point blurring. Rob climbed onto the chair, leant over. Rabs grabbed a razor and gave the area a quick once-over, then swabbed with alcohol.

'Time's short,' Rabs said. 'I think I might draw this one right on, if that's okay with you.'

'Sure – just no giant penises.'

'Aw, you're no fun.'

Rob recognised the pain but it didn't bother him anymore. After Ahmed's crazy bamboo-shoot technique, this was bliss. Ahmed. He zoned out for a while, trying not to think.

Rabs worked steadily on the tattoo. Then he asked, 'So when did they get him?'

'Tonight,' Rob replied. 'We tried phoning him. He didn't answer. Went over there and the wife was screaming over his body.'

'Shit. After all they went through.'

'Yep. I bet they thought, after the Fajar Baru, things couldn't get any worse.'

Rob drifted off, the buzz lulling him into a trance. As the ink went into his skin, he felt the memories moving down into a box in his brain. Like his dossier. A hole in the darkness. Cardinal would pay. Crow and Heathy would pay. One way or another.

'How'd they do it?'

Rob jerked, realised he'd been asleep. There hadn't been much chance to do much of that over the past couple of days. But he felt safe with Rabs.

'Shotgun.'

Rabs went back to work. Rob felt a dull ache in his lower back. If he had to sit here like this much longer, with his hip twisted towards Rabs, it would get really sore. He wished he had some of his painkillers, but he'd binned his stockpile at home after the incident at the bar. The damn things almost got him killed.

Outside, traffic droned past. And then something that was distinct from the sound of normal traffic. The big, heavy blast of a Harley. No, two.

'Steady,' Rabs said. 'Could be friendly.'

'Yeah. Right.'

Rabs switched off the machine.

'Over there. In the cupboard,' Rabs said.

Rob opened the cupboard. It was full of old tattoo magazines and books. He quickly lifted stacks of them and put them on the bench, then slipped himself inside. The cupboard smelt of mildew and old paper. He pulled the gun out of its holster, left the door open a crack.

The Harleys pulled up out the back. Engines cut off. From where he was hiding, he could see the doorway at the back of the studio. Heavy footsteps. He could imagine their heavy biker boots. The security gate at the back of the studio clanged open. They were inside.

Rabs' door opened and two men pushed through into the studio. Heathy and Crow. Rob cursed under his breath.

Heathy brandished an axe handle. Crow didn't appear to be armed, but he probably had a knife or something on him.

'Gentlemen,' Rabs said. Rob was amazed at how calm he sounded. 'I was just cleaning up.'

Rabs stepped to one side, towards the chair Rob had just been leaning on. Rob saw his shirt hanging over the back. *Fuck.*

'Rabs,' Crow said. 'We're looking for Rob. You seen him?'

'Not lately. He came in a few days ago for some work, but nah, not since then.'

Rabs stepped over to his trolley, blocking view of the shirt. The men moved further into the room, flanking Rabs. Rob rested on the balls of his feet, ready to spring out if they moved on the tattooist. There was no way he was going to let Rabs be added to the list.

'What do you want him for? Nothing good, by the looks,' Rabs nodded at the axe handle.

Heathy piped up. 'We just want to have a little chat.'

'Yeah, I've heard about your chats. You boys been busy tonight?'

'What the fuck's that supposed to mean?' Heathy stepped forward, getting in Rabs' face.

'Nothing,' Rabs said. He gently but firmly pushed Heathy back a step. 'Just looks like you've got a bit of tomato sauce on your t-shirt…'

As Heathy turned, Rob saw the bloodstain. While Heathy glanced down at the mess on his shirt, Rabs reached behind him and pulled Rob's shirt from view. He placed his other hand on the chair, then raised his fingers, palm out, towards the cupboard where Rob hid. *Wait.*

'You boys been running the Dreadnorts sausage sizzle?'

Heathy raised a tattooed hand and put it on the side of Rabs's head.

'You want to be careful asking questions, Rabs. Rob asked the wrong questions. So we're going to have a little chat with him. If you don't want us to have the same conversation with you, I suggest you shut your fucking mouth.'

Crow stepped closer. 'We love your work, Rabs. But you might find it hard to tattoo with broken fingers.'

Rabs, with nowhere else to go, sat back in the chair. He pushed the shirt onto the floor. 'Oh, I get it. You're the big men, right? Sorry, I didn't realise.'

Crow took a step backwards. 'Heathy, check out the front.'

Heathy went around the back of the chair, right past the cupboard. The stink of petrol, grease, sweat and blood trailed in his wake.

'Nuh. No-one out here.'

He returned to the room, stood with his back to the cupboard. Rob could put a round through his kneecap. From this range, it would take out his whole joint. He'd walk with a limp for the rest of his life. But Heathy was blocking Rabs and Crow. And Rob still didn't know what Crow was packing. He visualised it. Heathy going down, blood pulsing out of his leg. Rob trying to push out past Heathy's body and come up into a firing position. No, it was too risky.

'When he was here a couple of days ago, did he say anything about his plans?' Crow urged.

'I'm not his mum, Crow. I'm not his secretary. Why would he tell me his plans?'

'I don't fucking know. Maybe the silly bastard trusts you.'

Heathy snorted out a laugh. He shuffled to one side. Crow was on the other side of the room, looking around at the designs on the walls.

'If you happen to see Rob, or that slut of his, give us a yell, hey?'

Rabs said nothing.

'I know you've done a lot of work on Rob, but don't forget who pays the bills, okay?'

'Sure thing, Crow.'

Heathy followed Crow to the back door.

'This has been fun,' Rabs said. 'We should do this again some time.'

'Fucking cunt. Don't forget what I said.'

'Sure thing. Catch ya.'

They shuffled out the studio door, leaving both it and the back door open behind them. Rob could see through to the shadowy storage room. That was where they cut the drugs after they arrived from Afghanistan.

Moments later their Harleys fired up; Rob felt the reverberation beneath his feet. He trailed the sound up the side of the building, sat there listening while they disappeared into the traffic.

'Wait,' Rabs said.

He walked past the cupboard. Rob heard the beaded curtain clattering. A few moments later Rabs was back.

'All clear.'

Rob squeezed out of the cupboard, stretched his back, then moved to the corner of the room so he wouldn't be visible from either door. Rabs was flushed, and sweating. His chest heaved as though he'd just run a hundred metres.

'I mean it,' Rabs said, 'that was a lot of fun.' He tried to grin, but it withered on his face.

'I'm sorry,' Rob said.

Rabs waved it away. 'Don't be. They're murdering pricks.'

Rob turned to leave, then stopped. He pulled out his gun and offered it to Rabs.

'No. No, no, nope,' Rabs said, 'I don't do guns. Besides, you need it more than I do.'

'Take it.'

Rabs shook his head.

'Take it! Rabs, if they find out you've been helping me, they're gonna come back for you. I can't lose anyone else.'

Rabs folded his arms across his chest.

'Fine,' Rob said, 'I'll just leave it here.'

He clunked it down on the counter, and turned to leave.

'You always were a stubborn bastard!' Rabs called after him.

CHAPTER 29

Harry woke up with the now familiar throbbing. This time on his lower back. He rolled over and stared up at the ceiling, then pulled his iPhone from the charger. It was 5 a.m., and already stinking hot. He pulled the sweaty sheet off his body and set his feet on the floorboards.

He reached around and gingerly touched the new tattoo, then twisted so he could look at it. It was on his back, just above the hip, balancing out the crushed Black Hawk. He took a photo. Sat down on the bed and looked at it. An angel. Nothing cherubic about this one. He was big, pissed off, clutching a sword. Compared to the other tattoos, it was rough. You could tell it wasn't finished. Merely an outline. But Rob had made sure the names took priority.

More names, under the avenging angel's barely sketched feet. A name in Arabic script. It was at the top of the list so he assumed it was the woman in Afghanistan. Geoff. John. Ahmed – the Afghan Mullah Sensee.

A roll call of the fallen. Rob's personal list of people who must be avenged. Something he'd wanted to do himself, but instead it had fallen to Harry.

For once, Harry didn't need to try and unravel what the tattoo meant. He knew, because he'd been there with Rob when Rabs did it. For once, he could remember the whole dream. It was more like a memory.

Harry stripped off his pyjama pants and picked his sweaty running gear off the floor. His shorts and singlet stank, but that didn't matter. Soon he'd be on the road and adding more sweat, and he'd be far away, figuring out what the hell he was going to do next to end this thing.

Shoes on. Out the door. The air was cooler out here but he could feel something underneath, that intensity of summer. As soon as the sun hit, the day would begin heating up in earnest.

He set off down the road. He'd started to vary the run each day – part of Rob's training, he guessed. Vary your route in case someone was watching.

His feet slapped the bitumen, and soon he dropped into a rhythm, watching and yet immersed in his thoughts at the same time. He and Jess had worked out the meaning behind all of the tattoos, pretty much. Proving it was the next step.

Harry turned up the hill, feeling his muscles burn as they worked harder. The tattoo on his back throbbed, stinging slightly as the skin sweated. Once, the pain would have been a big deal. Now, he could barely feel it, and it certainly didn't bother him.

Into sunlight at the top of the hill. As expected, already hot. The sun burned his skin, drying up the sweat a little before he plunged down the other side, down the hill and back into shadow. This morning, he felt as though he could run forever. Arms pumping, chest heaving, sweat falling in fat drops to the road below. At the point where he would usually turn to head up to the water tower, he kept going. He had a vague idea of where he was, but he wasn't really seeing anything.

He was running down a dirt road, in the blazing sun. In army fatigues. Loaded up with a huge pack.

Every step sent a shockwave of pain through his body. Up ahead he could see another SAS candidate, shimmering through the heat haze. On the side of the road sat one of the selectors, face covered with a green scarf and sunglasses. He didn't bother talking to him. There was no point. They hardly ever talked back. When they did talk back, they never offered words of encouragement.

Ahead of him, the other candidate disappeared. When he got to him, he was sitting on the side of the road, piece of paper on his lap, trying to scrawl his name with a hand that was shaking so badly it could barely grip the pen. His face was a mask of pain, and disappointment. Another drop-out.

Harry heard the horn and saw the car in the same instance. *I'm dead.* But as he thought it he was already leaping, tucking his head under as the car roared out of the side street. He felt the car's bonnet against his back. Heard tyres squealing.

As he came out of the shoulder roll something in his lower spine gave way. He staggered, fell. White-hot spasms wracked his body, from his shoulder blades to his knees. The world greyed out. When he came to, a man was by his side, shaking his arm.

'Hey! Hey! You all right?'

He had glasses. Grey hair. Business shirt, with a tie flung over his shoulder. Around his neck hung a black lanyard, attached to some sort of ID card slotted into the shirt's pocket.

Harry tried to sit up, but the man put a hand on his shoulder. 'Don't. Just have a rest. You came down pretty hard.' He sounded annoyed.

The man looked around. The car had pulled up and its young driver was leaning out the window. 'Jesus, mate! Jesus!'

'Y…' Harry's throat closed. He could taste blood in his mouth. He cleared his throat. 'Yeah. Sorry.'

The driver cursed, slid back into his seat, and pulled out again into the traffic.

'Don't worry about it.' The man looked back at Harry. 'Just have a bit of a rest. You really should look where you're going though. I thought you were dead.'

Harry lay there. The concrete felt cool against his cheek. If he let himself go, he could feel the world spinning slightly. He breathed deeply, and the sensation passed.

An ant walked into his peripheral vision, and he flashed back to the first nightmare.

Well, he's definitely dead.

Harry forced himself up, ignoring the flash of pain from his back. Now that his body had cooled down, he felt himself cramping. He pulled his legs up underneath him, crossed them. His left knee throbbed. It was badly grazed and looked like it was going to swell. The good samaritan was down on his haunches, peering at Harry with real concern in his eyes. People passed by on either side, barely offering a glance. No-one else seemed to care.

'I'm okay,' Harry said. 'I'll be okay.'

'Do you have someone you can call?'

'Sure,' Harry said, although he didn't. Not really. He wasn't going to try and get Jess – she'd be on her way to work. Dave was at work. Christine? Yeah, and then he'd have to answer the questions. The lesser of two evils.

'Shit,' he said. 'I left my phone at home. I wasn't planning on coming so far.'

'That's okay. Use mine.'

The man handed over his phone. Harry considered just getting a bus home. But he was too exhausted. So he dialled Christine on the work number, which after so many years at the *Chronicle* was ingrained on his memory, and prepared his story.

Christine sat across the table, nursing her glass of water. It was the first time she'd visited his house, and would probably be the last time. Her opening statement was about the smell.

'Did something die in here?'

'Only my self-respect.' He opened some windows.

Harry made coffee. Despite the heat, he felt cold inside. When he got home he'd changed in the bathroom, had a shower. Then he realised that he hadn't brought any clean clothes in with him. Yeah, he could have just put his sweaty running clothes back on, but he couldn't bear to even look at them. And he realised he didn't want to hide the tattoos anymore. He wasn't ashamed of them. And sure, he couldn't explain them without lying or having the other person think him insane, but he was prepared to risk that with Christine.

'Holy shit,' she said, when he walked past. 'Holy, fucking, shit! Wait!'

He stood there, towel wrapped around him. She circled, examining the tattoos. Occasionally she'd stop, as though admiring a work of art in a gallery. She touched the poppies on his back. Goosebumps rose in answer.

'Harry.' It was all she could manage.

'Let me get dressed,' he said. For a moment he thought she was going to grab his arm. But she didn't.

He returned, sipped his coffee. Saw that Christine had

helped herself to a glass of water. She didn't say a word. But he could tell she was dying to.

'Look, it's no big deal,' Harry said.

She opened her mouth to argue but he held up a finger. 'You know this one,' Harry said. He pointed to his neck. She nodded. 'That was the first. They say that these things are addictive. Maybe they're right?' he continued.

Harry was impressed with himself. So far, he hadn't lied.

'Don't ask me about mid-life crises,' he said. 'Maybe that's what it is. But you know, maybe I don't want to go through my life being like everybody else. Maybe I want to do something different.'

Again, not a lie. He did want to do something different. For the first time since uni, he wanted to break a story that was worth breaking.

Christine held her palms up. 'Okay. Tattoos aside. What happened this morning?'

'I've been running every day. Maybe another aspect of this mid-life crisis I seem to be having. I usually do a block, turn up to the water tower, back down again. Something like that.

'I was bored. I wanted to push myself a little. I guess I chose the wrong day to do it.'

Christine nodded. 'It's thirty degrees out there! It's not even ten!'

She took a sip of water, as if to emphasise her point. 'And you should be drinking this, not that.' She nodded towards his coffee.

Harry shrugged. 'Water's next on the menu. Anyway, I really appreciate you coming to pick me up. I didn't have anyone else I could call.'

She stared at the table. 'That's okay,' she said, eventually.

258

Harry finished his coffee. Poured himself a glass of water. 'See?'

'So how's this scoop you're working on?'

Harry shivered. 'Yeah. I'm getting there.'

'You're not coming in to work today.'

'Well, I was…'

'That wasn't a question, Harry.' Christine finished her water and got up. She laid a hand on Harry's shoulder. 'Don't worry. I'll cover for you.'

'Thanks. For everything.'

Christine shrugged. 'You owe me.'

'I'll buy you a drink at the Christmas party.'

After Christine left, Harry shuffled around the house, jittery with nervous energy. He could feel the storm building inside himself, could feel the electricity in the air but couldn't do anything about it. Sweat poured off his body. He stripped down to his boxers and walked from room to room, the tin roof tick-tick-ticking as it expanded with the heat of the day. A dog barked somewhere nearby. Eventually he slumped back to his laptop, fired it up, tapping pen against pad as he waited for it to boot up.

There was an email from SASmate.

'Saw your message. I'm interested. But I've been slammed so many times I'm wary. Can you tell me more?'

Harry stared at the email. Hit 'Reply'.

'I have to be careful too. I've been burned before. I'm a reporter with the *Chermside Chronicle*. Trust me – I'll give you plenty of information before I ask you to commit. Do you use Skype? We can chat online if you feel better about that? This is my Skype username: haz_hendrick.'

Harry read through the email. Clicked 'Send'. There

wasn't much more he could do. SASmate, whoever he was, clearly wanted to engage. He'd seen this over the years at the *Chronicle*. People wanted to dish the dirt but they didn't want to be associated with it.

He went through his files. He was getting there, but he still had a long way to go. Without documents, a lot of what he had was hearsay. And when levelling it at a high-ranking politician – a high-ranking, incredibly popular politician – his story would need to be watertight. Already he was thinking that Miles would baulk at running it, no matter how good it was. It was too big for the *Chronicle*. He could sell it freelance, if he needed to. Hell, if it came to it, he'd set up a blog and publish it online.

He had documents showing that Swenson Constructions was in trouble. He hoped that those documents would show a massive drop-off in revenue, that couldn't solely be attributed to the GFC. He had witnesses that could put Crow and Heathy at the scene of a murder and an attempted murder. He had a line connecting Swenson to Cardinal, but on the surface that looked legitimate. Cardinal's property purchases were eccentric, but there was no law against that. Some might wonder where a former soldier found the cash, but then that could be explained away by Swenson helping him with his 'investments'. And he didn't have anything that linked Cardinal to the Dreadnorts. He didn't have any proof that Cardinal had been smuggling drugs into the country.

Harry got up and walked to the kitchen. He poured himself a drink of water, sculled it, then fetched a beer from the fridge. The VB carton sitting next to it was almost full of empties. He didn't remember drinking them. He'd really developed a taste for it.

When he got back to his computer, his Skype window was open. A message, from SASmate.

'You there?'

Harry sipped his beer, set it down beside him.

'Yeah.'

'So what's this info you've got?'

Harry considered, then set his fingers to the keys once more. 'It's tricky. Like I said, I've got to be careful.'

'Har. You sound like me.'

'I've got information that suggests a well-known politician has been doing some things he shouldn't.'

Harry sipped his beer. A pause. He imagined SASmate sitting in a dark room somewhere, the screen the only light in the room. It was stupid, assigning looks to someone he'd never met.

'Like what?' SASmate typed.

The cursor blinked. 'Oh, just the usual. Drug trafficking, rape, murder. What about you? What do you know about the crash?'

Harry flicked Skype to the background on his screen and watched the video of the Black Hawk coming in. In slow motion. It smashed against the deck, bounced, and dropped into the sea. He closed his eyes, seeing deep blue, the hull of the ship far above him. His lungs were screaming for air.

Opened his eyes. Flicked back to Skype. SASmate had replied.

'Well, let's just say I know for a fact it wasn't pilot error.'

Harry shook his head. 'I need more than that. At some point we're going to have to trust each other. Why don't we meet up. Where are you?'

'Brisbane. Same as you. What I want to know is, what's

261

a reporter on a shitty local rag doing chasing something that no-one else will touch with a barge pole?'

Harry considered. 'I came across some information. It led to some more information. I'm a journalist. That's what we do. We follow the story until the trail runs cold or we score a hit.'

Despite the heat, Harry felt goosebumps rising on his arms. A few weeks earlier, this wouldn't have applied to his journalistic endeavours. Now it did.

'Fair enough,' SASmate wrote. 'So let's line up this meeting.'

CHAPTER 30

The Thursday night crowd at the Liber Lounge was large enough that Harry and Jess could talk without worrying about people overhearing, but not so loud that they couldn't talk at all. They sat outside on the verandah, watching rush-hour traffic crawl by on Margaret Street below, the footpaths crowded with workers heading home or on to after-work drinks. A man in an unconvincing Santa suit had set up on the corner, and was urging passers-by to give him their loose change.

Jess was in her work clothes, a pristine dusky-pink blouse and dark pants. Hair down. She told Harry she used to wear it up, but then after the first tattoo decided wearing it down was the way to go. She didn't think the insurance company she worked for was quite ready for a tattooed team leader.

They sipped their drinks. A schooner of VB for Harry, large glass of white wine for Jess. Harry handed over his iPhone, with a photo of the latest tattoos: the Black Hawk and the avenging angel.

'I did some research on the names. Tim Edwards died in the Black Hawk crash in 2008. Tim was with Rob when they discovered the plantation. As were Geoff Lane and John Birmingham. Geoff and John died in an IED explosion in Helmand province, that same year.'

'What about this Middleton guy, and the Arabic script?'

'Middleton was the pilot off Fiji. Collateral damage.'

'And the Arabic?'

Harry shrugged. 'I got Bill to translate: Bibi Naderi. I couldn't find anything on her online. But my guess is she was the woman in the plantation.'

'How would he have known her name?'

'He must've tapped his contacts in Afghanistan to do some asking around for him.'

Jess sipped her drink. 'There were eight people on that chopper, right?'

Harry nodded.

'And presumably Geoff and John weren't the only ones caught up in that explosion?'

'No. Two others were injured.'

'Shit. So... Rob uncovers a massacre in Afghanistan. Tries to get some answers. And then, shortly after, his whole team dies in "accidents."'

'Yep.'

'Cardinal doesn't muck about.'

Harry shifted in his seat, trying to ease the discomfort in his back.

'Anything new on your end?' he asked.

'You could say that,' Jess replied. She turned and untucked her blouse at the back. The tattoo was still raw. It stretched from the bottom of her ribcage to the top of her hip, like Harry's avenging angel. But this was a cardplayer. Grinning, skeletal face. And it was holding the cards the wrong way around. Ten cards. An ace of hearts, five of diamonds, two of clubs, nine of spades, eight of spades, nine of hearts, five of hearts, two of spades and a four of clubs. A joker had been inserted between the two of clubs and the nine of spades.

'What was the nightmare?' Harry asked.

'You know how you told me that your sparrow tattoo appeared along with the memory of the fight at the pub?'

'The Shelter Bar, yeah.'

'They talked about getting out of Brisbane. They got as far as a shitty motel at the Gold Coast. Rob was zonked on the bed. Half a bottle of bourbon on the bedside table. He'd dumped the painkillers but then his back had gotten so bad he turned to booze instead.

'Kyla heard the Harleys booming into the forecourt. She tried to shake Rob awake but by the time he was with it, they were already hammering on the door.

'Rob reached under his pillow and she thought he must've had a gun there. But he didn't. It was just a scrap of paper. He shoved it into her front pocket. The door rattled on its hinges.

'They ran into the tiny bathroom and locked the door, just as the front door splintered inwards. Rob locked it but it was one of those shitty internal doors – it wasn't going to hold Dreadnorts back for any length of time.

'Kyla yanked the tiny window open. Rob braced himself against the door. They were thumping on it now, yelling to be let in. He told her to go. She didn't want to leave him. Someone massive hit the door and it cracked. She could see the sweat on Rob's brow and the way his legs were quivering. "Go," he hissed. "Or they win."

'She leant forward, kissed him, squeezed through the window and fell into the alleyway. Behind her she heard someone scream, but it wasn't Rob. She heard more Harleys approaching but the way the sound was reverberating she couldn't tell where they were coming from. So she ran for the streetlights and came out on one of the main roads. There were cars cruising past, towering apartment complexes everywhere she looked, and in the distance the sound of waves pounding the beach.

'She looked back. She could see the sign: Sea Breezes Motel. But from where she stood she couldn't see the front of the place. She ran across the road then, lost herself in Surfers Paradise.

'She was crying, cursing. She remembered the piece of paper and pulled it out of her pocket. It was a tattoo design. She laughed, in spite of herself.

'She went into the first tattoo parlour she found, and gave them the design.'

Jess looked down, took a big gulp of wine. Harry tried to make sense of the information.

'So, she escaped?' Harry said.

Jess shook her head. She wouldn't look at him.

'She felt like shit. She'd been let down so many times in her life that she knew intimately what it was like. Kyla clung to Rob's final words – *Go, or they win* – but she couldn't take much solace from them. She desperately wanted to go back for him, but knew there was no point.

'She went into hysterics while they were tattooing her. Laughing at the ridiculousness of it all. God knew what was happening to Rob, or had already happened to him, and here she was getting inked. The guy doing the tatt asked her if she was all right, and she just burst out crying. She told him to finish the fucking thing.'

'And then?' Harry reached across the table and laid his hand on Jess's. He felt giddy, touching her skin. She pulled away, pushed a strand of hair behind her ear.

'I can't… I can't talk about it right now. Maybe later.'

Harry stared at the tattoo.

'What do you think?' he said.

Jess shrugged. 'It's not exactly a winning hand. Nothing to grin about.'

She took another swallow of wine. She'd drunk half of it already.

'Oh,' she said. 'And Darren's moved out.'

'What!'

'Yeah. The night I brought Afsoon over – that was the final straw. I should have just lied. But I couldn't think of what to say. Lying isn't my forte. But, alternatively, I didn't know how to tell him the truth. So it was the worst of both possible worlds.'

Harry wanted to be sorry for this man he'd never met, but he didn't have it in him. Instead, he imagined taking Jess home, looking after her. He imagined coffee on the front steps with her. Walking up to the water tower.

'I'm sorry,' Harry said. 'I wish there was something I could do.'

Jess shrugged, sniffed. 'I think there's hope. Once all this mess is sorted out.'

She gestured to the air around her, as though the Liber Lounge or Brisbane in general was to blame. Her statement was one of blind optimism. Neither she nor Harry knew if they would ever sort it out, or what would happen when they did. Would the tattoos disappear? Would it stop more tattoos appearing? Or would the process continue, until they were totally consumed?

They finished their drinks. Jess bought another round. Harry watched her at the bar, felt a longing deep within himself that he hadn't experienced for a long time. Sighed it away. He watched the people in the street below.

'What are you thinking?' she said as she returned, placing the drinks down.

'Ah. Nothing. Bullshit,' he said.

'Hey, in case you think it's all bad news…' Jess reached up with one hand and pulled the black lanyard from around her neck, handing the memory key at the end of it to Harry. It was warm from her skin.

She smiled.

Harry raised his eyebrows. 'No way.'

Jess nodded. 'I think so. I've added a document in there, breaking it down. Four shell companies. I'm pretty sure they're shell companies. All doing a lot of business with Swenson Constructions until late 2008, when they pretty much drop off the face of the earth.'

'When you say "a lot of business…"'

'Millions. I did a business registry search on them and three of them are still listed,' she said. 'All based in Brisbane.'

'Why keep them?'

Jess shrugged. 'He might still be using them. Or he might have feared shutting them down in case it looked suss. Or maybe he wants to use them in the future to funnel some money out of the company. An insurance policy.'

Harry drank some beer. 'You said you're pretty sure?'

'It would be easy to check. All of them have a registered address. You can visit them. Chances are, there'll be a tiny office with a mail slot. If that.'

'Wow. Thank you. I want to kiss you.'

Jess looked away. Smiled. 'Let's propose a toast instead. Death to tyrants!'

Harry raised his glass to meet hers. Clinked. Drank. Saw Cardinal, torn apart by a sniper round.

'Oh, and I found an article about Rob and Kyla, about the incident at the Shelter Bar,' Jess said.

'Really? You trying to steal my job?'

'Ha. The article described Rob as "former SAS", said he was considered extremely dangerous and warned people not to approach him. They said Kyla was a nurse at the RBH, but was on extended leave for health reasons.'

Harry nodded.

A third round of drinks appeared and disappeared, and then a fourth. Harry and Jess moved on from tattoos and Rob and Kyla to general life. Growing up. School. Uni. Dreams, both those they'd achieved and those they hadn't. Harry loved everything about Jess. Her laugh. The way the corners of her eyes crinkled when she smiled. The unconscious gesture of smoothing strands of hair behind her ear. And she had a great body. She was smart. And she was with him. They were bound together.

Before he knew it, they were in a cab together, heading to his place.

CHAPTER 31

Harry felt strangely awkward when he ushered Jess into his house. Despite all that they shared. Despite feeling as though he knew her in ways he had never known a woman, including Bec. He felt suddenly coy.

'Take a seat,' he said, clearing some clothes off the lounge to make a space for them both. 'I'll get some wine.'

In the kitchen he poured two glasses, drank half of one, refilled. Stared out the kitchen window, into the back garden. Thunder boomed, the wind picked up. He closed his eyes, centring himself. Shook his head. He wanted to make love to her. Fuck the wine. He wanted to walk back in there, take her head in his hands and kiss her deeply. Run his hands down her body. He wanted to kiss every tattoo. Take the pain away and…

Harry opened his eyes. Is that what he wanted? Or what Rob wanted? And did Rob want Jess, or Kyla? Did it even matter anymore?

He carried the drinks back to the lounge room. Jess was going through his CD collection. She held up an Eminem CD, raised her eyebrows.

'It was a phase,' Harry said. Smiled.

She took her glass and they sat down together. He was

all too aware of her perfume, and the scent of her body. She slipped off her shoes and pulled her legs up under her. Their knees touched.

Harry sipped his wine.

'So… there's more to Kyla's story,' Jess said. 'And I know I have to tell you. But I couldn't back there.'

She gulped down some wine.

'Okay. So, Kyla got the tattoo. But just as they were finishing up, a bunch of Dreadnorts piled into the place. She thought someone had tipped them off.

'They grabbed her, dragged her outside. Bundled her into the back of a van. She expected Rob to be in there, but he wasn't. And that was the worst thing for her. She thought that must mean he was dead. Turns out, it was much worse than that.

'They… they brought her back to Brisbane. Through Brisbane. Up north. Well, you know where they took her, right?

'Dumped her in that field. Cardinal was waiting. No-one else. Just Cardinal. They dumped her on the ground and drove off. Her wrists and ankles were bound with cable ties. She lay there in the dirt, trying to sit up. She could hear traffic barrelling past on the highway but it may as well have been on the surface of the moon for all the good it would do her.

'He was on the phone. That was the thing that really blew her away. He was on the fucking phone.'

Jess shook her head, pressed her free hand against one of her eyes. Drank some more wine. Her hands were badly shaking now. Harry moved in, held her. He rested his head on the top of hers, breathing her in. She sniffed. Pushed him away gently.

'No, Harry. You need to hear this. He was on the phone to Rob. Well, to Crow and Heathy. They had Rob strapped to a chair, in that old skate rink at Paddington.'

Harry felt the hairs on the back of his neck stand up, thinking about the feeling he had, driving past it.

'They were trying to find out where he'd hidden the dossier. They were torturing him. Cardinal was… He was… It was as though he was on the phone to a friend, or a business colleague or something. Just stone cold. Calm. He smiled, looking at Kyla on the ground like that.

'And then he moved in.'

Jess finished the rest of her wine. She played with the empty glass. Stared into its depths.

'Jess, you don't have to…' Harry said.

'Yeah, I do. He put the phone on speaker, asked Crow to do the same. He… he had a knife. He cut Kyla's clothes off.

'Cardinal said, "Rob, I know you've got a stash of documents somewhere because I've heard the stories about what your slut here did to get them. So either she's going to tell me where they are, or you are."

'Then Cardinal laughed. "I'm going to enjoy this," he said.

'Kyla screamed. In spite of what she told herself she would do, she screamed. The pain was too much. And then, from the other end of the line, Crow said Rob wanted to say something. So Cardinal stopped.

'Rob was panting, hissing into the phone. When he spoke, his voice was thick, he could barely pronounce the words. They must've done a fair bit of work on him. He said, "Wait! Please, stop! Let her go. It's… it's somewhere special. Somewhere…"

'Kyla screamed again but not in pain, in anger. "Shut up! Rob, shut up! Don't! Or it's all for nothing…"

'Cardinal chuckled. "Touching," he said. "But I'm only just getting started."

'There was a loud noise, like splintering wood. Crow cursed. The sounds of a scuffle. Crow yelled out something about petrol, yelled at Heathy to put the fucking gun down. Then a noise, so loud the speaker distorted. And a moment of silence. Kyla screamed. She knew what the noise was. She remembered that Ahmed had been taken out with a shotgun.

'The line went dead. Cardinal was still smiling. "Looks like it's down to you," he said. "Where's the fucking dossier?"'

Harry was numb. He felt a pulsating sensation all over his body. His vision turned red.

'Fuck the article,' Harry said. 'I'm going to kill him. Kill all of those fuckers.'

Jess grabbed his arm. 'What!'

'Well, what do you want me to say, Jess? Afsoon said she thought it would require blood…'

'She said "maybe", Harry, "maybe."'

'Blood, Jess. This story I'm working on, I'm a fucking community journo. We're talking about the next prime minister of Australia. Jesus. Rob knows how to fix this. Rob knows.'

She squeezed his arm. 'I'm not finished, Harry. Don't you want to know what happens next?'

'No!'

'He raped her, Harry. He told her she could make it stop, by telling him where the dossier was. She told him that she didn't know. And by that point, she was too traumatised to lie. She really didn't know. He didn't care. He raped her, over and over again. And then he cut her. Told her he'd keep cutting until she told him what he wanted to know. She told him to fuck off. As the last drops of blood drained from her body, he raped her again.'

'Jess…'

'No! Get the fuck away from me, Harry. It didn't end there. Because of this fucking thing…' – she slapped the back of her neck – 'she was dead but still aware of everything. He slit her throat. He fucking cut her to pieces, Harry, and then he buried her. And I remember every fucking last moment.'

Jess sat there, panting. In one of the houses nearby, someone was watching a horror movie. Stage screams drifted across the gully.

'So don't tell me about rage, Harry. Don't tell me about what Rob's feeling. I know. A thousand times over. If I let Kyla do what she wanted, she'd take that knife to Cardinal and wouldn't stop until he was mincemeat.

'But I'll be damned if I'll give in to her, Harry. Because if we do, if we seek vengeance in that way, Andrew Cardinal wins. All the Andrew Cardinals out there win.

'We're better than that, Harry.'

'Are we?' Harry said. 'Have you seen the news lately?'

Jess hissed in frustration. She grabbed her bag and headed for the door.

'Jess. Don't leave like this, please.'

He followed, took her hand. She shook him away.

'Bye, Harry.'

CHAPTER 32

Harry sat fuming at his desk, unable to shake the anger and pessimism that had plagued him since the fight the previous night. He had gone over the argument with Jess time and time again, imagining himself speaking differently. But it always ended the same way – with her walking out. Several times he had picked up the phone to call her, only to set it down again. His feelings hadn't changed. The only way he could see to make things better with Jess was by lying, and there were too many lies in this sorry saga already.

'Harry?'

Harry started, looked over his shoulder. Christine was there, a copy of the paper in hand.

'Want to check it out?'

'Thanks.'

He took the paper from her, laid it out on the table. Another front-page lead for Christine. Page three also. Harry had managed a page-five lead, but he couldn't for the life of him remember writing it.

'Did I do any of this?' he asked.

Christine sat in her chair, raised one eyebrow. 'A little bit. How's the scoop you're working on?'

Harry nodded. 'Yeah. It's coming along.'

'Really?'

'Really. No, seriously. Trust me.'

'It's going to be Christmas soon, Harry. No-one will read it.'

Harry laughed. 'Oh, I think they'll read this one. It's a doozy.'

'Harry?'

He turned and saw Miles beckoning him from the door to his office. Harry followed him in.

'Close the door behind you,' Miles said.

Harry paused. But Miles wasn't looking at him. He closed the door and sat down.

'Christine has been keeping this paper running single-handedly.'

'I know. I'm working on something. It's slow.'

'What is it?'

'I can't tell you.'

'Harry!' It had been so long since he'd seen Miles angry that at first he didn't recognise it.

'You can't tell me? You can't tell me! How long have we worked together? I've stuck by you. I've never questioned why you'd want to work here for so long.

'I've understood that sometimes we have reasons. And when you told me you were working on something big, I didn't press you for details. I respected your professionalism.

'But we are not the *Brisbane Mail*, Harry. Even the *Brisbane Mail* can't fund investigative journalism. And we have a fraction of the money they have.

'Have you seen our circulation figures? Online ad sales? It's not pretty, Harry. I can't have it. I won't have it. Either you tell me what's going on, you confide in me, give me something, or you're gone.'

Harry sighed, tried to break it down for his boss. He kept bits back. The Rob stuff. Used the expression 'prominent politician' instead of referring directly to Andrew Cardinal. Told Miles about the drug operation, the Dreadnorts' involvement, and an edited summary of what Nick Swenson had told him, as well as what the spreadsheets showed. When he was done, Miles sat there, hand on mouth, still nodding even though Harry had finished talking.

Finally, he opened his mouth. He still looked pissed off. 'How much can you prove?'

Harry held his hands up, palms out. 'I have documentation on the money laundering. I have people who'll go on the record about the Dreadnorts. I'm working on another couple of angles. I still need to firm up the links with the politician.'

Miles shook his head. 'Harry. It's a hell of a story. But I mean it when I say we don't have the resources for investigative journalism. Christine's getting burned out. It's not hard work, not for someone like her, but there's so much of it to do.'

Harry nodded. 'I understand. Give me until the election,' he said. 'It'll come to a head by then… one way or another.'

Miles looked at Harry, adjusted his glasses. 'Have you apologised to Redwood yet?'

'No, but…'

'Well, get on it. This afternoon.'

Harry went back to his desk and checked his phone. Missed call. Tom. The counsellor. He'd left a message too, which Harry deleted without listening to. Harry had a feeling that by election day, just a week and a half away now, he'd be in need of plenty of counselling. But until then, he'd have to do without.

He went to work on the 'to do' list that was reaching critical. He powered through the tasks, pausing occasionally for a stroll into the office kitchen to make himself a coffee.

Harry's phone rang again. He picked it up, expecting Tom. Or maybe Jess.

'Hello?'

'Harry?'

It took Harry a moment to process the voice, so unexpected was the call. '*Bec*?'

'Hi.'

Harry's body dumped a load of adrenaline into his system. In a matter of seconds his face was flushed. His fingers and toes tingled. Palms sweaty. He was finding it hard to draw breath.

'Hi,' he managed. He felt dizzy. He closed his eyes, but that just made it worse.

'I… I just wanted to see how you're going?'

'Um… fine.'

'I ran into Christine in the city the other day.'

Now Harry did squeeze his eyes shut, wondering what Christine had told her.

'Oh yeah?' He glanced in her direction. But she was staring at the screen, pointedly not listening.

'She said you've got some tattoos.'

'Yeah, well, there's no law against it.'

'No, but I mean… wow. Bit of a change, hey?'

What? So he was now more exciting, because he had tattoos? He clamped his eyes shut and waited. Listened to her breathing. Could almost smell her perfume. He opened his eyes, grounding himself.

'Harry, the reason I called is… I wanted you to know… I've met someone,' she said.

Harry dropped into a pit. A grave. Twenty foot deep instead of the usual six. It was pitch black, but if he looked up he could see life somewhere up above him. Points of light against a night sky. He opened his mouth to speak, felt it fill with dirt.

Well, he's definitely dead.

Hyuck, hyuck, hyuck.

'I'm sorry. I wanted to tell you. I didn't want you to find out from someone else. And Christine said you were going on a date…'

Harry heaved. Swallowed. Took a deep breath. He couldn't speak. Bec filled the void.

'His name is Paul. He works at Queensland Health, in the PR department. You'd like him, Harry…'

'Stop. Bec. Stop. Thanks for telling me, but I don't need to know his fucking name. Goodbye.'

Harry hung up. She was still talking when he pushed the button.

He swivelled in his seat, until he was facing Christine.

'I'm sorry!' she said. 'I saw Bec in the city and…'

'Yes, she said.'

'I thought… I was just worried about you.'

Harry closed his eyes. All his tattoos throbbed. The sensation pulsed into his brain, latching onto the seed of a headache. Nourishing it. Making it grow.

'I didn't know she was seeing someone,' Christine said.

Harry held his hand out. 'Stop. Just… stop.'

He walked, without thought. Concentrating on putting one foot in front of the other. Out of the office. Down the stairs. Out of the building into a wall of hot, humid air. He thought of Chermside Shopping Centre. Endless noise. Chattering kids. Mobile phones.

He turned away from the shops, towards the main road, where lunchtime traffic crawled. Followed the cars headed towards the city. Walked. Picked up the pace. He wasn't in a trance, he was just walking, hands thrust into his pockets, feeling the heat beat down on his head. It was the wrong thing to do, with the headache now blooming inside his skull. But he needed to hurt himself a little. Without this, he'd punch a wall. Do something stupid. Buy a gun. Make a list. Kill some people.

Stop.

Who would he kill? Heathy. Crow. For starters. With a knife. He'd tie them down and stick them with holes.

Stop.

When the floor was tacky with their blood, he'd prod their bodies with the toes of his boot. Yep, they're definitely dead.

Fucking stop!

Andrew Cardinal. Andrew Cardinal was a tricky one. He'd have government security. Those guys were good. Sometimes they were even former SAS. It would be hard getting anywhere near Cardinal. He had said some crazy things about Afghanistan, about how Australia should invest more troops in the region. That made him even more of a target. A bomb was too risky, too unreliable. Civilians would get hurt. But a sniper rifle. A really good one. Harry had no idea what a really good sniper rifle looked like, and yet he could see one in his mind's eye. He also had no idea where he would get one. He shook his head. Yes, he did. Maybe.

In his mind he saw Andrew Cardinal arriving at the Brisbane Cultural Centre for the Labor Party launch, a week before polling day. Harry was across the river, in one of the office buildings. He was dressed as a cleaner. He had a cleaning trolley. And inside the trolley was the gun. He wouldn't go from the roof. No, not the roof. There would probably be security on all the roofs anywhere near the Cultural Centre, even that far away. And even if there wasn't, there would likely be air support. A Black Hawk or two, maybe even a gunship.

But from the office building. A shaped charge to take out the window just before he fired. Cardinal would be dead before…

'Fuck off! Rob – fuck off!'

Harry realised he'd spoken aloud. Looked around him. But there was no-one nearby. He was standing outside a used-car yard. A couple of people drifted between the shiny cars. Hot wind rattled the plastic flags. Inside an air-conditioned office, a fat salesman stood, waiting to see if there was any point venturing into the heat of the day.

'Fuck this.'

Harry turned around, heading back to the office.

CHAPTER 33

Harry stood outside Lutwyche Shopping Centre, sweating in the early afternoon sun. From one side the shopping mall's white facade beamed light and heat back at him. From the other, waves of pollution washed over him from the traffic on Lutwyche Road. He felt bad about letting Miles down. He felt even worse about lying to him after their conversation, telling him he was heading out to collect some vox pops on the election. He checked his watch, wishing he'd objected to SASmate's suggested meeting place. He didn't have a clue what this guy looked like. A nagging part of his brain insisted this was part of some elaborate trap. Cardinal was in military intelligence, after all.

He looked at his watch again. He was hoping to get over to the *Brisbane Mail* later in the afternoon, and one of Swenson's front companies was based in Bowen Hills, too. Harry planned on checking it out on the way over. Behind him, the automatic doors opened, giving Harry a brief waft of cool air, before the heat of the day swept it away.

'Harry Hendrick?'

Harry turned, squinting despite his sunglasses. The man had a long grey beard. Messy hair tucked under a Broncos cap. A faded Bridge to Brisbane t-shirt. Paint-stained shorts.

His arms were tanned, and marked with tattoos. He looked like he was in his mid-fifties.

'Yeah.'

'Jim. Jim Matthews,' he said, then grinned, revealing a mouth of misshapen, nicotine-stained teeth. 'SASmate.'

They shook hands. Jim's hands were rough, his grip suggested strength borne of hard work, not time at the gym.

'Come on, I'll buy you a drink,' Jim said.

They walked south, towards the city, past a row of worn-out-looking shops. Faded signs. Dirty windows. An abandoned laundromat. A tattoo parlour. Harry peered in, as he compulsively did these days, scanning the designs. He thought about Jess's cardplayer with the bad hand.

'Sorry about the odd meeting place,' Jim said. 'I just wanted to check you out, make sure you are who you said you are.'

'No worries. I would have done the same. Except I know nothing about you. I've checked out your posts online, but they don't really tell me much.'

The shops gave way to nondescript office blocks. The sorts of places Jess was talking about. Mail slots. Dirty glass. Names that meant nothing. Ahead of them, the road dropped away, revealing a vista of two giant fig trees and, beyond them, the city skyline. Trucks and cars churned the humid air as they waited at the pedestrian crossing.

'Yeah. I try not to get too involved in those forums,' Jim said. 'But you get sucked in. I'm on a disability pension now, so… you know. Not much else to do. It's stupid. When I got out of the army, one of me mates who was in security consulting said he didn't get out of bed for less than $800. And here I am, counting loose change to see if I can afford a beer.'

Harry nodded. He wasn't sure what to say. He didn't want to offer platitudes.

The Crown Hotel had been done up as an Irish bar in the mid-'90s, when that was all the rage. The current owners had pulled back a little. But it was still painted dark green, still had a miniature keg over the entrance, with a harp on its side. Someone had draped a bit of Christmas tinsel over it.

'I'll get them,' Harry said. 'What'll you have?'

'Just a XXXX. Thanks, mate.'

Harry returned with the beers to a table at the back of the room. He set the drinks down and sat opposite Jim. The first sip was heavenly, and he felt pangs of homesickness for his old life. Beer on the couch, watching the footy, waiting for Bec to come home.

'Cheers,' Harry said. 'So, what do you know about the crash?'

Jim grinned. Sipped his beer. 'Hang on a sec. Why do you want to know? What's it got to do with the *Chermside Chronicle*?'

Harry shook his head. 'We've been through this... Okay, fine.' Harry leant forward. Lowered his voice. 'I'm working on a story. It's not specifically about Chermside. It started with a local businessman, but it's spread much further than that.

'Like you, I suspect there's more to the crash than the official report makes out. I've got information that someone may have been trying to kill a couple of the guys on that Black Hawk. But I need to confirm the information and, ideally, find someone who's willing to go on the record.'

Jim nodded. 'Fair enough. I can help you out with the first part... and we'll see about the second.

'I was deployed with the SAS team on board the *Kanimbla*,' Jim said. 'So there was us, and there was this spook. Military intelligence guy. I never saw him. Well, at the time I didn't think I saw him.

'That morning, the morning of the crash, I went to check the bird. And there was this guy coming back from it. He had the coveralls on. Standard issue. He had gloves on, they were greasy.

'I didn't think anything of it. Why would you, right? Hundreds of people on the *Kanimbla*. Everyone with their jobs to do.

'At the last moment he looked up and I did this double-take. He had a tattoo, beside his eye. A tear. In the early morning light, it looked like blood.'

Harry felt the hairs on the back of his neck stand up. He kept his face neutral.

'It was weird. Facial tattoos stand out like dogs' balls in the ADF. Technically you're not meant to have them. Afterwards I thought, what was he doing out there? By himself. That early. An hour or so later, Tim and Justin were dead.'

Harry picked up his notebook. 'Do you mind if I take notes?'

Jim shook his head. His eyes were watering. He drank some more beer.

'So, I reported it, right? I reported what I saw. Reported the tattoo. No-one could remember a crew member with a tattoo like that.

'I don't know if they thought I was lying, originally. Or if they thought I was seeing things. That I wasn't fully awake, or that I was exhausted after the flight out from Perth. Both of which were true, by the way.

'I told them to check the security footage. There was a big block of time missing. No-one knew why. And that's when I got really suss. And the rest, as far as I'm concerned, was a big fucking exercise in covering your arse. No-one wanted to be lumbered with the blame. It made me sick when the report came back blaming Midsy. You know, they were all about fucking protecting the family, looking after his wife and kids. And then they dropped him in it. Dead men can't talk, right?'

Harry looked up. A little stunned. 'Right. Yeah, of course.'

'That's why I got out. And then I had problems… stress-related. Marriage fell apart. Blah blah blah.'

He waved it away. Drunk half his beer. Harry sipped his.

'Did you know Rob Johnson?' Harry asked.

Jim rubbed his face. 'Now there's a name I haven't heard in a while. He went missing. Him and that chick of his. What was her name?'

'Kyla.'

'Kyla! That's right. She was all right.'

'You knew them?'

'Ah. You know. You know everyone in the SAS. We're tight. I reckon there was something dodgy with that, as well.'

'How do you mean?'

'Come on. Someone fiddles with the Black Hawk. Rob survives. Only to go missing barely a year later. I think someone was tying up some loose ends.'

Jim peered at Harry. Harry stared down at his notebook.

'You do, too,' Jim said.

Harry looked up. 'Yeah. Yeah I do.'

After leaving Jim, Harry drove over to Bowen Hills.

He pulled into the car park, already knowing what he'd find. The place was deserted, a small block of offices tucked under the nest of highways that had sprung up over Brisbane's inner north. A hot, humid wind kicked up dust and chip packets. Old, yellowing copies of the *Chermside Chronicle* sat piled on the dirty tiles. He pulled to a stop outside Daybreak Imports. Climbed out of the car.

He barely recognised himself in the reflection in the glass. He seemed taller, bigger. The dodgy DIY tinting job on the windows distorted his face, making him look like a demon. He walked up to the doorway, tried pushing it open. Locked. He cupped his hands to the glass and peered inside. Mail on the floor. An old desk and broken office chair. A phone, but it wasn't even plugged in.

Harry took some photos with his phone, then climbed into his car and headed to the *Brisbane Mail*.

CHAPTER 34

Harry arrived at the *Brisbane Mail* expecting not only to be shown the door, but also to be thrown out of it. Or possibly through it. Redwood had had plenty of time to stew over the awards night debacle. Harry should have apologised sooner. He hoped this unexpected visit would smooth things over much better than a phone call or email could.

He waited at the front desk as the receptionist relayed his message. He was anticipating getting a 'He's not in', or 'He's in a meeting' or 'Fuck off and die'. Instead, the security door at the side of the reception desk buzzed and Redwood himself appeared, smiling.

'Harry Hendrick! Come on in.'

The smile caught Harry off guard, as did the invite. There was no need to go 'on in' anywhere. He could have delivered his apology quite easily in the foyer. But Redwood led Harry through the *Brisbane Mail*'s labyrinthine interior. Someone had strung up some tinsel on the walls. There was a plastic Christmas tree perched on a coffee table, but apparently the budget didn't stretch to decorations. Harry wondered if Redwood was planning on taking him to the newsroom, so he could administer some public humiliation.

Instead, he opened the glass-panelled door to an old office. There had been a name once on the frosted glass, but it had been scratched off. The blinds were down. Harry walked in, Redwood followed.

Redwood flicked the light switch, and a dusty fluorescent bulb cast blue-white light on the room. There was a scarred desk, yellowing newspaper clippings on the wall. Some framed, some stuck with Blu Tack. An old push-button phone.

Redwood wasn't quite so friendly once the door was closed.

'What do you want?' Redwood said.

'I just came here to…'

'Don't fucking give me that,' Redwood said. He was up in Harry's face. Harry backed away and ended up against the desk. 'What do you know?'

Redwood wasn't angry. He was scared. Harry gave him a gentle shove. Redwood staggered back. Stayed back. Harry gestured to the chair. Redwood sat down.

'Rob Johnson. He came to you with a story. Why didn't you chase it?'

'Are you writing something on this?'

'Don't fuck with me, Terry. Why didn't you chase it?'

Redwood rubbed his face.

'For Christ's sake, Harry, this could ruin me! I've got a wife, two kids I'm trying to put through school.'

Harry felt sweat dripping off his body. The aftertaste of beer in his mouth made him feel nauseated. He said nothing. Sometimes that was better.

'I don't know what it's like in your world, but when you work on a *real* paper, you can't chase everything,' Redwood said. 'You have to pick and choose. Rob came to me, told me this crazy shit about Cardinal murdering people in Afghanistan. Do you know how insane that is? He'd just won preselection!'

'You should have chased it.'

'I did! I did, Harry. I made some inquiries with a contact in the ADF. He said Rob had gone off the rails after the Black Hawk crash. Was pissed off about the compo he got. Said he was involved with these shady characters.

'And then I looked into that, and I found out that he was stalking various ADF personnel. That he had that woman of his – Kyla – trying to weasel information out of people. And yeah, that he'd been seen hanging out at that Stones Corner tattoo joint which, as you may or may not know, is popular with the Dreadnorts outlaw motorcycle gang.'

'Don't patronise me.'

Redwood licked his lips. 'Harry. I can forgive and forget what happened on the awards night, if you can forget about this story.

'Seriously, I'm doing you a favour here, buddy. You don't want to disappear down that rabbit hole, I can assure you. Just go back to your Meals on Wheels and your Chermside Bowls Club yarns.'

Redwood seemed to be about to say something else, then got up, crossed the room and pulled the door open. 'I've got work to do,' he said.

Harry blinked. 'So… you wanted to talk to me… and now you don't?'

'Come on, Harry. Or I'll call security.'

Harry moved towards the door.

'He had documents, Terry,' Harry said. 'Did you see them?'

Redwood said nothing. He didn't need to. His eyes said it all. Fear. Finally, he shrugged.

'Faked,' Redwood said. 'You should know all about that, right?'

Harry shook his head, walked past Redwood. 'I thought you had guts, Terry,' he said.

Redwood shook his head. 'Fuck off, Harry,' he said. 'Stay away from me.'

Harry sat slumped on the lounge, exhausted, hamburger wrappers and a growing collection of empty stubbies by his feet. Soon to be joined by the half-full beer in his hand. The news was on the TV, but he wasn't really seeing it. He was putting the pieces together in his mind. Making the connections, writing the story in his head. Figuring out what else he needed to make it work.

Andrew Cardinal appeared on the screen, and Harry forced himself to focus. Cardinal had arrived in Brisbane, ahead of tomorrow's official campaign launch. His wife and three kids were waiting for him at the airport. He kissed Mrs Cardinal, picked up his youngest daughter and swung her around. It reminded Harry of the scenes of soldiers returning from Afghanistan. Just what the spin doctor ordered.

It seemed impossible that this man's heart could be so dark and that he could hide such a side to his personality. Cardinal had killed people. With guns, with knives, with his bare hands. Harry stared at his own hands, thought about what Rob had done in Afghanistan.

Bad guys.

A gust of wind blew through the house. The back door slammed. Harry jumped.

291

'But it's all a matter of perspective, isn't it Rob?'

Harry's phone chimed. Ron Vessel: *We still on for tonight?*

After the Vessel interview had gone to press, Harry had organised to meet him when he was back in Brisbane. He dragged himself off the couch, remembering his argument with Jess.

We're better than that, Harry.

CHAPTER 35

Harry watched the big Ferris wheel turning against the backdrop of city lights. On his left, the Cultural Centre sat like a stack of toddler's blocks, lit up with special Christmas lights. On his right, the light and shade of Southbank parklands. The sound of kids playing at Kodak Beach carried on the warm night air.

Harry's phone buzzed. He pulled it out of his pocket.

I thought you were going to buy me a drink at the Christmas party?

Christine. Shit. He'd completely forgotten about it. It seemed weird that back in the normal world, normal things were still happening. It was a world he no longer belonged in. He slipped the phone back into his pocket.

Across the river, Harry could see people moving through the few offices with their lights on. Movers and shakers racking up Friday-night overtime to try and get ahead. Cleaners, giving the offices a quick once-over before knocking off.

He imagined Rob over there, laying the black case on the floor, opening it and assembling his sniper rifle. Setting it up, getting comfy. He didn't have Tim to help him this time, like he did back in Afghanistan, but it was a relatively easy shot. But there would be civilians everywhere, and he'd have limited time. Cardinal would climb out of his car almost where Harry was standing now, then walk into the Cultural Centre. Rob would have the time it took him to walk across that road.

Harry swapped his courier bag from one shoulder to the other. In it he had his laptop and notebook, in case Vessel wanted to make a last-minute statement. Pens, spare pens, and more spare pens. Vessel would be shocked. It was going to take him some time to absorb the information.

'Harry Hendrick!'

Harry jumped. He turned and saw Ron Vessel approaching with his big cheesy grin, hand outstretched. Harry shook it, trying to avoid letting Vessel crush his fingers. The politician gestured to the Brisbane Eye.

'Bit tacky for your photo, isn't it?' he said.

Harry shrugged. 'There're a few different angles. The Cultural Centre's in the background or, the other way, the city. You know, city boys make good.'

Ron didn't seem convinced.

'Doesn't the *Chronicle* hire photographers anymore?' he asked.

'Not on Friday nights. We chip in with the *Mail* for some social shots, but that's about it.'

Ron grunted. He seemed to sense something wasn't right.

'Come on, it won't take long,' Harry said.

'Okay. What the hell, right?'

Harry had organised the ride with the operators. They sounded a little dubious at first, until Harry told them he didn't want a free ride. Then they seemed to think that the article might drive a bit of extra traffic their way. As it was, business wasn't doing well. The Eye was named after a similar ride in London, but it was half the size, and Brisbane was half as impressive.

The wheel came to a stop and the doors opened. A young guy and girl climbed off, holding hands and clutching iPhones. Harry gestured and Ron climbed on. Harry followed, and they sat on either side of the pod. The girl's perfume lingered in the enclosed space.

'So, how does it feel to be the next Treasurer?' Harry asked.

Ron grinned. 'Now, now Harry. The campaign launch is tomorrow, and then there's a long, long week to election day. I think people will be surprised by how many want to maintain the status quo.

'I'm sure the PM has a few tricks up his sleeve for the final week of the campaign.'

The doors slid shut.

'Yeah, right,' Harry said. 'The prime minister's campaign is dead in the water. Andrew Cardinal is 15 points up.'

'It's not over until it's over.'

The wheel started moving. Slowly at first, stopping to let people off. They crept higher in the sky.

'Actually, Ron, I have an ulterior motive for asking you out here.'

Ron laughed. 'Well, you know, Harry, I'm married. It hasn't always been smooth sailing, but we're working out our problems so…'

Harry smiled, pushed on.

'Do you know what Andrew Cardinal did in Afghanistan?'

'It's classified. He worked for military intelligence.'

'Yeah, but do you know?'

Ron stared through Harry. They reached the top, then the Eye stopped. Below them, a CityCat crept down the river; city lights reflected in its wake like phosphorescence. Harry pulled out his laptop, opened it. It emerged out of sleep mode. Harry typed his password and brought up a copy of his notes. He handed it to Vessel.

Ron took the computer, rested it on his lap. He pulled out his reading glasses and peered down his nose at the screen.

'Not the best light in here,' he said.

'Andrew Cardinal was smuggling drugs into Australia. He was using the Dreadnorts MC to distribute them, and Swenson Constructions to launder the money. In 2005 he was involved in a massacre in Helmand province. Thirty people murdered. Men, women, kids. At least one woman brutally raped.'

Harry remembered her hijab, blowing along the rows of poppies. Ron stared down at the screen. Harry expected him to blanch. Expected him to say it was all a load of bullshit. When he laughed, it caught Harry off guard. Ron turned his head slightly, as if looking for someone else in the pod, even though it was barely big enough for the two of them.

'Nice one, Harry,' he said. 'Are you recording this?'

He grinned, looked for a hidden camera or microphone. Harry stared at him. The smile faltered.

'You're not serious?' Vessel said.

Harry nodded.

Vessel snorted out another laugh, but there was little mirth in this one. 'Harry, Andrew Cardinal is a war hero.'

'He's a drug dealer, rapist and murderer.'

Vessel shook his head. 'I know I said you should get out

of community newspapers. But fiction writing wasn't what I had in mind, Harry. Jesus!'

He thrust the laptop back at Harry.

'If I were you, I'd take this home and delete it. Who are your sources, Harry?'

Harry felt the heat rise to his face. His tattoos itched. He knew what Rob wanted to do to Vessel.

'My sources are my sources.'

'How much can you prove?'

'Most of it.' He thought of the dossier of documents, lying hidden somewhere in Brisbane. 'I'm working on verifying all of it.'

'Harry. You can't verify fairytales.'

The wheel was moving again now, arcing back towards the ground. Vessel leant forward. Harry could see the colour in his cheeks, the sweat on his brow. Fear, or anger?

'How many people know about this?'

Harry considered. 'My editor knows I'm working on something. But not the details.' He didn't mention Jess. Harry didn't think enlisting an insurance executive would strengthen his case.

'A word of advice, Harry. Keep it that way.'

The wheel came to a stop. The doors opened. Ron went to leave, then paused, looked back into the pod. 'Shit mate, you forgot your photos!'

He laughed, and then he was gone. Harry watched him leave, picking up two security guys on the way as he walked towards the ABC building. Harry eventually climbed out on shaky legs. Nausea gripped him. He made it down to the river before he threw up, his stomach constricting until all that was left was a spider's web trailing down from his mouth to the rocks below.

Beside him, light flashed, pushbike brakes squealed. Cops. Two of them.

'You okay, sir?' one of them asked.

Harry nodded.

'You been drinking?' the other said. The headlights on the bikes were so bright Harry could barely see their faces.

'I had a few beers,' Harry said. 'But I think I might have food poisoning. Dodgy burger.'

The cops stared at him.

'I caught the bus in,' he said, knowing he was over-explaining, but unable to stop himself.

'Better get yourself on another one home then, hadn't you?' the first one said.

Harry nodded. 'Yeah. Thanks.'

He shuffled along the river, walking until the waterside breeze and the anger welling inside him gave him a second wind.

Harry had expected that Vessel wouldn't want to believe what he was being told. The election was a week away. Harry's story would blow Labor out of the water, maybe for good. Vessel had been nurturing this dream for a long time. And he'd seen some dark and bloody days in the Labor caucus.

But to shut down Harry so quickly, without even hearing him out. Harry shook his head. He was going to have to work quickly now. Vessel would have been onto Cardinal right away. Spin doctors would be mobilised, lawyers readied. They would do everything they could to discredit Harry. And they would probably succeed. Unless Harry didn't give them the opportunity. He looked over at the buildings across the river.

CHAPTER 36

The bus pulled away, leaving Harry in a cloud of warm exhaust and swishing jacaranda leaves. He shouldered his courier bag. Two big Harleys roared past. Harry jumped, heart hammering. He watched as they disappeared around the corner.

He waited for a gap in the traffic, then crossed the road. Away from the main road, the pathway alternated between the orange glow of streetlights and inky darkness under the trees. Harry walked quickly. He wanted to get home. He needed to get this story finished. Get it moving. At the top of his street he glanced up at the water tower. There were lights on underneath it now, part of the new security arrangements. Harry could understand why Cardinal had thought it a spaceship.

'Harry! Wait up!'

Harry looked back towards the road. He saw the two silhouettes. He could tell by the way they were shuffling, almost running, that they weren't out for a late evening stroll.

They walked under a streetlight. Harry stopped dead, paralysed. One of them was tall. Greasy blond hair down to his collar. Celtic bands clawed up his neck. Heathy. The other one was shorter, overweight. Chin smeared with a dirty goatee. Crow.

Harry's heart rate jacked. His fingers felt numb. His breath came in short, sharp gasps. Black spots jumped in his peripheral vision. He knew he should run, but where to? He looked around for help. On one side, under the tower, was a steep rock wall. The houses on either side of the road were dark. He forced himself to breathe deeply.

Heathy and Crow dropped into darkness, barely a bus-length away now. Harry tried to remember his last fight, in high school. He struggled to recall any useful titbits from the taekwondo classes he'd attended for six months when he was a kid, until his mum left and money was too tight to pay for them. His mind went blank. As the Dreadnorts emerged into light again, Harry raised his arms to cover his chest and stomach as best he could, then ducked his head behind his fists.

Crow lumbered in. Harry dodged. Pain exploded in the side of his head. He staggered sideways, vision blurring. His tattoos were burning.

'Get on the other side of him!' Crow spat.

Heathy had dropped into a fighting stance. Harry saw the kick coming and threw his arm out to try and protect himself. Pain blasted up his forearm, pins and needles followed. Crow ducked forward and tried to pull the bag off Harry's arm. Harry twisted his arm through the strap and they fell together.

Harry felt Crow's breath on his face: stale garlic and bourbon. Harry lashed out with his fingers, grabbing the bikie's face and twisting. Crow roared in pain. Harry rolled away, felt another explosion of pain in his back. Caught a glimpse of Heathy lining up for another kick.

Harry clawed along the road, towards the rock wall, dragging his bag after him.

Crow pushed up onto his hands and knees, wiped blood away from his face. Heathy dived in. Harry rolled. The kick glanced off his thigh. Harry kept rolling, onto his back.

Get up, or you're dead!

Harry winced. He pushed himself to his hands and knees, then rose shakily to his feet.

'I'm done screwing around,' Crow said. He pulled a knife.

The tattoos pulsed on Harry's arms. He could feel something in his mind. Surging like a wave. Harry held it back, terrified. Then Heathy was on him again. Harry felt a blast of pain in his stomach, followed by a crack as his head snapped back against the rock wall. Stars danced in his eyes. The bag fell from his shoulder. Crow advanced with the knife.

Harry felt the surge again, and this time let it happen. For a moment the world was suffused with a deep blue glow. He sucked in a breath. His ears were ringing. Wind whistled through the trees. A TV blared. He could smell his sweat, and that of Crow and Heathy. Could taste the metallic tang of blood in his mouth.

Harry stepped away from the wall to meet them.

Heathy came in first, both hands out, trying to grab Harry. Harry pistoned his leg out, then watched stunned as Heathy doubled over and fell back to the ground.

Crow stabbed at him with the knife. Harry darted to one side, turned and thrust his leg back, but Crow dodged the kick. Crow slashed down. Harry parried the strike, barely noticing the lancing pain in his arm.

Harry backed up, wary of letting Heathy get behind him.

'Come on, you little fucker!' Crow said. 'Come on!'

Heathy ran for Harry's bag. Harry step-kicked in, driving Heathy against the wall. There was a solid crunch as the bikie's head impacted, and he dropped to the ground.

He turned in time to see Crow rushing in with the knife. Harry grabbed Crow's wrist, pulled him in close, twisting his hand into the bikie's shirt. He could feel the knife between them, could feel Crow's hot breath against his shirt. As he strained to hold the knife hand, blood pulsed down his wounded arm, warm and sticky.

'Take some martial arts classes, huh?' Crow said.

Crow snapped his elbow around. Harry threw his head back, taking the blow on the shoulder. Then brought his knee up, trying for a groin strike. He missed. Crow pushed him away. Harry grabbed for the knife. It sliced his hand but came away, bouncing on the road.

Heathy groaned, pushed himself to his feet. 'I thought you said this was going to be easy,' he said, then spat blood onto the road.

'It would be if you'd pull your fucking weight,' Crow replied.

Harry staggered back into the middle of the road, putting himself between them and the knife. His stomach churned. His bag was lying there, but they seemed to have decided that getting the bag alone wasn't enough now. Just down the road, traffic continued to pass, the drivers oblivious to the life-and-death struggle going on less than a hundred metres away.

Harry sucked in lungfuls of air. Blood was flowing from

his arm and the other hand now. Heathy and Crow started towards him, wary.

'Do you want to cut, or dig?' Harry said.

They stopped.

'What the fuck?' Heathy said. The streetlight caught the whites of his eyes.

'Doesn't matter,' Crow said, unsure of himself. 'Let's finish this.'

'It's not worth it,' Harry said. 'You kill me, the story's still going to come out.'

It was as though they didn't hear him. Crow lumbered in. Harry lashed out with his fist. Crow's head darted to one side at the last minute, the blow smacking against his cheek. Pain buzzed up Harry's arm. The bikie's head rocked back slightly, but momentum carried him forward. Before Harry could retreat the big man had him in a bear hug.

'That's it. Hold him,' Heathy said.

Harry tried to lift his knee, but Crow had him turned slightly. Harry pummelled Crow's sides with his fists. Crow grunted, but held firm. Out of the corner of his eye Harry saw Heathy step in and pick up the knife.

As Heathy launched himself, Harry slammed the heel of his boot against the top of Crow's kneecap. Crow screamed. His grip loosened and Harry burst free, the knife catching him on the way through.

'Fuck!' Heathy screamed.

Heathy lunged, grunted, bringing the knife across. Harry darted sideways and watched the blade slide past, feeling the passage of its arc. Slightly off balance, he grabbed Heathy's wrist, pulling the knife towards him. He lifted his leg and drove it into the bikie's ribcage. Heathy yelled. He tried to free himself. Harry twisted under Heathy's arm, curving the knife back around towards him. He saw it in his mind: the knife twisting under, slamming between Heathy's ribs.

'No!' Harry screamed.

He jerked his arm. The knife tore through Heathy's shirt and into the flesh below. The man staggered backwards, tripping over the kerb. The knife clattered across the bitumen, bounced off the gutter, and slipped down the stormwater drain.

Crow was on his side, shivering. Heathy lay beside him, panting. Heathy pressed a hand against his side, hissed in pain. The hand was black with blood, but the wound looked superficial, from what Harry could tell.

In the distance, a siren rose and fell through the late night air.

Harry stood over Heathy, pressed a boot against his throat. He could feel Rob, back in his cage, urging him to stomp. He resisted.

'Tell Cardinal he's going down,' Harry said.

He limped up to the top of his street to get his bag.

CHAPTER 37

Royal Brisbane Hospital glowed in the night, but Harry made it only as far as the smokers milling in the shadows before exhaustion overcame him. He staggered over to a low wall, sitting just as his legs gave way. He watched the nicotine addicts, some in wheelchairs, some with IV lines still attached. Bare feet shuffling in the dusty ground. An ambulance drove past, its lights and siren dead.

Harry texted Dave, and minutes later he saw a solid silhouette striding out of the light, into the darkness. Harry waved.

'What's going on?' Dave said.

'I'm in trouble.'

Dave glanced up at the hospital, then back at Harry.

'Dave, I'm in trouble and I don't know what to do.'

'You look like you're in shock,' Dave said. Then, when he got closer, 'Shit, you're bleeding.'

He took Harry's arm and studied it. Harry realised he was shivering.

'How did you get here? You didn't drive, did you?' Dave asked.

Harry tried to remember. He remembered getting off

the bus after talking to Vessel. He remembered figures running towards him. After that, it was just flashes. Pain. Blood. A knife clattering across the road. Then nothing.

'I don't know,' Harry said. 'Bus. I think.'

'Yep. You're in shock. Come on,' Dave said. He held a hand out.

Harry looked up. 'What?'

'Come on.' He grabbed Harry's hand and pulled him to his feet.

It was quiet for a Friday night; Dave was able to find a spare cubicle in Emergency. Harry lay on the bed, eyes fluttering closed, while Dave washed his arm with saline. He felt safe.

'You were lucky,' Dave said, swabbing the back of Harry's arm. 'No stitches required.'

He checked the hand. 'This thing will bleed like a bitch, but then hands always do.'

A head poked through the curtain. A woman with dark hair and bright eyes, holding a cup of tea. Dave took it from her.

'Thanks, Elva,' Dave said.

She looked from Dave to Harry, then back again. 'He hasn't been admitted, has he?'

Dave shook his head. 'He's a friend of mine. Cut himself shaving.'

'You're dead if they find out.'

Dave shrugged. 'I can always go back to pizza delivery,' he said. Elva smiled, then closed the curtain.

Harry tried climbing off the bed; the world spun around him.

'Whoa!' Dave said. 'Where do you think you're going?'

'I don't want you to get in trouble. I better…'

Dave planted a hand on Harry's chest. 'Let's just worry about you for a while. Here.'

Harry took the tea with a shaking hand. Sipped it. It was lukewarm, too sweet. He grimaced.

'Just drink it,' Dave said. He pulled together some bandages and started working on Harry's arm and hand.

Harry closed his eyes but when he did the world swam and he saw Crow's face, felt the knife-blade pressing against his stomach.

'Two Dreadnorts,' he said. 'They came after me.'

Dave stopped what he was doing. 'Dreadnorts? As in, outlaw motorcycle gang Dreadnorts?'

Harry nodded. 'I confronted Vessel tonight, at South Bank. He must've…'

Harry sucked in breath as Dave rubbed antiseptic into his arm, then sipped more tea. He'd never felt so tired.

Do you want to cut, or dig?

Harry's stomach cramped. Hot bile bubbled up his throat. He thrust the back of his hand against his lips as his stomach tensed again. Dave reached out and pulled a cardboard dish off the bedside table. He held it under Harry's mouth as he vomited the tea into it. Dave passed him a couple of tissues and he wiped his mouth.

'Feel better?' Dave said. 'Hang on. Ron Vessel. And Dreadnorts?'

'Cardinal is the link. They came after me, and somehow I beat them. Rob beat them.'

'Rob?'

'Yep. These were his tattoos. He was in the SAS. The guys who came after me are the same ones that took him and his girlfriend down. It was as if – it was as if he were in control. I was just along for the ride.'

Dave stopped working on the arm for a moment, and stared at Harry.

'He wanted me to kill them,' Harry whispered. 'He wanted me to destroy them.'

For a long time, Dave said nothing. Outside, a siren blared, then cut out. Shoes squeaked on linoleum.

'I told you, Harry,' Dave said. 'I told you to get out of there.'

'I couldn't.'

'I told you, and you stayed there, and now...'

'They're pieces of shit,' Harry said. Anger flared. 'They deserve it.'

Dave stared at Harry. 'That's Rob talking. No-one deserves to bleed to death in a back street, Harry.'

Harry felt a sullen rage pulsing behind his eyeballs. He forced it down, and the extreme fatigue overcame him again. He couldn't see a way out. But Rob could; Harry just didn't want to accept it.

'Then help me, Dave! Help me end this!' he pleaded.

'The best way I can think of to help you right now is to offer you somewhere safe to sleep,' Dave said.

Dave finished the dressing on Harry's hand, then rubbed his nose with his forearm. He tidied up, put Harry's vomit bowl into the hazardous-waste bin.

'You right to walk?' he asked.

Harry nodded.

'Come on then, you crazy bastard. Let's get you home.'

CHAPTER 38

Harry lay on the lounge, wide awake, watching and listening as the world came alive around him. Dave and Ellie's house was a blend of order and chaos. Neatly ironed uniforms hung off the ornate scrollwork between the lounge and dining rooms. Medical textbooks, scraps of paper and mouldy mugs covered the coffee table, which underneath housed Monopoly, Trivial Pursuit and a stack of battered Tom Clancy paperbacks. The only concession to the festive season was a string of Christmas lights, hanging over the TV. Outside, a kookaburra announced the arrival of dawn.

Perfect day for a run. But Harry's running days were over. He woke with the plan fully formed in his head, as though Rob had been busy, burning the midnight oil, so he could deliver it as a fait accompli when Harry opened his eyes. The borderline panic from the night before was gone, replaced by calm determination.

After returning from the hospital, Dave had put him in the shower and found him some old clothes. Harry considered popping home to get something instead, then realised that might not be such a smart move. They'd do.

He sat up, and pain tore through his body. His bandaged

arm throbbed, his fingertips tingling with pins and needles. His thigh muscles screamed. His shoulders cramped. His other arm, and his legs, were covered in bruises, and one ear pulsed sickly.

He picked up his phone and texted Jim, setting the wheels in motion. Then Harry took a deep breath and pulled himself to his feet, relieved to find that he could still walk.

Dave poked his head into the room from the kitchen. 'Want a coffee, old man?'

'Fuck off.'

Dave laughed, turned and carried two mugs out the back door onto the verandah. Multicoloured prayer flags fluttered in the warm breeze. Harry followed Dave outside.

Dave had cleared away enough beer bottles for the coffee cups.

'Good to see married life hasn't slowed you and Ellie down,' Harry said.

'I hardly think you're in any position to offer lifestyle advice.'

'Touché.'

Harry sipped his coffee. Wished he had his sunglasses. He checked his phone.

'So let me get this straight, because it was a bit much to take in last night,' Dave said. 'You told Vessel about the story you're working on. And then you got attacked by two Dreadnorts.'

Harry nodded. 'Not just Dreadnorts. The same guys who used to do Cardinal's dirty work.'

'So either Vessel is in on it…'

'… or he told Cardinal, and Cardinal set them on me.'

Dave sipped his coffee. 'Either way, it's not pretty.'

'No.'

'You should call the cops,' Dave said.

Harry shook his head.

'Why not? You were attacked last night. You know who these guys are.'

'I beat the shit out of them, Dave.'

'It was self-defence!'

Harry nodded. He couldn't tell Dave what he was thinking. He was thinking about Afsoon, talking about blood. He was thinking about what Rob wanted to do to those guys, and the repercussions of Harry not following through.

'Once the cops come in, it's going to get complicated, Dave. They're going to want to know the full story.'

'So tell them the full story!'

Harry shook his head again. 'The election is a week away. The cops are going to want to confiscate my computer, they're going to want me to hold back on the story...'

'Harry! This is your life! You can't fuck around!'

Harry didn't care about his life. He was thinking of someone else's life. Andrew Cardinal. The Cardinal juggernaut. This wasn't going to end until he stopped Cardinal. He and Jess wouldn't be safe until Cardinal was gone.

'Dave, listen to me. If Cardinal is elected, he'll have all kinds of power. The evidence I have, it won't stand up in a court of law. It's hearsay, mostly. Without the documents, all I've got is what a couple of people have told me, and what's up here,' he said, tapping the side of his head.

Dave looked as though he were about to push it further, then sighed. 'There's got to be a better way.'

They sat in silence for a while, drinking their coffee. Harry would have liked nothing better than for all of this to go away. For him to be able to hand it over to the cops.

GARY KEMBLE

But that wasn't going to work. Deep down, he knew that.

'At least let me take a look at your injuries,' Dave said.

Without waiting for a response he moved around the table, unclipped the fastener and wound the crepe bandage from Harry's hand and arm. The bandage was spotted with blood. He pulled it away, then gently removed the gauze pads. Down the road, someone fired up their lawn mower.

'Hang on a sec.'

When Dave disappeared inside, Harry checked his phone again. Dave returned with fresh gauze pads and smeared some antiseptic on the wounds. Harry sucked in breath.

'Don't be a baby,' Dave said.

He pressed the pads on top, then set to bandaging Harry's arm. When he was done, Harry flexed his hand. He could feel the cuts pulsing.

'Can't you just publish the story, see what happens?' Dave said.

'No. Been there, done that. I'm not going to press until it's watertight.'

Harry thought he sold the lie. There would be no story. Not from him anyway. And yet soon everyone would know his name. But Dave looked at him, and didn't look away until Harry stared down at the ground.

'Harry. I don't know what you're planning to do. But whatever it is – don't.'

Dave got up and went into the house. Harry texted Jim again, finished his coffee and followed Dave inside.

Harry sat on the old bench in the park. Above him, the jacaranda tree rustled in the breeze. At the end of the road he watched a 747 climbing in the sky. He felt totally

312

calm. He didn't know what it was like to be Rob, but he thought this was part of it. Understanding he was in danger, understanding he had to do dangerous things. Coming to terms with that and being at peace.

He smelt Jim's tobacco before he saw him. Harry twisted in his seat – wincing as the pain spiked up his back – and watched the former soldier shuffle down the steep slope from the road above.

'G'day,' Jim said.

'Hi.'

Jim sat down. 'No notepad today?'

'I think it's gone beyond notepads.'

Jim nodded, as though he knew it would come to this.

'I need a gun. Preferably a sniper rifle. And I need it today.'

'What! Harry…'

Harry didn't have time for a debate. He pulled off his shirt. Jim gasped. The colour drained out of his face. He started out of his seat but Harry grabbed his arm, dragged him back down.

'Look at me,' Harry said. He let Rob come forward.

Jim slumped in the seat, stunned. 'What the fuck?' he whispered.

'Rob's inside me. His spirit.'

'Bullshit.'

The plane climbed through the cerulean sky. A part of Harry wished he was on it. He cleared his throat. Wished he'd brought his water bottle with him.

'Whether you believe that bit or not, I've uncovered a lot,' Harry said. 'I've uncovered a drug-running operation. It's linked to a prominent developer – Brian Swenson. You've probably heard of him.'

'Heard of him? You can't drive fifty metres without seeing one of his construction sites!'

'Right. There's more. Dreadnorts MC are involved.' Harry gestured to the bruises on his face. 'I had a little run-in with them last night.'

'Shit, mate. You're lucky to be alive. But a sniper rifle's not…'

'There's more. Andrew Cardinal.'

Jim looked over at Harry. 'What about him?'

He felt a spring tensioning inside him. Like the hammer being pulled back on a pistol.

'You know he served in Afghanistan?'

'Yeah. Of course.'

'He was using his intel to run a drug-smuggling operation. He was involved in a massacre in Helmand province. And when he decided to go into politics, he tried to sever all links to that massacre.

'Rob. Kyla. Tim Daniels. John Birmingham. Geoff Lane. Ahmed. A local tattooist, Rabs.'

'Holy shit.'

Jim stared straight ahead, putting the pieces together in his mind. He nodded. 'Cardinal. Fuck me.'

'I was hoping to write a story on it, uncover Cardinal that way. But I've run out of time,' Harry said. 'And Cardinal can't be allowed to become prime minister. He'll have so much power that I won't be able to touch him.

'I need a gun. A fucking big one.'

Jim looked at Harry. Pulled out his phone and dialled. 'G'day, mate. It's Jim…'

Harry could hear a big voice on the other end of the line. Jim laughed. 'Fair ta middlin'. Hey, remember that product you got your hands on? The one you can't shift?' More mumbling. 'I've got a fella who's lookin' to buy. ASAP.'

Jim laughed again. 'Yeah, no worries ya fat bastard. Catch ya.'

He put his phone away. 'Done.'

'Can you do something else for me?'

Jim scratched his head. 'I don't do windows or foot rubs. If it's not one of those, try me.'

'I'm going to email you my story. What I've got of it. All my contacts. Everything. If… if anything happens to me, I want you to get it out there. I don't know how. But I need to know that the information doesn't die with me.'

'Sure.'

'Thanks.'

'No worries. Just go get the bastard.'

CHAPTER 39

Harry stood sweating outside the Dead Ringers MC clubhouse gates. Midday heat baked off the concrete under his feet and the green aluminium gates in front of him. Someone had hung a plastic Santa's head off the barbed wire on top. He looked back at his car. The road was lined with mechanics, small manufacturers that had somehow staved off the threat from China, and run-down offices with reflective glass and company names tacked to the windows.

Researching background for his article, Harry learnt that outlaw motorcycle clubs appealed to former military men. They craved the order, and the danger. Harry shook his head and stabbed a finger at the button on the faded grey intercom, glancing up at the security camera as he did so. Would the person on the other end see his fear?

There was a buzz. Somewhere, behind the barbed wire fence, a buzzer went off.

The speaker crackled. 'Yep?'

'Harry Hendrick. Here to see… uh, Chook.'

A pause. Then the electronic lock on the gate clicked open, and the gate started sliding back on its track. Harry walked through. The clubhouse was a low-set grey besser-block bunker with barred windows. Above the blue double doors a big sign proclaimed Dead Ringers MC, the club's patch next to it. Around the side of the clubhouse, an old Ford Falcon and three big Harley-Davidsons.

The door swung wide and Chook stepped out into the sunshine. Harry had seen blurry photos of him online. His hair was thinning and his big bushy beard had streaks of grey through it. The muscle in his tattooed arms had begun to turn to flab, and a pot belly pushed out over his faded jeans. Wraparound shades hid his eyes. He offered a hand.

'Mr Hendrick,' he said. 'You look like you had a rough night.'

Chook crushed Harry's fingers, pulled him closer.

'Yeah... work Christmas party.'

Chook grinned, showing two gold teeth. There was nothing friendly about the expression. Behind him came a rush of cool air, the sounds of blues and the crack of pool balls. The murmur of conversation. Then Chook pulled the door shut behind him, and brushed past Harry.

'Come on,' he said. 'Let's go for a drive.'

Harry followed him around the side of the building, looking back over his shoulder as they walked. The big gate was still open. Chook climbed into the Falcon and fired it up. A cloud of blue smoke filled the air as maybe six of its eight cylinders roared to life. Someone had attached plastic reindeer antlers above the doors. Heat and the stench of cigarettes engulfed Harry as he pulled the door open and climbed in. The ashtray was overflowing, the back seat covered in old clothes and faded porn magazines.

The Dead Ringers sergeant-at-arms revved the engine and the whole car shook. If possible, it was even louder in here than outside. If the Ford had a muffler, it wasn't doing its job. Chook put the car in gear and pulled out of the lot, pausing and looking over his shoulder, making sure the gate closed behind him.

He drove through the industrial estate.

'Thought you guys liked bikes?' Harry yelled.

Chook laughed. 'Yeah, you got one?'

Harry shook his head.

'Well, then. Besides, if you're bugged, or if I'm bugged or if the car's bugged, they won't get much out of it.'

The industrial estate gave way to battered, broken suburbia. Overgrown lawns, faded and flaking paintwork, rusty letterboxes.

'How long have you been sergeant-at-arms?' Harry asked.

'Coming up on twenty years now. Truth be told, I'm getting out.'

'Oh yeah?'

'Yeah. World is moving on. Club needs fresh blood.'

Chook took the car out onto a main road lined with fast-food outlets and used-car lots.

'So what happened? I heard two Dreadnorts got their arses handed to them.'

Harry sighed. The car was making his muscles ache again. 'I may have done the arse-handing.'

Chook laughed. 'You silly bastard. You shoulda finished them off. There's only one language these people understand.'

'Music?'

'Ha!' Chook threw his head back, slapped the steering wheel. The car veered slightly into the right-hand lane. The driver of the sedan next to them looked like he was going to make something of it, then saw Chook's battered face, big

318

beard and tattooed arm and thought better of it.

'You don't have much time. You know that, don't you? Depending on how those arseholes play this, you could have the whole of Dreadnorts MC after you by this time tomorrow.'

'I wasn't planning on waiting that long,' Harry said, checking his watch. He had two hours.

Chook blew some air through his lips. 'Well, no love lost between us and them, that's for sure. You wanna watch yourself.'

Harry looked out the window, watching the car yards drift past. He thought about Rob and Kyla, trying to flee Brisbane. He thought about the fight with Jess. At least she was out of the picture. Harry could see himself settling the reticle on Andrew Cardinal, breathing out, and squeezing the trigger. Beyond that was nothing. Darkness. Like being buried again.

Chook pulled off the main road again and back into suburbia. A more affluent area, McMansions lining the curved streets. Trees. Kids on bikes.

'Thing is, this military hardware is more trouble than it's worth,' Chook said, continuing a conversation that must've been running in his head. 'There's an inquiry going on down in Canberra. The feds are all over us at the moment.

'It'd be better for me to dump the military stuff in a creek somewhere.

'Jim and I go back a ways. I owe him one. But if I sell it to you, and some fucking copper turns up on my doorstep with an M82 in his hands, I'll break both your legs before I shoot you in the nuts. Witness protection, protective custody – none of that means shit if you cross me. Do you believe me?'

'Yeah.'

'Good.'

Chook guided the car through the estate, pulled up in front of a monstrous beige house with a triple garage. He pulled a remote control out of his pocket, and one of the big white doors opened. He looked over and caught Harry's expression.

'What? I made some good investments,' Chook said, grinning.

The car pulled into the garage. The door came down behind them.

'Don't mention the gun, okay?' Chook said. 'It's "the product" from now on, right?'

'Your house is bugged too?' Harry asked.

Chook shrugged. 'Better safe than sorry.'

Chook shut off the engine. Harry's ears rang.

On the other side of the garage, a Harley-Davidson stood in pieces. The engine was off, broken down on a white sheet. Behind it, on a tool board, a large Dead Ringers banner.

'Doin' a bit of work on her,' Chook said.

Chook led Harry through a white door at the back of the garage and into the house. He closed and locked the door behind them.

'Reinforced steel,' he said. 'Although you wouldn't know by looking at it.'

Tiled floor. White walls, with tasteful Christmas decorations adding a splash of colour. Lots of light coming through bi-folding sliding-glass doors at the back of the house. On the other side, a patio area and a pool.

'You've done all right for yourself,' Harry said.

Chook shrugged. 'I've got a good financial adviser.'

They passed through the kitchen, all stainless steel and marble, to a living room with a white leather lounge and a massive flat-screen TV. Christmas tree in the corner.

'3D, 4K, internet-ready,' Chook said, pointing at the TV. 'Take a seat.'

Harry sat on the cool leather while Chook pulled the curtains closed.

'Right. Let's see your cash,' he said.

Harry pulled out his wallet, which was bulging with fifties and hundreds. He counted the money. Chook nodded, scooped up the cash, and shoved it in his back pocket.

'Can I have a receipt?' Harry said.

'Har-har-har. Wait here.'

At one end of the room was another door, with a deadbolt lock. Harry guessed this door was reinforced steel, too. Chook jangled the keys, found the right one and slotted it in. He disappeared through the doorway. Harry looked around the room as he waited. He couldn't see any cameras, but he had the feeling of being watched. He leant forward, had a look at the magazines on the coffee table. *Australian Ink. Soldier of Fortune. Bacon Busters. Australian Financial Review.*

Chook came back with a large black plastic case. When he turned to lock the door, Harry noticed the money was gone from his back pocket.

'Here we go.'

Chook laid the case on the coffee table. It didn't have any markings. He opened it, revealing the M82. It was split into two main parts; three if you counted the magazine.

'You want me to… ?'

But Harry was already there. He assembled the rifle, checked the chamber was empty, then pulled the trigger. He grinned at the clunk of the firing pin coming forward. He'd never heard the noise before. But Rob had heard it countless times. He gently removed the scope and mounted it. For the first time since meeting him, Chook looked a little uneasy.

'Where did you say you learnt about… these products?'

'I didn't,' Harry said.

Harry hefted the weapon and looked through the sight. He liked the weight, even though he'd never take a shot from a standing position – at least, not without finding something to brace the barrel with. It was overkill for what he wanted, designed to take out armoured cars, but he'd rather have more power than not enough. He remembered Afghanistan, even though he'd never been there before. Finally, things were coming together.

Harry disassembled the rifle, placed it back in the case. Chook laid a box of ammo on the bench.

'Do you want accessories?'

Harry nodded, and put the ammo on top of the case.

'Got a few different sorts in there. Kinda like a bag of mixed lollies.'

He gestured to the guide. Different coloured tips for different types: tracer, armour-piercing, incendiary. Harry nodded.

'Anything else I can do you for?' Chook asked.

'Don't suppose you sell, uh, fancy dress?'

Chook raised his eyebrows.

CHAPTER 40

Harry parked his car, climbed out and looked down on the Queen Street Mall, packed with Christmas shoppers. He checked the time – thirty minutes to go – then called Bec, perching on the bonnet of his car while the phone rang. This wouldn't take long.

'Hello?'

'Bec?'

'Harry?' A pause. 'How are you?'

'Yeah. I'm… I'm getting there.'

He could hear noise at her end in the background. Plates, cutlery. He imagined Paul, cleaning up after Sunday lunch. He pushed the thought away.

'Bec. There's something I need to say to you.'

'Harry, you don't need to…'

'Yeah. I do. Bec, I still love you. Don't interrupt me because I need to say this. I don't care if you can't love me. That doesn't change the way I feel. I love you. I'll always love you.'

'Harry…'

'Do you remember when we came back from overseas? We were scrounging around, trying to find bits and pieces for our house. We bought that dodgy kettle?'

'Yeah. Of course.'

'That cup of tea. It tasted like shit, but you were right. You said, "This is the life". And you were right.'

'Oh, Harry…'

'I've got to go. I'll… I'll catch you later.'

He hung up. Stared at his phone. He wanted to call Christine, just to hear her voice one last time. But if he called her, he'd blab. And if he blabbed, she'd talk him out of going through with it.

There was a note for Jess, in with the documents he'd emailed to Jim.

Harry slipped the phone into his pocket and got ready.

Queen Street Mall was packed with sweaty election campaigners and Christmas shoppers, ducking in and out of the speciality shops, talking with friends, looking at their phones. Harry was dressed in Sunshine Air Conditioning-branded overalls and cap, with a Sunshine Air Conditioning identification card, belonging to Mr Hugh Bird. Chook, at no added charge, had given him a couple of matching stickers to plaster onto the M82's case

Harry let himself slip back, allowed Rob take over. This had to be done. There was no alternative.

The sign on the hoarding outside the shell of the Regent Cinema promised an 'exciting new residential development'. But the posters were faded, and there were no sounds of work coming from inside. At the bottom of the sign was a small Swenson Constructions logo.

The crowd thickened as Harry neared the intersection of Queen and Albert Streets – for some reason, despite all the landmarks in Brisbane, the Hungry Jack's there had become the place for young people to meet. There were two police officers leaning on a low wall, sunglasses hiding their eyes. As the crowd parted, Harry saw protesters, holding banners demanding more rights for asylum seekers. A woman with dreadlocks and a lip piercing thrust a copy of *Green Left* at him. Harry ignored her.

He kept walking, waiting to be stopped by the cops. He imagined doing what Dave wanted him to do – handing the whole sorry mess over to the police. If he threw enough mud, some of it might stick. It would only take one or two journalists to get curious, and God knows there were enough at *The Australian* looking for a chink in Andrew Cardinal's armour. What a coup! To stop dead the Cardinal juggernaut before election day!

Harry broke stride, almost stopped. His glance slipped sideways, down Albert Street to King George Square, where the giant Christmas tree stood. In his mind's eye he turned around, went back to the car. Drove to work and finished the article. Then he remembered sitting in the Vice Chancellor's office, wondering if he was going to be sued. Rob surfaced again. Rob couldn't force him to do anything, Harry thought. Not yet anyway. But ignoring him now was like ignoring a powerful itch. It felt better just to give in to it.

You print that story and it will pan out exactly as Vessel says it would. You'll be marked a crazy man, you'll be watched. It's now or never.

He started walking again. Slowly at first, then picking up pace. He fished out his phone and dialled. After eight rings it went to messagebank. *Challis Architects can't take your call right now...* Perfect.

Up by the casino, a Salvation Army band was playing a festive tune Harry couldn't quite place even though he'd heard it a thousand times. There was a small table set up nearby, red bunting and signs for the local Labor candidate. Most of the signs featured Andrew Cardinal. A young woman wearing a too-big ALP t-shirt offered him a flyer.

Harry shook his head, kept walking. There was no way he was going to get away with this. The mission might be a success, but Harry was going down for it. The girl handing out the *Green Left* would probably remember him, as would the ALP volunteer. His progress up Queen Street was being monitored by numerous security cameras. After the event, it would all be so obvious that something was wrong with this man. People would ask why. And they would never understand, even if Harry tried to explain it to them.

A helicopter thundered overhead. Harry looked up, shielding his eyes with his free hand. Harry had no idea what it was, but Rob did. Eurocopter Tiger with a 30mm cannon on the nose and a bunch of missiles, depending on how it was configured. Whatever it had, it would be bad news if they got wind of what Harry was up to.

At the end of the mall Victoria Bridge carried traffic over the river. Harry got his first sight of the Cultural Centre. The wind picked up, stirring the hot air, carrying the smell of mud and decay. He turned left, following George Street, parallel to the river.

Past the Land Administration Building, another sandstone relic of Queensland's colonial past. And then, right next to it, a bland concrete-and-glass office block, a remnant of the building boom in the '70s.

Harry welcomed the cold blast of air-conditioning as he strode through the automatic doors. There was a guard on duty, but Harry ignored him and headed straight for the lifts. Only people who weren't meant to be there asked permission. The guard didn't even look up from his book. Harry thumbed the lift button.

As he waited, he dropped down deep inside himself, preparing for the mission. Harry had done a story on the Challis brothers earlier that year. Chermside boys who'd started their own architectural firm, and then made it big (by Chermside standards) and moved into an office with river views. Harry had interviewed them there, and marvelled at the views of the Cultural Centre across the river.

The elevator arrived. Harry pressed the number ten, and the doors closed. Plenty of elevation. Great field of fire. Old locks. No visible security systems. Staff unlikely to be working weekends. Another plus: the glass windows facing the hallway had blinds.

The lift doors opened. Harry looked up and down the hallway to make sure it was clear, then moved to the office door. He pulled the lock picks out of his pocket. The lock was easy. Not easy for Harry, but easy for Rob. He knew how to pick a lock, although there'd been scant use for such skills in Afghanistan, where a boot or a shotgun would do the job just fine.

Harry shut the door behind him, closed the blinds on the windows that looked out to the hallway. The office was small. Two desks, dominated by high-end Macs with big screens. Every inch of wall space was occupied by bookcases or printouts of technical drawings. On the far side of the room: the window. Harry set his case down and walked over. He opened the blinds to the outside.

The brown mass of the river stretched out below. On its other side, the blocky structure of the Performing Arts Centre. Harry saw people gathering at the side doors, where

Cardinal would make his entrance. There was already a large crowd. Young people, families, children running around, red balloons bobbing along behind them. Possible collateral damage.

The thought sparked a vision of a woman lying on a bloody concrete floor. Her legs were spread. Her robes pulled up over her head.

Harry hefted a huge computer monitor off the desk, and set it on the floor. He dragged the desk and a chair over to the window. It was inevitable that the police would discover that this room was where the shot came from. But depending on the security systems in the building, that discovery may not be made until Monday morning. And by then it would all be over anyway.

Harry opened the case, assembled the M82. He checked that the mag was full. If Harry missed on the first shot, he could potentially still get Cardinal. The politician would be covered with security personnel, but from this range the rounds would easily penetrate a human shield.

Human shield? Innocent lives.

Harry suppressed the thought.

The windows didn't open, which meant that he'd have to cut a hole.

From his pocket he pulled out the glass cutter, also courtesy of Sunshine Air Conditioning, scratched a small circle on the window, then tapped the glass until it fell to the abandoned courtyard below. He put the cutter away, and lowered the blind halfway.

He sat on the chair, pulled the stock of the big gun to his shoulder, looked through the reticle. About four hundred metres. He looked at the people down below. How their clothing moved. How the balloons bobbed. A slight breeze came in off the river; nothing to get worried about. The M82 was good up to fifteen hundred metres. This should be a piece of piss.

Except for the civs everywhere. And the fact that Harry wasn't Rob. True, Rob was occupying his body, but it wasn't the same. That didn't make him Rob, or Rob him.

Harry pulled out his iPhone, opened his web browser. Streamed ABC News 24.

'And as you can see, the crowd is gathering here at the Cultural Centre in Brisbane, waiting for Andrew Cardinal's arrival. There's a real sense of occasion…'

Harry scanned the crowd through his scope and found the reporter doing her piece to camera. Picked out Cardinal's security detail. Six that he could see; there would be more out of sight. And more still would arrive with Cardinal. The gunship thundered overhead.

He checked the time on the phone. He scratched his arms through the shirt sleeves. His tattoos were itching. He reached around, rubbing the skin on his back. It flared like fire at his touch.

On the screen of his phone, footage of Andrew Cardinal's motorcade approaching. Harry grabbed the M82 and lifted the stock to his shoulder, keeping his finger outside the trigger guard for now.

'… and you can see that people are actually lining the streets now to get a look at the man who is very likely to be Australia's next prime minister…'

The scope was so good he could see their faces. People smiling, laughing. There were no protesters here. Probably their application to gather at Southbank had been refused, so they'd been relegated to the mall. Was he really going to end this? Could he really pull the trigger?

Harry's back burned intensely now. He saw screaming refugees engulfed by a giant wave. He saw a hijab, blowing between two rows of poppies. He saw a lone ant, walking in circles across a dirt floor.

Push it away. No time to fuck around now.

'… this is amazing. I've never seen anything like this…'

The motorcade stopped outside the Cultural Centre. Security climbed out first, scanning the crowd. The gunship hovered over Southbank. Shit. If it stayed there, he was in trouble. They'd be onto him in no time.

Andrew Cardinal climbed out of the car, followed by wife and kids. Waved to the crowd. The roar was so loud Harry heard it through the window, as well as on the video stream. Through the reticle he saw Cardinal's head, bobbing forward as he shook hands with well-wishers.

Harry began his breathing cycle. He pushed away the intense pain in his back. It was happening to someone else. It was happening to Rob. He saw Rob lying on his front, Rabs bent over him. Outlining an avenging angel.

It didn't matter now.

'… the crowd's engulfed him. They're literally mobbing him now…'

Shit!

He couldn't get a clear shot. Police moved in, trying to get Cardinal clear and move the people back. Andrew Cardinal was loving it. His family stood aside, letting the people have their moment with the next prime minister.

Through the reticle, Harry saw Andrew Cardinal's head bob up. Then someone moved in front of him. Harry waited.

You'll get the shot. Just wait.

When Cardinal moved towards the Cultural Centre

doors, he'd be clear of the crowd. He'd turn and… *bam*.

As predicted, Cardinal stepped away from the crowd. Turned. Offered one final wave.

Now.

Harry blinked the sweat out of his eyes. It took all the strength he could muster to resist the urge to curl his finger. The finger tightened slightly. Halfway. A little more. An intense itching sensation, in the centre of his brain. And all he had to do was…

'No!'

Harry pushed the gun away. The heavy stock clunked against the desk.

Rob surged; Harry lost control. His impulse was to return to the gun and fire every round in the magazine until it clicked empty, regardless of the target, regardless of how many innocents were killed in the process.

Instead, Harry tipped the other desk over, ripped books off the shelf, tore the drawings off the walls. On one side of the wall was a framed Wallabies jersey. Harry grabbed it and threw it at the window. Already weakened, the glass shattered, shards tumbling to the street below.

Harry punched the wall, ignoring the burst of pain up his arm. He kicked the bookshelf, sending design manuals tumbling across the floor. He came out of the fugue panting, leaning on the desk, looking at the gun as though he'd never seen it before. Outside, the gunship hovered, facing the office building. Had they seen the glass?

Harry disassembled the rifle, slotting the components back into the case quickly as the chopper buzzed across the river. His hand pulsed painfully. He ignored it, grabbing the case. The room was a disaster zone but there was nothing he could do about it. He ran for the elevator, pushed the button, then thought better of it and continued to the stairs. As he pushed through the door, he heard the lift pinging on his floor. He imagined the security guard, poking his nose in. How long before he figured out which office it was?

Halfway down the stairwell, Harry's phone started ringing. He glanced at the screen. Fred. He'd call him back.

He took the steps three at a time, his shoulder hitting the concrete wall at each landing. He stopped at the ground floor, panting. Then decided to take the stairs down to the car park.

In the basement, Harry shrugged out of the overalls and shoved them in the bin. He pulled the Sunshine Air Conditioning stickers off the case and put them in the bin also. Then he walked towards the fire exit door, case banging against his leg. Pushed through out onto George Street, then back towards Queen Street Mall.

Dazed, Harry looked at the teenagers gathered outside Hungry Jack's. Teenagers. Without a care in the world. He spotted some cops, but they were watching the teenagers, bored. The case suddenly felt incredibly heavy. Harry forced himself to continue until he was out of sight of the police, then found a spare bench and sat down, breathing heavily.

His phone rang again. Fred.

'Fred. I can't…'

'It's not Fred. It's Bill.'

'Bill?'

Harry felt sweat prickling his scalp.

'Harry, you'd better get over here.'

'Why? What's happened?'

'It's Fred…'

Harry felt the world drop away. His peripheral vision

disappeared. He felt as though he were staring down a long, dark tunnel.

'He's been attacked.'

'What? Where?'

'The ambos just arrived. Get over here.'

CHAPTER 41

Two paramedics wheeled Fred out on a gurney. For a moment Harry thought the white sheet was pulled over his face, and heavy dread settled on his chest. He saw the front page in his mind: *WWII vet dies in home invasion*.

Then the stretcher turned on the driveway and Harry realised the sheet was tucked up under Fred's chin, the old man's face so white it was barely indistinguishable.

Harry ran for the stretcher.

'How is he? What happened?'

The paramedics kept wheeling him towards the ambulance. 'It's his heart,' one of them said, dark glasses shielding his eyes from the afternoon sun. 'He's going to be okay. You his son?'

'No, just a friend.'

The other paramedic looked doubtfully at Harry's notebook, clutched in one hand. He didn't even remember grabbing it. Then the medico saw the look on Harry's face and his expression softened.

'Some mongrels roughed him up,' he said, shaking his head.

Harry looked up and saw Bill waiting at the top of the stairs. The screen door, the special 'burglar-proof' screen door, was hanging off its hinges.

'Was he hurt?'

'Bill reckons Fred gave as good as he got. But the fright. His heart gave out. Cops are meant to be here, when they can get their arses into gear.'

Harry looked down at Fred. The old man's chest rose and fell, his lungs rattled. Harry held his hand. It felt cool to the touch.

'You sure he's going to be okay?' Harry asked.

The paramedic with the sunglasses shrugged. 'As sure as we can be with someone his age. We're taking him to the Royal, if you want to catch him later.'

'Thanks.'

Harry walked up the garden. The anger was building again.

'Come in,' Bill said.

The first thing Harry noticed were the photos, because that was what he looked at every time he visited Fred. Two of them had fallen over. A few of the other knickknacks, like June's ballerina figurine, had fallen over too, and there were books strewn on the floor. Paperbacks, and a *Reader's Digest*.

'There were two guys,' Bill said. 'Filthy bikies.'

Harry stopped, staring at the TV, which had been tipped over.

'Bikies?'

He turned to Bill. His hands were shaking.

'Yeah. I came over to talk to him about the tower. I saw the two Harleys out front. Heard shouting from upstairs.'

Harry's eyes fell to the knife lying in the middle of the lounge-room floor. It was black with blood. There were smears on the carpet. Drops on the linoleum, leading to the front door.

Bill saw Harry's expression. 'That's not Fred's blood,' he said.

Suddenly, it all became too much for Bill and he dropped into one of the chairs around the dining table. Harry was sweating. He wanted to scream.

'They must've jimmied open the screen because when I got up here it was hanging like that. The whole thing's bent out of kilter,' Bill said.

'I heard one of them curse. When I got inside, there were two of them. Fred was over by the sideboard there, with that thing in his hand…' He gestured at the knife in the lounge room. 'White as a sheet. One of them – long greasy hair – was clutching his side, trying to staunch the flow of blood. The other one was moving in. Big fat bastard. Limping, he was.'

Harry nodded. He didn't need any further description. He knew who they were. He knew why they were here.

'I just yelled out. Screamed like a crazy man. Grabbed a frying pan…'

Harry noticed it on the dining table.

'… and just screamed at them. Fred collapsed. And they bolted. Fucking cowards.'

Bill shook his head. Harry walked over to the knife. He could feel Rob back there in his mind. The tattoos on his body were warm. Chook was right. These people only understood one thing.

Harry dropped to his haunches. What he'd first taken for a knife was actually a bayonet. Now he saw it properly, he wondered how he could have mistaken it for anything else.

'I saw him use that, in North Africa,' Bill said. Harry stared at the blood. He felt his own blood pulsing behind his eyes. Closed his eyes and saw a woman, spread-eagle on a cold concrete floor. Smelled the blood and the piss and he shit. Smelled the fear.

'You think you can leave it behind,' Bill said. 'The violence. The death. But part of it always comes back with you.'

Bill knelt beside Harry. 'He's never spoken about it. Not even to me. We were near El Alamein. Total chaos. We both ran out of ammo and suddenly we had a Kraut tank crew in our foxhole.

'Don't know who was more surprised, us or them. Fred didn't hesitate. And when I saw him going for it, I hooked in too. It wasn't pretty.'

Harry couldn't talk. He nodded. Took a deep breath. 'If the cops find this, he's going to be in the shit.'

Bill stared at him. 'If the cops find what?' He picked up the bayonet, took it down the hallway. Harry heard the bathroom sink filling up. Harry went to the kitchen, got a rag and mopped up the spots of blood.

When Bill returned, his face was wet. Harry washed out the rag and threw it in the bin.

'Good thing the cops are taking so long,' Harry said. 'Did you hear what they were saying? The bikies?'

Bill put his hands on his hips. 'Well, Fred was telling them to get the fuck out of his house. And they... You know already, don't you?'

Harry nodded. 'Yeah, but I need to hear you say it.'

'They were looking for you. "Where's Hendrick? Where's Hendrick?" Over and over again. What the fuck are you in for, Harry?'

'Trust me. You don't want to know.'

CHAPTER 42

The building site was just under a kilometre from the Dreadnorts' clubhouse. The place was meant to be for a new hotel with speciality shops underneath, before the global financial crisis sank it. Now it was just a concrete skeleton, surrounded by a collapsing temporary fence, scaffolding and broken streamers of faded caution tape.

Harry parked at the back of a run-down row of shops. He was barely there, operating on automatic while Rob looked after the finer points. Harry was exhausted, and he felt bad leaving Bill behind waiting for the cops. But Rob still had work to do. He got out, grabbed his knapsack, pulled the case out of the boot and walked towards the building site. He kept an eye out for watchers in his peripheral vision, but only stopped to check properly once he was standing in the shadow of one of the graffiti-scarred concrete pylons.

He scanned the surroundings. Cars passed by on the main road but there was a screen of bushes between the road and the building site. The stench of urine rose up from somewhere further back in the gloom, mixing with the more appetising aroma of roast chicken, coming from the shops over the way. Satisfied no-one was watching, he moved towards the back of the building site. The ground was covered in litter: beer bottles, chip and lolly packets, a bong fashioned out of a plastic orange-juice bottle, a used condom.

He found the disused scaffolding he'd spied from the road. Harry hefted the case, pushed it onto the lowest level. Then jumped and pulled himself up, his muscles bulging as he clambered onto the platform. It was a feat he would not have been able to accomplish a few weeks earlier. Rob had given him strength, and knowledge. That was the upside. The downside…

He picked up the case, pushed the thought away. Visualised Crow lying on the side of the road, shivering. Heathy, pulling his hand away, black with blood.

There's only one language these people understand.

I would say that this magic would require blood to satisfy it.

From the scaffolding he climbed onto the building, took the stairs to the second-highest level, then laid down the case and opened it. Assembled the gun while looking out across the mix of shops, suburbia and industrial estate. The clubhouse was a low-set brick building off in the middle distance.

As the light drained from the sky, Harry spread out a blanket and set up the gun. He opened the ammo case and chose a round with light-blue paint on the tip. He lay down, shifted his body weight until he was comfortable, and stared through the sight. His back throbbed. He focused on what he could see through the scope.

Tile roofs. Blur. Tin sheds. Blur. A low-set brick building. Dreadnorts MC sign over the double door.

The M82's round would go through that door from this distance, but that wasn't what Harry and Rob were interested in. The windows on the front of the building were screened on the outside, thick curtains on the inside. A round through the door or window would serve no purpose.

Other than the throbbing in his back, the wait was quite pleasant. There was a steady breeze up here, and unlike at road level, it was relatively cool and didn't stink of petrol and urine. In a nearby tree, noisy mynahs hassled a murder of crows until the big black birds got the hint and took flight, cawing at the indignity of it all.

Harry took another look through the sight, then rolled his neck to loosen it. He looked away. Saw a dead bird, tucked behind a concrete pylon. Its flesh was gone. All that remained was bleached bone and a few feathers.

An ant wandered across the concrete wall. *Do you want to cut, or dig?* Harry wondered how long it had taken it to climb this high. Whether it had come all the way from the ground, or whether the ants managed to survive on the seventh floor. What would they eat? There were tags up here – there were tags on the roof no doubt – but these were the tags of adventurers. There weren't as many as on the ground floor. So it's unlikely a colony of ants would survive on the meagre scraps brought by adventurous taggers.

Movement. Harry pressed his eye to the scope. The Harleys announced their presence as they came down the highway, and then Harry watched as they pulled up at the clubhouse in ones and twos. It was Church. All full members had to attend. That meant Heathy. That meant Crow. And, to be frank, Harry wanted to destroy the culture that had allowed these two scumbags to thrive. The culture that had facilitated Cardinal's rise to power.

The front gate opened. The Harleys pulled in and parked next to the LPG tanks lined up against the side of the building. The guys climbed off their hogs; they seemed to be laughing about something. They filed into the building.

When Heathy climbed off his bike, the white bandage wrapped around his torso glowed in the gloom. And Harry was glad to see Crow still walking with a pronounced limp. He wondered what they would tell their mates.

Harry flexed his fingers. Crow and Heathy lit up cigarettes, stood there smoking for a while. Harry settled the reticle on Heathy's forehead, caressed the trigger. But no, that wasn't quite what he was looking for. Harry wanted to give them something else to worry about.

Crow followed as Heathy sauntered around the side of the building. Harry followed them with the scope, then shifted his focus. Harry started his breathing routine. A small plume of smoke came out of Crow's mouth.

The M82 barked and kicked against his shoulder. The incendiary round covered the distance between Harry and the clubhouse in just over a second. There was a fraction of a second before the round ignited the gas in the LPG tanks at the side of the building.

There was a blinding flash, followed by a loud crack and whump as the fireball blasted into the sky, engulfing everything in a fifty-metre radius. The force of the blast threw Crow and Heathy across the forecourt. Harry watched them through the scope. At first he thought they were dead, but then they stirred, clawing their way along the ground with their backs on fire. Harry fancied he could hear their screams.

The side of the clubhouse was flaming rubble. The gum tree at the back of the compound ignited. The front doors burst open and Dreadnorts rushed out, one of them carrying a shotgun. The intensity of the heat pushed them back towards where Heathy and Crow were crawling.

Secondary explosions tore the air as more of the tanks cooked off. Crow was out the gates now. Heathy crawled after him, still on fire. One of the other bikies dragged him across the concrete, while another smothered the flames with a leather jacket. Other Dreadnorts, some injured, staggered out after them.

Sirens warbled through the streets below, from behind Harry on the main road. There was no reason for anyone to think this was anything other than a tragic accident. They would review the video footage from the security system. Unless it was a very good system, and unless they knew exactly what to look for, they would see nothing suspicious. No sign of forced entry. It would look as though one of the tanks had spontaneously ignited.

The fire brigade arrived first, red lights pulsing through the darkness. Through the scope Harry watched them assessing the danger, unravelling hoses and spraying the fire from a safe distance. An ambulance arrived, paramedics checking over Heathy and Crow, and the other injured bikies. The big man pushed them away, clambering to his feet and gesticulating. They shifted Heathy onto a stretcher, loaded him into the ambulance and took him away. Two police cars arrived next. Detectives would follow.

Harry's legs quivered. The sensation ran up his body. He pulled himself to his feet, turned away from the blanket. He made it a few steps across the concrete and then vomited. He stood, heaving, eyes watering, nose burning. His legs sagged and he dropped to the concrete as the world swam out of focus.

Harry's hands shook uncontrollably. He held them

between his knees, rolled onto his back. The breeze that had felt nice half an hour ago now felt Arctic. His teeth chattered.

His body convulsed again, but nothing came up this time. A steady throb built in the centre of his head. He crawled to his knapsack, pulled out a water bottle. The drink tasted metallic and warm and it was an effort to keep it down. He walked closer to the edge, then sat down leaning against a concrete pylon.

An unmarked police car pulled up and parked across the road from the Dreadnorts' clubhouse. The firies were dousing the last of the blaze. Through the smoke, Harry could see two detectives talking to a Dreadnort on the far side of the compound. One had his notebook out. The other had his hands on his hips. Harry doubted either of them would shed a tear about the accident.

Harry drifted. He was back under the house, staring at the crack in the concrete. He was under the slab, cocooned by the cold, dark earth. He was lying on the ground, while Crow and Heathy decided who was going to cut and who was going to dig.

CHAPTER 43

Harry kept his eyes down as he exited the elevator, glancing up briefly to get his bearings. He ignored the nurses' station, instead following the directions Dave had texted him.

Dave was waiting outside the room when Harry arrived. He looked scared, and he had good reason to be. Dave had taken Heathy to the wrong room, on the wrong floor.

'Don't be long,' Dave said. 'There're cops downstairs. It won't take them long to figure out he's missing.'

Dave opened the door for Harry, then closed it behind him.

The room was dimly lit. There were a couple of chairs. A blank TV bolted to the wall. A window looking out on the northern suburbs. And Heathy, lying in his bed, white covers pulled up around him. His head was bandaged. His arms were lying on top of the covers, enclosed in beige pressure bandages. A heart-rate monitor bleeped at his side.

Harry grabbed a chair and wedged it under the door handle. Heathy looked up. He was clearly expecting a nurse, or a doctor, or the cops.

'What the…'

Harry pulled up the other chair, sat down. Opened his notebook.

'What do you know about Rob and Kyla's disappearance?'

'Fuck you.'

This close, Harry could smell singed hair. Could see the blistering skin beside Heathy's eye, causing the tear tattoo to bulge.

'Okay,' Harry said. 'Here's what I know. I know that you and Crow served with Andrew Cardinal in Afghanistan. I know that you took part in rape and mass murder while you were over there. I know that you helped Cardinal set up a drugs operation here. And that you brokered a deal with Brian Swenson to launder the money…'

Heathy grinned, then winced as the damaged skin pulled tight. He chuckled. 'There's a difference between knowing and proving, Harry. A big difference.'

Harry felt Rob trying to surge, but Harry needed information.

'Where are the cops, Harry?' Heathy said. Harry's eyes darted to one side. Heathy's grin grew, despite his burned and blistered lips. 'Naughty, naughty. Your friend brought me to the wrong room, didn't he?'

'I know that you and Crow tried to wipe out all links to the operation when Cardinal decided to go straight. I know about the Black Hawk sabotage. The IED Crow planted. I know about Rabs. Ahmed. Rob and Kyla.'

Heathy reached over for the remote control and turned on the TV. Canned laughter issued forth. He laughed.

'My lips are sealed, buddy,' he said. He glanced at the TV, then back at Harry. 'Did you have fun the other night? I said to Crow afterwards, we should have gone in with the knives earlier. Like Cardinal did with…'

Rob surged again, and this time Harry couldn't hold him back. Harry leapt out of his chair, grabbed Heathy's chin and squeezed. Heathy cried out. Harry leant over him.

'Look! Look at me!'

Heathy looked. His eyes widened. The heart monitor beeped faster. Harry opened his shirt. 'Look, you piece of shit.'

Harry showed off Rob's tattoos. Heathy shook his head.

'No. No-no-no!'

'Yep.'

'You're dead. You're fucking dead!'

Harry leant over the bed. Heathy struggled to free himself from the covers, but they were pulled too tight and he was too weak. He lashed out with his hand and Harry caught it. Squeezed. Leant forward with his other hand and shoved it against Heathy's mouth, stifling the scream. He felt warm fluid seep over his fingers as the blisters burst.

'Heathy. You're going to tell me what I want to know.'

Harry grabbed his pen, pressed it against the side of Heathy's eyeball. Held the bikie's head steady with his other hand. Heathy was sweating now, his skin grey under the red burns. Harry pushed back. Rob retreated slightly.

'It's Rob,' Harry said. 'Believe it, Heathy. Tell him what he wants to know.'

Heathy panted, whimpered. 'You know it all!' he yelled. The pen jerked forwards, pressing deep under Heathy's eyeball.

'Shhhhhh,' Harry said.

'You know it all. Why do you need me to tell you? Those fuckers in Afghanistan. They deserved it, right? Blowing us up every day. Every fucking day. IEDs. RPGs. Having to live with that shit and for what? For what the ADF thought it was worth? Deployment allowance?

'Bullshit. That's bullshit. If we didn't make money out of those poppies, they would've. More money for the Taliban. More money for the warlords.'

'What about the kids? And rape? Did she deserve it?'

Heathy's chest heaved. Tears flowed out of the corners of his eyes. 'That was Cardinal,' Heathy said, barely a whisper. 'Cardinal. He's fucking sick.'

'And you let him do it?'

Heathy shrugged.

'What about Vessel? How much does he know?'

Heathy's eyes lost focus. He stared straight ahead. Outside, Dave was talking to someone. Harry couldn't make out the words. Footsteps, heading away from the door.

Harry climbed onto the bed. He laid his knee against Heathy's arm and pressed. Heathy groaned. His eyes rolled back in his head. Harry slapped his face.

'What. About. Vessel?'

'He's… he's like Cardinal's controller. Keeps him on track.' Heathy shook his head. 'Helps him find an outlet for his… his urges.'

'Urges?'

'You know… like Kyla.'

Rob surged forward again, so hard that Harry almost blacked out. Harry grabbed Heathy's hair through the bandages and squeezed. Shoved the pen sideways in Heathy's mouth to muffle the scream.

'What do you mean?' He removed the pen.

'Vessel sets up meetings. Women. Women who won't be missed.'

Harry's mind reeled. Outside, there was a commotion. Dave's voice rose. This time, Harry could make out the words. He thrust his hand over Heathy's mouth.

'I've been told we could use this room!'

Someone mumbling.

'Well, go and check it!'

Footsteps. A knock on the door. Harry was running out of time.

'One last question, Heathy,' he said.

Heathy's eyes moved to the door. Harry pressed the pen against his eyeball again. 'I swear to god, I will kill you if I have to.'

'Okay,' Heathy said. 'Okay.'

'Where's the dossier?'

'The what?'

'The information. The stuff Rob had.'

Heathy laughed. Flinched as the pen stabbed towards his eye. 'The dossier? You think I know? That's why we came after you. After the old guy. Cardinal and Vessel think you've got it. They're shitting themselves!'

Rob tried to surge again and Harry dragged himself away from the bed, groaning in frustration. If he stayed here any longer, he'd find himself up on murder charges.

Heathy shook his head. 'You had it all mapped out, ya silly prick. All except the most important part! Watch ya back.'

Harry removed the chair from under the door handle, opened the door a crack, looked up and down the corridor. Dave had moved a few metres towards the nurses' station, anticipating the return of whoever had rightful claim on the room. He looked back at Harry.

'Go. Get the fuck outta here,' Dave mouthed.

Harry slipped out of the room and down the corridor away from the nurses' station, taking the fire exit to head downstairs.

CHAPTER 44

Fred looked like he was sleeping, or dead. Lying in the bed, staring out the window with glazed eyes. His papery skin looked translucent in the pale light filtering through the windows. Harry stood in the doorway, barely breathing.

Fred sensed him standing there and turned his head.

'I thought visiting hours were over,' he said, waving Harry in and wincing as the cannula pulled at his arm. 'What time is it?'

'About nine. When you know a nurse you can almost get away with murder,' Harry said, thinking of Dave's pinched expression as he snuck out from Heathy's room. 'I can't stay long.'

'You all right?' Fred said. 'You look a bit peaky.'

Harry rubbed his face. 'Exhausted. Trying to tie up a few loose ends. You know how it is. Anyway, you're the one who had the heart attack.'

Fred waved it away. 'Yeah. Just gave me a bit of a fright, that's all.'

'You had a heart attack.'

'Yeah, well that's what happens when blokes my age get a bit of a fright.'

He looked back out the window.

'I'm sorry,' Harry said.

'Nah. Don't be. Old busybody like me – it's bound to happen sooner or later.'

'But if I hadn't…'

'Harry. Come on. You're doing your job, right?'

Harry sat in silence. There was so much he'd done lately that wasn't his job at all. It was Rob's job. Getting the bad guys. But Fred was almost up on his elbows now, ready for a fight. So Harry said nothing until he settled down again.

'Besides, let's face it, if someone is out to get us, I'm safer here,' he said.

Harry thought of Heathy, one floor up. But he didn't consider him a threat anymore. 'I think you'll be pretty safe now, regardless.'

Once he was out of the hospital, he pulled out his phone. It had been such a massive day. He was beyond exhausted. But Rob drew from a well of strength Harry didn't know a person could possess. He dialled the number, muttering to himself as the phone rang over and over again. Finally, she answered.

'Jess?'

'Harry?' she sounded sleepy. 'What time is it?'

'It's late. I'm sorry. It's been a hell of a day. Can I come over?'

'What? Where are you?'

'Please.'

Silence.

'Of course. Drive… drive safely.'

In the car, he called Dave.

'Haven't I done enough for you tonight?' he said. He

sounded like he was only half-joking, but that was fair enough.

'Thank you,' Harry said.

'Did you get what you needed?'

'No. I'm sorry.'

Dave hissed in frustration. 'Harry. Take it to the cops.'

'I can't. I need to finish this.'

A pause. 'Is that why you called me, so we could have this fight all over again?'

'No. I called to warn you. Do you and Ellie have somewhere to stay until this blows over?'

Dave cursed. 'You really are stretching our friendship, mate.'

'I know. I'm sorry. A carton of beer isn't going to cover this one, is it?'

A pause.

'Throw in a bottle of Bundy and you're getting closer. Don't worry about it. I'll give Simmo a call. Where are you going to camp?'

'I'm going to pick up Jess and then see if Christine can put us up for a while.'

'Burning all your bridges, mate. Good to see.'

'Yep. To the ground. I'll give you a call when I know anything new. Take care.'

'Thanks, mate. You too.'

CHAPTER 45

Harry pulled up outside Jess's place. Relief flooded through him when he saw the curtain twitch and her face peer out. She met him at the front door wearing just a singlet and underpants.

'I'm sorry,' he said.

'No, it was…'

Harry placed his fingertips gently against her lips. 'No, don't do that. I'm sorry.'

She looked up at him, then stepped up and kissed him on the lips. He kissed her too, hands on the back of her head, entwined in her hair. Like that, they shuffled into the house. Harry shouldered the front door closed. Jess dragged him to the bedroom.

They kissed again, more deeply this time. He pulled away, took off his shirt and then her singlet. He touched her bare skin, kissed her tattoos, kissing away the pain they represented. Goosebumps rose on her skin.

She tugged at his pants. He eased her down onto the bed. All thoughts of Cardinal, Vessel and everything else were wiped away. And then he was inside her. They writhed against each other, kissed and bit each other, clawed at each other.

His tattoos burned on his skin, like petrol had ignited just under the surface. He cried out, part pain part ecstasy. Squeezed his eyes shut. Below him, Jess mirrored his cries. There was an echo. He opened his eyes. His breath caught. Jess was sheathed in a delicate azure light. Her tattoos burned a deep, electric blue.

She too opened her eyes, and from the expression on her face he could tell that she saw it as well, on him. Then she pulled him down to her, into her, and they kissed. The room spun. Everything that he saw and heard felt doubled up.

In the moment of her release he heard two women crying out, their voices overlapping.

Harry slumped down on top of Jess, whispering in her ear. He didn't recognise the words. They weren't his. He slid off her, to the side, the pillow cool against his face.

'What was that?' he said.

Jess didn't answer. Because she knew he knew. Harry drifted, listening to her breathing, and the sound of the wind outside. The pain from the tattoos disappeared as quickly as it appeared. Just the now-familiar ache in his lower back. He thought he was going to drift off to sleep, and then he spoke.

'I was across the river, at the launch today, staring through the scope at Cardinal,' he said. 'Rob was so angry when I didn't pull the trigger.'

Jess rolled to face him. 'This morning, I found myself standing by the front door, in a daze. I'd packed a bag. You know, hat, sunscreen, paperback to read on the train, a kitchen knife... Kyla wanted to stab him.'

Harry thought about the back-up plans Rob had set in place. If he hadn't been able to get a sniper's rifle, he would have wanted an assault rifle. If he couldn't get an assault rifle, a pistol or a shottie would have done. If not those, then a knife, just as Kyla had been planning.

Harry ran his hand down her arm. 'Whatever happens, I'm here for you,' he said.

Jess snuggled into him. Harry kissed the tattoo on her arm.

He thought sleep would come easily, but it didn't. He lay in bed, watching the gauzy curtains billow slightly in the breeze. His eyes roamed the room. Wedding photos of Jess and her husband sat on top of the dark wooden dresser. Suits and shirts hung in the walk-in wardrobe. On the wall beside the bedroom door hung a framed map of Brisbane, commemorating Expo '88, with clowns and mime artists and mascots cavorting.

You had it all mapped out, ya silly prick. Except the most important part.

Goosebumps rose on Harry's arm. He stared at the map, but saw Tim in Afghanistan, checking the map and calling in the coordinates of the massacre.

Right around Brisbane's western suburbs, we're moving to protect icons that have been allowed to rot for too long.

Harry saw a map of Christmas Island, surrounded by lines, with areas shaded red. Then the Expo '88 map came into focus, his eyes settled on the clown, waving at the camera.

It's not exactly a winning hand.

'Oh shit,' Harry said. 'How could I have missed it?'

CHAPTER 46

Jess, Dave and Christine stood around Christine's kitchen table as Harry rolled out a Quantity Surveying map of Brisbane. It was marked with little red crosses.

Harry flicked through the photos on his phone, until he found the one of Jess's cardplayer.

'It never made any sense, right? What sort of hand is this? What sort of game involves holding that many cards?' Harry said.

Dave started to speak. Harry cut him off. 'I know there are such games, but in tattoos?'

He zoomed in. 'And see here, on the third card?' he said.

Christine squinted. 'It's like a full stop.'

'Exactly. Read the numbers out to me.'

Christine took the phone and read out the numbers. Harry looked up and down the side of the map, at the numbers written there. He picked up his red pencil and a ruler.

'I'll have to estimate a bit, because the scale doesn't go down that far.'

Harry marked each side of the map at the right spot. 'Grab that piece of string, Dave,' he said.

He looked up at Christine and shook his head in

admiration. Despite his arse-hattery on awards night, when he and Jess had rocked up on her doorstep on Sunday morning she didn't bombard him with questions. She just said, 'How can I help?'

Dave picked up the string, held it to the dot Harry had drawn. Harry did the same on the other side, bisecting the map about a third of the way down.

'Rob was meant to get the other tattoo, the longitude. But they ran out of time. Kyla only managed to get hers because she escaped the bikie raid. It was the last tattoo she ever got. And it represents this line across Brisbane.'

Dave assessed. 'That's a lot of ground to cover.'

'Yeah. Except, we don't have to. We know that Cardinal developed a penchant for property investment after Rob and Kyla went missing. He's has been buying up little pieces of property all over the city. Places of significance.'

'But why?' Dave said.

'Because of the last thing Rob said. He told them that the dossier was hidden somewhere…'

'Somewhere special,' Jess said.

Harry traced the line, until it intersected with one of the red crosses he'd drawn earlier. Dave squinted, trying to make sense of the map.

'It's Paddington water tower,' Harry said.

'Fuck me,' Dave said.

'Rob lived just over the other side from where Cardinal's dad lived,' Harry said. 'It was close, convenient.'

'Why not a safety deposit box?' Jess asked.

'He was worried about it falling into the wrong hands. He knew Cardinal had some powerful friends. Assumed police might be among those friends.'

'Shit,' Christine said. 'Surely they would have searched

it. Cardinal's had his grubby little hands on it for long enough.'

Harry shrugged. 'If they searched, they didn't find it. I'm guessing that's why the big push to restore the tower rather than knock it down. You knock something down, who knows what's going to come tumbling out of it.'

Dave stood up. 'Well then, let's go, right?'

'He's got the place under surveillance,' Harry said.

'So what? We get the evidence and we take it to the police.'

'If we get that far,' Jess said.

'What? They've got people waiting around the corner?'

Jess shrugged. 'Maybe. Crow is still out there, right? Heathy's probably checked himself out of hospital. They're not exactly in Cardinal's good books at the moment. They'd be looking to make amends.'

Harry took the string away, folded up the map. 'I don't think it's going to be a case of opening up the water tower and "Ta-dah!"'

'And we don't know exactly what's in the dossier,' Jess said. 'We need to make sure we've got time to sort through it, without bikies after us.'

'Vessel and Cardinal know that Heathy and Crow failed. They're going to suspect I had something to do with the attack on the clubhouse.

'Look, Saturday's election day. They're going to be extremely busy. They'll think they've won. We can't make a mistake with this. We've only got one shot. We just need to lie low until then.'

CHAPTER 47

Harry and Christine sat at her kitchen table, laptops open. Jess looked over Harry's shoulder. He was working on two articles, with Jess's help. One about Rob and Kyla's murder. The other about what happened in Afghanistan. Harry was flicking between his articles and several news sites for updates. Election-day polling booths were closed; votes were being counted. Pundits were still predicting a Labor whitewash. Harry hadn't voted. He added it to the mental list of bad things he'd done lately, alongside almost assassinating Andrew Cardinal and demolishing a bikie clubhouse.

After the map revelation, Jess had suggested they write up what they already knew, even though they didn't have access to the documents that would allow them to verify the story. If nothing else, it had helped the time pass faster in the lead-up to Saturday and eased the frustration of watching Vessel and Cardinal cavorting on national television, as it became clearer that nothing was going to stop them. Christine returned to work on Tuesday. Dave decided it would be too risky going back to the hospital, so had called in sick, as had Jess. Dave and Ellie were hanging out at the granny flat at Simmo's place.

Christine was writing some pen pictures of Vessel, Cardinal and Swenson, and some other key players. She'd already managed to dig up Keith 'Crow' Crowther and Heath 'Heathy' Travill's real names, and write a piece on their involvement with Dreadnorts MC.

Harry checked his watch. It was getting dark. Christine looked up. 'Heard from Dave yet?'

'No. I left a message on his phone. Maybe he's had enough of the insanity.'

It was weird though. In spite of everything, Dave had been there for him. It seemed odd that at the critical moment he'd bug out. Harry picked up his phone for the umpteenth time to check he hadn't missed a message somehow. He left his computer and went into the lounge room, checking the bag of gear they'd gathered for their water tower visit: torches, a rope ladder, crowbar.

'Harry,' Jess called out to him. 'Your phone.'

She handed it to him. He looked at the screen. Relief ran through him.

'Dave! Where…'

'Not quite, Harry, although he is here with me. It's Keith. You may know me as Crow. I'll put Davey on.'

'Harry?' He was terrified.

'Dave!'

Thunder boomed. The line crackled.

'Harry. I'm sorry. I went home for my surfboard. Stupid…'

There was the crack of flesh on flesh, and then a muffled yell.

'Dave? Dave!'

'He's okay,' Crow said. 'Just a love tap.'

'He doesn't know anything!'

'We know he doesn't, Harry. Me and Heathy were after you and when we saw this cunt rock up, we figured he owed us one.

'Heathy told me all about what happened at the hospital. You reckon Rob's inside you? Well, Rob knows where the documents are.'

'If I knew where they were…'

'Shut it! I want the documents, Harry. Don't fuck me around. Do whatever mumbo-jumbo seance bullshit you need to do to get Rob to spill his guts. If you can't, your mate's gonna be spilling his. You've got fifteen minutes.'

Harry's stomach rolled. The hairs stood up on his arms. 'Okay. Where?'

'The old skate rink. I'm guessing you know where it is.'

The line went dead. Outside, thunder boomed again, and rain splattered down. The world closed in on Harry and he wanted to smash it all apart. *I should've pulled the trigger. I should've pulled that fucking trigger.* Then he felt Jess's hand on his shoulder. He sat down on the floor, put this head in his hands and sucked in a deep breath. Let it out and sucked in another.

'What? What is it?' Jess said.

'Crowther,' Harry said. 'He's got Dave. Shit!' He stood up and rubbed his face. Christine walked into the room from the kitchen, a concerned look on her face.

'He wants me to try and summon Rob, or something.'

'Can you even do that?' Jess said.

Harry looked up, sweat stung his eye. 'No. I don't think so. It doesn't work like that. But we know where the documents are now.'

'So you're just going to tell him?' Christine said.

'What do you want me to do, Chris? He's got Dave. This isn't a fucking movie!'

'I know it's not, Harry,' she said. 'But you've worked your arse off on this. You go down there and give them what they want and Cardinal gets away with it all. Again.'

'I've got fifteen minutes.'

'Shit!' Christine went back to the kitchen. Harry could hear her pounding away on a keyboard. 'I'll be damned if these fuckers get away with this.'

'What are you doing?' He and Jess followed her back to the kitchen.

'Putting all this stuff in the cloud. And emailing it to Miles, and me, and you.'

Harry shook his head. 'It doesn't matter, Chris. Without the documents, it's meaningless.'

'Bullshit, Harry! That is total bullshit. Don't you get it? You had most of the story. You got it yourself! Rob didn't know about the Swenson connection. He didn't know about the property deals.'

Harry pressed his hands against his eyelids. 'It doesn't matter. It's over.'

'Harry, come on. Do you really think delivering yourself to them is going to save you?'

Harry shook his head. 'Have you got a better idea?'

'Yeah. Yeah, I do.'

CHAPTER 48

The Paddington skating rink was rapidly returning to the state nature intended. Weeds pushed themselves up from the charred remains of the building where thousands of teenagers once spent their Saturday nights. A couple of young gum trees reached for the open roof. As the wind picked up, chip packets and sheets of old newspaper rustled around in the darkness, looking for escape. Harry peered up through the skeletal remains of the skate rink's roof. The stars were gone, obscured by clouds. Every now and then lightning flickered through them, followed a couple of seconds later by a boom of thunder. Jess snaked her fingers through his.

They waited. A gentle rain fell. Harry started to think that this was a trap, or that he'd gone to the wrong place and Dave was already dead. Then a car pulled up outside, headlights panning across the open doorway. Car doors opened and shut, and a silhouette appeared in the doorway of the rink. Crow waited, hiding behind Dave, letting his eyes adjust to the gloom. He moved forward towards Harry and pushed Dave down onto the ground. Dave's hands were tied behind his back, his face mottled with bruises and dried blood.

'Harry, I'm sorry, don't…'

Crow silenced him with a kick, and pointed his gun at him.

'Harry Hendrick! Or should I call you Rob?' he said. As he emerged from the gloom, the light fell across his face. He was grinning. He turned to Jess. 'Strange idea for a date, but whatever floats ya boat, I guess.'

Heathy appeared behind them, took up position halfway between Crow and Harry. He had a big black shotgun. His face was a mess of half-healed scabs.

'Did you choose this place because of Rob? This is where you killed him, right?' Harry said.

Crow snorted. 'Fun times. That's all ancient history, Harry. He was too nosy for his own good. Just like you.'

Jess stepped forward. 'Rob and Kyla didn't deserve what happened to them. They deserve justice.'

This time Crow laughed out loud. 'And what good would that do? Huh? We've all made mistakes. You've made mistakes, right?'

'Mistakes? Is that what you call what you and Cardinal did to those people in Afghanistan? To Ahmed? Rabs? You sabotaged a fucking Black Hawk, for Christ's sake!' He peered into the darkness behind Crow. 'And what you did to Kyla? Rape? Murder? Just a mistake?'

'Jeez, mate, and you call yourself a journo,' Crow said. 'I'll cop it on the chin for most of that but not Kyla. I had nothing to do with Kyla. I was a little busy with Rob. Fingers don't break themselves, y'know. Kyla was all the Chief's work.'

'Andrew Cardinal?' Jess prompted.

'It's one of his specialities. He took her out to Swenson's new block of land. And she didn't come back.'

Heathy snorted.

Lightning flashed, gleaming off the dull metal of Heathy's shotgun. Thunder boomed and for a moment Harry thought he'd pulled the trigger.

'Where are the documents, Rob?'

Dave looked up. 'Harry, don't…'

'Shut it, sunshine,' Crow said. He knelt down behind him, picked up Dave's head and slammed it against the floorboards. With his other hand he pressed the gun into Dave's side, then looked up at Harry. 'You know what a nine-millimetre round will do to his guts from this range? It'll fuck him up but won't kill him. Next time there's thunder, I'm pullin' the trigger.'

Harry could feel Rob back there, but if Rob had any answers, he wasn't sharing. Crow and Dave were a good five metres away, too far to try and rush them. Heathy now had his shotgun up, aiming at him and Jess. He glanced into the darkness. He'd just have to trust Christine.

'Okay! Okay!' he said. 'It's in the water tower! The documents are in the water tower.'

Crow's brow furrowed, he turned his head to one side. Harry's hands shook violently, rain fell into his eyes. Lightning flashed and thunder followed a second or so later. Dave cried out. Crow took the gun away from Dave's side.

'Interesting,' he said. 'Because we searched the water tower, came away with zilcho.'

'I swear,' Harry said. 'That's where they are.' Doubts flew through Harry's mind. What if his map theory was wrong? What if he'd read the map wrong? What if someone else had found the documents and they weren't there anymore?

'If you're lying to me, you know how this ends, right?'

'Get on the floor, both of you,' Heathy said. 'Hands behind your backs.'

Harry lowered himself to the wet floor. He could feel Rob calculating, working out the odds of escape. In the corner of his eye he saw Crow yanking Dave to his feet, as Heathy laid his shotgun on the ground. Harry grunted as Heathy dropped a knee into his back, then pulled his hands together. He grimaced as a cable tie bit into his wrists. As Heathy moved to secure Jess, he looked to her and mouthed 'Sorry'. She blinked it away and shook her head with reassurance.

Heathy slammed his foot down in the small of Harry's back, sending an explosion of pain through him. He started to black out, and Heathy grabbed his hair and shook him awake.

'That's for that shit you pulled in the hospital,' he said, then laughed. *Hyuck, hyuck, hyuck.*

He dragged Harry to his feet. Then Jess.

'Come on, let's go,' Crow said.

CHAPTER 49

In the back seat of Crow and Heathy's battered Ford Falcon, Harry sat slouched against the door, waves of pain washing over him. Jess was wedged in the middle between him and Dave. Harry's hands were going numb, but the worst of it was the nausea-inducing throb coming from the small of his back. The radio was on, tuned to election coverage. Heathy climbed into the passenger seat, while Crow stood out in the rain, talking on his phone. On the other side of the weed-strewn parking lot, Saturday-night traffic streamed along Waterworks Road.

Crow climbed in. 'He's going to meet us there.'

'Isn't that a bit risky?' Heathy said.

'Yeah, well neither of us are in the running for employee of the month, are we?'

He slammed the door and gunned the engine. Heathy cranked the radio.

'Didn't know you were into politics,' Crow said.

'… and as you just heard, Andrew Cardinal has left his election party at the Eastern Suburbs Leagues Club. We're not exactly sure where he's going…'

'Well,' Heathy said, 'It's more interesting when it's interactive.'

Crow pulled out into the Saturday-night traffic. The now-torrential rain pounded on the roof of the car. A woman ran across the road, dress plastered to her skin, trying to protect herself from the deluge with her clutch. Harry willed her to turn around and look. But what would she see? A car full of people. Big deal.

The car powered down Enoggera Terrace, past old Queenslanders and trendy restaurants, then onto Kennedy Terrace, heading through a maze of back streets towards the water tower. The windscreen wipers could barely keep up with the rain. Lightning carved the sky into pieces and the radio buzzed.

'Ever seen an incoming prime minister leave his own victory party so early?' the presenter said.

'Well, the last words of his victory speech were "Let's get to work", so maybe he's leading by example…'

Dave sat slumped forward in the seat, blood dripping from his lips.

'I'm so sorry, Dave,' Harry said. 'You were right, we should have gone to the police.'

Dave shrugged. 'Yeah, maybe. It doesn't matter. This isn't your fault, Harry. It's these fuckers in the front.'

Heathy turned in his seat. 'Yeah, yeah. Just settle, petal. Once Harry finds our gear for us, we'll set you on your merry way and you can kiss and make up.'

Harry doubted that was the case. He doubted any of them would live to tell the tale. Harry had stepped through the veil between the normal world and the underworld, and he'd dragged Jess and Dave with him.

As they pulled up outside the water tower, the car triggered a set of spotlights. The rain had eased off slightly, the drizzle drifting through the sickly yellow light. Crow turned off the engine. From next door came the sounds of someone splashing in a pool, and election coverage competing with the pop music blaring over the sound system. Another seat was called for Labor, and a cheer went up.

'Wouldn't have thought of this area as a Labor stronghold,' Heathy said.

'What isn't a Labor stronghold these days?' Crow replied.

Crow fished around in his pockets for his cigarettes, tapped one out and lit up. The smell of the smoke, coupled with the odour of the decaying upholstery, made Harry feel sick. A set of headlights appeared from the other end of the street, the car moving at a crawl.

'It's showtime,' Crow said. He and Heathy climbed out of the car.

'Harry,' Dave said. 'If I don't get out of this, and you do, tell Ellie I love her.'

'Dave…' But he had no words.

A big black BMW pulled up. The passenger door opened, and in that moment Harry saw Vessel in the driver's seat. He drew a small amount of satisfaction from the fact that the smug expression from that night on the Brisbane Eye was gone, replaced by fear. Then the door slammed, the light went out, and Vessel was just a silhouette, a faceless man again.

Cardinal strode over to the Falcon, suit flapping in the wind.

'Where is he? Where is the shit? Give me your gun.'

Crow handed over his pistol. Cardinal pulled open the door, yanked Harry out by his shirt and thrust him up against the side of the car. He jammed the pistol up under his chin.

GARY KEMBLE

'Come on,' he said. 'Let's go get us some documents.'

He turned on Heathy and Crow. 'Seeing as you two numbnuts are incapable of doing anything but fucking up lately, I'll keep this simple. Heathy, grab the backpack out of the car and come with me. Harry and Jess are coming up with us. Crow, make sure this one doesn't escape. Do you think you can manage that without a gun?'

'Sure, boss,' Crow said.

Cardinal thrust Harry to one side and reached into the car for Jess. She tried to kick him but he grabbed her hair and yanked her out, dropping her in the mud. He put his boot on her back and pushed down. Harry moved forward but then Heathy was there, shotgun raised. Cardinal pocketed the gun and pulled out a pen knife. He opened the blade.

'New fucking prime minister, and look what I'm doing,' he muttered. 'Micromanaging this clusterfuck.'

He sliced Jess's cable tie, then did the same for Harry, who rubbed some feeling back into his wrists.

Cardinal pointed the gun at Jess's head. 'Come on, move it!'

Lightning lanced down and thunder boomed as the storm intensified further. Cardinal opened the gate and they filed through. Heathy went first. Then Jess and Harry. Cardinal followed them. Across the sodden ground and up the ladder. Wind threatened to tear them from the structure and throw them into space. Harry risked a look down and saw Crow watching Dave in the car.

Cardinal marched them along the maintenance gangway under the tank, to the final ladder. Harry looked up, as Heathy climbed over the edge and disappeared out of view, and then Jess. A few short weeks ago he wouldn't have been

370

able to climb up there in this weather, even with a gun to his head.

As if on cue, Cardinal prodded him with his gun.

'Move.'

CHAPTER 50

On the edge of the tower roof, on the side facing away from the city, was a square hatch secured with a padlock.

'Cover me,' Cardinal said. Heathy already had the shotgun trained on Harry and Jess. Cardinal fished in his pockets for his keys. He fumbled them, and they clanged against the steel. Cardinal got on his knees, found the key and unlocked the hatch.

He pulled the cover back, letting it bang against the top of the tower.

'Pass me the backpack,' he said to Heathy.

Cardinal fished out a torch and handed it to Harry.

'Down you go,' Cardinal said. 'No fucking about, mate. You know what will happen to Jess if you do. I've killed so many people, a couple more won't make any difference.'

Harry shone the torch through the hatch, down into the darkness. There were handholds, leading to the bottom of the tank.

Again he felt fear. What if the documents weren't here any more? Why hadn't Cardinal found them already? But there was no way back now. Just down.

Harry shuffled through the hatch, slotting his feet into the holds, trying to ignore the sick pulsing pain in his back. With the torch shoved in his back pocket he climbed down, feeling his way. After the cacophony of the storm, it was silent down here. He stepped off the bottom rung into a thick layer of silt, which puffed up around his feet. Dirt that had been in the water maybe, or the result of the tank decaying from the inside out. He pulled out the torch and shone it around, noting the footprints and holes in the silt from a previous search. Amazingly, there was life down here. Moss, fungi, surviving on a tiny amount of light and moisture. Life goes on, Harry thought.

He looked up as Cardinal clambered down, awkwardly holding on one-handed so he could wave the pistol at Harry. Again, Harry could feel Rob back there, assessing the situation, looking for a way out that didn't involve sacrificing any more innocent lives.

'Look at me,' Cardinal said when he reached the bottom, pressing the gun against Harry's chest. His voice echoed so much Harry could barely understand him. Cardinal was wet, bedraggled; hair messed up. He looked less like the politician, and more like the intel officer wreaking havoc in Helmand. He thrust Harry against the side of the water tower, and grabbed his chin.

'You in there, Rob? Hello? You never really got it, did you? Power. You were good at sneaking around and taking out towelheads from a distance, but you couldn't handle the true dirty work.

'You made the mistake of thinking life is a team sport when it's really one-on-one contact. Everyone is your enemy. Until you can understand that, you'll never win.'

He thrust Harry's head to one side.

'Come on, then,' Cardinal said. 'Commune with the spirit world.'

The tattoos warmed Harry's skin. The torch flickered. In that moment of darkness, Harry saw a familiar blue glow. He closed his eyes, remembering the night he and Jess made love. The sensation of seeing the world through two sets of eyes. He dropped into Rob's breathing routine, then lowered himself to his hands and knees.

Dust tickled his nostrils. He ignored it. Cardinal paced and cursed and fired more threats at him. Harry shut him out. He would wait. He had to wait. Like Harry, Cardinal was out of options.

A sensation of weightlessness filled him. In his mind's eye he saw himself floating out of his body, looking down on himself. No, not himself. Rob. Rob, dressed in a tight green t-shirt and jeans. Next to him was a package, wrapped in black plastic and sealed with silver duct tape. There was a bag and some tools, and a circle of metal about the size of an open umbrella.

Harry dug into the dirt by his feet, his back pulsing in pain. Eventually, he revealed a round piece of metal, riveted to the bottom of the tank.

Harry opened his eyes and looked up. 'Your knife. Give me your knife.'

Cardinal laughed. 'Are you fucking crazy?'

'It's where the water used to flow,' he said. 'They covered it when the tank was decommissioned. You want the documents, then I need your knife.'

Cardinal reached into his pants pocket and threw Harry the knife. He moved a couple of steps back and brandished the gun.

Harry unfolded the blade. Again Rob assessed the

374

situation. There was a small chance he could get to Cardinal without being shot. An even smaller chance he could get to Cardinal without a shot being fired. No chance of getting out of the tank without Heathy blowing his head off and murdering Jess. He turned back to the base of the water tank and slipped the knife blade under the edge of the metal, twisting to lever it up. Eventually, he made a gap big enough to get his fingers into.

From above: 'Boss?' The echo: *osssss, ossss, ossss.*

Harry looked up and saw Heathy peering down into the tank, dripping with rainwater. Cardinal cursed. 'Yeah, hang on.'

Harry put the knife down and heaved on the plate, biting back a scream. It came loose with a loud shriek. He slid it to one side. In the shallow cavity sat a rectangular package, wrapped in black plastic and sealed with duct tape.

'Open it,' Cardinal said.

'Boss!'

'Yes! For fuck's sake! I see your face again and I'll put a bullet in it!'

Harry took the knife and slid it through the plastic. A large, metallic-green fire-proof document case. Harry wiped his forehead.

Cardinal dumped the backpack at his feet. 'Get it in there and let's move.'

Harry loaded the case into the backpack. He reached again for the knife but Cardinal got to it first, closing the blade and slipping it back into his pocket. Harry grimaced as he slung the pack over his shoulder. His pain-wracked body was drenched in sweat.

'Come on!' Cardinal's eyes gleamed in the darkness.

Harry's feet clanged on the ladder rungs as he ascended. He'd never felt so tired or defeated.

CHAPTER 51

Harry climbed onto the roof of the tower into rain that was now coming down so hard it almost hurt. Heathy was bent over, trying to keep his feet as he stood over Jess. Nearby trees thrashed back and forth. The sky boiled with thunder and lightning.

At first he thought the red and blue lights strobing off the nearby houses were a figment of his imagination. Then he saw how Heathy's face snapped from side to side, like a caged animal. Harry followed his gaze and saw a street full of cop cars. Further up the road, a white van with a satellite dish on the roof and a TV channel logo on the side edged past a police barrier.

Cardinal clambered up after him. The smile withered on his face.

'What the fuck?'

'They came out of nowhere,' Heathy said. 'They got Crow!'

'Crow! Crow? Who gives a fucking shit! I'm standing here with my fucking balls hanging out!'

A gust of wind pummelled the tower. Cardinal staggered, then regained his footing. He grabbed Harry and pressed the gun against his head.

'What's going on?' he yelled. 'Why are the cops here?'

'Your boys confessed.'

He glared at Heathy. 'What the fuck is he talking about?'

Heathy shrugged.

'Back at the skate rink,' Harry yelled. 'A colleague of mine was recording. Live-streamed it to the internet. She followed us here and got the audio of you spilling your guts.'

Cardinal's head swivelled frantically back and forth, looking for a woman with a camera. He couldn't see her. He was probably blinded by the police flashers. But Harry could. Standing just outside the fence, still recording. Harry didn't know if she'd managed to get any useable audio from the top of the tower, or inside it, but it didn't matter anymore. He had Andrew Cardinal, standing in front of countless cops, waving a gun around.

'It's over, Cardinal.'

Harry pulled open his shirt, revealing the mic taped to his chest. Cardinal lashed out with his gun, catching Harry in the side of the head. Black spots bloomed across his vision. The top of the water tower skewed out of view as his head lurched, and he stumbled and fell.

'Truss 'em up,' Cardinal said.

Heathy hesitated. 'Boss. We're surrounded.'

Cardinal turned the gun on him. 'I said truss them up!'

Heathy pushed Jess down on the water tower and reached into his back pocket. He pulled out a cable tie and secured her hands in front of her. Then he strode across the tower and secured Harry's hands behind him. Jess was crying. Harry felt rage bloom inside him. He saw Jess but he also saw Kyla. A blue, shimmering mirage. The tattoos pulsing off her body like an aura.

Cardinal turned his head to the skies and howled.

'How? How, how, how.' He walked to Harry and slammed his shoe against Harry's face, mashing his lips against the steel. Harry grunted and spat blood. 'How does some shit-stain from the fucking *Chronicle* do this? Tell me! I killed them all! Left that fucking tattooist a vegetable. There were no loose ends! How, Harry? How!

'Tell me, and I'll kill you quick.'

'There are cops everywhere, Cardinal,' Harry said, but the wind whipped away his words. Cardinal leant down.

'What's that, Harry?'

Cardinal rolled him over onto his back, straddled him.

'Cops… everywhere.'

'Oh yeah, but they'll dick around for ages down there. No air support tonight. No snipers – we're at the highest point in the inner west. Thunder to disguise the gunshots. Plenty of time to have some fun with you and your lady friend. Just like we did with Rob and Kyla. I'm gonna kill you fuckers… again, and then I'm going to blow my brains out.'

Lightning raged across the sky, thunder roaring almost simultaneously, so loud Harry felt it in his chest. Cardinal yanked the microphone off Harry's chest and cast it aside.

'It was Rob, wasn't it? These fucking tattoos,' Cardinal said. He jabbed his pistol into one of them.

'I told the boys to get rid of all the tattoos,' he yelled. 'Didn't I, Heathy? Did they do what they were fucking told? No, of course not. Hard to get good fucking help. For identification purposes. You know, in case the body was found. But after…' he looked up into the storm, then back at Harry, 'I realised it was more than that.'

'Because of your dad.'

'At first I thought he was going loopy-loo. Then he

strung himself up. I thought it died with him. Some kind of revenge mojo. Eye for an eye, and all that.'

Lightning struck at the end of the street. Thunder so loud it rattled the ground. Cardinal whooped. Heathy peered over his shoulder, away from Jess, watching in horror as the street continued to fill with police.

'Oh well,' Cardinal said. 'It ends now.' He put the gun down and pulled the knife out. Harry saw what was coming and tried to buck him off, but he was too tired, his back too sore. Cardinal grinned. He opened the blade, grabbed a patch of Harry's inked skin and started sawing. Harry screamed.

Harry heard a low growling noise. Cardinal looked up. Jess, her body wreathed in an electric blue corona. She sprang and landed on him, knocking him off Harry and sending the gun skittering off the side of the water tower. The tattoos burned through her clothes, sending wisps of smoke into the air.

Heathy turned, waving his shotgun, looking for a clear shot. Harry rolled onto his side and pushed himself onto his knees. Cardinal was back on his feet. He closed his fists and turned on Jess but she was too fast for him, leaping up and wrapping her legs around his waist.

Harry welcomed Rob's surge. Hands still behind his back and body bent double, he charged at Heathy. The shotgun went off, pellets grazing his back. Harry drove his shoulder into Heathy's stomach. The bikie fell backwards, gasping for air. He groped for the shotgun. Harry stomped on his fingers, then with the other foot kicked the shottie off the side of the tower.

Cardinal slammed his fists into Jess's kidneys and spun around, trying to shake her off. They teetered towards the edge. She gripped on tighter than ever. With both hands, she grabbed his face and ripped down, nails slicing his forehead and cheeks open. He screamed, blinking away the blood flowing into his eyes.

He snapped his head forward, catching the bridge of Jess's nose. She cried out and fell off him, landing hard against the steel. She rolled away, back onto her knees, shaking her head to clear it. Harry kicked at Heathy, stomping down again as the bikie rolled away from him. His tattoos burned. He could feel the heat through his damp clothes, could smell the stench of singed meat. Blood pulsed from his wounds. Heathy rolled again, pushed himself back up onto his feet. But when he tried to stand his left boot slipped off the side of the water tower. His hands grasped at a mobile-phone antenna, but slipped. He dropped, screaming into the darkness.

Jess launched herself at Cardinal again, but he was ready for her this time. He lashed out at her shoulder. Jess staggered backwards, but left something there, standing toe-to-toe with Cardinal. A blue aura, like an after-image burning on Harry's retinas. More than an aura. A woman, sketched in blue light. Longer hair than Jess. Tattoos up both arms, shimmering in the night like jewels. Cardinal's eyes widened. Truly fearful for the first time.

'No!' he yelled.

Then Kyla's ghost was pulled back into Jess's body.

Harry ran for Cardinal, screaming as a burning sensation ripped through his arms. And then he saw Rob's arms, ghostly blue, reaching out from his body, while his own arms remained tied behind his back. Rob's arms grabbed Cardinal around the waist and lifted him off his feet, propelling him towards the edge. Harry screamed again, agony pulsing through his flesh as Rob tore free of his body.

The rain dropped away. Harry saw the world through two sets of eyes. Nausea washed over him. Cardinal tried to wriggle free.

'You can't hurt me,' Cardinal screamed. 'You're dead.'

Jess ran screaming at Cardinal.

At the last moment Kyla tore free of Jess, who slumped to the ground, one arm hanging over the tower's edge. Cardinal's feet slipped on the wet steel. His face contorted in rage. His arms pinwheeled. For a moment his face cleared; he realised his fight was over. And then he, Rob and Kyla plummeted from view. Only Cardinal screamed.

Again Harry saw the world through two sets of eyes: St Elmo's fire danced off the mobile-phone towers; the earth, bathed in the red and blue of police lights, rushed towards him. Harry felt the tower, firm under his feet; and he felt the crushing impact as Rob hit the ground.

'Jess!' Harry sat down heavily, slipped his tied hands under his bum and legs. He shuffled to where Jess lay unmoving at the edge, and with his tied hands outstretched he pulled her back towards him. She grabbed onto Harry and he looped his hands over her head. They held each other as the strange St Elmo's fire intensified around them. Harry tasted the coppery tang of blood. The hairs on his arms and legs stood on end. His skin was burning. Far below, someone screamed. A corona of light bloomed, reaching up to the sky.

'Oh shit,' Harry said.

And the world exploded in white.

EPILOGUE

Harry sat on his front step, watching the restoration crew work on the water tower. Despite Cardinal's motives for wanting to protect the tower, new Labor leader and Prime Minister Carol Lawler decided to stand behind his decision, saying that it would stand as a monument to Cardinal's victims and as a reminder of the need for eternal vigilance in the battle against corruption. That was the way Labor was spinning it, anyway.

Jess came out with two cups of tea, handed one to Harry and eased down next to him. His mending skin stretched tight as he reached for the cup. Lightning flowers, the doctor called them. She said they'd fade over time, as would the headaches and the ringing in his ears. She seemed perplexed by the fact that the burns seemed more pronounced in some places than others, and didn't always follow the path the electricity took through his body, as Lichtenberg figures usually did.

'Lightning is strange,' the doctor had concluded, shrugging. 'You're lucky to be alive.'

That suited Harry and Jess just fine. Neither of them wanted to explain the tattoos that had mysteriously appeared and then been torn off their bodies. The only tattoo that survived was the one on his neck. He wasn't surprised to see Jess's was still there, too.

'Do you think this government will survive?' Jess asked, sipping her tea.

'I don't know. The Opposition is baying for blood,' he said.

When Harry woke up in hospital, head throbbing and body on fire, the last thing he could remember was placing his sights on the back of Andrew Cardinal's head. For a few terrifying moments he thought he'd gone through with it. Short-term memory loss was another symptom of lightning strike, the doctor said. But slowly it came back to him: cracking the code, Dave's kidnap, finding the documents, and the life-and-death struggle on the top of the tower.

As soon as he was out of ICU, Christine was there, with her laptop and the metallic-green fire-proof document case, much to the chagrin of his doctor. The nurses shooed her away but as soon as they were gone, she was back. Tenacious didn't even begin to cover it. Harry read through the notes he'd written up, but it was like something a stranger had written. Rob's memories were gone. Harry didn't believe a word he'd written until he started sifting through the documents in the case.

Transcripts of conversations – Kyla and Rob talking to various military officials, and to Terry Redwood. Military intel documents, signed by Cardinal and his superiors. Photos taken in Afghanistan. Police reports detailing the various sins of Crow and Heathy after they left the army and joined the Dreadnorts. Surveillance photos of key players. Cardinal had been careful, had kept his distance, but Rob still managed to get a photo of him and Heathy and Crow, laughing and sharing a beer together. And there, at the bottom of the case, an old piece of cloth. The bloodstains on the hijab were almost black now.

While in hospital Harry and Jess had been under police protection. It meant they had the room to themselves, and the press were kept at bay. The journalists knew part of the story – they'd seen the skating rink confessions on YouTube; they'd heard the audio from the top of the water tower. All of that had been enough to land Vessel and Crow in jail. Cardinal and Heathy would have to answer to a higher power.

But no-one knew the full story. So Harry wrote, or he dictated and Christine wrote. Dave dropped by with coffee, limping slightly but still giving Harry sass for taking so long to finish the bloody thing and for landing him in the doghouse with Ellie. And when it was done and checked and legalled, Miles ran the story in the *Chermside Chronicle*. Harry was offered a lot of money to publish the story elsewhere, but he turned down all the offers. They'd all get their claws into it as soon as it hit the streets, but he wanted Miles to have a rare taste of glory.

The former government howled for a new election, arguing that a party led by a psychopath and a man willing to keep his mouth shut for a taste of power wasn't fit to rule. New prime minister Carol Lawler and her party clung on for all they were worth, and the spin doctors pointed out that Labor had won in a huge landslide, with the Coalition ousted all the way from Perth to Brisbane. You elect a party, not a prime minister, they said.

Sitting on the front step, Jess leant against Harry. 'You going to stay here?'

He nodded. While they were in hospital the police had

come to Harry's house, dug up Rob's body, and forensics had had their way with the place. Rob and Kyla had been given a proper burial.

'Yeah. It's peaceful… now.'

He'd had visits in the hospital, from Dave, Christine, Sandy and Fred. They brought cards, chocolates, flowers. Sandy the psychic gave him a big hug, like Harry was her long-lost son. All of them wanted to give him updates about the latest developments in the story. Ron Vessel charged with accessory to murder, and a bunch of other stuff. Brian Swenson's arrest and subsequent fatal heart attack. Terry Redwood brought in to answer allegations of perverting the course of justice.

Harry didn't want to hear it. He knew everything was back in balance. He could feel it. He had no interest in writing a follow-up. There was no follow-up. This was the end.

A week after he arrived home, Christine told him the *Brisbane Mail* had offered her a job. He told her to hold out for something better. Then he switched his phone off, sick of journalists – mostly people he'd gone to uni with – calling him for 'the story behind the story'. He was scared to think how many messages would be waiting for him next time he switched it on.

'Darren phoned me,' Jess said. 'He wants to meet me. He wants to talk.'

Harry watched the workers on top of the tower. He was expecting it. Maybe that's why he didn't feel sad.

'How do you feel?' he said.

She shrugged. 'I think you know.'

Harry nodded. He'd had a message from Bec before he turned his phone off. She said she wanted to talk to him.

Wanted to see him again, even if just as friends. He hadn't responded yet.

'I think I need to talk to him,' Jess said.

'Yeah. That sounds like a good idea.'

'I... I don't regret it. Any of it. But...'

Harry looked at her. She was beautiful. Strong and smart and beautiful. But there was no connection, now that Rob and Kyla were gone.

'I know,' he said. He leant forward, kissed her on the lips.

They finished their tea in silence. Jess touched Harry's shoulder, got up and went inside.

Harry stretched his legs out, leant back, and enjoyed the sunshine.

ACKNOWLEDGEMENTS

It has been a long, long road, but certainly not a lonely journey.

Thank you to the following:

Alex Adsett, my agent, for making sure this book wasn't left to languish in a bottom drawer, like a corpse in a shallow grave.

Angela Meyer and Echo Publishing for taking a punt on a debut author. Cat Camacho and the Titan Books team for keeping the dream alive in the UK and the US.

Kate Eltham for teaching me how to write grant applications, and the Australia Council for giving me time to write.

Angela Slatter for the flensing and your belief in the book. The fact that the flensing wasn't as severe as I feared it might be gave me hope that maybe I truly had something worth reading. Claudine Ryan, my 'book counsellor', for your help with the initial structural edit – you saw some true horrors. Critique partner Chris McMahon – I'm not sure how much work we got done during those Friday-evening sessions at the Irish Club, but it sure was fun. And to my beta readers – your thoughtful feedback improved the book no end.

Everyone who helped with my sometimes weird research questions, and everyone who cheered me on via social media during the first draft (you can follow me on Twitter: @garykemble). There's nothing like a public shaming to get those fingers tap-tap-tapping. Thank you to Davin at Brunswick Ink Tattoo, and Matt Cunnington and the Westside Tattoo crew. (I thought about getting a tattoo, then chickened out).

My dad for not encouraging me to be an accountant or engineer (both noble professions but I would have sucked at them and been miserable). Carolynne for those kitchen book chats. Mum for always believing in me and reading every short story I had published, even though you don't like horror. I'm sorry you couldn't be here to read the finished product, but I'm glad you got to read the first draft. (And fuck cancer.)

My wife, Amelia, for giving me time to write and for those times when I was with you but my mind was with Harry. My kids, Eamon and Aurora. You are everything to me.

If you want to read about some real-life action heroes, check out *The Amazing SAS* (Ian McPhedran) and *SAS Sniper* (Rob Maylor). If you want two very different perspectives on bikie culture, read *Dead Man Running* (Ross Coulthart and Duncan McNab) and *The Brotherhoods* (Arthur Veno).

The Paddington water tower was heritage listed in 2000. It is very well looked after and doesn't wear a crown of mobile-phone towers.

The Border Protection Bill (2001) was never enacted. It passed the House of Representatives but was knocked back in the Senate. At time of writing, the current government's Operation Sovereign Borders had resulted in 15 vessels being turned back from Australian waters.

Gary Kemble's award-winning short fiction has been published in magazines and anthologies in Australia and abroad, and his non-fiction has appeared in newspapers, magazines and online. Born in England, Gary now lives in Brisbane with his wife and kids, where he is the Social Media Co-ordinator for national news broadcaster ABC News. *Strange Ink* is his first novel.

For more fantastic fiction, author events, exclusive
excerpts, competitions, limited editions and more

VISIT OUR WEBSITE
titanbooks.com

LIKE US ON FACEBOOK
facebook.com/titanbooks

FOLLOW US ON TWITTER
@TitanBooks

EMAIL US
readerfeedback@titanemail.com